OMNIBUS EDITIONS BY THE SAME AUTHOR IN VIKING/PENGUIN

Indian Thought: A Miscellany

Malgudi Landscapes: The Best of R.K. Narayan

A Town Called Malgudi

The World of Malgudi

Indian Epics Retold

The Magic of Malgudi

R.K. NARAYAN

The Magic of Malgudi

Swami and Friends
The Bachelor of Arts
The Vendor of Sweets

Edited with an introduction by
S. Krishnan

VIKING

VIKING

Penguin Books India (P) Ltd., 11 Community Centre, Panchsheel Park, New Delhi 110 017, India
Penguin Books Ltd., 27 Wrights Lane, London W8 5TZ, UK
Penguin Putnam Inc., 375 Hudson Street, New York, NY 10014, USA
Penguin Books Australia Ltd., Ringwood, Victoria, Australia
Penguin Books Canada Ltd., 10 Alcorn Avenue, Suite 300, Toronto, Ontario, M4V 3B2, Canada
Penguin Books (NZ) Ltd., Cnr Rosedale and Airborne Roads, Albany, Auckland, New Zealand

First published in Viking by Penguin Books India 2000

Copyright © R.K. Narayan 2000
Introduction copyright © S. Krishnan 2000

Swami and Friends was first published in London by Hamish Hamilton, 1935
The Bachelor of Arts was first published in Great Britain by Thomas Nelson and Sons Limited, 1937
The Vendor of Sweets was first published in Great Britain by The Bodley Head, 1967

10 9 8 7 6 5 4 3 2 1

Typeset in *Casablanca* by SÜRYA, New Delhi
Printed at Chaman Offset Printers, New Delhi

Contents

Introduction

IN SHOW-BUSINESS PARLANCE, one might say that *The Magic of Malgudi* comprises three acts, each depicting a stage in a man's life—the small schoolboy (*Swami and Friends*); the adolescent poised on the verge of manhood (*The Bachelor of Arts*); and the confused, middle-aged man (*The Vendor of Sweets*). The novels also provide an interesting study of the development of the style and imagination of R.K. Narayan. The first two display the vigour and vivacity of the young man whose memories of his earlier years were still strong—he was only twenty-four when he started writing *Swami and Friends*, and hardly thirty when he launched into *The Bachelor of Arts*. *The Vendor of Sweets* came thirty years later when Narayan had had a number of splendid novels to his credit. Along with *The Painter of Signs*, it also showed him moving with the times, coming to grips with a Malgudi which was slowly changing.

R(asipuram) K(rishnaswami Iyer) Narayan Swami was born on 10 October, 1906 in his grandmother's house in Madras where he spent his first fifteen years. He then moved to Mysore where his father had become headmaster of a prestigious high school. The lakes and hills, the flowering trees, the beautiful buildings and the salubrious climate of Mysore so different from hot and dusty Madras, and the opportunity to live with his siblings for the first time wrought a change in Narayan. He started taking long walks with friends, and more importantly he had free access to the books and magazines in the school library as the son of the headmaster. He read voraciously and pretty soon after, tried his hand at writing, his early melodramatic pieces being greatly admired by his friends.

Shortly after this he started contributing to journals in Madras and reporting for newspapers. His big moment during this period was when *Punch* accepted one of his articles and paid him for it, but this was a flash in the pan, so to say.

Between 1930 and 1932 he finished writing *Swami and Friends* and tried to find a publisher for it in the UK. In this he was supported by a close friend, Purna, who took the manuscript to publisher after publisher with no success. Narayan got so desperate that in a moment of total self-disgust he advised Purna to tie a stone to the manuscript and drop it into the Thames. But good luck was just round the corner. Purna showed the manuscript to Graham Greene, who liked it well enough to send it to the publisher, Hamish Hamilton, who in turn published it, shortening in the process Narayan Swami to Narayan and the book's title from *Swami the Tate* to *Swami and Friends* (Tate was an eminent bowler of those days, and Swami's bowling ability brought him the nickname.)

The book is an absolute delight, a little masterpiece. Narayan had not become old enough to have forgotten his school days, and his sketches of students and teachers are quite vividly portrayed. Swami is a student of the first form, four feet tall and probably about ten years old. He revels in his friendships with important people like the class monitor and the class bully. The novel cannot be summarized as it is necessarily episodic, Swami moving from one catastrophe to another. He walks out—rather runs out of the Albert Mission School as the headmaster tries to punish him for enthusiastically taking part in a political rally. He joins the Board School, but here too, when he is about to be punished by the headmaster for not attending the drill classes, he runs away. This requires some explanation. His friends had formed a cricket club of which he was the best bowler. But by the time Swami finished his drill class it was always too late to get in some cricket practice. So he manages to get himself dismissed from school and happily explains to his captain that though he had left the school for good he would show up for the big match. But having left the school, and now his home in an act of defiance, Swami keeps walking along the main road and gets lost. He is found by a cartman who takes him to the Forest Officer who manages to return him to his family. By now the big match is over and the captain turns his face against him as their team had lost. The novel ends with the captain leaving Malgudi on account of his father's transfer to another town.

This is a very bare outline but for a first-time novelist Narayan packs a lot of interesting and lively material into it and crafts beautifully the world seen through the eyes of this lovable small boy. Each character created in this novel is true to life and takes the reader back to his own childhood. Also, the teachers are very true to the types one has known at school. Swami's family is described wonderfully well, especially the changes that occur when a baby is born to Swami's mother. And Granny, in whose lap Swami always takes refuge and who knows nothing about cricket, seems so much like someone who Dickens could have created.

Swami and Friends is so well-rounded and so near perfection that one might be forgiven for wondering how the author was going to follow up this difficult act. What Narayan followed *Swami* with was *The Bachelor of Arts*. He must have started work on it while waiting for *Swami* to be published—*Swami* was published in 1935 and *The Bachelor of Arts* came out in 1937, with Graham Greene acting the midwife again. I have said this before and I say it again, that each time I reread one of Narayan's novels, I think it is his best. When I reread *The Bachelor of Arts* after several years, I was truly astonished at the enormous progress Narayan had made since *Swami* in regard to style, characterization, and development of the theme. (Of course, this is not to denigrate *Swami and Friends* at all as it is in a class by itself. In fact most aficionados of Narayan always think of *Swami and Friends* first when they think of Narayan's works.) *The Bachelor of Arts* flows so easily and smoothly that it seems to have written itself. From the moment Chandran, the protagonist, allows himself to be arm-twisted into agreeing to be the prime mover in a union debate on, 'In the opinion of this house, historians should be slaughtered first,' (and Chandran is a history student) we follow his career with the greatest of interest. Narayan is no longer writing about schoolboys but about senior college students, and he adapts his style to the changed theme remarkably well. He lets his characters smoke cigarettes and watch late cinema shows. They laze around, go to the college library once in a while, chat about irrelevant things, promenade on the banks of the Sarayu and get home about 8.30 p.m. This carefree life comes to an abrupt stop only when the month of November looms around. It is only six months now for the all-important final examination, passing which will get one the Bachelor of Arts degree. Chandran makes all sorts of resolutions, including preparing a personal timetable for his study at home. All things must come to an end however, and all too soon, the last classes are over. 'There would be no more college for him from tomorrow. He would return to it a fortnight hence for the examination and (hoping for the best) pass it, and pass out into the world, forever out of Albert College. He felt very tender and depressed.'

Chandran acquires his BA but spends the next few months doing nothing, reading books from the public library, and toying with the idea of going to England for further study. It is then that his whole life changes—he sees a girl on the banks of the Sarayu and promptly falls in love with her. After several days of this one-way ocular communion, he follows her carefully one evening and realizes that she lives in a house opposite a lodge in which his college friend, Mohan, occupies a room. Through Mohan's cooperation, he learns the name of the girl—Malathi—and her family background. He musters enough courage to tell his parents that he wants to marry Malathi. At first his parents resist the idea as they feel that Malathi's parents are of inferior social status, but finally they agree as they can't bear to watch Chandran's unhappiness. Formal parleys are initiated, astrologers brought in, and then the blow falls. The horoscopes do not match, and indicate that a flaw in Chandran's meant an early death for his bride. Chandran rants and raves but Malathi's parents do not want to take a chance. (There is an irony here. A couple of years earlier Narayan had married his wife against astrological warnings. Happy in his marriage, he must have thought the idea of Chandran's possible marriage being wrecked by horoscopes a dramatic one, but his own wife died about two years after the publication of *The Bachelor of Arts*.) Chandran is shattered when he realizes that Malathi was actually being married to someone else, and cannot bear to stay in Malgudi any longer. His parents send him to Madras for a change, but instead of going to his uncle's as planned, he takes a room in a lodge. Here he runs into Kailas, a well-heeled drunk who takes Chandran under his wing. After a day of rattling around, Kailas takes Chandran to a bar, but Chandran refuses to drink anything, and on the spur of the moment, tells Kailas he has promised his mother never to touch alcohol. Here occurs one of the most delightful passages in all Narayan's work. 'This affected Kailas profoundly. He remained solemn for a moment and said, "Then don't. Mother is a sacred object. It is a commodity whose value we don't realize as long as it is with us. One must lose it to know what a precious possession it is. If I had my mother I should have studied in a college and become a respectable person. After this, where do you think I am going?" "I don't know." "To the houe of a prostitute." He remained reflective for a moment and said with a sigh, "As long as my mother lived she said every minute—Do this. Don't do that. And I remained a good son to her. The moment she died I changed. It is a rare commodity, sir. Mother is a rare commodity." ' Then Kailas drags Chandran to a brothel. (' "Is this Kokilam's house?" "What does a name matter? You are welcome to my poor abode, sir." It was a middle-aged woman. "You are right," said Kailas, greatly pleased.') Terrified by these experiences, Chandran manages to get away from Kailas, and spends the night on the road.

In the morning he finds a barber, gets his head shaved, obtains some ochre clothes and starts wandering wherever his feet might take him, begging food, eating fruits and vegetables. After a few weeks of such wandering, he tires of it, longs for Malgudi, and gets back with the help of a postmaster. He has exorcized Malathi from his system. The rest of the novel deals with Chandran becoming the representative of a newspaper, marrying a beautiful girl his parents have chosen, to whom he becomes utterly devoted.

The Bachelor of Arts is a young man's book. Chandran's passion for Malathi is not very different from Narayan's own love for the girl whom he married in the face of astrological warnings. Some of the themes he used here would recur in his later work, particularly Chandran's brief career as a sanyasi which Narayan puts to effective use in *The Guide*. Drunkards keep appearing in his stories probably because he had a young uncle, a dedicated alcoholic, with whom he had some amusing but terrifying experiences. In my opinion, *The Bachelor of Arts*, considering especially that it is only the second novel that he wrote, occupies a high place in Narayan's work.

The Vendor of Sweets came out thirty years later. In between Narayan had produced quite a few of his masterly series of novels about Malgudi and its denizens which brought him international fame. They were translated into several languages, brought him many awards, and one of them in particular, *The Guide*, was dramatized and filmed, and remains a best-seller among his works. When

Narayan started to write *The Vendor of Sweets*, Malgudi was changing, perhaps not in externals, but in atmosphere and attitudes, with which some people were able to come to terms, but other could not. Jagan, the prosperous vendor of sweets and the protagonist of the novel, is one of the latter. The novel opens with a delightful but up-in-the-air homily by Jagan. ' "Conquer taste, and you will have conquered the self," said Jagan to his listener, who asked, "Why conquer the self?" Jagan said, "I do not know, but all our sages advise us so." ' The key words are 'I do not know.' Jagan is a true follower of Mahatma Gandhi—he reads the Bhagavad Gita all the time, wears only clothes made from the yarn he spins daily, he believes in naturopathy and eats and drinks only the food he cooks and the water he boils. Withal he is a very prosperous seller of sweets, and makes a lot of money, some of which he stashes away and does not show in his income tax returns. He is a widower with one son, Mali. It is the relationship between father and son that provides the drama in the novel. Jagan feels an inarticulate affection for Mali that is not returned. Especially after the mother's death, father and son seem to go their separate ways, though Jagan would like to stay close to his son. Things go on like this, with the two living practically like strangers in the huge ancestral house. Then one day Mali announces his intention of giving up his studies and going to America to become a writer—and this he does. While Jagan is proud to have a son in America and talks about it incessantly to whoever might listen, he is also perturbed deep inside as to whether he would meet another person altogether when Mali returned. One can then well imagine Jagan's mental travail when Mali returns with a mountain of luggage, and a Korean-American girl tagging along as his wife. Pretty soon Mali makes his intentions clear—with American collaboration he wants to build a story-writing machine, and popularize it all over the country. For this project he wants to raise a huge amount of money, a hefty share of which he expected his father to dole out. The Korean wife, with whom Jagan has established a friendly relationship, tells him that she and Mali are not really married, and Mali, who has been living high in the expectation of raising becoming rich overnight starts leading a debauched life much to the consternation of his father.

In a way it is a simple story about the conflict between generations. Though Narayan resolves the tangle in his usual amiable and practical style, his artistry lies in giving the story vivid

life, by showing a changing Malgudi which can take in its stride a
local boy consorting with a foreign girl. Nowhere expect in Jagan's
own mind does the conflict persist. Jagan's Malgudi is the Malgudi
we have always known; his struggles about what people might think
of his son's behaviour are all mental and inner-directed. Several of
Narayan's characters tend to soliloquize to themselves, but Jagan is
the master of them all.

If I might end on a personal note, the magic of Malgudi touched me
in 1942 when I had joined a college to read for my MA degree in
English. One of my professors introduced me to it. During the war
years Narayan's books were not easily available—many perished in
the blitzkreig of London—but I caught up with his work soon
afterwards, and I believe I have read all his novels and short stories,
and most of his occasional writings. In 1957 I met him in person in
New York just after he had finished writing his most successful
novel, *The Guide*, and have kept in touch with him since then. I have
no doubt in my mind that he is the finest writer of English in India,
and it has been a great privilege to introduce his work to an even
larger readership than he already has, and to a new generation.
    I am sure that reading these masterpieces in this omnibus
volume will be a delightful treat to the reader, bringing home to the
mind Narayan's myriad variety under an apparent simplicity.

S. Krishnan

(S. Krishnan has also edited and introduced the following omnibus editions
by R.K. Narayan: *Indian Thought: A Miscellany*, *Malgudi Landscapes: The Best
of R.K. Narayan*, *A Town Called Malgudi*, *The World of Malgudi* and *Indian
Epics Retold*.)

The Magic of Malgudi

Swami and Friends

CHAPTER ONE

MONDAY MORNING

IT WAS MONDAY morning. Swaminathan was reluctant to open his eyes. He considered Monday specially unpleasant in the calendar. After the delicious freedom of Saturday and Sunday, it was difficult to get into the Monday mood of work and discipline. He shuddered at the very thought of school: that dismal yellow building; the fire-eyed Vedanayagam, his class-teacher; and the Head Master with his thin long cane . . .

By eight he was at his desk in his 'room', which was only a corner in his father's dressing-room. He had a table on which all his things, his coat, cap, slate, ink-bottle, and books, were thrown in a confused heap. He sat on his stool and shut his eyes to recollect what work he had for the day: first of course there was Arithmetic—those five puzzles in Profit and Loss; then there was English—he had to copy down a page from his Eighth Lesson, and write dictionary meanings of difficult words; and then there was Geography. And only two hours before him to do all this heap of work and get ready for the school!

Fire-eyed Vedanayagam was presiding over the class with his back to the long window. Through its bars one saw a bit of the drill ground and a corner of the veranda of the Infant Standards. There were huge windows on the left showing vast open grounds bound at the other extreme by the railway embankment.

To Swaminathan existence in the classroom was possible only because he could watch the toddlers of the Infant Standards falling over one another, and through the windows on the left see the 12.30 mail gliding over the embankment, booming and rattling while passing over the Sarayu Bridge.

The first hour passed off quietly. The second they had Arithmetic. Vedanayagam went out and returned in a few minutes in the role of an Arithmetic teacher. He droned on monotonously. Swaminathan was terribly bored. His teacher's voice was beginning to get on his nerves. He felt sleepy.

The teacher called for home exercises. Swaminathan left his seat, jumped on the platform, and placed his note-book on the table. While the teacher was scrutinizing the sums, Swaminathan was gazing on his face, which seemed so tame at close quarters. His criticism of the teacher's face was that his eyes were too near each other, that there was more hair on his chin than one saw from the bench, and that he was very very bad-looking.

His reverie was disturbed. He felt a terrible pain in the soft flesh above his left elbow. The teacher was pinching him with one hand, and with the other, crossing out all the sums. He wrote 'Very Bad' at the bottom of the page, flung the note-book in Swaminathan's face, and drove him back to his seat.

Next period they had History. The boys looked forward to it eagerly. It was taken by D. Pillai, who had earned a name in the school for kindness and good humour. He was reputed to have never frowned or sworn at the boys at any time. His method of teaching History conformed to no canon of education. He told the boys with a wealth of detail the private histories of Vasco da Gama, Clive, Hastings, and others. When he described the various fights in History, one heard the clash of arms and the groans of the slain. He was the despair of the Head Master whenever the latter stole along the corridor with noiseless steps on his rounds of inspection.

The Scripture period was the last in the morning. It was not such a dull hour after all. There were moments in it that brought stirring pictures before one: the Red Sea cleaving and making way for the Israelites; the physical feats of Samson; Jesus rising from the grave; and so on. The only trouble was that the Scripture master, Mr Ebenezar, was a fanatic.

'Oh, wretched idiots!' the teacher said, clenching his fists. 'Why do you worship dirty, lifeless, wooden idols and stone images? Can they talk? No. Can they see? No. Can they bless you? No. Can they take you to Heaven? No. Why? Because they have no life. What did your gods do when Mohammed of Gazni smashed them to pieces, trod upon them, and constructed out of them steps for his lavatory?

If those idols and images had life, why did they not parry Mohammed's onslaughts?'

He then turned to Christianity. 'Now see our Lord Jesus. He could cure the sick, relieve the poor, and take us to Heaven. He was a real God. Trust him and he will take you to Heaven; the kingdom of Heaven is within us.' Tears rolled down Ebenezar's cheeks when he pictured Jesus before him. Next moment his face became purple with rage as he thought of Sri Krishna: 'Did our Jesus go gadding about with dancing girls like your Krishna? Did our Jesus go about stealing butter like that arch-scoundrel Krishna? Did our Jesus practise dark tricks on those around him?'

He paused for breath. The teacher was intolerable today. Swaminathan's blood boiled. He got up and asked, 'If he did not, why was he crucified?' The teacher told him that he might come to him at the end of the period and learn it in private. Emboldened by this mild reply, Swaminathan put to him another question, 'If he was a God, why did he eat flesh and fish and drink wine?' As a brahmin boy it was inconceivable to him that a God should be a non-vegetarian. In answer to this, Ebenezar left his seat, advanced slowly towards Swaminathan, and tried to wrench his left ear off.

Next day Swaminathan was at school early. There was still half an hour before the bell. He usually spent such an interval in running round the school or in playing the Digging Game under the huge tamarind tree. But today he sat apart, sunk in thought. He had a thick letter in his pocket. He felt guilty when he touched its edge with his fingers.

He called himself an utter idiot for having told his father about Ebenezar the night before during the meal.

As soon as the bell rang, he walked into the Head Master's room and handed him a letter. The Head Master's face became serious when he read:

Sir,

I beg to inform you that my son Swaminathan of the First Form, A Section, was assaulted by his Scripture Master yesterday in a fanatical rage. I hear that he is always most insulting and provoking in his references to the Hindu religion. It is bound to have a bad effect upon the boys. This is not the place for me to dwell upon the necessity for toleration in these matters.

I am also informed that when my son got up to have
a few doubts cleared, he was roughly handled by the same
teacher. His ears were still red when he came home last
evening.

The one conclusion that I can come to is that you do
not want non-Christian boys in your school. If it is so, you
may kindly inform us as we are quite willing to withdraw
our boys and send them elsewhere. I may remind you that
Albert Mission School is not the only school that this town,
Malgudi, possesses. I hope you will be kind enough to
inquire into the matter and favour me with a reply. If not,
I regret to inform you, I shall be constrained to draw the
attention of higher authorities to these un-Christian
practices.

I have the honour to be,
> Sir,
> Your most obedient servant,
>> W.T. SRINIVASAN.

When Swaminathan came out of the room, the whole school
crowded round him and hung on his lips. But he treated inquisitive
questions with haughty indifference.

He honoured only four persons with his confidence. Those
were the four that he liked and admired most in his class. The first
was Somu, the Monitor, who carried himself with such an easy air.
He set about his business, whatever it was, with absolute confidence
and calmness. He was known to be chummy even with the teachers.
No teacher ever put a question to him in the class. It could not be
said that he shone brilliantly as a student. It was believed that only
the Head Master could reprimand him. He was more or less the
uncle of the class.

Then there was Mani, the mighty good-for-nothing. He towered
above all the other boys of the class. He seldom brought any books
to the class, and never bothered about homework. He came to the
class, monopolized the last bench, and slept bravely. No teacher
ever tried to prod him. It was said that a new teacher who once tried
it very nearly lost his life. Mani bullied all strangers that came his
way, be they big or small. People usually slunk aside when he
passed. Wearing his cap at an angle, with a Tamil novel under his
arm, he had been coming to the school ever since the old school

peon could remember. In most of the classes he stayed longer than his friends did. Swaminathan was proud of his friendship. While others crouched in awe, he could address him as 'Mani' with gusto and pat him on the back familiarly. Swaminathan admiringly asked whence Mani derived his power. Mani replied that he had a pair of wooden clubs at home with which he would break the backs of those that dared to tamper with him.

Then there was Sankar, the most brilliant boy of the class. He solved any problem that was given to him in five minutes, and always managed to border on 90 per cent. There was a belief among a section of the boys that if only he started cross-examining the teachers the teachers would be nowhere. Another section asserted that Sankar was a dud and that he learnt all the problems and their solution in advance by his sycophancy. He was said to receive his 90 per cent as a result of washing clothes for his masters. He could speak to the teachers in English in the open class. He knew all the rivers, mountains and countries in the world. He could repeat History in his sleep. Grammar was child's play to him. His face was radiant with intelligence, though his nose was almost always damp, and though he came to the class with his hair braided and with flowers in it. Swaminathan looked on him as a marvel. He was very happy when he made Mani see eye to eye with him and admit Sankar to their company. Mani liked him in his own way and brought down his heavy fist on Sankar's back whenever he felt inclined to demonstrate his affection. He would scratch his head and ask where the blithering fool of a scraggy youngster got all that brain from and why he should not part with a little of it.

The fourth friend was Samuel, known as the 'Pea' on account of his size. There was nothing outstanding about him. He was just ordinary, no outstanding virtue of muscle or intellect. He was as bad in Arithmetic as Swaminathan was. He was as apprehensive, weak and nervous about rings as Swaminathan was. The bond between them was laughter. They were able to see together the same absurdities and incongruities in things. The most trivial and unnoticeable thing to others would tickle them to death.

When Swaminathan told them what action his father had taken in the Scripture Master affair, there was a murmur of approval. Somu was the first to express it, by bestowing on his admirer a broad grin. Sankar looked serious and said, 'Whatever others might say, you did right in setting your father to the job.' The mighty

Mani half closed his eyes and grunted an approval of sorts. He was only sorry that the matter should have been handled by elders. He saw no sense in it. Things of this kind should not be allowed to go beyond the four walls of the classroom. If he were Swaminathan, he would have closed the whole incident at the beginning by hurling an ink bottle, if nothing bigger was available, at the teacher. Well, there was no harm in what Swaminathan had done; he would have done infinitely worse by keeping quiet. However, let the Scripture Master look out: Mani had decided to wring his neck and break his back.

Samuel the Pea found himself in an acutely embarrassing position. On the one hand, he felt constrained to utter some remark. On the other, he was a Christian and saw nothing wrong in Ebenezar's observations, which seemed to be only an amplification of one of the Commandments. He felt that his right place was on Ebenezar's side. He managed to escape by making scathing comments on Ebenezar's dress and appearance and leaving it at that.

The class had got wind of the affair. When the Scripture period arrived there was a general expectation of some dramatic denouement. But nothing happened. Ebenezar went on as merrily as ever. He had taken the trouble that day to plod through *Bhagavad Gita*, and this generous piece of writing lends itself to any interpretation. In Ebenezar's hand it served as a weapon against Hinduism.

His tone was as vigorous as ever, but in his denunciation there was more scholarship. He pulled *Bhagavad Gita* to pieces, after raising Hinduism on its base. Step by step he was reaching the sublime heights of rhetoric. The class Bible lay uncared for on the table.

The Head Master glided in.

Ebenezar halted, pushing back his chair, and rose, greatly flurried. He looked questioningly at the Head Master. The Head Master grimly asked him to go on. Ebenezar had meanwhile stealthily inserted a finger into the pages of the closed Bible. On the word of command from the Head Master, he tried to look sweet and relaxed his brow, which was knit in fury. He then opened his book where the finger marked and began to read at random. It happened to be the Nativity of Christ. The great event had occurred. There the divine occupant was in the manger. The Wise

Men of the East were faithfully following the Star.

The boys attended in their usual abstracted way. It made little difference to them whether Ebenezar was making a study of Hinduism in the light of *Bhagavad Gita* or was merely describing the Nativity of Christ.

The Head Master listened for a while and, in an undertone, demanded an explanation. They were nearing the terminal examination and Ebenezar had still not gone beyond the Nativity. When would he reach the Crucifixion and Resurrection, and begin to revise? Ebenezar was flabbergasted. He could not think of anything to say. He made a bare escape by hinting that that particular day of the week, he usually devoted to a rambling revision. Oh, no! He was not as far behind as that. He was in the proximity of the Last Supper.

At the end of the day Swaminathan was summoned to the Head Master's room. As soon as he received the note, he had an impulse to run home. And when he expressed it, Mani took him in his hands, propelled him through to the Head Master's room, and gave him a gentle push in. Swaminathan staggered before the Head Master.

Ebenezar was sitting on a stool, looking sheepish. The Head Master asked: 'What is the trouble, Swaminathan?'

'Oh—nothing, sir,' Swaminathan replied.

'If it is nothing, why this letter?'

'Oh!' Swaminathan ejaculated uncertainly.

Ebenezar attempted to smile. Swaminathan wished to be well out of the whole affair. He felt he would not mind if a hundred Ebenezars said a thousand times worse things about the gods.

'You know why I am here?' asked the Head Master.

Swaminathan searched for an answer: the Head Master might be there to receive letters from boys' parents; he might be there to flay Ebenezar alive; he might be there to deliver six cuts with his cane every Monday at twelve o'clock. And above all why this question?

'I don't know, sir,' Swaminathan replied innocently.

'I am here to look after you,' said the Head Master.

Swaminathan was relieved to find that the question had such a simple answer.

'And so,' continued the Head Master, 'you must come to me if you want any help, before you go to your father.' Swaminathan furtively glanced at Ebenezar, who writhed in his chair.

'I am sorry,' said the Head Master, 'that you should have been so foolish as to go to your father about this simple matter. I shall look into it. Take this letter to your father.'

Swaminathan took the letter and shot out of the room with great relief.

CHAPTER TWO

RAJAM AND MANI

RIVER SARAYU WAS the pride of Malgudi. It was some ten minutes' walk from Ellaman Street, the last street of the town, chiefly occupied by oilmongers. Its sandbanks were the evening resort of all the people of the town. The Municipal President took any distinguished visitor to the top of the Town Hall and proudly pointed to him the Sarayu in moonlight, glistening like a silver belt across the North.

The usual evening crowd was on the sand. Swaminathan and Mani sat aloof on a river-step, with their legs dangling in the water. The *peepul* branches overhanging the river rustled pleasantly. A light breeze played about the boughs and scattered stray leaves on the gliding stream below. Birds filled the air with their cries. Far away, near Nallappa's Mango Grove, a little downstream, a herd of cattle was crossing the river. And then a country cart drawn by bullocks passed, the cart-man humming a low tune. It was some fifteen minutes past sunset and there was a soft red in the west.

'The water runs very deep here, doesn't it?' Mani asked.

'Yes, why?'

'I am going to bring Rajam here, bundle him up, and throw him into the river.'

Rajam was a fresh arrival in the First A. He had sauntered into the class on the reopening day of the Second Term, walked up to the last bench, sat beside Mani, and felt very comfortable indeed till Mani gave him a jab in the ribs, which he returned. He had impressed the whole class on the very first day. He was a newcomer; he dressed very well—he was the only boy in the class who wore socks and shoes, a fur cap and tie, and a wonderful coat and knickers. He came to the school in a car. As well as all this, he proved to be a very good student too. There were vague rumours that he had come from some English boys' school somewhere in Madras. He spoke very good English, 'exactly like a "European" '; which meant that few in the school could make out what he said. Many of his class-mates could not trust themselves to speak to him, their fund of broken English being small. Only Sankar, the genius of the class, had the courage to face him, though his English sounded halting and weak before that of Rajam.

This Rajam was a rival to Mani. In his manner to Mani he assumed a certain nonchalance to which Mani was not accustomed. If Mani jabbed, Rajam jabbed; if Mani clouted, he clouted; if Mani kicked, he kicked. If Mani was the overlord of the class, Rajam seemed to be nothing less. And add to all this the fact that Rajam was a regular seventy-percenter, second only to Sankar. There were sure indications that Rajam was the new power in the class. Day by day as Mani looked on, it was becoming increasingly clear that a new menace had appeared in his life.

All this lay behind his decision on the river-step to bundle up Rajam and throw him into the river. Swaminathan expressed a slight fear: 'You forget that his father is the police superintendent.' Mani remained silent for a while and said, 'What do I care? Some night I am going to crack his shoulders with my clubs.'

'If I were you, I would keep out of the way of policemen. They are an awful lot,' said Swaminathan.

'If you were me! Huh! But thank God I am not you, a milk-toothed coward like you.'

Swaminathan bit his lips and sighed.

'And that reminds me,' said the other, 'you are in need of a little warning. I find you hanging about that Rajam a bit too much. Well, have a care for your limbs. That is all I can say.'

Swaminathan broke into loud protestations. Did Mani think that Swaminathan could respect anyone but him, Mani the dear old friend and guide? What made him think so? As far as Swaminathan could remember, he had never been within three yards of Rajam. Oh, how he hated him! That vile upstart! When had Mani seen him with Rajam? Oh, yes. It must have been during the Drawing period on Monday. It was Rajam who had come and talked to him in spite of the cold face that Swaminathan had turned to him. That ass had wanted a pencil sharpener, which he did not get, as he was promptly directed to go to a shop and buy it if he needed it so urgently. Oh, there was no comparison between Rajam and Mani.

This pleased Mani greatly. For the first time that evening he laughed, and laughed heartily too. He shook Swaminathan and gave such an affectionate twist to his ear that Swaminathan gave a long howl. And then he suddenly asked, 'Did you bring the thing that I wanted?'

'Oh, Mani! I beg a hundred pardons of you. My mother was all the time in the kitchen. I could not get it.' ('It' referred to lime pickles.)

'You are a nasty little coward—oh, this riverbank and the fine evening. How splendid it would have been! . . .'

Swaminathan was to act as a cord of communication between Rajam and Mani. They were sitting in the last bench with their backs against the yellow wall. Swaminathan sat between Rajam and Mani. Their books were before them on the desks; but their minds were busy.

Mani wrote on a piece of paper: 'Are you a man?' and gave it to Swaminathan, who pushed it across to Rajam, putting on as offensive a look as possible. Rajam read it, crumpled it, and threw it away. At which Mani wrote another note repeating the question, with the addition: 'You are the son of a dog if you don't answer this,' and pushed it across. Rajam hissed into Swaminathan's face, 'You scoundrel, don't disturb me,' and crumpled the letter up.

Further progress was stopped.

'Swaminathan, stand up,' said the teacher. Swaminathan stood up faithfully.

'What is Lisbon famous for?' asked the teacher.

Swaminathan hesitated and ventured, 'For being the capital of Spain.'

The teacher bit his moustache and fired a second question, 'What do you know about the Indian climate?'

'It is hot in summer and cold in winter.'

'Stand up on the bench!' roared the teacher. And Swaminathan stood up without a protest. He was glad that he was given this supposedly degrading punishment instead of the cane.

The teacher resumed his lessons: Africa was a land of forests. Nile was the most important river there. Did they understand? What did he say? He selected someone from the first bench to answer this question. (Nile was the most important river in Africa, the boy answered promptly, and the teacher was satisfied.) What was Nile? (The most important river in Africa, a boy answered with alacrity and was instantly snubbed for it, for he had to learn not to answer before he was asked to.) Silence. Silence. Why was there such a lot of noise in the class? Let them go on making a noise and they would get a clean, big zero in the examination. He would see to that . . .

Swaminathan paid no attention to the rest of the lessons. His mind began to wander. Standing on the bench, he stood well over the whole class. He could see so many heads, and he classified them according to the caps: there were four red caps, twenty-five Gandhi caps, ten fur caps, and so on.

When the work for the day was over, Swaminathan, Mani and Rajam adjourned to a secluded spot to say what was in their minds. Swaminathan stood between them and acted as the medium of communication. They were so close that they could have heard each other even if they had spoken in whispers. But it was a matter of form between enemies to communicate through a medium. Mani faced Swaminathan steadily and asked, 'Are you a man?' Swaminathan turned to Rajam and repeated, 'Are you a man?' Rajam flared up and shouted, 'Which dog doubts it?' Swaminathan turned to Mani and said ferociously, 'Which dirty dog doubts it?'

'Have you the courage to prove that you are a man?' asked Mani.

Swaminathan turned to Rajam and repeated it.

'How?'

'How?' repeated Swaminathan to Mani.

'Meet me at the river, near Nallappa's Grove, tomorrow evening.'

'—near Nallappa's Grove,' Swaminathan was pleased to echo.

'What for?' asked Rajam.

'To see if you can break my head.'

'Oh, to pieces,' said Rajam.

Swaminathan's services were dispensed with. They gave him no time to repeat their words. Rajam shouted in one ear, and Mani in the other.

'So we may expect you at the river tomorrow,' said Swaminathan.

'Yes,' Rajam assured them.

Mani wanted to know if the other would come with guards. No, he would not. And Mani voiced another doubt: 'If anything happens to you, will you promise to keep it out of your father's knowledge?' Rajam promised, after repudiating the very suggestion that he might act otherwise.

Nallappa's Grove stood a few yards before them. It was past six and the traffic for the day between the banks was over. The usual evening crowd was far behind them. Swaminathan and Mani were squatting on the sand. They were silent. Mani was staring at the ground, with a small wooden club under his arm. He was thinking: he was going to break Rajam's head in a short while and throw his body into the river. But if it should be recovered? But then how could they know that he had done it? But if Rajam should conk and trouble him at night as a spirit? Since his grandfather's death, he was sleeping alone. What if Rajam should come and pull his hair at night? After all it would be better not to kill him. He would content himself with breaking his limbs and leaving him to his fate. If he should batter his head, who was going to find it out? Unless of course—he cast a sly look at Swaminathan, who was blinking innocently . . . unless of course Swaminathan informed the police.

At the sound of the creaking of boots, they turned and found that Rajam had come. He was dressed in khaki, and carried under his arm an air-gun that was given to him a couple of months ago on his birthday. He stood very stiff and said: 'Here I am, ready.'

'You are late.'

'Yes.'

'We will start.'

Rajam shouldered his gun and fired a shot in the air. Mani was startled. He stood still, his club down.

'You heard the shot?' asked Rajam. 'The next is going to be into your body, if you are keen upon a fight.'

'But this is unfair. I have no gun while you have . . . It was to be a hand-to-hand fight.'

'Then why have you brought your club? You never said anything about it yesterday.'

Mani hung his head.

'What have I done to offend you?' asked Rajam.

'You called me a sneak before someone.'

'That is a lie.'

There was an awkward pause. 'If this is all the cause of your anger, forget it. I won't mind being friends.'

'Nor I,' said Mani.

Swaminathan gasped in astonishment. In spite of his posing before Mani, he admired Rajam intensely, and longed to be his friend. Now is was the happiest conclusion to all the unwanted trouble. He danced with joy. Rajam lowered his gun, and Mani dropped his club. To show his goodwill, Rajam pulled out of his pocket half a dozen biscuits.

The river's mild rumble, the rustling of the *peepul* leaves, the half-light of the late evening, and the three friends eating, and glowing with new friendship—Swaminathan felt at perfect peace with the world.

CHAPTER THREE

SWAMI'S GRANDMOTHER

IN THE ILL-VENTILATED dark passage between the front hall and the dining-room, Swaminathan's grandmother lived with all her belongings, which consisted of an elaborate bed made of five carpets, three bedsheets and five pillows, a square box made of jute fibre, and a small wooden box containing copper coins, cardamoms, cloves, and arecanut.

After the night meal, with his head on Granny's lap, nestling close to her, Swaminathan felt very snug and safe in the faint atmosphere of cardamom and cloves.

'Oh, Granny!' he cried ecstatically, 'you don't know what a great fellow Rajam is.' He told her the story of the first enmity between Rajam and Mani and the subsequent friendship.

'You know, he has a real police dress,' said Swaminathan.

'Is it? What does he want a police dress for?' asked Granny.

'His father is the Police Superintendent. He is the master of every policeman here.' Granny was impressed. She said that it must be a tremendous office indeed. She then recounted the days when her husband, Swaminathan's grandfather, was a powerful Sub-Magistrate, in which office he made the police force tremble before him, and the fiercest dacoits of the place flee. Swaminathan waited impatiently for her to finish the story. But she went on, rambled, confused, mixed up various incidents that took place at different times.

'That will do, Granny,' he said ungraciously. 'Let me tell you something about Rajam. Do you know how many marks he gets in Arithmetic?'

'He gets all the marks, does he, child?' asked Granny.

'No, silly. He gets ninety marks out of one hundred.'

'Good. But you must also try and get marks like him . . . You know, Swami, your grandfather used to frighten the examiners with his answers sometimes. When he answered a question, he did it in a tenth of the time that others took to do it. And then, his answers would be so powerful that his teachers would give him two hundred marks sometimes . . . When he passed his FA he got such a big medal! I wore it as a pendant for years till—when did I remove it? Yes, when your aunt was born . . . No, it wasn't your aunt . . . It was when your father was born . . . I remember on the tenth day of confinement . . . No, no. I was right. It was when your aunt was born. Where is that medal now? I gave it away to your aunt—and she melted it and made four bangles out of it. The fool! And such flimsy bangles too! I have always maintained that she is the worst fool in our family . . .'

'Oh, enough, Granny! You go on bothering about old unnecessary stories. Won't you listen to Rajam?'

'Yes, dear, yes.'

'Granny, when Rajam was a small boy, he killed a tiger.'

'Indeed! The brave little boy!'

'You are saying it just to please me. You don't believe it.'

Swaminathan started the story enthusiastically: Rajam's father was camping in a forest. He had his son with him. Two tigers came upon them suddenly, one knocking down the father from behind. The other began chasing Rajam, who took shelter behind a bush and shot it dead with his gun. 'Granny, are you asleep?' Swaminathan asked at the end of the story.

'No, dear, I am listening.'

'Let me see. How many tigers came upon how many?'

'About two tigers on Rajam,' said granny.

Swaminathan became indignant at his grandmother's inaccuracy. 'Here I am going hoarse telling you important things and you fall asleep and imagine all sorts of nonsense. I am not going to tell you anything more. I know why you are so indifferent. You hate Rajam.'

'No, no, he is a lovely little boy,' Granny said with conviction, though she had never seen Rajam. Swaminathan was pleased. Next moment a new doubt assailed him. 'Granny, probably you don't believe the tiger incident.'

'Oh, I believe every word of it,' Granny said soothingly. Swaminathan was pleased, but added as a warning: 'He would shoot anyone who called him a liar.'

Granny expressed her approval of this attitude and then begged leave to start the story of Harischandra, who, just to be true to his word, lost his throne, wife, and child, and got them all back in the end. She was halfway through it when Swaminathan's rhythmic snoring punctuated her narration, and she lay down to sleep.

Saturday afternoon. Since Saturday and Sunday came so rarely, to Swaminathan it seemed absurd to waste at home, gossiping with Granny and Mother or doing sums. It was his father's definite orders that Swaminathan should not start loafing in the afternoon and that he should stay at home and do schoolwork. But this order was seldom obeyed.

Swaminathan sat impatiently in his 'study', trying to wrest the meaning out of a poem in his *English Reader*. His father stood before the mirror, winding a turban round his head. He had put on his silk coat. Now only his spectacles remained. Swaminathan watched his progress keenly. Even the spectacles were on. All that remained now was the watch.

Swaminathan felt glad. This was the last item and after that Father would leave for the Court. Mother came in with a tumbler of water in one hand and a plate of betel leaves and nuts in the other. Frank drank the water and held out his hand. She gave him a little arecanut and half a dozen neatly-rolled betel leaves. He put them all into his mouth, chewing them with great contentment. Swaminathan read at the top of his voice the poem about a woolly sheep. His father fussed about a little for his tiny silver snuff-box and the spotted kerchief, which was the most unwashed thing in that house. He hooked his umbrella on his arm. This was really the last signal for starting. Swaminathan had almost closed the book and risen. His father had almost gone out of the room. But—Swaminathan stamped his foot under the table. Mother stopped Father and said: 'By the way, I want some change. The tailor is coming today. He has been pestering me for the last four days.'

'Ask him to come tomorrow,' Father said. Mother was insistent. Father returned to his bureau, searched for the keys, opened it, took out a purse, and gave her the change. 'I don't know how I am going to manage things for the rest of the month,' he said peering into the purse. He locked the bureau, and adjusted his turban before the mirror. He took a heavy pinch of snuff, and wiping his nose with his kerchief, walked out. Swaminathan heaved a sigh of relief.

'Bolt the door,' came Father's voice from the street door. Swaminathan heard the clicking of the bolts. He sat at the window, watched his father turn the corner, and then left his post.

His mother was in the kitchen giving instructions to the cook about the afternoon coffee. Granny was sitting up in her bed. 'Come here, boy,' she cried as soon as she saw him.

'I can't. No time now.'

'Please. I will give you three pies,' she cried.

Swaminathan ignored the offer and dashed away.

'Where are you going?' Mother asked.

'I have got to go,' Swaminathan said with a serious face.

'Are you going to loaf about in the sun?'

'Certainly not,' he replied curtly.

'Wander about recklessly and catch fever? . . .'

'No, mother, I am not going to wander about.'

'Has your father not asked you to stay at home on holidays?'

'Yes, but my Drawing Master has asked me to see him. I suppose even then I should not go.' He added bitterly: 'If I fail in the Drawing examination I think you will be pleased.'

Swaminathan ran down Grove Street, turned to his right, threaded his way through Abu Lane, stood before a low-roofed, dingy house, and gave a low whistle. He waited for a second and repeated it. The door chain clanked, the door opened a little, and Mani's head appeared and said: 'Fool! My aunt is here, don't come in. Go away and wait for me there.'

Swaminathan moved away and waited under a tree. The sun was beating down fiercely. The street was almost deserted. A donkey was standing near a gutter, patiently watching its sharp shadow. A cow was munching a broad, green, plantain leaf. Presently Mani sneaked out of his house.

Rajam's father lived in Lawley Extension (named after the mighty engineer Sir Frederick Lawley, who was at one time the Superintending Engineer for Malgudi Circle), which consisted of about fifty neat bungalows, mostly occupied by government officials. The Trunk Road to Trichinopoly passed a few yards in front of these houses.

Swaminathan and Mani were nervously walking up the short drive leading to Rajam's house. A policeman in uniform cried to them to stop and came running towards them. Swaminathan felt like turning and fleeing. He appealed to Mani to speak to the policeman. The policeman asked what they were doing there. Mani said in a tone in which overdone carelessness was a trifle obvious: 'If Rajam is in the house, we are here to see him. He asked us to come.' The policeman at once became astonishingly amiable and took them along to Rajam's room.

To Mani and Swaminathan the room looked large. There were chairs in it, actually chairs, and a good big table with Rajam's books arranged neatly on it. What impressed them most was a timepiece on the table. Such a young fellow to own a timepiece! His father seemed to be an extraordinary man.

Presently Rajam entered. He had known that his friends were waiting for him, but he liked to keep them waiting for a few minutes, because he had seen his father doing it. So he stood for a few minutes in the adjoining room, biting his nails. When he could keep away no longer, he burst in upon his friends.

'Sit down, boys, sit down,' he cried when he saw them standing.

In a few minutes they were chatting about odds and ends, discussing their teachers and school-mates, their parents, toys, and games.

Rajam took them to a cupboard and threw it open. They beheld astounding things in it, miniature trains and motors, mechanical marvels, and a magic-lantern with slides, a good many large picture-books, and a hundred other things. What interested Mani most was a grim air-gun that stood in a corner. Rajam gave them permission to handle anything they pleased. In a short while Swaminathan was running an engine all over the room. Mani was shooting arrow after arrow from a bow, at the opposite wall. When he tired of it, he took up the gun and devastated the furniture around with lead balls.

'Are you fellows, any of you, hungry?' Rajam asked.

'No,' they said half-heartedly.

'Hey,' Rajam cried. A policeman entered.

'Go and ask the cook to bring some coffee and tiffin for three.' The ease and authority with which he addressed the policeman filled his friends with wonder and admiration.

The cook entered with a big plateful of eatables. He set down the plate on the table. Rajam felt that he must display his authority.

'Remove it from the table, you—' he roared at the cook. The cook removed it and placed it on a chair.

'You dirty ass, take it away, don't put it there.'

'Where am I to put it, Raju?' asked the cook.

Rajam burst out: 'You rascal, you scoundrel, you talk back to me?'

The cook made a wry face and muttered something.

'Put it on the table,' Rajam commanded. The cook obeyed, mumbling: 'If you are rude, I am going to tell your mother.'

'Go and tell her, I don't care,' Rajam retorted.

He peered into a cup and cursed the cook for bringing it so dirty. The cook looked up for a moment, quietly lifted the plate, and saying, 'Come and eat in the kitchen if you want food,' went away with it.

This was a great disappointment to Swaminathan and Mani, who were waiting with watering mouths. To Rajam it was a terrible moment. To be outdone by his servant before his friends! He sat still for a few minutes and then said with a forced laugh: 'The scoundrel, that cook is a buffoon . . . Wait a minute.' He went out.

After a while he returned, carrying the plate himself. His friends were a bit astonished at this sign of defeat. Obviously he could not subdue the cook. Swaminathan puzzled his head to find out why Rajam did not shoot the cook dead, and Mani wanted to ask if he could be allowed to have his own way with the cook for a few minutes. But Rajam set their minds at rest by explaining to them: 'I had to bring this myself. I went in and gave the cook such a kick for his impertinence that he is lying unconscious in the kitchen.'

CHAPTER FOUR

'WHAT IS A TAIL?'

THE GEOGRAPHY MASTER was absent, and the boys of the First A had leisure between three and three-forty-five on Wednesday.

Somehow Swaminathan had missed his friends and found himself alone. He wandered along the corridor of the Infant Standards. To Swaminathan, who did not really stand over four feet, the children of the Infant Standards seemed ridiculously tiny. He felt vastly superior and old. He was filled with contempt when he saw them dabbling in wet clay, trying to shape models. It seemed such a meaningless thing to do at school! Why, they could as well do those things resembling elephants, mangoes, and whatnots, in the backyards of their houses. Why did they come all the way to a school to do this sort of thing? Schools were meant for more serious things like Geography, Arithmetic, Bible, and English.

In one room he found all the children engaged in repeating simultaneously the first two letters of the Tamil alphabet. He covered his ears and wondered how the teacher was able to stand it. He passed on. In another room he found an ill-clad, noisy crowd of children. The noise that they made, sitting on their benches and swinging their legs, got on his nerves. He wrinkled his brow and twisted his mouth in the hope of making the teacher feel his resentment but unfortunately the teacher was sitting with his back to Swaminathan.

He paused at the foot of the staircase leading to the senior classes—the Second and the Third Forms. He wanted to go up and inspect those classes which he eagerly looked forward to joining. He took two or three steps up, and changed his mind. The Head Master might be up there, he always handled those classes. The teachers too were formidable, not to speak of the boys themselves, who were snobs and bullies. He heard the creak-creak of sandals far off and recognized the footsteps of the Head Master. He did not want to be caught there—that would mean a lot of unsatisfactory explanations.

It was with pleasant surprise that he stumbled into his own set, which he had thought was not at school. Except Rajam and Mani all the rest were there. Under the huge tamarind tree they were playing some game. Swaminathan joined them with a low, ecstatic cry. The response disappointed him. They turned their faces to him with a faint smile, and returned to their game. What surprised Swaminathan most was that even the genial Somu was grim. Something seemed to be wrong somewhere. Swaminathan assumed an easy tone and shouted: 'Boys, what about a little place for me in the game?' Nobody answered this. Swaminathan paused and announced that he was waiting for a place in the game.

'It is a pity, we can't take more,' Sankar said curtly.

'There are people who can be very efficient as Tails,' said the Pea. The rest laughed at this.

'You said Tail, didn't you?' asked Sankar. 'What makes you talk of Tail now?'

'It is just my pleasure. What do *you* care? It doesn't apply to you anyway,' said the Pea.

'I am glad to hear it, but does it apply to anyone here?' asked Sankar.

'It may.'

'What is a Tail?'

'A long thing that attaches itself to an ass or a dog.'

Swaminathan could comprehend very little except that the remark contained some unpleasant references to himself. His cheeks grew hot. He wanted to cry.

The bell rang and they ran to their class. Swaminathan slunk to his seat with a red face.

It was the English period presided over by Vedanayagam. He was reading the story of the old man who planted trees for posterity and was paid ten rupees by a king. Not a word reached Swaminathan's brain, in which there was only dull pain and vacuity. If he had been questioned he would have blundered and would have had to spend the rest of the hour standing on the bench. But his luck was good.

The period was over. He was walking home alone, rather slowly, with a troubled heart. Somu was going a few yards in front of him. Swaminathan cried out: 'Somu, Somu . . . Somu, won't you stop?' Somu stopped till the other came up.

After a brief silence Swaminathan quavered: 'What is the matter with you fellows?'

'Nothing very particular,' replied Somu. 'By the way, may I inform you that you have earned a new name?—The Tail, Rajam's Tail, to be more precise. We aren't good enough for you, I believe. But how can everyone be a son of a Police Superintendent?' With that he was off.

This was probably Swaminathan's first shock in life. It paralysed all his mental processes. When his mind started working again, he faintly wondered if he had been dreaming. The staid Somu, the genial Somu, the uncle Somu, was it the same Somu that had talked to him a few minutes ago? What was wrong in liking and going about with Rajam? Why did it make them so angry?

He went home, flung his coat and cap and books on the table, gulped down the cold coffee that was waiting for him, and sat on the *pyol*, vacantly gazing into the dark intricacies of the gutter that adorned Vinayaka Mudali Street. A dark volume of water was rushing along. Odd pieces of paper, leaves, and sticks floated by. A small piece of tin was gently skimming along. Swaminathan had an impulse to plunge his hand in and pick it up. But he let it go. His mind was inert. He watched the shining bit float away. It was now at the end of the compound wall; now it had passed under the tree. Swaminathan was slightly irritated when a brick obstructed the progress of the tin. He said that the brick must either move along or stand aside without interfering with the traffic. The piece of tin released itself and dashed along furiously, disappeared round a bend at the end of the street. Swaminathan ran in, got a sheet of paper, and made a boat. He saw a small ant moving about aimlessly. He carefully caught it, placed it in the boat, and lowered the boat into the stream. He watched its quick motion in rapture. He held his breath when the boat with its cargo neared a danger zone formed by stuck-up bits of straw and other odds and ends. The boat made a beautiful swerve to the right and avoided destruction. It went on and on. It neared a fatal spot where the waters were swirling round and round in eddies. Swaminathan was certain that his boat was nearing its last moment. He had no doubt that it was going to be drawn right to the bottom of the circling eddies. The boat whirled madly round, shaking and swaying and quivering. But providentially a fresh supply of water from the kitchen in the neighbour's house pushed it from behind out of danger. But it rushed on at a fearful speed, and Swaminathan felt that it was going to turn turtle. Presently it calmed, and resumed a normal speed. But when it passed under a tree, a thick dry leaf fell down and upset it. Swaminathan ran frantically to the spot to see if he could at least save the ant. He peered long into the water, but there was no sign of the ant. The boat and its cargo were wrecked beyond recovery. He took a pinch of earth, uttered a prayer for the soul of the ant, and dropped it into the gutter.

In a few days Swaminathan got accustomed to his position as the enemy of Somu and company.

All the same, now and then he had an irresistible desire to talk to his old friends. When the Scripture Master pursed his lips and scratched his nose, Swaminathan had a wild impulse to stamp on the Pea's leg and laugh, for that was a joke that they had never failed to enjoy day after day for many years past. But now Swaminathan smothered the impulse and chuckled at it himself, alone. And again, when the boy with the red cap nodded in his seat and woke up with a start every time his head sank down, Swaminathan wanted to whisper into the Pea's ear: 'Look at that fellow, third on the first bench, red cap—Now he is falling off again—' and giggle; but he merely bit his lips and kept quiet.

Somu was looking in his direction. Swaminathan thought that there was friendliness in his look. He felt a momentary ecstasy as he realized that Somu was willing to be friendly again. They stared at each other for a while, and just as Swaminathan was beginning to put on a sweet friendly look, Somu's expression hardened and he turned away.

Swaminathan was loitering in the compound. He heard familiar voices behind, turned round, and saw Somu, Sankar, and the Pea, following him. Swaminathan wondered whether to stop and join them, or wait till they had passed and then go in the opposite direction. For it was awkward to be conscious of the stare of three pairs of hostile eyes behind one's ears. He believed that every minute movement of his body was being watched and commented on by the three followers. He felt that his gait was showing unfavourably in their eyes. He felt they were laughing at the way in which he carried his books. There was a slight itching on his nape, his hand almost rose, but he checked it, feeling that the scratching would be studiously watched by the six keen eyes.

He wanted to turn to his right and enter the school hall. But that would be construed as cowardice; they would certainly think that he was doing it to escape from them. He wanted to run away, but that would be no better. He wanted to turn back and get away in the opposite direction, but that would mean meeting them square in the face. So, his only recourse was to keep on walking as best as he could, not showing that he was conscious of his followers. The same fellows ten days ago, what they were! Now what formidable creatures they had turned out to be! Swaminathan was wonderstruck at the change.

It was becoming unendurable. He felt that his legs were taking a circular motion, and were twining round each other when he walked. It was too late to turn and dash into the school hall. He had passed it. Now he had only one way of escape. He must run. It was imperative. He tried a trick. He paused suddenly, turned this way and that, as if looking for something, and then cried aloud: 'Oh, I have left my note-book somewhere,' raised his hand and was off from the spot like a stag.

CHAPTER FIVE

'FATHER'S' ROOM

IT WAS SATURDAY and Rajam had promised to come in the afternoon. Swaminathan was greatly excited. Where was he to entertain him? Probably in his own 'room'; but his father often came in to dress and undress. No, he would be at Court, Swaminathan reminded himself with relief. He cleaned his table and arranged his books so neatly that his father was surprised and had a good word to say about it. Swaminathan went to his grandmother. 'Granny,' he said, 'I have talked to you about Rajam, haven't I?'

'Yes. That boy who is very strong but never passes his examination.'

'No no. That is Mani.'

'Oh, now I remember, it is a boy who is called the Gram or something, that witty little boy.'

Swaminathan made a gesture of despair. 'Look here Granny, you are again mistaking the Pea for him. I mean Rajam, who has killed tigers, whose father is the Police Superintendent, and who is great.'

'Oh,' Granny cried, 'that boy, is he coming here? I am so glad.'

'H'm . . . But I have got to tell you—'

'Will you bring him to me? I want to see him.'

'Let us see,' Swaminathan said vaguely, 'I can't promise. But I have got to tell you, when he is with me, you must not call me or come to my room.'

'Why so?' asked Granny.

'The fact is—you are, well you are too old,' said Swaminathan with brutal candour. Granny accepted her lot cheerfully.

That he must give his friend something very nice to eat, haunted his mind. He went to his mother, who was squatting before a cutter with a bundle of plantain leaves beside her. He sat before her, nervously crushing a piece of leaf this way and that, and tearing it to minute bits.

'Don't throw all those bits on the floor. I simply can't sweep the floor any more,' she said.

'Mother, what are you preparing for the afternoon tiffin?'

'Time enough to think of it,' said Mother.

'You had better prepare something very nice, something fine and sweet. Rajam is coming this afternoon. Don't make the sort of coffee that you usually give me. It must be very good and hot.' He remembered how in Rajam's house everything was brought to the room by the cook. 'Mother, would you mind if I don't come here for coffee and tiffin? Can you send it to my room?' He turned to the cook and said: 'Look here, you can't come to my room in that *dhoti*. You will have to wear a clean, white *dhoti* and shirt.' After a while he said: 'Mother, can you ask Father to lend me his room for just an hour or two?' She said that she could not as she was very busy. Why could he himself not go and ask?

'Oh, he will give more readily if you ask,' said Swaminathan.

He went to his father and said: 'Father, I want to ask you something.' Father looked up from the papers over which he was bent.

'Father, I want your room.'

'What for?'

'I have to receive a friend,' Swaminathan replied.

'You have your own room,' Father said.

'I can't show it to Rajam.'

'Who is this Rajam, such a big man?'

'He is the Police Superintendent's son. He is—he is not ordinary.'

'I see. Oh! Yes, you can have my room, but be sure not to mess up the things on the table.'

'Oh, I will be very careful. You are a nice father, Father.'

Father guffawed and said: 'Now run in, boy, and sit at your books.'

Rajam's visit went off much more smoothly that Swaminathan had anticipated. Father had left his room open; Mother had prepared some marvel with wheat, plum and sugar. Coffee was really good. Granny had kept her promise and did not show her senile self to Rajam. Swaminathan was only sorry that the cook did not change his *dhoti*.

Swaminathan seated Rajam in his father's revolving chair. It was nearly three hours since he had come. They had talked out all subjects—Mani, Ebenezar, trains, tiger-hunting, police, and ghosts.

'Which is your room?' Rajam asked.

Swaminathan replied with a grave face: 'This is my room, why?'

Rajam took time to swallow this. 'Do you read such books?' he asked, eyeing the big gilt-edged law books on the table. Swaminathan was embarrassed.

Rajam made matters worse with another question.

'But where are your books?' There was just a flicker of a smile on his lips.

'The fact is,' said Swaminathan, 'this table belongs to my father. When I am out, he meets his clients in this room.'

'But where do you keep your books?'

Swaminathan made desperate attempts to change the topic: 'You have seen my grandmother, Rajam?'

'No. Will you show her to me? I should love to see her,' replied Rajam.

'Wait a minute then,' said Swaminathan and ran out. He had one last hope that Granny might he asleep. It was infinitely safer to show one's friends a sleeping Granny.

He saw her sitting on her bed complacently. He was disappointed. He stood staring at her, lost in thought.

'What is it, boy?' Granny asked. 'Do you want anything?'

'No. Aren't you asleep? Granny,' he said a few minutes later, 'I have brought Rajam to see you.'

'Have you?' cried Granny. 'Come nearer, Rajam. I can't see your face well. You know I am old and blind.'

Swaminathan was furious and muttered under his breath that his Granny had no business to talk all this drivel to Rajam.

Rajam sat on her bed. Granny stroked his hair and said that he had fine soft hair, though it was really short and prickly. Granny asked what his mother's name was, and how many children she had. She then asked if she had many jewels. Rajam replied that his mother had a black trunk filled with jewels, and a green one containing gold and silver vessels. Rajam then described to her Madras, its lighthouse, its sea, its trams and buses, and its cinemas. Every item made Granny gasp with wonder.

When Swaminathan entered the class, a giggle went round the benches. He walked to his seat hoping that he might not be the cause of the giggling. But it continued. He looked about. His eyes travelled up to the black-board. His face burnt red. On the board was written in huge letters, 'TAIL'. Swaminathan walked to the black-board and rubbed it off with his hands. He turned and saw Sankar's head bent over his note-book, and the Pea was busy unpacking his satchel. Without a word Swaminathan approached the Pea and gave him a fierce slap on his cheek. The Pea burst into tears and swore that he did not do it. He cast a sly look at Sankar, who was absorbed in some work. Swaminathan turned to him and slapped his face also.

Soon there was pandemonium, Sankar, Swaminathan and the Pea rolling over, tearing, scratching and kicking one another. The bell rang. Rajam, Somu and Mani entered. The teacher came in and stood aghast. He could do little more than look on and ejaculate. He was the old Tamil pundit, the most helpless teacher in the school.

Somu and Mani parted the fighters. The teacher ascended the platform and took his seat. The class settled down. Somu got up and said: 'Sir, please let us go out. We do not want to disturb the class.' The teacher demurred; but already Mani had gone out, pushing Swaminathan and the Pea before him. Somu followed him with Sankar.

They came to a lonely spot in the field adjoining the school. There was tense silence for a while, and Mani broke it: 'What is wrong with you, you little rogues?' All three started to speak at once. Swaminathan's voice was the loudest: 'He—the Pea—wrote TAIL—Big Tail—on the black-board—big—'

'No—I didn't, you—' screamed the Pea.

'The other two wrote it,' cried Swaminathan, pointing at Sankar.

'Rascal! Did you see me?' howled Sankar.

Mani covered their mouths with his hands. 'What is a Tail, anyway?' he asked, not having been told anything about it till then.

'They call me Rajam's Tail,' sobbed Swaminathan.

A frozen expression came over Mani's face, and he asked, 'And who dares to talk of Rajam here?'

'Oh, dare!' repeated Somu.

'If any of you fellows have done it—' growled Mani, looking at the trembling Sankar and the Pea.

'If they have, what can you do?' asked Somu with a contemptuous smile.

'What do you mean, Somu, what do you mean?'

'Look here, Mani,' Somu cried, 'for a long time I have been waiting to tell you this: you think too much of yourself and your powers.' Mani swung his hand and brought it down on Somu's nape. Somu pushed it away with a heavy blow. Mani aimed a kick at Somu, which would send him rolling. Somu stepped aside and delivered one himself which nearly bent the other.

The three youngsters could hardly believe their eyes. Somu and Mani fighting! They lost their heads. They thought that Somu and Mani were killing each other. They looked accusingly at one another, and then ran towards the school.

They burst in upon the Head Master, who gathered from them with difficulty that in the adjacent field two murders were being committed at that very moment. He was disposed to laugh at first. But the excitement and seriousness on the boys' faces made him check his laughter and scratch his chin. He called a peon and with him set off to the field.

The fighters, rolling and rolling, were everywhere in the field. The Head Master and the peon easily picked them apart, much to the astonishment of Swaminathan, who had thought till then that the strength that Somu or Mani possessed was not possessed by anyone else in the world.

CHAPTER SIX

A FRIEND IN NEED

ONE AFTERNOON THREE weeks later, Swaminathan stood before Mani's house and gave a low whistle. Mani joined him. They started for Rajam's house, speculating on the way what the surprise (which Rajam had said he would give them if they saw him that afternoon) might be.

'I think,' said Swaminathan, 'Rajam is merely joking. It is merely a trick to get us to his house.' He was very nearly pushed into a gutter for this doubt.

'Probably he has bought a monkey or something,' Swaminathan ventured again. Mani was gracious enough to admit that it might be so. They thought of all possible subjects that might surprise them, and gave up the attempt in the end.

Their thoughts turned to their enemies. 'You know what I am going to do?' Mani asked. 'I am going to break Somu's waist. I know where he lives. He lives in Kabir Street, behind the market. I have often seen him coming out at nights to a shop in the market for betel leaves. I shall first fling a stone at the municipal lamp and put it out. You have no idea how dark Kabir Street is . . . I shall wait with my club, and as soon as he appears—he will sprawl in the dust with broken bones . . .' Swaminathan shuddered at the thought. 'And that is not all,' said Mani, 'I am going to get that Pea under my heel and press him to the earth. And Sankar is going to hang by his tuft over the Sarayu, from a *peepul* branch . . .'

They stopped talking when they reached Rajam's house.

The gate was bolted, and they got up the wall and jumped in. A servant came running towards them. He asked, 'Why did you climb the wall?'

'Is the wall your property?' Mani asked and burst into laughter.

'But if you had broken your ribs—' the servant began.

'What is that to you? Your ribs are safe, are they not?' Swaminathan asked ungraciously and laughed.

'And just a word more,' Mani said. 'Do you happen to be by any chance the Police Superintendent's son?'

'No, no,' replied the servant.

'Very well then,' replied Mani, 'we have come to see and talk to the Police Superintendent's son.' The servant beat a hasty retreat.

They banged their fists on Rajam's door. They heard the clicking of the latch and hid themselves behind the pillar. Rajam peeped out and shut the door again.

They came out, stood before the door, and wondered what to do. Swaminathan applied his mouth to the keyhole and mewed like a cat. Mani pulled him away and putting his mouth to the hole barked like a dog. The latch clicked again, and the door opened slightly. Mani whispered to Swaminathan, 'You are a blind kitten, I will be a blind puppy.'

Mani fell down on his knees and hands, shut his eyes tight, pushed the door with his head, and entered Rajam's room in the role of a blind puppy. Swaminathan crawled behind him with shut eyes, mewing for all he was worth. They moved round and round the room, Rajam adding to the interest of the game by mewing and barking in answer every few seconds. The blind puppy brushed its side against a leg, and thinking that it belonged to Rajam, softly bit the calf muscle. Imagine its confusion when it opened its eyes and saw that it was biting its enemy, Somu! The blind kitten nestled close to a leg and scratched it with its paw. Opening its eyes, it found that it was fondling a leg that belonged to its enemy, Sankar.

Mani remained stunned for a moment, and then scrambled to his feet. He looked around, his face twitching with shame and rage. He saw the Pea sitting in a corner, his eyes twinkling with mischief, and felt impelled to take him by the throat. He turned round and saw Rajam regarding him steadily, his mouth still quivering with a smothered grin.

As for Swaminathan he felt that the best place for himself would be the darkness and obscurity under a table or a chair.

'What do you mean by this, Rajam?' Mani asked.

'Why are you so wild?'

'It was your fault,' said Mani vehemently. 'I didn't know—' He looked around.

'Well, well. I didn't ask you to crawl and bark, did I?'

Somu and company laughed. Mani glared round, 'I am going away, Rajam. This is not the place for me.'

Rajam replied, 'You may go away, if you don't want me to see you or speak to you any more.'

Mani fidgeted uneasily. Rajam took him aside and soothed him. Rajam then turned to Swaminathan, who was lost in bottomless misery. He comforted and flattered him by saying that it was the best imitation of a cat and dog that he had ever witnessed in his life. He admitted that for a few minutes he wondered whether he was watching a real cat and a dog. They would get prizes if they did it in fairs. If Swaminathan and Mani would be good enough to repeat the fun, he would be delighted, and even ask his father to come and watch.

This was soothing. Swaminathan and Mani felt proud of themselves. And after the round of eating that followed, they were perfectly happy, except when they thought of the other three in the room.

They were in this state of mind when Rajam began a lecture on friendship. He said impressive things about friendship, quoting from his book the story of the dying old man and the faggots, which proved that union was strength. A friend in need was a friend indeed. He then started giving hair-raising accounts of what hell had in store for persons who fostered enmity. According to Rajam, it was written in the Vedas that a person who fostered enmity should be locked up in a small room, after his death. He would be made to stand, stark naked, on a pedestal of red-hot iron. There were beehives all around with bees as big as lemons. If the sinner stepped down from the pedestal, he would have to put his foot on immense scorpions and centipedes that crawled about the room in hundreds—

(A shudder went through the company.)

—The sinner would have to stand thus for a month, without food or sleep. At the end of a month he would be transferred to another place, a very narrow bridge over a lake of boiling oil. The bridge was so narrow that he would be able to keep only one foot on it at a time. Even on the narrow bridge there were plenty of wasp nests and cactus, and he would be goaded from behind to move on. He would have to balance on one foot, and then on another, for ages and ages, to keep himself from falling into the steaming lake below, and move on indefinitely . . .

The company was greatly impressed. Rajam then invited everyone to come forward and say that they would have no more enemies. If Sankar said it, he would get a bound note-book; if Swaminathan said it, he would get a clock-work engine; if Somu said it, he would get a belt; and if Mani said it, he would get a nice pocket-knife; and the Pea would get a marvellous little pen.

He threw open the cupboard and displayed the prizes. There was silence for some time as each sat gnawing his nails. Rajam was sweating with his peace-making efforts.

The Pea was the first to rise. He stood before the cupboard and said, 'Let me see the fountain-pen.' Rajam gave it him. The Pea turned it round and round and gave it back without any comment. 'Why don't you like it?' Rajam asked. The Pea kept staring into the cupboard and said, 'Can I have that box?' He pointed at a tiny box with a lot of yellow and black designs on it and a miniature Taj Mahal on its lid. Rajam said, 'I can't give you that. I want it.' He paused. He had two more boxes like that in his trunk. He changed his mind, 'No. I don't want it. You can take the box if you like.'

In a short while, Mani was sharpening a knife on his palm; Somu was trying a belt on; Sankar was fingering a thick bound note-book; and Swaminathan was jealously clasping a green engine to his bosom.

CHAPTER SEVEN

A NEW ARRIVAL

MOTHER HAD BEEN abed for two days past. Swaminathan missed her very much in the kitchen, and felt uncomfortable without her attentions. He was taken to her room, where he saw her lying dishevelled and pale on her bed. She asked him to come nearer. She asked him why he was looking emaciated and if he was not eating and sleeping well. Swaminathan kept staring at her blankly. Here seemed to be a different Mother. He was cold and reserved when he spoke to her. Her appearance depressed him. He wriggled himself from her grasp and ran out.

His Granny told him that he was going to have a brother. He received the news without enthusiasm.

That night he was allowed to sleep on Granny's bed. The lights kept burning all night. Whenever he opened his eyes, he was conscious of busy feet scurrying along the passage. Late at night Swaminathan woke up and saw a lady doctor in the hall. She behaved as if the house belonged to her. She entered Mother's room, and presently out of the room came a mingled noise of whispers and stifled moans. She came out of the room with a serious face and ordered everybody about. She commanded even Father to do something. He vanished for a moment and reappeared with a small bottle in his hand. He hovered about uncertainly. The hushed voices, hurry, seriousness, agitation, hot water, and medicine— preparations for ushering a new person into the world—were too bewildering for Swaminathan's comprehension. Meanwhile Granny kept asking something of everybody that passed by, and no one bothered to answer her.

What did it matter? The five carpets in Granny's bed were

cosy; her five pillows were snug; and Granny's presence nearby was reassuring; and above all, his eyelids were becoming heavy. What more did he want? He fell asleep.

The Tamil pundit, with his unshaven face and the silver-rimmed spectacles set askew on his nose, was guiding the class through the intricacies of Tamil grammar. The guide was more enthusiastic than his followers. A continual buzz filled the air. Boys had formed themselves into small groups and carried on private conversations. The Pundit made faint attempts to silence the class by rapping his palms on the table. After a while, he gave up the attempt and went on with his lecture. His voice was scarcely audible.

Sankar and a few others sat on the first bench with cocked-up ears and busy pencils.

Swaminathan and the Pea sat on the last bench.

'I say, Pea,' said Swaminathan, 'I got a new brother this morning.'

The Pea was interested. 'How do you like him?'

'Oh, like him! He is hardly anything. Such a funny-looking creature!' said Swaminathan, and gave what he thought was an imitation of his little brother: he shut his eyes, compressed his lips, folded his hands on his chest, protruded his tongue, and tilted his head from side to side. The Pea laughed uncontrollably. 'But,' Swaminathan said, 'this thing has a wonderful pair of hands, so small and plump, you know! But I tell you, his face is awful, red, red like chilli.'

They listened to the teacher's lecture for a few minutes. 'I say, Swami,' said the Pea, 'these things grow up soon. I have seen a baby that was just like what your brother is. But you know, when I saw it again during Michaelmas I could hardly recognize it.'

CHAPTER EIGHT

BEFORE THE EXAMINATIONS

IN APRIL, JUST two weeks before the examinations, Swaminathan realized that his father was changing—for the worse. He was becoming fussy and difficult. He seemed all of a sudden to have made up his mind to harass his son. If the latter was seen chatting with his Granny, he was told sourly, 'Remember, boy, there is an examination. Your Granny can wait, not your examination.' If he was seen wandering behind his mother, he was hunted down and sent to his desk. If his voice was heard anywhere after the Taluk Office gong had struck nine, a command would come from his father's room, 'Swami, why haven't you gone to bed yet? You must get up early and study a bit.' This was a trying period in Swaminathan's life. One day he was piqued enough to retort, 'Why are you so nervous about my examination?'

'Suppose you fail?'

'I won't.'

'Of course you won't if you study hard and answer well . . . Suppose you fail and all your class-mates go up, leaving you behind? You can start doing just what you like on the very day your examination closes.'

Swaminathan reflected: suppose the Pea, Mani, Rajam and Sankar deserted him and occupied Second A? His father was right. And then his father drove home the point, 'Suppose all your juniors in the Fifth Standard become your class-mates?'

Swaminathan sat at Decimals for half an hour.

At school everybody seemed to be overwhelmed by the thought of the examinations. It was weeks since anybody had seen a smile on

Sankar's face. Somu had become brisk and businesslike. The Pea
took time to grasp jokes, and seldom gave out any. And as for
Rajam, he came to the school at the stroke of the first bell, took
down everything the teacher said, and left at the stroke of the last
bell, hardly uttering a dozen words to anybody. Mani was beginning
to look worried and took every opportunity to take Sankar aside and
have his doubts (that arose from time to time as he plodded through
his texts) cleared. He dogged the steps of the school clerk. There
was a general belief in the school that the clerk was omniscient and
knew all the question papers of all the classes.

One day Mani went to the clerk's house and laid a neat bundle
containing fresh brinjals at his feet. The clerk was pleased and took
Mani in and seated him on a stool.

The clerk looked extremely amiable and Mani felt that he
could ask anything at that moment and get it. The clerk was
murmuring something about his cat, a lank ill-fed thing, that was
nestling close to him. Most of what he was saying did not enter
Mani's head. He was waiting feverishly to open the topic of
question papers. The clerk had meanwhile passed from cats to eye-
flies; but it made little difference to Mani, who was waiting for the
other to pause for breath to launch his attack. 'You must never let
these eye-flies buzz near your eyes. All cases of eyesore can be
traced to it. When you get eyesore the only thing you can do is to
take a slice of raw onion . . .'

Mani realized that the other would not stop, and butted in,
'There is only a week more for the examinations, sir . . .'

The clerk was slightly puzzled: 'Yes, indeed, a week more . . .
You must take care to choose only the juicy variety, the large juicy
variety, not the small onion . . .'

'Sir,' Mani interrupted, ignoring the juicy variety, 'I am much
worried about my examination.' He tried to look pathetic.

'I am glad. If you read well, you will pass,' said the Oracle.

'You see, sir, I am so worried, I don't sleep at nights, thinking
of the examination . . . If you could possibly tell me something
important . . . I have such a lot to study—don't want to study
unnecessary things that may not be necessary for the examination.'
He meandered thus. The clerk understood what he was driving at,
but said, 'Just read all your portions and you will pass.' Mani
realized that diplomacy was not his line. He asked bluntly, 'Please
tell me, sir, what questions we are getting for our examination.'

The clerk denied having any knowledge of the question papers.

Mani flattered him by asking, if he did not know the questions, who else would. By just a little more of the same judicious flattery the clerk was moved to give what Mani believed to be 'valuable hints'. In spite of the fact that he did not know what the First Form texts were, the clerk ventured to advise, 'You must pay particular attention to Geography. Maybe you will have to practise map-drawing a lot. And in Arithmetic make it a point to solve at least five problems every day, and you will he able to tackle Arithmetic as easily as you swallow plantains.'

'And what about English?'

'Oh, don't worry about that. Have you read all your lessons?'

'Yes, sir,' Mani replied without conviction.

'It is all right then. You must read all the important lessons again, and if you have time, yet again, and that will be ample.'

These answers satisfied Mani greatly. On his way home, he smiled to himself and said that the four annas he had invested on brinjals was not after all a waste.

Mani felt important. He secretly pitied his class-mates, who had to do coolie work without valuable hints to lighten their labour. He felt he ought to share his good secret with Swaminathan without divulging the source.

They were going home from the school. They stopped for a while at the junction of Vinayak Mudali and Grove Streets before parting ways. Mani said, 'Young man, have you any idea what we are getting for the examination?'

'Nothing outside the covers of the text-books.'

Mani ignored the humour. 'Now listen to me carefully, last night from seven to ten, do you know what I did?'

'Munched groundnuts?'

'Idiot, don't joke. I made two maps of India, two of Africa, and one map of Europe.'

'Say all the maps in the Atlas.'

'Maybe,' Mani said, not quite liking the remark, 'but I do it with some definite purpose . . . It may be that I know one or two questions. But don't let the other fellows know anything about it. I may get into trouble.' Swaminathan was taken in by the other's seriousness and inferred a moral.

Reaching home, Swaminathan felt rather dull. His mother was not at home. Granny was not in a talkative mood. He related to her some exciting incidents of the day: 'Granny, guess what happened in our school today. A boy in First C stabbed another in the forearm with a penknife.'

'What for?' asked Granny mechanically.

'They were enemies.' Finding that it fell flat, he brought out the big event of the day. 'Granny, Granny, here is another thing. The Head Master knocked his toe against a door-post and oh! there was such a lot of blood! He went limping about the school the whole day. He couldn't take the Third Form and so they had leave, the lucky fellows!'

'Is it?' asked Granny.

Swaminathan perceived, to his intense disgust, that his Granny was in one of her dull sleepy moods.

He strayed near the swing-cradle of his little brother. Though at first he had been sceptical of his brother's attractions and possibilities, now day by day he was finding him more interesting. This little one was now six months old and was charming. His attainments were: he made shrill noises whenever he saw anybody; thrust his fists into his mouth and damped his round arms up to the elbow; vigorously kicked the air; and frequently displayed his bare red gums in a smile. Swaminathan loved every inch of him. He would spend hours balancing himself on the edge of the cradle and trying to make him say 'Swaminathan'. The little one would gurgle, and Swaminathan would shriek, pretending that it was the other's futile version of his name.

Now he peered in and was disappointed to find the baby asleep. He cleared his throat aloud and coughed in the hope of waking him. But the baby slept. He waited for a moment, and tiptoed away, reminding himself that is was best to leave the other alone, as he had a knack of throwing the house in turmoil for the first half-hour, whenever he awoke from sleep.

Staying at home in the evenings was extremely irksome. He sighed at the thought of the sand-banks of the Sarayu and Mani's company. But his father had forbidden him to go out till the examinations were over. He often felt he ought to tell his father what he thought of him. But somehow when one came near doing it, one failed. He would have to endure it after all only for a week . . . The thought that he would have to put up with his travails only for a week at worst gave him fresh energy.

He sat at his table and took out his Atlas. He opened the political map of Europe and sat gazing at it. It puzzled him how people managed to live in such a crooked country as Europe. He wondered what the shape of the people might be who lived in places where the outline narrowed as in a cape, and how they managed to escape being strangled by the contour of their land. And then another favourite problem began to tease him: how did those mapmakers find out what the shape of a country was? How did they find out that Europe was like a camel's head? Probably they stood on high towers, and copied what they saw below. He wondered if he would be able to see India as it looked in the map, if he stood on the top of the Town Hall. He had never been there nor ever did he wish to go there. Though he was incredulous, tailor Ranga persistently informed him that there was a torture chamber in the top storey of the Town Hall to which Pathans decoyed young people.

He shook himself from his brown study and copied the map of Europe. He kept the original and his own copy side by side and congratulated himself on his ability to draw, though his outline looked like some strange animal that had part bull's face and part camel's.

It was past seven by now and his father came home. He was greatly pleased to see his son at work. 'That is right, boy,' he said looking at the map. Swaminathan felt that that moment was worth all his suffering. He turned over the pages and opened out the map of Africa.

Two days before his examination he sat down to draw up a list of his needs. On a piece of paper he wrote:

Unruled white paper	20 sheets
Nibs	6
Ink	2 bottles
Clips	
Pins	

He nibbled his pencil and re-read the list. The list was disappointing. He had never known that his wants were so few. When he first sat down to draw the list he had hoped to fill two or three imposing pages. But now the cold lines on the paper numbered only five. He scrutinized the list again: 'Unruled white paper—20 sheets.' He asked himself why he was so particular about the paper's being unruled. It was a well-known fact that, try as he would, his lines had a tendency to curl up towards the right-hand corner of the paper. That would not do for examinations. He had better keep a stock of ruled paper. And then 'Nibs'. He wondered how many nibs one would need for an examination. One? Two? Five? . . . And then the 'Ink' column worried him. How much of it did one buy? After that he had trouble with Clips and Pins. He not only had not the faintest idea of the quantity of each that he would need but was totally ignorant of the unit of purchase also. Could one go to a shop and demand six pins and six clips without offending the shopman?

At the end the list was corrected to:

Unruled white paper	20 sheets
Ruled white paper	10 sheets
Black ink	1 bottle
Clips	3-6-12
Pins	6-12

The list was not satisfactory even now. After pondering over it, he added 'Cardboard Pad—One' and 'One Rupee for Additional Expenses'.

His father was busy in his office. Swaminathan stood before him with the list in his hand. Father was absorbed in his work and did not know that Swaminathan was there. Swaminathan suddenly realized that it would be better to approach his father at some other time. He could be sure of a better reception if he opened the question after food. He tiptoed out. When he was just outside the door, his father called out, 'Who is that?' There was no friendliness in the tone. 'Who is that, I say?' roared Father again and was at his side with a scowling face before Swaminathan could decide whether to sneak out or stop and answer.

'Was it you?'

'Yes.'

'You idiot, why couldn't you answer instead of driving me hoarse calling out "Who is that? Who is that?" . . . A man can't have peace in this house even for a second. Here I am at work—and every fifth second somebody or other pops in with some fool question or other. How am I to go on? Go and tell your mother that she can't come to my room for the rest of the day. I don't care if the whole battalion of oil-mongers and vegetable women come and clamour for money. Let her drive them out. Your mother seems to think—What is that paper in your hand?'

'Nothing, Father,' Swaminathan answered, thrusting the paper into his pocket.

'What is that?' Father shouted, snatching the list. Reading it with a terrific scowl, he went back to his chair. 'What is this thing?'

Swaminathan had to cough twice to find his voice. 'It is—my—examination list.'

'What examination list?'

'My examinations begin the day after tomorrow, you know.'

'And yet you are wandering about the house like an unleashed donkey! What preposterous list is this? Do you think rupees, annas and pies drop from the sky?' Swaminathan did not think so, but something nearly so. Father pulled out a drawer and peering into it said: 'You can take from me anything you want. I haven't got clips. You don't need them. And then the pad, why do you want a pad? Are there no desks in your rooms? In our days slates were good enough for us. But now you want pen, paper, ink, and pad to keep under the paper . . .' He took out an awful red pencil and scored out the 'Pad' from the list. It almost gashed the list. He flung it back at Swaminathan, who looked at it sadly. How deliciously he had been dreaming of going to Ameer Mart, jingling with coins, and buying things!

He was just going out when Father called him back and said: 'Here, boy, as you go, for goodness' sake, remove the baby from the hall. I can't stand his idiotic cry . . . What is the matter with him? . . . Is your mother deaf or callous? The child may cry till he has fits, for aught she cares . . .'

CHAPTER NINE

SCHOOL BREAKS UP

WITH DRY LIPS, parched throat, and ink-stained fingers, and exhaustion on one side and exaltation on the other, Swaminathan strode out of the examination hall on the last day.

Standing in the veranda, he turned back and looked into the hall and felt slightly uneasy. He would have felt more comfortable if all the boys had given their papers as he had done, twenty minutes before time. With his left shoulder resting against the wall, Sankar was lost to the world. Rajam, sitting under the second ventilator, between two Third-Form boys, had become a writing machine. Mani was still gazing at the rafters, scratching his chin with the pen. The Pea was leaning back in his seat, revising his answers. One supervisor was drowsing in his chair; another was pacing up and down, with an abstracted look in his eyes. The scratchy noise of active nibs, the rustle of papers, and the clearing of the throats, came through the brooding silence of the hall.

Swaminathan suddenly wished that he had not come out so soon. But how could he have stayed in the hall longer? The Tamil paper was set to go on till five o'clock. He had found himself writing the last line of the last question at four-thirty. Out of the six questions set, he had answered the first question to his satisfaction, the second was doubtful, the third was satisfactory, the fourth, he knew, was clearly wrong (but then, he did not know the correct answer). The sixth answer was the best of the lot. It took only a minute to answer it. He had read the question at two minutes to four-thirty, started answering a minute later, and finished it at four-thirty. The question was: 'What moral do you infer from the story of the Brahmin and the Tiger?' (A brahmin was passing along the edge of a pond. A tiger hailed him from the other bank and offered him a gold bangle. The brahmin at first declined the offer, but when the tiger protested its innocence and sincerity and insisted upon his taking the bangle, he waded through the water. Before he could hold out his hand for the bangle, he was inside the tiger.) Swaminathan had never thought that this story contained a moral. But now he felt that it must have one since the question paper mentioned it. He took a minute to decide whether the moral was: 'We must never accept a gold bangle when it is offered by a tiger' or 'Love of gold bangle costs one one's life'. He saw more logic in the latter and wrote it down. After writing, he looked at the big hall clock. Half an hour more! What had he to do for half an hour? But he felt awkward to be the first to go out. Why could not the others be as quick and precise as he?

He had found it hard to kill time. Why wasn't the paper set for two and a half hours instead of three? He had looked wistfully at the veranda outside. If only he could pluck up enough courage to hand in the paper and go out—he would have no more examinations for a long time to come—he could do what he pleased—roam about the town in the evenings and afternoons and morning—throw away the books—command Granny to tell endless tales.

He had seen a supervisor observing him, and had at once pretended to be busy with the answer paper. He thought that while he was about it, he might as well do a little revision. He read a few lines of the first question and was bored. He turned over the leaves and kept gazing at the last answer. He had to pretend that he was revising. He kept gazing at the moral of the tiger story till it lost all its meaning. He set his pen to work. He went on improving the little dash under the last line indicating the end, till it became an elaborate complicated pattern.

He had looked at the clock again, thinking that it must be nearly five now. It was only ten minutes past four-thirty. He saw two or three boys giving up their papers and going out, and felt happy. He briskly folded the paper and wrote on the flap the elaborate inscription:

'Tamil Tamil
W.S. Swaminathan
1st Form A Section
Albert Mission School
Malgudi
South India
Asia.'

The bell rang. In twos and threes boys came out of the hall. It was
a thorough contrast to the preceding three hours. There was the din
of excited chatter.

'What have you written for the last question?' Swaminathan
asked a class-mate.

'Which? The moral question? . . . Don't you remember what
the teacher said in the class? . . . "Love of gold cost the brahmin
his life." '

'Where was gold there?' Swaminathan objected. 'There was
only a gold bangle. How much have you written for the question?'

'One page,' said the class-mate.

Swaminathan did not like this answer. He had written only a
line. 'What! You should not have written so much.'

A little later he found Rajam and Sankar. 'Well, boys, how did
you find the paper?'

'How did you find it?' Sankar asked.

'Not bad,' Swaminathan said.

'I was afraid only of Tamil,' said Rajam. 'Now I think I am safe.
I think I may get passing marks.'

'No. Certainly more. A Class,' Sankar said.

'Look here,' Swaminathan said, 'some fools have written a page
for that moral question.'

'I wrote only three-quarters of a page,' Rajam said.

'And I only a little more than half,' said Sankar, who was an
authority on these matters.

'I too wrote about that length, about half a page,' lied
Swaminathan as a salve to his conscience, and believed it for the
moment.

'Boys, do you remember that we have no school from tomorrow?'

'Oh, I forgot all about it,' Rajam said.

'Well, what are you going to do with yourselves?' somebody
asked.

'I am going to use my books as fuel in the kitchen,' Swaminathan
said.

'My father has bought a lot of books for me to read during the
vacation, *Sinbad the Sailor*, *Alibaba*, and so on,' said, Sankar.

Mani came throwing up his arms and wailing: 'Time absolutely
insufficient. I could have dashed off the last question.'

The Pea appeared from somewhere with a huge streak of ink
on his left cheek. 'Hello Sankar, first class?'

'No. May hardly get thirty-five.'

'You rascal, you are lying. If you get a first class, may I cut off your tuft?' Mani asked.

The bell rang again fifteen minutes later. The whole school crowded into the hall. There was joy in every face and good-fellowship in every word. Even the teachers tried to be familiar and pleasant. Ebenezar, when he saw Mani, asked: 'Hello, block-head, how are you going to waste your vacation?'

'I am going to sleep, sir,' Mani said, winking at his friends.

'Are you likely to improve your head by the time you return to the school?'

'How is it possible, sir, unless you cut off Sankar's head and present it to me?' A great roar of laughter followed this. There would have been roars of laughter at anything; the mood was such. In sheer joy the Drawing Master was bringing down his cane on a row of feet because, he said, he saw some toes growing to an abnormal length.

The Head Master appeared on the platform, and after waiting for the noise to subside, began a short speech, in which he said that the school would remain closed till the nineteenth of June and open again on the twentieth. He hoped that the boys would not waste their time but read story-books and keep glancing through the books prescribed for their next classes to which, he hoped, most of them were going to be promoted. And now a minute more, there would be a prayer, after which the boys might disperse and go home.

At the end of the prayer the storm burst. With the loudest, lustiest cries, the gathering flooded out of the hall in one body. All through this vigorous confusion and disorder, Swaminathan kept close to Mani. For there was a general belief in the school that enemies stabbed each other on the last day. Swaminathan had no enemy as far as he could remember. But who could say? The school was a bad place.

Mani did some brisk work at the school gate, snatching from all sorts of people ink-bottles and pens, and destroying them. Around him was a crowd seething with excitement and joy. Ecstatic shrieks went up as each article of stationery was destroyed. One or two little boys feebly protested. But Mani wrenched the ink-bottles from their hands, tore their caps, and poured ink over their clothes. He had a small band of assistants, among whom Swaminathan was prominent. Overcome by the mood of the hour, he had spontaneously emptied his ink-bottle over his own head and had drawn frightful dark circles under his eyes with the dripping ink.

A policeman passed in the road. Mani shouted: 'Oh, policeman, policeman! Arrest these boys!' A triumphant cry from a hundred throats rent the air. A few more ink-bottles exploded on the ground and a few more pens were broken. In the midst of it Mani cried: 'Who will bring me Singaram's turban? I shall dye it for him.'

Singaram, the school peon, was the only person who was not affected by the spirit of liberty that was abroad, and as soon as the offer to dye his turban reached his ears, he rushed into the crowd with a big stick and dispersed the revellers.

CHAPTER TEN

THE COACHMAN'S SON

SWAMINATHAN HAD TWO different attachments: one to Somu, Sankar, and the Pea—a purely scholastic one, which automatically ceased when the school gates closed; his other attachment was more human—to Rajam and Mani. Now that they had no school, they were free from the shackles of time, and were almost always together, and arranged for themselves a hectic vacation.

Swaminathan's one consuming passion in life now was to get a hoop. He dreamt of it day and night. He feasted on visions of an ex-cycle wheel without spokes or tyre. You had only to press a stick into the groove and the thing would fly. Oh, what joy to see it climb small obstacles, and how gently it took curves! When running it made a steady hum, which was music to the ear. Swaminathan thought that anybody in Malgudi would understand that he was coming, even a mile away, by that hum. He sometimes kept awake till ten-thirty in the night, thinking of this hoop. He begged everyone that he came across, from his father's friends to a municipal sweeper that he knew, to give him a cycle wheel. Now he could not set his eyes on a decent bicycle without his imagination running riot over its wheels. He dreamt one night that he crossed the Sarayu near Nallappa's Grove 'on' his wheel. It was a vivid dream; the steel wheel crunched on the sandy bed of the river as it struggled and heaved across. It became a sort of horse when it reached the other bank. It went back home in one leap, took him to the kitchen, and then to his bed, and lay down beside him. This was fantastic; but the early part of the dream was real enough. It nearly maddened him to wake to a hopeless morning.

In sheer despair he opened his heart to a coachman—a casual

acquaintance of his. The coachman was very sympathetic. He agreed that existence was difficult without a hoop. He said that he would be able to give Swaminathan one in a few hours if the latter could give him five rupees. This was an immense sum, which Swaminathan hoped to possess in some distant future when he should become as tall as his father. He said so. At which the coachman gave a convincing talk on how to get it. He wanted only six pies to start with; in a short time he would make it six annas, and after that convert it to six rupees. And Swaminathan could spend the five out of the six rupees on the hoop and the balance of one rupee just as he pleased. Swaminathan declared that nothing would give him greater happiness than giving that extra rupee to the coachman. If any doubts arose in Swaminathan's mind, they were swept away by the other's rhetoric. The coachman's process of minting higher currency was this: he had a special metal pot at home in which he kept all base copper coins together with some mysterious herb (whose name he would not reveal even if he were threatened with torture). He kept the whole thing, he said, buried in the ground, he squatted on the spot at dead of night and performed some yoga, and lo, when the time came, all the copper was silver. He could make even gold, but to get the herbs for it, he would have to walk two hundred and fifty miles across strange places, and he did not consider it worth all that exertion.

Swaminathan asked him when he might see him again as he had to think out and execute a plan to get six pies. The coachman said that if the other did not get the money immediately he would not be available for weeks to come as his master was going away and he would have to go away too. Swaminathan cringed and begged him to grant him six hours and ran home.

He first tried Granny. She almost shed tears that she had no money, and held her wooden box upside down to prove how hard up she was.

'I know, Granny, you have a lot of coins under your pillows.'

'No, boy. You can search if you like.'

Swaminathan ordered Granny to leave the bed and made a thorough search under the pillows and the carpets.

'Why do you want money now?' Granny asked.

'If you have what I want, have the goodness to oblige me. If not, why ask futile questions?'

Granny cried to Mother: 'If you have money, give this boy six pies.' But nobody was prepared to oblige Swaminathan. Father dismissed the request in a fraction of a second, which made Swaminathan wonder what he did with all the money that he took from his clients.

He now tried a last desperate chance. He fell on his hands and knees, and resting his cheek on the cold cement floor, peered into the dark space under his father's heavy wardrobe. He had a wild notion that he might find a few coins scattered there. He thrust his hand under the wardrobe and moved it in all directions. All that he was able to collect was a disused envelope musty with cobwebs and dust, a cockroach, and pinches of fine dust.

He sometimes believed that he could perform magic, if only he set about it with sufficient earnestness. He also remembered Ebenezer's saying in the class that God would readily help those that prayed to him.

He secured a small cardboard box, placed in it a couple of pebbles, and covered them with fine sand and leaves. He carried the box to the *puja* room and placed it in a corner. It was a small room in which a few framed pictures of gods hung in the wall, and a few bronze and brass idols kept staring at Swaminathan from a small carved wooden pedestal. A permanent smell of flowers, camphor and incense hung in the air.

Swaminathan stood before the gods and with great piety informed them of the box and its contents, how he expected them to convert the two pebbles into two three-pie coins, and why he needed money so urgently. He promised that if the gods helped him, he would give up biting his thumb. He closed his eyes and muttered: 'Oh, Sri Rama! Thou hast slain Ravana though he had ten heads, can't you give me six pies? . . . If I give you the six pies now, when will you give me the hoop? I wish you would tell me what that herb is . . . Mani, shall I tell you the secret of getting a hoop? Oh, Rama! Give me six pies and I will give up biting my thumb for a year . . .'

He wandered aimlessly in the backyard persuading himself that in a few minutes he could return to the *puja* room and take his money—transmuted pebbles. He fixed a time limit of half an hour.

Ten minutes later he entered the *puja* room, prostrated himself before the gods, rose, and snatching his box, ran to a secluded place in the backyard. With a fluttering heart he opened the box. He emptied it on the ground, ran his fingers through the mass of sand

and leaves, and picked up the two pebbles. As he gazed at the cardboard box, the scattered leaves, sand, and the unconverted pebbles, he was filled with rage. The indifference of the gods infuriated him and brought tears to his eyes. He wanted to abuse the gods, but was afraid to. Instead, he vented all his rage on the cardboard box, and kicked it from place to place and stamped upon the leaves and sand. He paused and doubted if the gods would approve of even this. He was afraid that it might offend them. He might get on without money, but it was dangerous to incur the wrath of the gods; they might make him fail in his examinations, or kill Father, Mother, Granny, or the baby. He picked up the box again and put back into it the sand, the leaves, and the pebbles, that were crushed, crumpled and kicked a minute ago. He dug a small pit at the root of a banana tree and buried the box reverently.

Ten minutes later he stood in Abu Lane, before Mani's house, and whistled twice or thrice. Mani did not appear. Swaminathan climbed the steps and knocked on the door. As the door-chain clanked inside, he stood in suspense. He was afraid he might not be able to explain his presence if anyone other than Mani should open the door. The door opened, and his heart sank. A big man with bushy eyebrows stood before him. 'Who are you?' he asked.

'Who are you? Where is Mani?' Swaminathan asked. This was intended to convey that he had come to see Mani but was quite surprised to meet this other person, and would like to know who it was, whom he had the pleasure of seeing before him. But in his confusion, he could not put this sentiment in better form.

'You ask me who I am in my own house?' bellowed Bushy-Eyebrows. Swaminathan turned and jumped down the steps to flee. But Bushy-Eyebrows ordered: 'Come here, little man.' It was impossible to disobey this command. Swaminathan slowly advanced up the steps, his eyes bulging with terror. Bushy-Eyebrows said: 'Why do you run away? If you have come to see Mani, why don't you see him?' This was logic absolute.

'Never mind,' Swaminathan said irrelevantly.

'Go in and see him, little man.'

Swaminathan meekly entered the house. Mani was standing behind the door, tame and unimpressive in his domestic setting. He and Swaminathan stood staring at each other, neither of them uttering a single word. Bushy-Eyebrows was standing in the doorway with his back to them, watching the street. Swaminathan pointed a timid finger and jerked his head questioningly. Mani whispered: 'Uncle.' The uncle suddenly turned round and said: 'Why do you stand staring at each other? Did you come for that? Wag your tongues, boys.' After this advice he stepped into the street to drive away two dogs that came and rolled in front of the house, locked in a terrible fight. He was now out of earshot. Swaminathan said: 'Your uncle? I never knew. I say, Mani, can't you come out now? . . . No? . . . I came on urgent business. Give me—urgent—six pies—got to have it—coachman goes away for weeks—may not get the chance again—don't know what to do without hoop . . .' He paused. Mani's uncle was circling round the dogs, swearing at them and madly searching for stones. Swaminathan continued: 'My life depends on it. If you don't give it, I am undone. Quick, get the money.'

'I have no money, nobody gives me money,' Mani replied.

Swaminathan felt lost. 'Where does your uncle keep his money? Look into that box . . .'

'I don't know.'

'Mani, come here,' his uncle cried from the street, 'drive away these devils. Get me a stone.'

'Rajam, can you lend me a policeman?' Swaminathan asked two weeks later.

'Policeman! Why?'

'There is a rascal in this town who has robbed me.' He related to Rajam his dealings with the coachman. 'And now,' Swaminathan said continuing his tale of woe, 'whenever he sees me, he pretends not to recognize me. If I got to his house, I am told he is not at home, though I can hear him cursing somebody inside. If I persist, he sends word that he will unchain his dog and kill me.'

'Has he a dog?' asked Rajam.

'Not any that I could see.'

'Then why not rush into his house and kick him?'

'It is all very well to say that. I tremble whenever I go to see him. There is no knowing what coachmen have in their houses . . . He may set his horse on me.'

'Let him, it isn't going to eat you,' said Mani.

'Isn't it? I am glad to know it. You come with me one day to tailor Ranga and hear what he has to say about horses. They are

sometimes more dangerous than even tigers,' Swaminathan said
earnestly.

'Suppose you wait one day and catch him at the gate?' Rajam
suggested.

'I have tried it. But whenever he comes out, he is on his coach.
And as soon as he sees me, he takes out his long whip. I get out of
his reach and shout. But what is the use? That horse simply flies!
And to think that he has duped me of two annas!'

'It was six pies, wasn't it?'

'But he took from me twice again, six pies each time . . .'

'Then it is only an anna and a half,' Rajam said.

'No, Rajam, it is two annas.'

'My dear boy, twelve pies make an anna, and you have paid
thrice, six pies each time; that is eighteen pies in all, one anna and
a half.'

'It is a useless discussion. Who cares how many pies make an
anna?' Swaminathan said.

'But in money matters, you must be precise—very well, go on,
Swami.'

'The coachman first took from me six pies, promising me the
silver coins in two days. He dodged me for four days and demanded
six more pies, saying that he had collected herbs for twelve pies. He
put me off again and took from me another six pies, saying that
without it the whole process would fail. And after that, every time
I went to him he put me off with some excuse or other; he often
complained that owing to the weather the process was going on
rather slowly. And two days ago he told me that he did not know
me or anything about my money. And now you know how he
behaves—I don't mind the money, but I hate his boy—that dark
rascal. He makes faces at me whenever he sees me, and he has
threatened to empty a bucketful of drain-water on my head. One
day he held up an open penknife. I want to thrash him; that will
make his father give me back my two annas.'

Next day Swaminathan and Mani started for the coachman's house.
Swaminathan was beginning to regret that he had ever opened the
subject before his friends. The affair was growing beyond his
control. And considering the interest that Rajam and Mani displayed
in the affair, one could not foresee where it was going to take them
all.

Rajam had formed a little plan to decoy and kidnap the coachman's son. Mani was his executive. He was to befriend the coachman's son. Swaminathan had very little part to play in the preliminary stages. His duty would cease with pointing out the coachman's house to Mani.

The coachman lived a mile from Swaminathan's house, westward, in Keelacheri, which consisted of about a dozen thatched huts and dingy hovels, smoke-tinted and evil-smelling, clustering together irregularly.

They were now within a few yards of the place. Swaminathan tried a last desperate chance to stop the wheel of vengeance.

'Mani, I think the coachman's son has returned the money.'

'What!'

'I think . . .'

'You think so, do you? Can you show it to me?'

Swaminathan pleaded: 'Leave him alone, Mani. You don't know what troubles we shall get into by tampering with that boy . . .'

'Shut up or I will wring your neck.'

'Oh, Mani—the police—or the boy himself—he is frightful, capable of anything.' He had in his heart a great dread of the boy. And sometimes in the night would float before him a face dark, dirty and cruel, and make him shiver. It was the face of the coachman's son.

'He lives in the third house,' Swaminathan pointed out.

At the last moment Mani changed his plan and insisted upon Swaminathan's following him to the coachman's house. Swaminathan sat down in the road as a protest. But Mani was stubborn. He dragged Swaminathan along till they came before the coachman's house, and then started shouting at him.

'Mani, Mani, what is the matter?'

'You son of a donkey,' Mani roared at Swaminathan and swung his hand to strike him.

Swaminathan began to cry. Mani attempted to strangle him. A motley crowd gathered round them, urchins with prodigious bellies, women of dark aspect, and their men. Scurvy chickens cackled and ran hither and thither. The sun was unsparing. Two or three mongrels lay in the shade of a tree and snored. A general malodour of hencoop and unwashed clothes pervaded the place.

And now from the hovel that Swaminathan had pointed out as

the coachman's, emerged a little man of three feet or so, ill-clad and unwashed. He pushed his way through the crowd and, securing a fine place, sucked his thumb and watched the fight in rapture. Mani addressed the crowd indignantly, pointing at Swaminathan: 'This urchin, I don't know who he is, all of a sudden demands two annas from me. I have never seen him before. He says I owe him that money.' Mani continued in this strain for fifteen minutes. At the end of it, the coachman's son took the thumb out of his mouth and remarked: 'He must be sent to the gaol.' At this Mani bestowed an approving smile upon him and asked: 'Will you help me to carry him to the police station?'

'No,' said the coachman's son, being afraid of police stations himself.

Mani asked: 'How do you know that he must be taken to the police station?'

'I know it.'

'Does he ever trouble you similarly?' asked Mani.

'No,' said the boy.

'Where is the two annas that your father took from me?' asked Swaminathan, turning to the boy his tear-drenched face. The crowd had meanwhile melted, after making half-hearted attempts to bring peace. Mani asked the boy suddenly: 'Do you want this top?' He held a shining red top. The boy put out his hand for the top.

Mani said: 'I can't give you this. If you come with me, I will give you a bigger one. Let us become friends.'

The boy had no objection. 'Won't you let me see it?' he asked. Mani gave it to him. The boy turned it in his hand twice or thrice and in the twinkling of an eye disappeared from the place. Mani took time to grasp the situation. When he did grasp it, he saw the boy entering a hovel far off. He started after him.

When Mani reached the hovel, the door was closed. Mani knocked a dozen times, before a surly man appeared and said that the boy was not there. The door was shut again. Mani started knocking again. Two or three menacing neighbours came round and threatened to bury him alive if he dared to trouble them in their own locality. Swaminathan was desperately appealing to Mani to come away. But it took a great deal more to move him. He went on knocking.

The neighbours took up their position a few yards off, with handfuls of stones, and woke the dogs sleeping under the tree.

It was only when the dogs came bouncing towards them that Mani shouted 'Run' to Swaminathan, and set an example himself.

A couple of stones hit Swaminathan on the back. One or two hit Mani also. A sharp stone skinned Mani's right heel. They became blind and insensible to everything except the stretch of road before them.

CHAPTER ELEVEN

IN FATHER'S PRESENCE

DURING SUMMER MALGUDI was one of the most detested towns in south India. Sometimes the heat went above a hundred and ten in the shade, and between twelve and three any day in summer the dusty blanched roads were deserted. Even donkeys and dogs, the most vagrant of animals, preferred to move to the edge of the street, where cat-walks and minor projections from buildings cast a sparse strip of shade, when the fierce sun tilted towards the west.

But there is this peculiarity about heat: it appears to affect only those that think of it. Swaminathan, Mani and Rajam would have been surprised if anybody had taken the trouble to prove to them that the Malgudi sun was unbearable. They found the noon and the afternoon the most fascinating part of the day. The same sun that beat down on the head of Mr Hentel, the mill manager, and drove him to Kodaikanal, or on the turban of Mr Krishnan, the Executive Engineer, and made him complain that his profession was one of the hardest, compelling him to wander in sun and storm, beat down on Swaminathan's curly head, Mani's tough matted hair, and Rajam's short wiry crop, and left them unmoved. The same sun that baked the earth so much that even Mr Retty, the most Indianized of the 'Europeans', who owned a rice mill in the deserted bungalow outside the town (he was, by the way, the mystery man of the place: nobody could say who he was or where he had come from; he swore at his boy and at his customers in perfect Tamil and always moved about in shirt, shorts, and sandalled feet), screamed one day when he forgetfully took a step or two barefoot, was the same sun that made the three friends loathe to remain under a roof.

They were sitting on a short culvert, half a mile outside the municipal limits, on the Trunk Road. A streak of water ran under the culvert on a short stretch of sand, and mingled with the Sarayu farther down. There was no tree where they sat, and the sun struck their heads directly. On the sides of the road there were paddy fields; but now all that remained was scorched stubble, vast stretches of stubble, relieved here and there by clustering groves of mango or coconut. The Trunk Road was deserted but for an occasional country cart lumbering along.

'I wish you had done just what I had asked you to do and nothing more,' said Rajam to Mani.

Swaminathan complained: 'Yes, Rajam. I just showed him the coachman's son and was about to leave him, just as we had planned, when all of a sudden he tried to murder me . . .' He shot an angry glance at Mani.

Mani was forlorn. 'Boys, I admit that I am an idiot. I thought I could do it all by the plan that came to my head on the spot. If I had only held the top firmly, I could have decoyed him, and by now he would have been howling in a lonely shed.' There was regret in his tone.

Swaminathan said, nursing his nape: 'It is still paining here.' After the incident at Keelacheri, it took three hours of continuous argument for Mani to convince Swaminathan that the attack on him was only sham.

'You needn't have been so brutal to Swami,' said Rajam.

'Sirs,' Mani said, folding his hands, 'I shall stand on my head for ten minutes, if you want me to do it as a punishment. I only pretended to scratch Swami to show the coachman's boy that I was his enemy.'

A jingling was now heard. A closed mat-covered cart drawn by a white bullock was coming down the road. When it had come within a yard of the culvert, they rose, advanced, stood in a row, and shouted: 'Pull up the animal, will you?'

The cart driver was a little village boy.

'Stop the cart, you fool,' cried Rajam.

'If he does not stop, we shall arrest him and confiscate his cart.' This was Swaminathan.

The cart driver said: 'Boys, why do you stop me?'

'Don't talk,' Mani commanded, and with a serious face went round the cart and examined the wheels. He bent down and scrutinized the bottom of the cart: 'Hey, cart-man, get down.'

'Boys, I must go,' pleaded the driver.

'Whom do you address as "boys"?' asked Rajam menacingly. 'Don't you know who we are?'

'We are the Government Police out to catch humbugs like you,' added Swaminathan.

'I shall shoot you if you say a word,' said Rajam to the young driver. Though the driver was incredulous, he felt that there must be something in what they said.

Mani tapped a wheel and said: 'The culvert is weak, we can't let you go over it unless you show us the pass.'

The cart driver jabbered: 'Please, sirs, let me go—I have to be there.'

'Shut up,' Rajam commanded.

Swaminathan examined the animal and said: 'Come here.'

The cart driver was loath to get down. Mani dragged him from his seat and gave him a push towards Swaminathan.

Swaminathan scowled at him, and pointing at the sides of the animal, asked: 'Why have you not washed the animal, you blockhead?'

The villager replied timidly: 'I have washed the animal, sir.'

'But why is this here?' Swaminathan asked, pointing at a brown patch.

'Oh, that! The animal has had it since its birth, sir.'

'Birth? Are you trying to teach me?' Swaminathan shouted and raised his leg to kick the cart driver.

They showed signs of relenting.

'Give the rascal a pass, and be done with him,' Rajam conceded graciously. Swaminathan took out a pencil stub and a grubby pocket-book that he always carried about him on principle. It was his habit to note down all sorts of things: the number of cycles that passed him, the number of people going barefoot, the number going with sandals or shoes on, and so forth.

He held the paper and pencil ready. Mani took hold of the rope of the bullock, pushed it back, and turned it the other way round. The cart driver protested. But Mani said: 'Don't worry. It has got to stand here. This is the boundary.'

'I have to go this way, sir.'

'You can turn it round and go.'

'What is your name?' asked Rajam.

'Karuppan,' answered the boy.

Swaminathan took it down.

'Age?'

'I don't know, sir.'

'You don't know? Swami, write a hundred,' said Rajam.

'No sir, no sir, I am not a hundred.'

'Mind your business and hold your tongue. You are a hundred. I will kill you if you say no. What is your bullock's name?'

'I don't know, sir.'

'Swami, write "Karuppan" again.'

'Sir, that is my name, not the bullock's.'

They ignored this and Swaminathan wrote 'Karuppan' against the name of the bullock.

'Where are you going?'

'Sethur.'

Swaminathan wrote it down.

'How long will you stay there?'

'It is my place, sir.'

'If that is so, what brought you here?'

'Our headman sent ten bags of coconut to the railway shed.'

Swaminathan entered every word in his note-book. Then all three signed the page, tore it off, gave it to the cart driver, and permitted him to start.

Much to Swaminathan's displeasure, his father's courts closed in the second week of May, and Father began to spend the afternoons at home. Swaminathan feared that it might interfere with his afternoon rambles with Rajam and Mani. And it did. On the very third day of his vacation, Father commanded Swaminathan, just as he was stepping out of the house: 'Swami, come here.'

Father was standing in the small courtyard, wearing a *dhoti* and a banian, the dress which, for its very homeliness, Swaminathan detested to see him in; it indicated that he did not intend going out in the near future.

'Where are you going?'

'Nowhere.'

'Where were you yesterday at this time?'

'Here.'

'You are lying. You were not here yesterday. And you are not going out now.'

'That is right,' Mother added, just appearing from somewhere. 'There is no limit to his loafing in the sun. He will die of sunstroke if he keeps on like this.'

Father would have gone on even without Mother's encouragement. But now her words spurred him to action. Swaminathan was asked to follow him to his 'room' in his father's dressing-room.

'How many days is it since you have touched your books?' Father asked as he blew off the fine layer of dust on Swaminathan's books, and cleared the web that an industrious spider was weaving between a corner of the table and the pile of books.

Swaminathan viewed this question as a gross breach of promise. 'Should I read even when I have no school?'

'Do you think you have passed the BA?' Father asked.

'I mean, Father, when the school is closed, when there is no examination, even then should I read?'

'What a question! You must read.'

'But, Father, you said before the examinations that I needn't read after they were over. Even Rajam does not read.' As he uttered the last sentence, he tried to believe it; he clearly remembered Rajam's complaining bitterly of a home tutor who came and pestered him for two hours a day thrice a week. Father was apparently deaf to Swaminathan's remarks. He stood over Swaminathan and set him to dust his books and clean his table. Swaminathan vigorously started blowing off the dust from the book covers. He caught the spider carefully, and took it to the window to throw it out. He held it outside the window and watched it for a while. It was swinging from a strand that gleamed in a hundred delicate tints.

'Look sharp! Do you want a whole day to throw out the spider?' Father asked. Swaminathan suddenly realized that he might have the spider as his pet and that it would be a criminal waste to throw it out. He secretly slipped it into his pocket and, after shaking an empty hand outside the window, returned to his duty at the desk.

'Look at the way you have kept your English text! Are you not ashamed of yourself?' Swaminathan picked up the oily red-bound *Fourth Reader*, opened it, and banged together the covers, in order to shake off the dust, then rubbed the oily covers violently with his palm.

'Get a piece of cloth, boy. That is not the way to clean things. Get a piece of cloth, Swami,' Father said, half kindly and half impatiently.

Swaminathan looked about and complained, 'I can't find any here, Father.'

'Run and see.'

This was a welcome suggestion. Swaminathan hurried out. He first went to his grandmother.

'Granny, get me a piece of cloth, quick.'

'Where am I to go for a piece of cloth?'

'Where am I to go?' he asked peevishly and added quite irrelevantly, 'If one has got to read even during holidays, I don't see why holidays are given at all.'

'What is the matter?'

This was his opportunity to earn some sympathy. He almost wept as he said: 'I don't know what Rajam and Mani will think, waiting for me there, if I keep on fooling here. Granny, if Father cannot find any work to do, why shouldn't he go and sleep?'

Father shouted across the hall: 'Did you find the cloth?'

Swaminathan answered: 'Granny hasn't got it. I shall see if Mother has.' His mother was sitting in the back corridor on a mat, with the baby sleeping on her lap. Swaminathan glared at her. Her advice to her husband a few minutes ago rankled in his heart. 'You are a fine lady, Mother,' he said in an undertone. 'Why don't you leave us poor folk alone?'

'What?' she asked, unconscious of the sarcasm, and having forgotten what she had said to her husband a few minutes ago.

'You needn't have gone and carried tales against me. I don't know what I have done to you.' He would have enjoyed prolonging this talk, but Father was waiting for the duster.

'Can you give me a piece of cloth?' he asked, coming to business.

'What cloth?'

'What cloth! How should I know? It seems I have got to tidy up those—those books of mine. A fine way of spending the holidays!'

'I can't get any now.'

'H'm. You can't, can you?' He looked about. There was a piece of cloth under the baby. In a flash, he stooped, rolled the baby over, pulled out the cloth, and was off. He held his mother responsible for all his troubles, and disturbing the baby and snatching its cloth gave him great relief.

With fierce satisfaction he tilted the table and tipped all the things on it over the floor, and then picked them up one by one, and arranged them on the table. Father watched him: 'Is this how you arrange things? You have kept all the light things at the bottom and the heavy ones on top. Take out those note-books. Keep the Atlas at the bottom.' Mother came in with the baby in her arms and complained to Father, 'Look at that boy, he has taken the baby's cloth. Is there nobody to control him in this house? I wonder how long his school is going to be kept closed.' Swaminathan continued his work with concentrated interest. Father was pleased to ignore Mother's complaint; he merely pinched the sleeping baby's cheeks, at which Mother was annoyed and left the room.

Half an hour later Swaminathan sat in his father's room in a chair, with a slate in his hand and pencil ready. Father held the Arithmetic book open and dictated: 'Rama has ten mangoes with which he wants to earn fifteen annas. Krishna wants only four mangoes. How much will Krishna have to pay?'

Swaminathan gazed and gazed at this sum, and every time he read it, it seemed to acquire a new meaning. He had the feeling of having stepped into a fearful maze . . .

His mouth began to water at the thought of mangoes. He wondered what made Rama fix fifteen annas for ten mangoes. What kind of a man was Rama? Probably he was like Sankar. Somehow one couldn't help feeling that he must have been like Sankar, with his ten mangoes and his iron determination to get fifteen annas. If Rama was like Sankar, Krishna must have been like the Pea. Here Swaminathan felt an unaccountable sympathy for Krishna.

'Have you done the sum?' Father asked, looking over the newspaper he was reading.

'Father, will you tell me if the mangoes were ripe?'

Father regarded him for a while and smothering a smile remarked: 'Do the sum first. I will tell you whether the fruits were ripe or not, afterwards.'

Swaminathan felt utterly helpless. If only Father would tell him whether Rama was trying to sell ripe fruits or unripe ones! Of what avail would it be to tell him afterwards? He felt strongly that the answer to this question contained the key to the whole problem. It would be scandalous to expect fifteen annas for ten unripe mangoes. But even if he did, it wouldn't be unlike Rama, whom Swaminathan was steadily beginning to hate and invest with the darkest qualities.

'Father, I cannot do the sum,' Swaminathan said, pushing away the slate.

'What is the matter with you? You can't solve a simple problem in Simple Proportion?'

'We are not taught this kind of thing in our school.'

'Get the slate here. I will make you give the answer now.' Swaminathan waited with interest for the miracle to happen. Father studied the sum for a second and asked: 'What is the price of ten mangoes?'

Swaminathan looked over the sum to find out which part of the sum contained an answer to this question. 'I don't know.'

'You seem to be an extraordinary idiot. Now read the sum. Come on. How much does Rama expect for ten mangoes?'

'Fifteen annas of course,' Swaminathan thought, but how could that be its price, just price? It was very well for Rama to expect it in his avarice. But was it the right price? And then there was the obscure point whether the mangoes were ripe or not. If they were ripe, fifteen annas might not be an improbable price. If only he could get more light on this point!

'How much does Rama want for his mangoes?'

'Fifteen annas,' replied Swaminathan without conviction.

'Very good. How many mangoes does Krishna want?'

'Four.'

'What is the price of four?'

Father seemed to delight in torturing him. How could he know? How could he know what that fool Krishna would pay?

'Look here, boy. I have half a mind to thrash you. What have you in your head? Ten mangoes cost fifteen annas. What is the price of one? Come on. If you don't say it—' His hand took Swaminathan's ear and gently twisted it. Swaminathan could not open his mouth because he could not decide whether the solution lay in the realm of addition, subtraction, multiplication, or division. The longer he hesitated, the more violent the twist was becoming. In the end when Father was waiting with a scowl for an answer, he received only a squeal from his son. 'I am not going to leave you till you tell me how much a single mango costs at fifteen annas for ten.' What was the matter with Father? Swaminathan kept blinking. Where was the urgency to know its price? Anyway, if Father wanted to know so badly, instead of harassing him, let him go to the market and find it out. The whole brood of Ramas and Krishnas, with their endless transactions with odd quantities of mangoes and fractions of money, was getting disgusting.

Father admitted defeat by declaring: 'One mango costs fifteen over ten annas. Simplify it.'

Here he was being led to the most hideous regions of Arithmetic, Fractions. 'Give me the slate, Father. I will find it out.' He worked and found at the end of fifteen minutes: 'The price of one mango is three over two annas.' He expected to be contradicted any moment. But Father said: 'Very good, simplify it further.' It was plain sailing after that. Swaminathan announced at the end of half an hour's agony: 'Krishna must pay six annas,' and burst into tears.

At five o'clock when he was ready to start for the club, Swaminathan's father felt sorry for having worried his son all afternoon. 'Would you like to come with me to the club, boy?' he asked when he saw Swaminathan sulking behind a pillar with a woebegone face. Swaminathan answered by disappearing for a minute and reappearing dressed in his coat and cap. Father surveyed him from head to foot and remarked: 'Why can't you be a little more tidy?' Swaminathan writhed awkwardly.

'Lakshmi,' Father called, and said to Mother when she came: 'there must be a clean dress for the boy in the box. Give him something clean.'

'Please don't worry about it now. He is all right. Who is to open the box? The keys are somewhere . . . I have just mixed milk for the baby—' said Mother.

'What has happened to all his dresses?'

'What dresses? You haven't bought a square inch of cloth since last summer.'

'What do you mean? What has happened to all the pieces of twill I bought a few months ago?' he demanded vaguely, making a mental note at the same time to take the boy to the tailor on Wednesday evening. Swaminathan was relieved to find Mother reluctant to get him a fresh dress, since he had an obscure dread that his father would leave him behind and go away if he went in to change. A car hooted in front of the house. Father snatched his tennis racket from a table and rushed out, followed by Swaminathan. A gentleman, wearing a blazer that appealed to Swaminathan, sat at the wheel, and said 'Good evening,' with a grin. Swaminathan was at first afraid that this person might refuse to take him in the car. But his fears were dispelled by the gentleman's saying amiably: 'Hello, Srinivasan, are you bringing your boy to the club? Right O!' Swaminathan sat in the back seat while his father and his friend occupied the front.

The car whizzed along. Swaminathan was elated and wished that some of his friends could see him then. The car slid into a gate and came to a stop amidst half a dozen other cars.

He watched his father playing tennis, and came to the conclusion that he was the best player in all the three courts that were laid side by side. Swaminathan found that whenever his father hit the ball, his opponents were unable to receive it and so let it go and strike the screen. He also found that the picker's life was one of grave risks.

Swaminathan fell into a pleasant state of mind. The very fact that he was allowed to be present there and watch the game gave him a sense of importance. He would have something to say to his friends tomorrow. He slowly moved and stood near the screen behind his father. Before stationing himself there, he wondered for a moment if the little fellow in khaki dress might not object. But the little fellow was busy picking up balls and throwing them at the players. Swaminathan stayed there for about ten minutes. His father's actions were clearer to watch from behind, and the twang of his racket when hitting the ball was very pleasing to the ear.

For a change Swaminathan stood looking at the boy in khaki dress. As he gazed, his expression changed. He blinked fast as if he disbelieved his eyes. It was the coachman's son, only slightly transformed by the khaki dress! Now the boy had turned and seen him. He grinned maliciously and hastily took out of his pocket a penknife, and held it up. Swaminathan was seized with cold fear. He moved away fast, unobtrusively, to his former place, which was at a safe distance from his enemy.

After the set when his father walked towards the building, Swaminathan took care to walk a little in front of him and not behind, as he feared that he might get a stab any minute in his back.

'Swami, don't go in front. You are getting between my legs.' Swaminathan obeyed with a reluctant heart. He kept shooting glances sideways and behind. He stooped and picked up a stone, a sharp stone, and held it ready for use if any emergency should arise. The distance from the tennis court to the building was about a dozen yards, but to Swaminathan it seemed to be a mile and a half.

He felt safe when he sat in a chair beside his father in the card-room. A thick cloud of smoke floated in the air. Father was shuffling and throwing cards with great zest. This was the safest place on earth. There was Father and any number of his friends,

and let the coachman's son try a hand if he liked. A little later
Swaminathan looked out of the window and felt disturbed at the
sight of the stars. It would be darker still by the time the card game
was finished and Father rose to go home.

An hour later Father rose from the table. Swaminathan was in
a highly nervous state when he got down the last steps of the
building. There were unknown dangers lurking in the darkness
around. He was no doubt secure between Father and his friend.
That thought was encouraging. But Swaminathan felt at the same
time that it would have been better if all the persons in the card-
room had escorted him to the car. He needed all the guarding he
could get, and some more. Probably by this time the boy had gone
out and brought a huge gang of assassins and was waiting for him.
He could not walk in front as, in addition to getting between his
father's legs, he had no idea which way they had to go for the car.
Following his father was out of the question, as he might not reach
the car at all. He walked in a peculiar side-step which enabled him
to see before him and behind him simultaneously. The distance
was interminable. He decided to explain the danger to Father and
seek his protection.

'Father.'

'Well, boy?'

Swaminathan suddenly decided that his father had better not
know anything about the coachman's son, however serious the
situation might be.

'What do you want, boy?' Father asked again.

'Father, are we going home now?'

'Yes.'

'Walking?'

'No. The car is there, near the gate.'

When they came to the car, Swaminathan got in first and
occupied the centre of the back seat. He was still in suspense.
Father's friend was taking time to start the car. Swaminathan was
sitting all alone in the back seat, very far behind Father and his
friend. Even now, the coachman's son and his gang could easily pull
him out and finish him.

The car started. When its engine rumbled, it sounded to
Swaminathan's ears like the voice of a saviour. The car was outside
the gate now and picked up speed. Swaminathan lifted a corner of
his *dhoti* and mopped his brow.

CHAPTER TWELVE

BROKEN PANES

ON THE 15TH of August 1930, about two thousand citizens of
Malgudi assembled on the right bank of the Sarayu to protest
against the arrest of Gauri Sankar, a prominent political worker of
Bombay. An earnest-looking man clad in *khaddar* stood on a wooden
platform and addressed the gathering. In a high, piercing voice, he
sketched the life and achievements of Gauri Sankar, and after that
passed on to generalities. 'We are slaves today,' he shrieked, 'worse
slaves than we have ever been before. Let us remember our
heritage. Have we forgotten the glorious periods of *Ramayana* and
Mahabharata? This is the country that has given the world a
Kalidasa, a Buddha, a Sankara. Our ships sailed the high seas and
we had reached the height of civilization when the Englishman ate
raw flesh and wandered in the jungles nude. But now what are we?'
He paused and said on the inspiration of the moment, without
troubling to verify the meaning: 'We are slaves of slaves.' To
Swaminathan, as to Mani, this part of the speech was
incomprehensible. But five minutes later the speaker said something
that seemed practicable: 'Just think for a while. We are three
hundred and thirty-six million, and our land is as big as Europe
minus Russia. England is no bigger than our Madras Presidency and
is inhabited by a handful of white rogues and is thousands of miles
away. Yet we bow in homage before the Englishman! Why are we
become, through no fault of our own, docile and timid? It is the
bureaucracy that has made us so, by intimidation and starvation.
You need not do more. Let every Indian spit on England, and the
quantity of saliva will be enough to drown England . . .'
    '*Gandhi ki Jai!*' shouted Swaminathan involuntarily, deeply

stirred by the speaker's eloquence at this point. He received a fierce dig from Mani, who whispered: 'Fool! Why can't you hold your tongue?'

Swaminathan asked: 'Is it true?'

'Which?'

'Spitting and drowning the Europeans.'

'Must be, otherwise do you think that fellow would suggest it?'

'Then why not do it? It is easy.'

'Europeans will shoot us, they have no heart,' said Mani. This seemed a satisfactory answer, and Swaminathan was about to clear up another doubt, when one or two persons sitting around frowned at him.

For the rest of the evening Swaminathan was caught in the lecturer's eloquence; so was Mani. With the lecturer they wept over the plight of the Indian peasant; resolved to boycott English goods, especially Lancashire and Manchester cloth, as the owners of those mills had cut off the thumbs of the weavers of Dacca muslin, for which India was famous at one time. What muslin it was, a whole piece of forty yards could be folded and kept in a snuff box! The persons who cut off the thumbs of such weavers deserved the worst punishment possible. And Swaminathan was going to mete it out by wearing only *khaddar*, the rough homespun. He looked at the dress he was just then wearing, in chagrin. 'Mani,' he said in a low voice, 'have you any idea what I am wearing?'

Mani examined Swaminathan's coat and declared: 'It is Lancashire cloth.'

'How do you know it?'

Mani glared at him in answer.

'What are you wearing?' asked Swaminathan.

'Of course *khaddar*. Do you think I will pay a pie to those Lancashire devils? No. They won't get it out of me.'

Swaminathan had his own doubts over this statement. But he preferred to keep quiet, and wished that he had come out nude rather than in what he believed to be Lancashire cloth.

A great cry burst from the crowd: '*Bharat Matha ki Jai!*' And then there were cries of: '*Gandhi ki Jai!*' After that came a kind of mournful 'national' song. The evening's programme closed with a bonfire of foreign cloth. It was already dark. Suddenly the darkness was lit up by a red glare. A fire was lighted. A couple of boys wearing Gandhi caps went round begging people to burn their foreign cloth. Coats and caps and upper cloth came whizzing through the air and fell with a thud into the fire, which purred and crackled and rose high, thickening the air with smoke and a burnt smell. People moved about like dim shadows in the red glare. Swaminathan was watching the scene with little shivers of joy going down his spine. Somebody asked him: 'Young man, do you want our country to remain in eternal slavery?'

'No, no,' Swaminathan replied.

'But you are wearing a foreign cap.'

Swaminathan quailed with shame. 'Oh, I didn't notice,' he said, and removing his cap flung it into the fire with a feeling that he was saving the country.

Early next morning as Swaminathan lay in bed watching a dusty beam of sunlight falling a few yards off his bed, his mind, which was just emerging from sleep, became conscious of a vague worry. Swaminathan asked himself what that worry was. It must be something connected with school. Homework? No. Matters were all right in that direction. It was something connected with dress. Bonfire, bonfire of clothes. Yes. It now dawned upon him with an oppressive clearness that he had thrown his cap into the patriotic bonfire of the previous evening; and of course his father knew nothing about it.

What was he going to wear for school today? Telling his father and asking for a new cap was not practicable. He could not go to school bareheaded.

He started for the school in a mood of fatalistic abandon, with only a coat and no cap on. And the fates were certainly kind to him. At least Swaminathan believed that he saw the hand of God in it when he reached the school and found the boys gathered in the road in front of the school in a noisy irregular mob.

Swaminathan passed through the crowd unnoticed till he reached the school gate. A perfect stranger belonging to the Third Form stopped him and asked: 'Where are you going?' Swaminathan hesitated for a moment to discover if there was any trap in this question and said: 'Why—er . . . Of course . . .'

'No school today,' declared the stranger with emphasis, and added passionately, 'one of the greatest sons of the Motherland has been sent to gaol.'

'I won't go to school,' Swaminathan said, greatly relieved at this unexpected solution to his cap problem.

The Head Master and the teachers were standing in the front veranda of the school. The Head Master looked careworn. Ebenezar was swinging his cane and pacing up and down. For once, the boys saw D. Pillai, the History teacher, serious, and gnawing his close-clipped moustache in great agitation. The crowd in the road had become brisker and noisier, and the school looked forlorn. At five minutes to ten the first bell rang, hardly heard by anyone except those standing near the gate. A conference was going on between the teachers and the Head Master. The Head Master's hand trembled as he pulled out his watch and gave orders for the second bell. The bell that at other times gave out a clear rich note now sounded weak and inarticulate. The Head Master and the teachers were seen coming toward the gate, and a lull came upon the mob.

The Head Master appealed to the boys to behave and get back to their classes quietly. The boys stood firm. The teachers, including D. Pillai, tried and failed. After uttering a warning that the punishment to follow would be severe, the Head Master withdrew. Thundering shouts of *'Bharat Mata ki Jai!'* *'Gandhi ki Jai!'* and *'Gauri Sankar ki Jai!'* followed him.

There were gradual unnoticed additions of all sorts of people to the original student mob. Now zestful adult voices could be detected in the frequent cries of *'Gandhi ki Jai!'*

Half a dozen persons appointed themselves leaders, and ran about crying: 'Remember, this is a hartal. This is a day of mourning. Observe it in the proper spirit of sorrow and silence.'

Swaminathan was an unobserved atom in the crowd. Another unobserved atom was busily piling up small stones before him, and flinging them with admirable aim at the panes in the front part of the school building. Swaminathan could hardly help following his example. He picked up a handful of stones and searched the building with his eyes. He was disappointed to find at least seventy per cent of the panes already attended to.

He uttered a sharp cry of joy as he discovered a whole ventilator, consisting of small square glasses, in the Head Master's room, intact! He sent a stone at it; and waited with cocked-up ears for the splintering noise as the stone hit the glass, and the final shivering noise, a fraction of a second later, as the piece crashed on the floor. It was thrilling.

A puny man came running into the crowd announcing excitedly,

'Work is going on in the Board High School.'

This horrible piece of news set the crowd in motion. A movement began towards the Board High School, which was situated at the tail-end of Market Road.

When it reached the Board High School, the self-appointed leaders held up their hands and requested the crowd to remain outside and be peaceful, and entered the school. Within fifteen minutes, trickling in by twos and threes, the crowd was in the school hall.

A spokesman of the crowd said to the Head Master, 'Sir, we are not here to create a disturbance. We only want you to close the school. It is imperative. Our leader is in gaol. Our Motherland is in the throes of war.'

The Head Master, a wizened owl-like man, screamed, 'With whose permission did you enter the building? Kindly go out. Or I shall send for the police.'

This was received with howling, jeering and hooting. And following it, tables and benches were overturned and broken, and window-panes were smashed. Most of the Board School boys merged with the crowd. A few, however, stood apart. They were first invited to come out; but when they showed reluctance, they were dragged out.

Swaminathan's part in all this was by no means negligible. It was he who shouted 'We will spit on the police' (though it was drowned in the din), when the Head Master mentioned the police. The mention of the police had sent his blood boiling. What brazenness, what shamelessness, to talk of police—the nefarious agents of the Lancashire thumb-cutters! When the pandemonium started, he was behind no one in destroying the school furniture. With tremendous joy he discovered that there were many glass panes untouched yet. His craving to break them could not be fully satisfied in his own school. He ran round collecting ink-bottles and flung them one by one at every pane that caught his eye. When the Board School boys were dragged out, he felt that he could not do much in that line, most of the boys being as big as himself. On the flash of a bright idea, he wriggled through the crowd and looked for the Infant Standards. There he found little children huddled together and shivering with fright. He charged into this crowd with such ferocity that the children scattered about, stumbling and falling. One unfortunate child who shuffled and moved awkwardly received individual attention. Swaminathan pounced upon him, pulled out his cap, threw it down and stamped on it, swearing at him all the time. He pushed him and dragged him this way and that and then gave him a blow on the head and left him to his fate.

Having successfully paralysed work in the Board School, the crowd moved on in a procession along Market Road. The air vibrated with the songs and slogans uttered in a hundred keys by a hundred voices. Swaminathan found himself wedged in among a lot of unknown people, in one of the last ranks. The glare from the blanched treeless Market Road was blinding. The white dust stirred up by the procession hung like thin mist in the air and choked him. He could see before him nothing but moving backs and shoulders and occasionally odd parts of some building. His throat was dry with shouting, and he was beginning to feel hungry. He was just pondering whether he could just slip out and go home, when the procession came to a sudden halt. In a minute the rear ranks surged forward to see what the matter was.

The crowd was now in the centre of Market Road, before the fountain in the square. On the other side of the fountain were drawn up about fifty constables armed with *lathis*. About a dozen of them held up the procession. A big man, with a cane in his hand and a revolver slung from his belt, advanced towards the procession. His leather straps and belts and the highly-polished boots and hose made him imposing in Swaminathan's eyes. When he turned his head Swaminathan saw to his horror that it was Rajam's father! Swaminathan could not help feeling sorry that it should be Rajam's father. Rajam's father! Rajam's father to be at the head of those traitors! The Deputy Superintendent of Police fixed his eyes on his wrist-watch and said, 'I declare this assembly unlawful. I give it five minutes to disperse.' At the end of five minutes he looked up and uttered in a hollow voice the word, 'Charge.'

In the confusion that followed Swaminathan was very nearly trampled upon and killed. The policemen rushed into the crowd, pushing and beating everybody. Swaminathan had joined a small group of panic-stricken runners. The policemen came towards them with upraised *lathis*. Swaminathan shrieked to them, 'Don't kill me. I know nothing.' He then heard a series of dull noises as the *lathis* descended on the bodies of his neighbours. Swaminathan saw blood streaming from the forehead of one. Down came the *lathis* again. Another runner fell down with a groan. On the back of a third the *lathis* fell again and again.

Swaminathan felt giddy with fear. He was running as fast as his legs could carry him. But the policemen kept pace with him; one of them held him up by his hair and asked, 'What business have you here?'

'I don't know anything, leave me, sirs,' Swaminathan pleaded.

'Doing nothing! Mischievous monkey!' said the grim, hideous policeman—how hideous policemen were at close quarters!—and delivering him a light tap on the head with the *lathi*, ordered him to run before he was kicked.

Swaminathan's original intention had been to avoid that day's topic before his father. But as soon as Father came home, even before taking off his coat, he called Mother and gave her a summary of the day's events. He spoke with a good deal of warmth. 'The Deputy Superintendent is a butcher,' he said as he went in to change. Swaminathan was disposed to agree that the Deputy Superintendent was a butcher, as he recollected the picture of Rajam's father looking at his watch, grimly ticking off seconds before giving orders for massacre. Father came out of the dressing room before undoing his tie, to declare, 'Fifty persons have been taken to the hospital with dangerous contusions. One or two are also believed to be killed.' Turning to Swaminathan he said, 'I heard that schoolboys have given a lot of trouble, what did you do?'

'There was a strike . . .' replied Swaminathan and discovered here an opportunity to get his cap problem solved. He added, 'Oh, the confusion! You know, somebody pulled off the cap that I was wearing and tore it to bits . . . I want a cap before I start for school tomorrow.'

'Who was he?' Father asked.

'I don't know, some bully in the crowd.'

'Why did he do it?'

'Because it wats foreign . . .'

'Who said so? I paid two rupees and got it from the Khaddar Stores. It is a black *khaddar* cap. Why do you presume that you know what is what?'

'I didn't do anything. I was very nearly assaulted when I resisted.'

'You should have knocked him down. I bought the cap and the cloth for your coat on the same day in the Khaddar Stores. If any man says that they are not *khaddar*, he must be blind.'

'People say that it was made in Lancashire.'

'Nonsense. You can ask them to mind their business. And if you allow your clothes to be torn by people who think this and that, you will have to go about naked, that is all. And you may also tell them that I won't have a pie of mine sent to foreign countries. I know my duty. Whatever it is, why do not you urchins leave politics alone and mind your business? We have enough troubles in our country without you brats messing up things . . .'

Swaminathan lay wide awake in bed for a long time. As the hours advanced, and one by one as the lights in the house disappeared, his body compelled him to take stock of the various injuries done to it during the day. His elbows and knees had their own tales to tell: they brought back to his mind the three or four falls that he had had that day. One was—when—yes, when Rajam got down from his car and came to the school, and Swaminathan had wanted to hide himself, and in the hurry stumbled on a heap of stones, and there the knees were badly skinned. And again when the policemen charged, he ran and fell flat before a shop, and some monster ran over him, pinning him with one foot to the ground.

Now as he turned there was a pang about his hips. And then he felt as if a load had been hung from his thighs. And again as he thought of it, he felt a heavy monotonous pain in the head—the merciless rascals! The policeman's *lathi* was none too gentle. And he had been called a monkey! He would—he would see—to call him a monkey! He was no monkey. Only they—the policemen—looked like monkeys, and they behaved like monkeys too.

The Head Master entered the class with a slightly flushed face and a hard ominous look in his eyes. Swaminathan wished that he had been anywhere but there at that moment. The Head Master surveyed the class for a few minutes and asked, 'Are you not ashamed to come and sit there after what you did yesterday?' Just as a special honour to them, he read out the names of a dozen or so that had attended the class. After that he read out the names of those that had kept away, and asked them to stand on their benches. He felt that that punishment was not enough and asked them to stand on their desks. Swaminathan was among them and felt humiliated at that eminence. Then they were lectured. When it was over, they were asked to offer explanations one by one. One said that he had had an attack of headache and therefore could not come to the school. He was asked to bring a medical certificate. The second said that while he had been coming to the school on the previous day, someone had told him that there would be no school, and he had gone back home. The Head Master replied that if he was going to listen to every loafer who said there would be no school, he deserved to be flogged. Anyway, why did he not come to the school and verify? No answer. The punishment was pronounced: ten days' attendance cancelled, two rupees fine, and the whole day to be spent on the desk. The third said that he had had an attack of headache. The fourth said that he had had stomach-ache. The fifth said that his grandmother died suddenly just as he was starting for the school. The Head Master asked him if he could bring a letter from his father. No. He had no father. Then, who was his guardian? His grandmother. But the grandmother was dead, was she not? No. It was another grandmother. The Head Master asked how many grandmothers a person could have. No answer. Could he bring a letter from his neighbours? No, he could not. None of his neighbours could read or write, because he lived in the more illiterate parts of Ellaman Street. Then the Head Master offered to send a teacher to this illiterate locality to ascertain from the boy's neighbours if the death of the grandmother was a fact. A pause, some perspiration, and then the answer that the neighbours could not possibly know anything about it, since the grandmother died in the village. The Head Master hit him on the knuckles with his cane, called him a street dog, and pronounced the punishment: fifteen days' suspension.

When Swaminathan's turn came, he looked around helplessly. Rajam sat on the third bench in front, and resolutely looked away. He was gazing at the blackboard intently. But yet the back of his head and the pink ears were visible to Swaminathan. It was an intolerable sight. Swaminathan was in acute suspense lest that head should turn and fix its eyes on his; he felt that he would drop from the desk to the floor, if that happened. The pink ears three benches off made him incapable of speech. If only somebody would put a blackboard between his eyes and those pink ears!

He was deaf to the question that the Head Master was putting to him. A rap on his body from the Head Master's cane brought him to himself.

'Why did you keep away yesterday?' asked the Head Master, looking up. Swaminathan's first impulse was to protest that he had

never been absent. But the attendance register was there. 'No—
no—I was stoned. I tried to come, but they took away my cap and
burnt it. Many strong men held me down when I tried to come . . .
When a great man is sent to gaol . . . I am surprised to see you a
slave of the Englishmen . . . Didn't they cut off—Dacca Muslin—
Slaves of slaves . . .' These were some of the disjointed explanations
which streamed into his head, and which, even at that moment, he
was discreet enough not to express. He had wanted to mention a
headache, but he found to his distress that others beside him had
had one. The Head Master shouted, 'Won't you open your mouth?'
He brought the cane sharply down on Swaminathan's right shoulder.
Swaminathan kept staring at the Head Master with tearful eyes,
massaging with his left hand the spot where the cane was laid. 'I
will kill you if you keep on staring without answering my question,'
cried the Head Master.

'I—I—couldn't come,' stammered Swaminathan.

'Is that so?' asked the Head Master, and turning to a boy said,
'Bring the peon.'

Swaminathan thought: 'What, is he going to ask the peon to
thrash me? If he does any such thing, I will bite everybody dead.'
The peon came. The Head Master said to him, 'Now say what you
know about this rascal on the desk.'

The peon eyed Swaminathan with a sinister look, grunted, and
demanded, 'Didn't I see you break the panes? . . .'

'Of the ventilators in my room?' added the Head Master with
zest.

Here there was no chance of escape. Swaminathan kept staring
foolishly till he received another whack on the back. The Head
Master demanded what the young brigand had to say about it. The
brigand had nothing to say. It was a fact that he had broken the
panes. They had seen it. There was nothing more to it. He had
unconsciously become defiant and did not care to deny the charge.
When another whack came on his back, he ejaculated, 'Don't beat
me, sir. It pains.' This was an invitation to the Head Master to bring
down the cane four more times. He said, 'Keep standing here, on
this desk, staring like an idiot, till I announce your dismissal.'

Every pore in Swaminathan's body burnt with the touch of the
cane. He had a sudden flood of courage, the courage that comes of
desperation. He restrained the tears that were threatening to rush
out, jumped down, and, grasping his books, rushed out muttering,
'I don't care for your dirty school.'

CHAPTER THIRTEEN

THE 'MCC'

SIX WEEKS LATER Rajam came to Swaminathan's house to announce that he forgave him all his sins—starting with his political activities, to his new acquisition, the Board High School air, by which was meant a certain slowness and stupidity engendered by mental decay.

After making his exit from Albert Mission School in that theatrical manner (on the day following the strike), Swaminathan became so consistently stubborn that a few days later his father took him to the Board School and admitted him there. At first Swaminathan was rather uncertain of his happiness in the new school. But he excited the curiosity that all newcomers do, and found himself to his great satisfaction the centre of attraction in Second C. All his new class-mates, remarkably new faces, often clustered round him to see him and hear him talk. He had not yet picked the few that he would have liked to call his chums. He still believed that his Albert Mission set was intact, though, since the reopening in June, the set was not what it had been before. Sankar disappeared, and people said that his father had been transferred; Somu was not promoted, and that meant he was automatically excluded from the group, the law being inexorable in that respect; the Pea was promoted, but he returned to the class exactly three months late, and he was quite full up with medical certificates, explanations, and exemptions. He was a man of a hundred worries now, and passed his old friends like a stranger. Only Rajam and Mani were still intact as far as Swaminathan was concerned. Mani saw him every day. But Rajam had not spoken to him since the day when his political doings became known.

And now this afternoon Swaminathan was sitting in a dark corner of the house trying to make a camera with a cardboard box and a spectacle lens. In his effort to fix the lens in the hole that was one round too large, he was on the point of losing his temper, when he heard a familiar voice calling him. He ran to the door.

'Hello! Hello! Rajam,' he cried, 'why didn't you tell me you were coming?'

'What is the thing in your hand?' Rajam asked.

'Oh,' Swaminathan said, blushing.

'Come, come, let us have a look at it.'

'Oh, it is nothing,' Swaminathan said, giving him the box.

As Rajam kept gazing at the world through the hole in the cardboard box, Swaminathan said, 'Akbar Ali of our class has made a marvellous camera.'

'Has he? What does he do with it?'

'He has taken a lot of photos with it.'

'Indeed! Photos of what?'

'He hasn't yet shown them to me, but they are probably photos of houses, people, and trees.'

Rajam sat down on the door-step and asked, 'And who is this Akbar Ali?'

'He is a nice Mohammedan, belongs to our class.'

'In the Board High School?' There was just a suspicion of a sneer in his tone. Swaminathan preferred to ignore this question and continued, 'He has a bicycle. He is a very fine Mohammedan, calls Mohammed of Gazni and Aurangzeb rascals.'

'What makes you think that they were that?'

'Didn't they destroy our temples and torture the Hindus? Have you forgotten the Somnathpur god? . . .'

'We brahmins deserve that and more,' said Rajam. 'In our house my father does not care for new-moon days and there are no annual ceremonies for the dead.' He was in a debating mood, and Swaminathan realized it and remained silent. Rajam said, 'I tell you what, it is your Board High School that has given you this mentality.'

Swaminathan felt that the safest course would be to agree with him. 'You are right in a way. I don't like the Board High School.'

'Then why did you go and join it?'

'I could not help it. You saw how beastly our Head Master was. If you had been in my place, you would have kicked him in the face.'

This piece of flattery did not soothe Rajam. 'If I were you I would have kept clear of all your dirty politics and strikes.' His father was a Government servant, and hence his family was anti-political.

Swaminathan said, 'You are right. I should have remained at home on the day of the strike.' This example of absolute submissiveness touched Rajam. He said promptly that he was prepared to forgive Swaminathan his past sins and would not mind his belonging to the Board School. They were to be friends as of old. 'What would you say to a cricket team?' Rajam asked.

Swaminathan had not thought of cricket as something that he himself could play. He was, of course, familiar with Hobbs, Bradman, and Duleep, and vainly tried to carry their scores in his head, as Rajam did. He filched pictures of cricket players, as Rajam did, and pasted them in an album, though he secretly did not very much care for those pictures—there was something monotonous about them. He sometimes thought that the same picture was pasted in every page of the album.

'No, Rajam, I don't think I can play. I don't know how to play.'

'That is what everybody thinks,' said Rajam. 'I don't know how myself, though I collect pictures and scores.'

This was very pleasing to hear. Probably Hobbs too was shy and sceptical before he took the bat and swung it.

'We can challenge a lot of teams, including our School Eleven. They think they can't be beaten,' said Swaminathan.

'What! The Board School mugs think that! We shall thrash them. Oh, yes.'

'What shall we call it?'

'Don't you know? It is the MCC,' said Rajam.

'That is Hobbs's team, isn't it? They may drag us before a court if we take their name.'

'Who says that? If we get into any trouble, I shall declare before the judge that MCC stands for Malgudi Cricket Club.'

Swaminathan was a little disappointed. Though as MCC it sounded imposing, the name was really a bit tame. 'I think we had better try some other name, Rajam.'

'What would you suggest?'

'Well—I am for "Friends Eleven".'

'Friends Eleven?'

'Or say "Jumping Stars"?' said Swaminathan.

'Oh, that is not bad, not bad you know.'

'I do think it would be glorious to call ourselves "Jumping Stars"!'

Rajam instantly had a vision of a newspaper report: 'The Jumping Stars soundly thrashed the Board High School Eleven.' 'It is a beauty, I think,' he cried, moved by the vision. He pulled out a piece of paper and a pencil, and said, 'Come on, Swami, repeat the names that come to your head. It would be better to have a long list to select from. We shall underline "Jumping Stars" and "MCC" and give them special consideration. Come on.'

Swaminathan remained thoughtful and started, ' "Friends Eleven" . . . "Jumping Stars" . . . "Friends Union" . . .'

'I have "Friends Union" here already,' Rajam said, pointing to the list.

Swaminathan went on: ' "Excelsiors" . . .'

'I have got it.'

' "Excelsior Union" . . . "Champion Eleven" . . .' A long pause.

'Are you dried up?' Rajam asked.

'No, if Mani were here, he would have suggested a few more names . . . "Champion Eleven".'

'You have just said it.'

' "Victory Union Eleven" . . .'

'That is very good. I think it is very very good. People would be afraid of us.' He held the list before him and read the names with great satisfaction. He had struggled hard on the previous night to get a few names. But only 'Friends Union' and 'Excelsiors' kept coming till he felt fatigued. But what a lot of names Swaminathan was able to reel off. 'Can you meet me tomorrow evening, Swami? I shall get Mani down. Let us select a name.'

After a while Swaminathan asked, 'Look here, do you think we shall have to pay tax or something to the Government when we start the team?'

'The Government seems to tax everything in this world. My father's pay is about five hundred. But nearly two hundred and over is demanded by the Government. Anyway, what makes you think that we shall have to pay tax?'

'I mean—if we don't pay tax, the Government may not recognize our team or its name and a hundred other teams may take the same name. It might lead to all sorts of complications.'

'Suppose we have two names?' asked Rajam.

'It is not done.'

'I know a lot of teams that have two names. When I was in Bishop Waller's, we had a cricket team that we called—I don't remember the name now. I think we called it "Cricket Eleven" and "Waller's Cricket Eleven". You see, one name is for ordinary use and the other is for matches.'

'It is all very well for a rich team like your Waller's. But suppose the Government demands two taxes from us?'

Rajam realized at this point that the starting of a cricket team was the most complicated problem on earth. He had simply expected to gather a dozen fellows on the maidan next to his compound and play, and challenge the world. But here were endless troubles, starting with the name that must be unique, Government taxes, and so on. The Government did not seem to know where it ought to interfere and where not. He had a momentary sympathy for Gandhi; no wonder he was dead against the Government.

Swaminathan seemed to be an expert in thinking out difficulties. He said, 'Even if we want to pay, whom are we to pay the taxes to?' Certainly not to His Majesty or the Viceroy. Who was the Government? What if somebody should take the money and defraud them, somebody pretending to be the Government? Probably they would have to send the taxes by Money Order to the Governor! Well, that might be treason. And then what was the amount to be paid?

They sat round Rajam's table in his room. Mani held before him a catalogue of Messrs Binns, the Shop for Sports Goods. He read, 'Junior Willard Bats, Seven Eight, made of finest seasoned wood, used by Cambridge Junior Boys' Eleven.'

'Let me have a look at it . . .' said Rajam. He bent over the table and said, 'Seems to be a fine bat. Have a look at it, Swami.' Swaminathan craned his neck and agreed that it was a fine bat, but he was indiscreet enough to say, 'It looks like any other bat in the catalogue.' Mani's left hand shot out and held his neck and pressed his face close to the picture of the bat: 'Why do you pretend to be a cricket player if you cannot see the difference between Junior Willard and other bats? You are not fit to be even a sweeper in our team.' After this admonition the hold was relaxed.

Rajam asked, 'Swami, do you know what the catalogue man calls the Junior Willard? It seems it is the Rolls-Royce among the junior bats. Don't you know the difference between the Rolls-Royce and other cars?'

Swaminathan replied haughtily, 'I never said I saw no difference between the Rolls-Royce and other cars.'

'What is the difference?' urged Rajam.

Mani laughed and teased, 'Come on. If you really know the difference, why don't you say it?'

Swaminathan said, 'The Rolls costs a lakh of rupees, while other cars cost about ten thousand; a Rolls has engines made of silver, while other cars have iron engines.'

'Oh, oh!' peered Rajam.

'A Rolls never gives trouble, while other cars always give trouble; a Rolls engine never stops; a Rolls-Royce never makes a noise, while other cars always make a noise.'

'Why not deliver a lecture on the Rolls-Royce?' asked Mani.

'Swami, I am glad you know so much about the Rolls-Royce. I am at the same time ashamed to find you knowing so little about Willard Junior. We had about a dozen Willard Juniors when I was in Bishop Waller's. Oh! What bats! There are actual springs inside the bat, so that when you touch the ball it flies. There is fine silk cord wound round the handle. You don't know anything, and yet you talk! Show me another bat which has silk cord and springs like the Willard.'

There was a pause, and after that Rajam said, 'Note it down, Swami.' Swaminathan noted down on a paper, 'Vilord june-ear bat.' And looking up asked, 'How many?'

'Say three. Will that do, Mani?'

'Why waste money on three bats? Two will do . . .'

'But suppose one breaks in the middle of a match?' Rajam asked.

'Do you suppose we are going to supply bats to our opponents? They will have to come provided with bats. We must make it clear.'

'Even then, if our bat breaks we may have to stop playing.'

'Two will do, Rajam, unless you want to waste money.'

Rajam's enthusiasm was great. He left his chair and sat on the arm of Mani's chair, gloating over the pictures of cricket goods in the catalogue. Swaminathan, though he was considered to be a bit of a heretic, caught the enthusiasm and perched on the other arm of the chair. All the three devoured with their eyes the glossy pictures of cricket balls, bats, and nets.

In about an hour they selected from the catalogue their team's requirements. And then came the most difficult part of the whole affair—a letter to Messrs Binns, ordering goods. Bare courtesy made Rajam offer the authorship of the letter to Mani, who declined it. Swaminathan was forced to accept it in spite of his protests, and he sat for a long time chewing his pencil without producing a word: he had infinite trouble with spelling, and the more he tried to be correct the more muddled he was becoming; in the end he sat so long thinking of spelling that even such words as 'the' and 'and' became doubtful. Rajam took up the task himself. Half an hour later he placed on the table a letter:

From
MCC (And Victory Union Eleven),
Malgudi.

To
Messrs Binns,
Sportsmen,
Mount Road,
Madras.

Dear Sir,
Please send to our team two Junior Willard bats, six balls, wickets and other things quick. It is very urgent. We shall send you money afterwards. Don't fear. Please be urgent.
      Yours obediently,
                    CAPTAIN RAJAM (Captain).

This letter received Swaminathan's benedictions. But Mani expressed certain doubts. He wanted to know whether 'Dear' could stand at the beginning of a letter to a perfect stranger. 'How can you call Binns "Dear Sir"? You must say "Sir".'

Rajam's explanation was: 'I won't say "Sir". It is said only by clerks. I am not Binns's clerk. I don't care to address him as "Sir".'

So this letter went as it was.

After this exacting work they were resting, with a feeling of relief, when the postman came in with a card for Rajam. Rajam read it and cried, 'Guess who has written this?'

'Binns.'

'Silly. It must be our Head Master.'

'Somebody.'

'J.B. Hobbs.'

'It is from Sankar,' Rajam announced joyfully.

'Sankar! We had almost forgotten that old thief.' Swaminathan and Mani tore the card from Rajam's hand and read:

MY DEAR FRIEND,

I am studying here because my father came here. My mother is also here. All of us are here. And we will be only here. I am doing well. I hope you are doing well. It is very hot here. I had fever for three days and drank medicine. I hope I will read well and pass the examination. Is Swami and Mani doing well! It is very hot here. I am playing cricket now. I can't write more.

> With regards,
> Your dearest friend,
> SANKAR.

P.S. Don't forget me.

S

They were profoundly moved by this letter, and decided to reply at once.

Three letters were ready in an hour. Mani copied Sankar's letter verbatim. Swaminathan and Rajam wrote nearly similar letters: they said they were doing well by the grace of God; they hoped that Sankar would pass and also that he was doing well; then they said a lot about their cricket team and hoped that Sankar would become a member; they also said that Sankar's team might challenge them to a match.

The letters were put into a stamped envelope, and the flap was pasted. It was only then that they felt the need of knowing Sankar's address. They searched all parts of Sankar's card. Not a word anywhere, not even the name of the town he was writing from. They tried to get this out of the postmark. But a dark curved smudge on the stamp cannot be very illuminating.

The MCC and its organizers had solid proof that they were persons of count when a letter from Binns came addressed to the Captain, MCC, Malgudi. It was a joy, touching that beautiful envelope and turning it over in the hand. Binns were the first to recognize the MCC, and Rajam took a vow that he would buy every bit that his team needed from that great firm. There were three implications in this letter that filled Rajam and his friends with rapture: (1) that His Majesty's post office recognized their team was proved by the fact that the letter addressed to the captain was promptly delivered to him; (2) that they were really recognized by such a magnificent firm as Binns of Madras was proved by the fact that Binns cared to reply in a full letter and not on a card, and actually typed the letter! (3) Binns sent under another cover carrying four annas postage a huge catalogue. What a tribute!

The letter informed the captain that Messrs Binns thanked him for his letter and would be much obliged to him if he would kindly remit 25 per cent with the order and the balance could be paid against the VPP of the railway receipt.

Three heads buzzed over the meaning of this letter. The trouble was that they could not understand whether Binns were going to send the goods or not. Mani promised to unravel the letter if somebody would tell him what 'obliged' meant. When they turned the pages of a dictionary and offered him the meaning, he was none the wiser. He felt that it was a meaningless word in that place. 'One thing is clear,' said Rajam, 'Binns thanks us for our letter. So I don't think this letter could mean a refusal to supply us goods.' Swaminathan agreed with him, 'That is right. If he did not wish to supply you with things, would he thank you? He would have abused you.' He scrutinized the letter again to make sure that there was no mistake about the thanks.

'Why has the fool used this word?' Mani asked, referring to 'obliged' which he could not pronounce. 'It has no meaning. Is he trying to make fun of us?'

'He says something about 25 per cent. I wish I knew what it was,' said Rajam.

Swaminathan could hardly contain himself, 'I say, Rajam, I am surprised that you cannot understand this letter; you got 60 per cent in the last examination.'

'Have you any sense in you? What has that to do with this. Even a BA cannot understand this letter.'

In the end they came to the conclusion that the letter was sent to them by mistake. As far as they could see, the MCC had written nothing in their previous letter to warrant such expressions as 'obliged', 'remit', and '25 per cent'. It could not be that the great firm of Binns were trying to make fun of them. Swaminathan pointed out 'To the Captain, MCC' at the beginning of the letter.

But he was told that it was also a part of the mistake.

This letter was put in a cover with a covering letter and dispatched. The covering letter said:

'We are very sorry that you sent me somebody's letter. We are returning this somebody's letter. Please send our things immediately.'

The MCC were an optimistic lot. Though they were still unhonoured with a reply to their second letter, they expected their goods to arrive with every post. After ten days they thought they would start playing with whatever was available till they got the real bats, etc. The bottom of a dealwood case provided them with three good bats, and Rajam managed to get three used tennis balls from his father's club. The Pea was there, offering four real stumps that he believed he had somewhere in his house. A neat slip of ground adjoining Rajam's bungalow was to be the pitch. Everything was ready. Even if Binns took a month more to manufacture the goods specially for the MCC (as they faintly thought probable), there need be no delay in starting practice. By the time the real bats and the balls arrived, they would be in form to play matches.

Rajam had chosen from his class a few who, he thought, deserved to become members of the MCC.

At five o'clock on the opening day, the MCC had assembled, all except the Pea, for whom Rajam was waiting anxiously. He had promised to bring the real stumps. It was half an hour past time and yet he was not to be seen anywhere.

At last his puny figure was discovered in the distance. There was a catch in Rajam's heart when he saw him. He strained his eyes to find out if the Pea had the things about him. But since the latter was coming from the west, he was seen in the blaze of the evening sun. All the twelve assembled in the field shaded their eyes and looked. Some said that he was carrying a bundle, while some thought that he was swinging his hands freely.

When he arrived, Rajam asked, 'Why didn't you tell us that you hadn't got the stumps?'

'I have still got them,' protested the Pea, 'I shall bring them tomorrow. I am sure my father knows where they are kept.'

'You kept us waiting till now. Why did you not come earlier and tell us that you could not find them?'

'I tell you, I have been spending hours looking for them everywhere. How could I come here and tell you and at the same time search?'

A cloud descended upon the gathering. For over twenty hours every one among them had been dreaming of swinging a bat and throwing a ball. And they could have realized the dream but for the Pea's wickedness. Everybody looked at him sourly. He was isolated. Rajam felt like crying when he saw the dealwood planks and the tennis balls lying useless on the ground. What a glorious evening they could have had if only the stumps had been brought!

Amidst all this gloom somebody cast a ray of light by suggesting that they might use the compound wall of Rajam's bungalow as a temporary wicket.

A portion of the wall was marked off with a piece of charcoal, and the captain arranged the field and opened the batting himself. Swaminathan took up the bowling. He held a tennis ball in his hand, took a few paces, and threw it over. Rajam swung the bat but missed it. The ball hit the wall right under the charcoal mark. Rajam was bowled out with the very first ball! There was a great shout of joy. The players pressed round Swaminathan to shake him and pat him on the back; he was given on the very spot the title, 'Tate'.

CHAPTER FOURTEEN

GRANNY SHOWS HER IGNORANCE

WORK WAS RATHER heavy in the Board High School. The amount of homework given at the Albert Mission was nothing compared to the heap given at the Board. Every teacher thought that his was the only subject that the boys had to study. Six sums in Arithmetic, four pages of 'hand-writing copy', dictionary meanings of scores of tough words, two maps, and five stanzas in Tamil poetry, were the average homework every day. Swaminathan sometimes wished that he had not left his old school. The teachers here were ruthless beings; not to speak of the drill three evenings a week, there were scout classes, compulsory games, etc. after the regular hours every day; and missing a single class meant half a dozen cane cuts on the following day. The wizened spectacled man was a repulsive creature, with his screeching voice; the Head of the Albert Mission had a majestic air about him in spite of all his defects.

All this rigour and discipline resulted in a life with little scope for leisure. Swaminathan got up pretty early, rushed through all his homework, and rose just in time to finish the meal and reach the school as the first bell rang. Every day, as he passed the cloth shop at the end of Market Road, the first bell reached his ears. And just as he panted into the class, the second bell would go off. The bell lacked the rich note of the Albert Mission gong; there was something mean and nasal about it. But he soon got accustomed to it.

Except for an hour in the afternoon, he had to be glued to his seat right till four-thirty in the evening. He had lost the last-bench habit (it might be because he no longer had Mani's company in the classroom). He sat in the second row, and no dawdling easygoing nonsense was tolerated there; you sat right under the teacher's nose. When the four-thirty bell rang, Swaminathan slipped his pencil into his pocket and stretched his cramped aching fingers. The four-thirty bell held no special thrill. You could not just dash out of the class with a howl of joy. You had to go to the drill ground and stand in a solemn line, and for three-quarters of an hour the Drill Master treated you as if you were his dog. He drove you to march left and right, stand at attention, and swing the arms, or climb the horizontal or parallel bars, whether you liked it or not, whether you knew the thing or not. For aught the Drill Master cared, you might lose your balance on the horizontal bars and crack your skull.

At the end of this you ran home to drink coffee, throw down the books, and rush off to the cricket field, which was a long way off. You covered the distance half running, half walking, moved by the vision of a dun field sparsely covered with scorched grass, lit into a blaze by the slant rays of the evening sun, enveloped in a flimsy cloud of dust, alive with the shouts of players stamping about. What music there was in the thud of the bat hitting the ball! Just as you took the turn leading to Lawley Extension, you looked at the sun, which stood poised like a red-hot coin on the horizon. You hoped it would not sink. But by the time you arrived at the field, the sun went down, leaving only a splash of colour and light in the sky. The shadows already crept out, and one or two municipal lanterns twinkled here and there. You still hoped you would be in time for a good game. But from about half a furlong away you saw the team squatting carelessly round the field. Somebody was wielding the bat rather languidly, bowled and fielded by a handful who were equally languid—the languor that comes at the end of a strenuous evening in the sun.

In addition to the misery of disappointment, you found Rajam a bit sore. He never understood the difficulties of a man. 'Oh, Swami, why are you late again?'

'Wretched drill class.'

'Oh, damn your drill classes and scout classes! Why don't you come early?'

'What can I do, Rajam? I can't help it.'

'Well, well. I don't care. You are always ready with excuses. Since the new bats, balls and things arrived, you have hardly played four times.'

Others being too tired to play, eventually you persuaded the youngest member of the team (a promising, obedient boy of the Fifth Standard, who was admitted because he cringed and begged Rajam perseveringly) to bowl while you batted. And when you tired of it, you asked him to hold the bat and started bowling, and since you were the Tate of the team, the youngster was rather nervous. And again you took up batting, and then bowling, and so on. It went on till it became difficult to find the ball in the semi-darkness and the picker ran after small dark objects on the ground, instead of after the ball. At this stage a rumour started that the ball was lost and caused quite a stir. The figures squatting and reposing got busy, and the ball was retrieved. After this the captain passed an order forbidding further play, and the stumps were drawn for the day, and soon all the players melted in the darkness. You stayed behind with Rajam and Mani, perched upon Rajam's compound wall, and discussed the day's game and the players, noting the improvement, stagnation, or degeneration of each player, till it became quite dark and a peon came to inform Rajam that his tutor had come.

One evening, returning home from the cricket field, after parting from Mani at the Grove Street junction, Swaminathan's conscience began to trouble him. A slight incident had happened during the early evening when he had gone home from the school to throw down the books and start for the cricket field. He had just thrown down the books and was running towards the kitchen, when Granny cried, 'Swami, Swami. Oh, boy, come here.'

'No,' he said as usual and was in a moment out of her sight, in the kitchen, violently sucking coffee out of a tumbler. He could still hear her shaky querulous voice calling him. There was something appealing in that weak voice, and he had a fit of pity for her sitting and calling people who paid no heed to her. As soon as he had drunk the coffee, he went to her and asked, 'What do you want?'

She looked up and asked him to sit down. At that he lost his temper and all the tenderness he had felt for her a moment back. He raced, 'If you are going to say what you have to say as quickly as possible . . . If not, don't think I am a silly fool . . .'

She said, 'I shall give you six pies. You can take three pies and bring me a lemon for three pies.' She had wanted to open this question slowly and diplomatically, because she knew what to expect from her grandson. And when she asked him to sit down, she did it as the first diplomatic move.

Without condescending to say yes or no, Swaminathan held out his hand for the coins and took them. Granny said, 'You must come before I count ten.' This imposition of a time-limit irritated him. He threw down the coins and said, 'If you want it so urgently, you had better go and get it yourself.' It was nearing five-thirty and he wanted to be in the field before sunset. He stood frowning at her as if giving her the choice of his getting the lemon late when he returned from the field, or not at all. She said, 'I have a terrible pain in the stomach. Please run out and come back, boy.' He did not stay there to hear more.

But now all the excitement and exhilaration of the play being over, and having bidden the last 'good night', he stood in the Grove and Vinayak Mudali Street junction, as it were face to face with his soul. He thought of his grandmother and felt guilty. Probably she was writhing with pain at that very moment. It stung his heart as he remembered her pathetic upturned face and watery eyes. He called himself a sneak, a thief, an ingrate, and a hardhearted villain.

In this mood of self-reproach he reached home. He softly sat beside Granny and kept looking at her. It was contrary to his custom. Every evening as soon as he reached home he would dash straight into the kitchen and worry the cook. But now he felt that his hunger did not matter.

Granny's passage had no light. It had only a shaft falling from the lamp in the hall. In the half-darkness, he could not see her face clearly. She lay still. Swaminathan was seized with a horrible passing doubt whether she might not be dead—of stomach-ache. He controlled his voice and asked, 'Granny, how is your pain?' Granny stirred, opened her eyes and said, 'Swami, you have come! Have you had your food?'

'Not yet. How is your stomach-ache, Granny?'

'Oh, it is all right. It is all right.'

It cost him all his mental powers to ask without flinching, 'Did you get the lemon?' He wanted to know it. He had been feeling genuinely anxious about it. Granny answered this question at once, but to Swaminathan it seemed an age—a terrible stretch of time during which anything might happen, she might say anything, scold him, disown him, swear that she would have nothing more to do with him, or say reproachfully that if only he had cared to go and purchase the lemon in time, he might have saved her and that she was going to die in a few minutes. But she simply said, 'You did right in not going. Your mother had kept a dozen in the kitchen.'

Swaminathan was overjoyed to hear this good news. And he expressed this mood of joy in: 'You know what my new name is? I am Tate.'

'What?'

'Tate.'

'What is Tate?' she asked innocently. Swaminathan's disappointment was twofold: she had not known anything of his new title, and failed to understand its rich significance even when told. At other times he would have shouted at her. But now he was a fresh penitent, and so asked her kindly, 'Do you mean to say that you don't know Tate?'

'I don't know what you mean.'

'Tate, the great cricket player, the greatest bowler on earth. I hope you know what cricket is.'

'What is that?' Granny asked. Swaminathan was aghast at this piece of illiteracy. 'Do you mean to say, Granny, that you don't know what cricket is, or are you fooling me?'

'I don't know what you mean.'

'Don't keep on saying "I don't know what you mean". I wonder what the boys and men of your days did in the evenings! I think they spent all the twenty-four hours in doing holy things.'

He considered for a second. Here was his Granny stagnating in appalling ignorance; and he felt it his duty to save her. He delivered a short speech setting forth the principles, ideals, and the philosophy of the game of cricket, mentioning the radiant gods of that world. He asked her every few seconds if she understood, and she nodded her head, though she caught only three per cent of what he said. He concluded the speech with a sketch of the history and the prospects of the MCC. 'But for Rajam, Granny,' he said, 'I don't know where we should have been. He has spent hundreds of rupees on this team. Buying bats and balls is no joke. He has plenty of money in his box. Our team is known even to the Government. If you like, you may write a letter to the MCC and it will be delivered to us promptly. You will see us winning all the cups in Malgudi, and in course of time we shall show even the Madras fellows what cricket is.' He added a very important note: 'Don't imagine all sorts of fellows can become players in our team.'

His father stood behind him, with the baby in his arms. He asked, 'What are you lecturing about, young man?'

Swaminathan had not noticed his father's presence, and now writhed awkwardly as he answered, 'Nothing . . . Oh, nothing, Father.'

'Come on. Let me know it too.'

'It is nothing—Granny wanted to know something about cricket and I was explaining it to her.'

'Indeed! I never knew Mother was a sportswoman. Mother, I hope Swami has filled you with cricket-wisdom.'

Granny said, 'Don't tease the boy. The child is so fond of me. Poor thing! He has been trying to tell me all sorts of things. You are not in the habit of explaining things to me. You are all big men . . .'

Father replied, pointing at the baby, 'Just wait a few days and this little fellow will teach you all the philosophy and the politics in the world.' He gently clouted the baby's fat cheeks, and the baby gurgled and chirped joyfully. 'He has already started lecturing. Listen attentively, Mother.' Granny held up her arms for the baby. But Father clung to him tight and said, 'No. No. I came home early only for this fellow's sake. I can't. Come on, Swami, I think we had better sit down for food. Where is your mother?'

The captain sternly disapproved of Swaminathan's ways. 'Swami, I must warn you. You are neglecting the game. You are not having any practice at all.'

'It is this wretched Board School work.'

'Who asked you to go and join it? They never came and invited you. Never mind. But let me tell you. Even Bradman, Tate, and everybody spends four to five hours on the pitch every day, practising, practising. Do you think you are greater than they?'

'Captain, listen to me. I do my best to arrive at the field before five. But this wretched Board High School time-table is peculiar.'

A way out had to be found. The captain suggested, 'You must see your Head Master and ask him to exempt you from extra work till the match is over.' It was more easily said than done, and Swaminathan said so, conjuring up before his mind a picture of the wizened face and the small dingy spectacles of his Head Master.

'I am afraid to ask that monster,' Swaminathan said. 'He may detain me in Second Form for ages.'

'Indeed! Are you telling me that you are in such terror of your

Head Master? Suppose I see him?'

'Oh, please don't, Captain. I beg you. You don't know what a vicious being he is. He may not treat you well. Even if he behaves well before you, he is sure to kill me when you are gone.'

'What is the matter with you, Swami? Your head is full of nonsense. How are we to go on? It is two months since we started the team, and you have not played even for ten days . . .'

Mani, who had stretched himself on the compound wall, now broke in: 'Let us see what your Head Master can do. Let him say yes or no. If he kills you I will pulp him. My clubs have had no work for a long time.'

There was no stopping Rajam. The next day he insisted that he would see the Head Master at the school. He would not mind losing a couple of periods of his own class. Mani offered to go with him but was advised to mind his business.

Next morning at nine-thirty Swaminathan spent five minutes rubbing his eyes red, and then complained of headache. His father felt his temples and said that he would be all right if he dashed a little cold water on his forehead.

'Yes, Father,' Swaminathan said and went out. He stood outside Father's room and decided that if cold water was a cure for headache he would avoid it, since he was praying for that malady just then. Rajam was coming to see the Head Master, and it would be unwise to go to school that morning. He went in and asked, 'Father, did you say cold water?'

'Yes.'

'But don't you think it will give me pneumonia or something? I am also feeling feverish.'

Father felt his pulse and said, 'Now run to school and you will be all right.' It was easier to squeeze milk out of a stone than to get permission from Father to keep away from school.

He whispered into his Granny's ear, 'Granny, even if I die, I am sure Father will insist on sending my corpse to the school.' Granny protested vehemently against this sentiment.

'Granny, a terrible fever is raging within me and my head is splitting with headache. But yet, I mustn't keep away from school.'

Granny said, 'Don't go to school.' She then called Mother and said, 'This child has fever. Why should he go to school?'

'Has he?' Mother asked anxiously, and fussed over him. She felt his body and said that he certainly had a temperature.

Swaminathan said pathetically, 'Give me milk or something, Mother. It is getting late for school.' Mother vetoed this virtuous proposal. Swaminathan faintly said, 'But Father may not like it.' She asked him to lie down on a bed and hurried along to Father's room. She stepped into the room with the declaration, 'Swami has fever, and he can't go to school.'

'Did you take his temperature?'

'Not yet. It doesn't matter if he misses the school for a day.'

'Anyway, take his temperature,' he said. He feared that his wife might detect the sarcasm in his suggestion, and added as a palliative, 'that we may know whether a doctor is necessary.'

A thermometer stuck out of Swaminathan's mouth for half a minute and indicated normal. Mother looked at it and thrust it back into his mouth. It again showed normal. She took it to Father, and he said, 'Well, it is normal,' itching to add, 'I knew it.' Mother insisted, 'Something has gone wrong with the thermometer. The boy has fever. There is no better thermometer than my hand. I can swear that he has 100.2 now.'

'Quite likely,' Father said.

And Swaminathan, when he ought to have been at school, was lying peacefully, with closed eyes, on his bed. He heard a footstep near his bed and opened his eyes. Father stood over him and said in an undertone, 'You are a lucky fellow. What a lot of champions you have in this house when you don't want to go to school!' Swaminathan felt that this was a sudden and unprovoked attack from behind. He shut his eyes and turned towards the wall with a feeble groan.

By the afternoon he was already bedsore. He dreaded the prospect of staying in bed through the evening. Moreover, Rajam would have already come to the school in the morning and gone.

He went to his mother and informed her that he was starting for the school. There was a violent protest at once. She felt him all over and said that he was certainly better but in no condition to go to school. Swaminathan said, 'I am feeling quite fit, Mother. Don't get fussy.'

On the way to the school he met Rajam and Mani. Mani had his club under his arm. Swaminathan feared that these two had done something serious.

Rajam said, 'You are a fine fellow! Where were you this morning?'

'Did you see the Head Master, Rajam?'

'Not yet. I found that you had not come, and did not see him. I want you to be with me when I see him. After all it is your business.'

When Swaminathan emerged from the emotional chaos which followed Rajam's words, he asked, 'What is Mani doing here?'

'I don't know,' Rajam said. 'I found him outside your school with his club, when he ought to have been in his class.'

'Mani, what about your class?'

'It is all right,' Mani replied, 'I didn't attend it today.'

'And why your club?' Swaminathan asked.

'Oh! I simply brought it along.'

Rajam asked, 'Weren't you told yesterday to attend your class and mind your business?'

'I don't remember. You asked me to mind my business only when I offered to accompany you. I am not accompaning you. I just came this way, and you have also come this way. This is a public road.' Mani's jest was lost on them. Their minds were too busy with plans for the impending interview.

'Don't worry, young men,' Mani said. 'I shall see you through your troubles. I will talk to the Head Master, if you like.'

'If you step into his room, he will call the police,' Swaminathan said.

When they reached the school, Mani was asked to go away, or at worst wait in the road. Rajam went in, and Swaminathan was compelled to accompany him to the Head Master's room.

The Head Master was sleeping with his head between his hands and his elbows resting on the table. It was a small stuffy room with only one window opening on the weatherbeaten side-wall of a shop; it was cluttered with dust-laden rolls of maps, globes, and geometrical squares. The Head Master's white cane lay on the table across two ink-bottles and some pads. The sun came in a hot dusty beam and fell on the Head Master's nose and the table. He was gently snoring. This was a possibility that Rajam had not thought of.

'What shall we do?' Swaminathan asked in a rasping whisper.

'Wait,' Rajam ordered.

They waited for ten minutes and then began to make gentle noises with their feet. The Head Master opened his eyes and without taking his head from his hands, kept staring at them vacantly, without showing any sign of recognition. He rubbed his eyes, raised his eyebrows three times, yawned, and asked in a voice thick with sleep, 'Have you fellows no class?' He fumbled for his spectacles and put them on. Now the picture was complete—wizened face and dingy spectacles calculated to strike terror into the hearts of Swaminathans. He asked again, 'To what class do you fellows belong? Have you no class?'

'I don't belong to your school,' Rajam said defiantly.

'Ah, then which heaven do you drop from?'

Rajam said, 'I am the captain of the MCC and have come to see you on business.'

'What is that?'

'This is my friend W.S. Swaminathan of Second C studying in your school . . .'

'I am honoured to meet you,' said the Head Master turning to Swaminathan. Rajam felt at that moment that he had found out where the Board High School got its reputation from.

'I am the captain of the MCC.'

'Equally honoured . . .'

'He is in my team. He is a good bowler . . .'

'Are you?' said the Head Master, turning to Swaminathan.

'May I come to the point?' Rajam asked.

'Do, do,' said the Head Master, 'for heaven's sake, do.'

'It is this,' Rajam said, 'he is a good bowler and he needs some practice. He can't come to the field early enough because he is kept in the school every day after four-thirty.'

'What do you want me to do?'

'Sir, can't you permit him to go home after four-thirty?'

The Head Master sank back in his chair and remained silent. Rajam asked again, 'What do you say, sir, won't you do it?'

'Are you the Head Master of this school or am I?'

'Of course you are the Head Master, sir. In Albert Mission they don't keep us a minute longer than four-thirty. And we are exempted from drill if we play games.'

'Here I am not prepared to listen to your rhapsodies on that pariah school. Get out.'

Mani, who had been waiting outside, finding his friends gone too long, and having his own fears, now came into the Head Master's room.

'Who is this?' asked the Head Master, looking at Mani sourly.

'What do you want?'

'Nothing,' Mani replied and quietly stood in a corner.

'I can't understand why every fellow who finds nothing to do comes and stands in my room.'

'I am the Police Superintendent's son,' Rajam said abruptly.

'Is that so? Find out from your father what he was doing on the day a gang of little rascals came in and smashed these windows ... What is the thing that fellow has in his hand?'

'My wooden club,' Mani answered.

Rajam added, 'He breaks skulls with it. Come out, Mani, come on, Swami. There is nothing doing with this—this madcap.'

CHAPTER FIFTEEN

BEFORE THE MATCH

THE MCC'S CHALLENGE to a 'friendly' match was accepted by the Young Men's Union, who kept themselves in form with indefatigable practice on the vacant site behind the Reading Room, or when the owner of this site objected, right in the middle of Kulam Street. The match was friendly in nought but name. The challenge sent by the MCC was couched in terms of defiance and threat.

There were some terrifying conditions attached to the challenge. The first condition was that the players should be in the field promptly at eleven noon. The second was that they should carry their own bats, while the stumps would be graciously supplied by the MCC. The third was not so much a plain condition as a firm hint that they would do well to bring and keep in stock a couple of their own balls. The reason for this was given in the pithy statement 'that your batsmen might hit your own balls and not break ours'. The next was the inhospitable suggestion that they had better look out for themselves in regard to lunch, if they cared to have any at all. The last condition was perhaps the most complicated of the lot, over which some argument and negotiation ensued: 'You shall pay for breaking bats, balls, wickets and other damages.'

The YMU captain was rather puzzled by this. He felt that it was irrelevant in view of the fact that there were conditions 2 and 3, and if they broke any bats and balls at all, it would be their own property, and the MCC's anxiety to have the damage made good was unwarranted. He was told that the stumps belonged to the MCC anyway, and there was also the YMU's overlooking clauses 2 and 3. At which the YMU captain became extremely indignant and asked why if the MCC was so impoverished, it should not come and play in their (YMU's) own pitch and save them the trouble of carrying their team about. The stinging rejoinder occurred to the indignant Rajam exactly twenty minutes after the other captain had left, that it could not be done as the MCC did not think much of a match played in the middle of Kulam Street, if the owner of the vacant site behind the Reading Room should take it into his head to object to the match. Before he left, the YMU captain demanded to be told what 'other damages' in the last clause meant. Rajam paused, looked about, and pointed to the windows and tiles of a house adjoining the MCC field.

The match was to be played on Sunday two weeks later.

Rajam lost all peace of mind. He felt confident that his team could thrash the YMU. He himself could be depended upon not to let the team down. Mani was steady if unimpressive. He could be depended upon to stop with his head, if necessary, any ball. His batting was not bad. He had a peculiar style. With his bat he stopped all reasonable approaches to the wicket and brought the best bowlers to a fainting condition. Rajam did not consider it worth while to think of the other players of the team. There was only one player who caused him the deepest anxiety day and night. He was a dark horse. On him rested a great task, a mighty responsibility. He was the Tate of the team, and he must bowl out all the eleven of the other team. But he looked uncertain. Even with the match only a fortnight off, he did not seem to care for practice. He stuck to his old habit of arriving at the field when darkness had fallen on the earth. 'Swami,' Rajam pleaded, 'please do try to have at least an hour's practice in the evenings.'

'Certainly Rajam, if you can suggest a way . . .'

'Why not tell your Head Master that . . .'

'Oh, no, no,' Swaminathan cried, 'I am grateful to you for your suggestion. But let us not think of that man. He has not forgotten your last visit yet.'

'I don't care. What I want is that you should have good practice. If you keep any batsman standing for more than five minutes, I will never see your face again. You needn't concern yourself with the score. You can leave it to us . . .'

Just seven days before the march, Swaminathan realized that his evenings were more precious than ever. As soon as the evening bell rang, he lined up with the rest in the drill ground. But contrary to the custom, he had not taken off his coat and cap. All the others were in their shirts, with their *dhotis* tucked up. The Drill Master, a square man with a protruding chest, a big moustache sharpened at the ends, and a silk turban wound in military style, stood as if he posed before a camera, and surveyed his pupils with a disdainful side-glance. The monitor called out the names from the greasy register placed on the vaulting horse. The attendance after an interminable time was over and the Drill Master gave up his pose, came near the file, and walked from one end to the other, surveying each boy sternly. Swaminathan being short came towards the end of the file. The Drill Master stopped before him, looked him up and down, and passed on muttering: 'You won't get leave. Coat and cap off.' Swaminathan became desperate and pursued him: 'Sir, I am in a terrible state of health. I can't attend drill today. I shall die if I do. Sir, I think I shall—' He was prancing behind the Drill Master.

The Drill Master had come to the last boy and yet Swaminathan was dogging him. He turned round on Swaminathan with a fierce oath: 'What is the matter with you?'

'Sir, you don't understand my troubles. You don't even care to ask me what I am suffering from.'

'Yes, yes, what exactly is ailing you now?'

Swaminathan had at first thought of complaining of headache, but now he saw that the Drill Master was in a mood to slight even the most serious of headaches. He had an inspiration and said: 'Sir, the whole of last night I was delirious.' The Drill Master was stunned by this piece of news. 'You were delirious! Are you mad?'

'No, sir. I didn't sleep a wink last night. I was delirious. Our doctor said so. He has asked me not to attend drill for a week to come. He said that I should die if I attended drill.'

'Get away, young swine, before I am tempted to throttle you. I don't believe a word. But you are a persevering swine. Get out.'

The intervening period, about half an hour, between leaving the drill ground and reaching the cricket field, was a blur of hurry and breathlessness. Everybody at the field was happy to see him so early. Rajam jumped with joy.

On the whole everything was satisfactory. The only unpleasant element in all this was an obsession that the Drill Master might spy him out. So that, when they dispersed for the evening, Swaminathan stayed in Rajam's house till it was completely dark, and then skulked home, carefully avoiding the lights falling on the street from shop-fronts.

The next morning he formed a plan to be free all the evenings of the week. He was at his desk with the *Manual of Grammar* open before him. It was seven-thirty in the morning, and he had still two and a half hours before him for the school.

He did a little cautious reconnoitring: Mother was in the baby's room, for the rhythmic creaking of the cradle came to his ears. Father's voice was coming from the front room; he was busy with his clients. Swaminathan quietly slipped out of the house.

He stood before a shop in front of which hung the board: 'Doctor T. Kesavan, L.M. & S. Sri Krishna Dispensary.' The doctor was sitting at a long table facing the street. Swaminathan found that the doctor was alone and free, and entered the shop.

'Hallo, Swaminathan, what is the matter?'

'Nothing, sir. I have come on a little business.'

'All well at home?'

'Quite. Doctor, I have got to have a doctor's certificate immediately.'

'What is the matter with you?'

'I will tell you the truth, Doctor. I have to play a match next week against the Young Men's Union. And I must have some practice. And yet every evening there is Drill Class, Scouting, some dirty period or other. If you could give me a certificate asking them to let me off at four-thirty, it would help the MCC to win the match.'

'Well, I could do it. But is there anything wrong with you?'

Swaminathan took half a second to find an answer: 'Certainly, I am beginning to feel of late that I have delirium.'

'What did you say?' asked the doctor anxiously.

Swaminathan was pleased to find the doctor so much impressed, and repeated that he was having the most violent type of delirium.

'Boy, did you say delirium? What exactly do you mean by delirium?'

Swaminathan did not consider it the correct time for cross-examination. But he had to have the doctor's favour. He answered: 'I have got it. I can't say exactly. But isn't it some, some kind of stomach-ache?'

The doctor laughed till a great fit of coughing threatened to choke him. After that he looked Swaminathan under the eye, examined his tongue, tapped his chest, and declared him to be in the pink of health, and told him he would do well to stick to his drill if he wanted to get rid of delirium. Swaminathan again explained to him how important it was for him to have his evenings free. But the doctor said: 'It is all very well. But I should be prosecuted if I gave you any such certificate.'

'Who is going to find it out, Doctor? Do you want our MCC to lose the match?'

'I wish you all success. Don't worry. I can't give you a certificate. But I shall talk to your Head Master about you and request him to let you off after four-thirty.'

'That will do. You are very kind to me, Doctor.'

At four-thirty that evening, without so much as thinking of the Scouting Class in the quadrangle of the school, Swaminathan went home and then to the cricket field. Next day he had Drill Class, and he did not give it a thought. He was having plenty of practice. Rajam said: 'Swami, you are wonderful! All that you needed was a little practice. What have you done about your evening classes?'

'It is a slight brain-work, my boy. Our doctor has told the Head Master that I should die if I stayed in school after four-thirty. I got him to do it. What do you think of it?'

Mani dug him in the ribs and cried: 'You are the brainiest fellow I have ever seen.' Rajam agreed with him, and then was suddenly seized with worry: 'Oh, I don't know if we shall win that match. I will die if we lose.'

Mani said: 'Here, Rajam, I am sick of your talks of defeat. Do you think those monkey-faced fools can stand up to us?'

'I shall write to the papers if we win,' said Rajam.

'Will they print our photos?' Tate asked.

'Without doubt.'

It was during the Geography hour on Friday that the Head Master came to the class, cane in hand. The Geography Master, Mr Rama Rao, a mild elderly person, rose respectfully. The Head Master gave the full benefit of his wizened face to the class. His owl-like eyes were fixed upon Swaminathan, and he said: 'Get up.'

Swaminathan got up.

'Come here.'

Swaminathan 'came' there promptly.

'Show your shameless face to the class fully.'

Swaminathan now tried to hide his face. The Head Master threw out his arm and twisted Swaminathan's neck to make him face the class, and said: 'This great man is too busy to bother about such trivial matters as Drill and Scouting, and has not honoured these classes with his presence since last Monday.' His lips twisted in a wry smile. The class considered it safer to take the cue, and gently giggled. Even on the Geography Master's face there appeared a polite smile.

'Sir, have you any explanation to give?' the Head Master asked.

With difficulty Swaminathan found his voice and answered: 'It was the doctor—didn't the doctor talk to you about me, sir?'

'What doctor talk about what?'

'He said he would,' answered Swaminathan faintly.

'If you talk in enigmas I shall strip you before the class and thrash you.'

'Dr Kesavan said—'

'What about Dr Kesavan?'

'He said he would talk to you about me and get me exemption from Drill and other extra periods. He said that I should die if I attended Drill for some days to come.'

'And pray what is your trouble?'

'He thinks it is some—some kind—of—delirium, you know.' He had determined to avoid this word since he met the doctor last, but at this critical moment be blundered into it by sheer habit.

The Head Master turned to the teacher and raised his brow. He waited for some time and said: 'I am waiting to hear what other words of truth and wisdom are going to drop from your mouth.'

'Sir, I thought he had talked to you. He said he would . . .'

'I don't care to have every street mongrel come and tell me what to do in my school with my boys. It is a good thing that this Surgeon-General did not come. If he had, I would have asked the peon to bash his head on the table.'

Swaminathan realized that the doctor had deceived him. He remembered the genial smile with which the doctor had said that he would see the Head Master. Swaminathan shuddered as he realized what a deep-dyed villain Dr Kesavan was behind that genial smile. He would teach that villain a lesson; put a snake into his table-drawer; he would not allow that villain to feel his pulse even if he (Swaminathan) should be dying of fever. Further plans of revenge were stopped by a flick of the cane on his knuckles. The Head Master held the cane ready and cried: 'Hold out your hand. Six on each hand for each day of absence, and the whole of the next lesson on the bench. Monitor, you had better see to it. And remember W.S. Swaminathan, if you miss a single class again, I shall strip you in the school hall and ask the peon to cane you. You can't frighten me with your superintendents of police, their sons, grandsons, or grandfathers. I don't care even if you complain to His Majesty.' He released Swaminathan's neck and raised the cane.

Another moment and that vicious snake-like cane, quivering as if with life, would have descended on Swaminathan's palm. A flood of emotion swept him off his feet: a mixture of fear, resentment, and rage. He hardly knew what he was doing. His arm shot out, plucked the cane from the Head Master's hand, and flung it out of the window. Then he dashed to his desk, snatched his books, and ran out of the room. He crossed the hall and the veranda in a run, climbed the school gate because the bolt was too heavy for him, and jumped into the end of Market Road.

He sat under a tree on the roadside to collect his thoughts. He had left the school to which he would never go back as long as that tyrant was there. If his father should hear of it, he would do heaven knew what. He would force him to go back, which would be impossible . . . He had got out of two schools in this fashion. There were no more schools in Malgudi. His father would have to send him to Trichinopoly or Madras. But probably the Board High School Head Master would write to all the schools, telling them who Swaminathan was. He would not be admitted to any school. So he would have to work and earn . . . He might get some rupees— and he could go to hotels and buy coffee and tiffin as often as he pleased. What divine sweets the Bombay Anand Bhavan made! There was some green slab on the top left of the stall, with almonds stuck on it. He had always wanted to eat it, but lacked the courage to ask the hotel man, as he believed it to be very costly . . . His father would not allow him to remain in the house if he did not go to school. He might beat him. He would not go home that day nor on any other day. He could not face his father. He wondered at the same time where he could go. Anywhere. If he kept walking along Market Road where would it lead him? Probably to Madras. Could he reach Bombay and England if he went further? He could work in any of those places, earn money and do what he pleased. If he should go by train . . . But what to do for money? There might not be much trouble about that. The station master was an amiable man, and Swaminathan knew him.

The school bell rang, and Swaminathan rose to hurry away. The boys might come out, stand around, and watch him as if he were something funny.

He hurried along Market Road, turned to his right, along Smith Street, and taking a short-cut through some intricate lanes, stood before his old school, the Albert Mission. The sight of the deep yellow building with its top-storey filled him with a nostalgia for old times. He wished he had not left it. How majestic everything there now seemed! The Head Master, so dignified in his lace-turban, so unlike the grubby wretch of the Board. Vedanayagam, Ebenezar, even Ebenezar. D.P. Pillai, how cosy and homely his history classes were! Swaminathan almost wept at the memory of Somu and the Pea . . . All his friends were there, Rajam, Somu, Mani, and the Pea, happy, dignified, and honoured within the walls of the august Albert Mission School. He alone was out of it, isolated, as if he were a leper. He was an outcast, an outcast. He was filled with a sudden self-disgust. Oh, what would he not give to be back in the old school! Only, they would not take him in. It was no use. He had no more schools to go to in Malgudi. He must run away to Madras and work. But he had better see Rajam and Mani before going away.

He lingered outside the school gate. He had not the courage to enter it. He was the enemy of the school. The peon Singaram might assault him and drive him out if he saw him. He discreetly edged close to the massive concrete gate-post which screened him from a direct view of the school. He had to meet Rajam and Mani. But how? He stood still for a few minutes and formed a plan.

He went round behind the school. It was a part of the building that nobody frequented. It was a portion of the fallow field adjoining the school and terminating in the distant railway embankment. Swaminathan had not seen this place even once in all the six or seven years that he had spent at the school. Here the school compound wall was covered half with moss, and the rear view of the school was rather interesting. From here Swaminathan could see only the top half of the building, but even that presented a curious appearance. For instance, he could not at once point out where his old Second A was situated. He rolled up a stone to the foot of the wall, and stood on it. He could just see the school compound now.

It was about twelve, the busiest hour in the school, and there was not a single person in the compound. He waited. It was tedious waiting. After a short time, a very small person came out of the First Standard, to blow his nose. The three sections of the First Standard were in a block not a dozen yards from Swaminathan.

Swaminathan whistled softly, and the very small person did not hear. Swaminathan repeated the whistling, and the very small person turned and started as if he saw an apparition. Swaminathan beckoned to him. The small person took just a second to decide whether to obey the call of that apparition or to run back to the class. Swaminathan called him again. And the very small man drew towards him as if in a hypnotic state, staring wildly.

Swaminathan said: 'Would you like to have an almond peppermint?'

The very small man could hardly believe his ears. Here was a man actually offering almond peppermints! It could not be true. There was probably some fraud in it. Swaminathan repeated the offer and the small man replied rather cautiously that he would like to have the peppermint.

'Well, then,' Swaminathan said, 'you can't have it just now. You will have to earn it. Just go to Second Form A and tell M. Rajam that somebody from his house wants him urgently and bring him over here, and then hold out your hand for the peppermint. Maybe you will be given two.' The small man stood silent, assimilating every detail of the question, and then with a puckered brow asked: 'Where is Second Form A?'

'Upstairs.'

'Oh!' the boy ejaculated with a note of despair, and stood ruminating.

'What do you say?' Swaminathan asked, and added: 'Answer me before I count ten. Otherwise the offer is off. One, two, three—'

'You say it is upstairs?' the boy asked.

'Of course, I do.'

'But I have never gone there.'

'You will have to now.'

'I don't know the way.'

'Just climb the stairs.'

'They may—they may beat me if I am seen there.'

'If you care for the almond peppermint you will have to risk it. Say at once whether you will go or not.'

'All right. Wait for me.' The very small man was off.

Ten minutes later he returned, followed by Rajam. Rajam was astonished to see Swaminathan's head over the wall. 'What are you doing here?'

'Jump over the wall. I want you very urgently, Rajam.'

'I have got a class. I can't come out now.'

'Don't be absurd. Come on. I have something very urgent to say.'

Rajam jumped over the wall and was by his side.

Swaminathan's head disappeared from view. A pathetic small voice asked over the wall: 'Where is my peppermint?'

'Oh, I forgot you, little one,' Swaminathan said reappearing, 'come on, catch this.' He tossed a three-pie coin at the other.

'You said almond peppermint,' the boy reminded.

'I may say a thousand things,' Swaminathan answered brusquely. 'But isn't a three-pie coin sufficient? You can buy an almond peppermint if you want.'

'But you said two almond peppermints.'

'Now be off, young man. Don't haggle with me like a brinjal seller. Learn contentment,' said Swaminathan and jumped down from the stone.

'Rajam, do you know what has happened in the school today? I have fought with the Head Master. I am dismissed. I have no more schools or classes.'

'You fought with the Head Master?'

'Yes, he came to assault me about the drill attendance, and I wrenched his hand, and snatched the cane ... I don't believe I shall ever go back to the school. I expect there will be a lot of trouble if I do.'

'What a boy you are!' exclaimed Rajam. 'You are always in some trouble or other wherever you go. Always, always—'

'It was hardly my fault, Rajam,' Swaminathan said, and tried to vindicate himself by explaining to him Dr Kesavan's villainy.

'You have no sense, Swami. You are a peculiar fellow.'

'What else could I do to get the evenings off for practice? The YMU are no joke.'

'You are right, Swami. I watched the fellows at practice this morning. Tley have morning practice too. They are not bad players. There is one Mohideen, a dark fellow, oh, you know—you will have to keep an eye on him. He bats like Bradman. You will have to watch him. There is another fellow, Shanmugam. He is a dangerous bowler. But there is one weakness in Mohideen. He is not so steady on the leg side . . . Swami, don't worry about anything for some time to come. You must come in the morning too tomorrow. We have got to beat those fellows.'

Swaminathan had really called Rajam to bid him good-bye, but now he changed his mind. Rajam would stop him if he came to know of his adventurous plans. He wasn't going to tell Rajam, nor anybody about it, not even Mani. If he was stopped, he would have no place to stay in. The match was still two days off. He would go away without telling anyone, somehow practice on the way, come back for a few hours on the day of the match, disappear once again, and never come back to Malgudi—a place which contained his father, a stern stubborn father, and that tyrant of a Head Master . . . And no amount of argument on his part could ever make his father see eye to eye with him. If he went home, Father might beat him, thrash him, or kill him, to make him return to the Board High School. Father was a tough man . . . He would have to come back on the day of the match, without anybody's knowledge. Perhaps it would not be necessary. He asked suddenly: 'Rajam, do you think I am so necessary for the match?'

Rajam regarded him suspiciously and said: 'Don't ask such questions.' He added presently: 'We can't do without you, Swami. No. We depend upon you. You are the best bowler we have. We have got to give those fellows a beating. I shall commit suicide if we lose. Oh, Swami, what a mess you have made of things! What are you going to do without a school?'

'I shall have to join a workshop or some such thing.'

'What will your father say when he hears of it?'

'Oh, nothing. He will say it is all right. He won't trouble me,' Swaminathan said.

'Swami, I must get back to the class. It is late.' Rajam rose and sprinted towards the school, crying: 'Come to the field early. Come very soon, now that you are free . . .'

CHAPTER SIXTEEN

SWAMI DISAPPEARS

SWAMINATHAN'S FATHER FELT ashamed of himself as he approached Ellaman Street, the last street of the town, which turned into a rough track for about a hundred yards, and disappeared into the sands of the Sarayu river. He hesitated for a second at the end of Market Road, which was bright with the lights of a couple of late shops and a street gas-lamp, before he turned to plunge into the darkness and silence of Ellaman Street. A shaft of greenish light from the gas-lamp fell athwart Ellaman Street, illuminating only a few yards of the street and leaving the rest in deep gloom. A couple of municipal lanterns smouldered in their wicks, emphasizing the darkness around.

Swaminathan's father felt ashamed of himself. He was going to cross the street, plod through the sand, and gaze into the Sarayu— for the body of his son! His son, Swami, to be looked for in the Sarayu! It seemed to him a ridiculous thing to do. But what could he do? He dared not return home without some definite news of his son, good or bad. The house had worn a funereal appearance since nine o'clock. His wife and his old mother were more or less dazed and demented. She—his wife—had remained cheerful till the Taluk Office gong struck ten, when, her face turning white, she had asked him to go and find out from Swaminathan's friends and teachers what had happened to him.

He did not know where Swaminathan's Head Master lived. He had gone to the Board School and asked the watchman, who misdirected him and made him wander over half the town without purpose. He could not find Mani's house. He had gone to Rajam's house, but the house was dark, everybody had gone to bed, and he felt that it would be absurd to wake up the household of a stranger to ask if they had seen his son. From what he could get out of the servant sleeping in the veranda, he understood that Swaminathan had not been seen in Rajam's house that evening. He had then vaguely wandered in the streets. He was doing it to please his wife and mother. He had not shared in the least his wife's nervousness. He had felt all along that the boy must have gone out somewhere and would return, and then he would treat him with some firmness and nip this tendency in the bud. He had spent nearly an hour thus and gone home. Even his mother had left her bed and was hobbling agitatedly about the house, praying to the god of the Thirupathi Hills and promising him rich offerings if he should restore Swaminathan to her safe and sound. His wife stood like a stone image, looking down the street. The only tranquil being in the house was the youngest member of the family, whose soft breathings came from the cradle, defying the gloom and heaviness in the house.

When Swaminathan's father gave his wife the news—or no news—that he had gathered from his wanderings, he had assumed a heavy aggressive cheerfulness. It had lasted for a while, and gradually the anxiety and the nervousness of the two women infected him. He had begun to feel that something must have happened to his son—a kidnapping or an accident. He was trying to reason out these fears when his wife asked in a trembling voice: 'Did you search in the hospital?' and broke into a hysterical cry. He received this question with apparent disdain while his mind was conjuring up a vision of his son lying in a pulp in the hospital. He was struggling to erase this picture from his mind when his mother made matters worse with the question: 'Tell me—tell me—where could the boy have gone? Were you severe with him for anything this morning?' He was indignant at this question. Everybody seemed to be holding him responsible for Swaminathan's disappearance. Since nine o'clock he had been enduring the sly references and the suspicious glances. But this upset him, and he sharply asked his mother to return to her bed and not to let her brain concoct silly questions. He had after that reviewed his behaviour with his son since the morning, and discovered with surprise and relief that he had not seen him the whole day. The boy had risen from bed, studied, and gone to school, while he had shut himself up in his room with his clients. He then wondered if he had done anything in the past two or three days. He was not certain of his memory, but he felt that his conduct was blameless. As far as he could remember there had not been any word or act of his that could have embittered the boy and make him do—do—wild things. It was nearing twelve and he found his wife still sobbing. He tried to console her and rose to go out saying, again with a certain loud cheerfulness: 'I am going out to look for him. If he comes before I return, for Heaven's sake don't let him know what I am out for. I don't care to appear a fool in his eyes.'

He had walked rather briskly up Hospital Road, but had turned back, after staring at the tall iron gate of the hospital. He told himself that it was unnecessary to enter the hospital, but in fact knew that he lacked the courage. That very window in which a soft dim light appeared might have behind it the cot containing Swaminathan all pulped and bandaged. He briskly moved out of Hospital Road and wandered about rather aimlessly through a few dark lanes around the place. With each hour, his heart became heavier. He had slunk past Market Road, and now entered Ellaman Street.

He swiftly passed through Ellaman Street and crossed the rough foot-path leading to the river. His pace slackened as he approached the river. He tried to convince himself that he was about to do a piece of work which was a farce. But if the body of his son, sodden and bloated, should be seen stuck up among the reeds, and rocking gently on the ripples . . . He shut his eyes and prayed: 'Oh, God, help me.'

He looked far up and down the river which was gliding along with gentle music. The massive *peepul* trees overhanging the river sighed to the night. He started violently at the sight of the flimsy shadow of some branch on the water; and again as some float kept tilting against the moss-covered parapet with muffled thuds.

And then, still calling himself a fool, he went to the Malgudi Railway Station and walked a mile or so along the railway line, keenly examining the iron rails and the sleepers. The ceaseless hum and the shrill whistle of night insects, the whirring of bats, and the croaking of frogs, came through the awful loneliness of the night. He once stooped with a shudder to put his finger on some wet patch on the rails. As he held up the finger and examined it in the starlight and found that it was only water and not blood, he heaved a sigh of relief and thanked God.

THE DAY OF THE MATCH

A NARROW ROAD branching to the left of the Trunk Road attracted Swaminathan because it was shaded by trees bearing fruits. The white ball-like wood-apple, green figs, and the deep purple eugenia, peeped out of thick green foliage. He walked a mile and did not like the road. It was utterly deserted and silent. He wished to be back in the Trunk Road in which there was some life and traffic, though few and far between: some country cart lumbering along; or an occasional motor-car with trunks and bedding strapped behind, whizzing past and disappearing in a cloud of dust; or groups of peasants moving on the edge of the road. But this branch road oppressed him with its stillness. Moreover, he had been wandering for many hours away from home, and now longed to be back there. He became desperate at the thought of home. What fine things the cook prepared! And how Mother always insisted upon serving ghee and curds herself! Oh! how he would sit before his leaf and watch Mother open the cupboard and bring out the aluminum curd-pot, and how soft and white it was as it noiselessly fell on the heap of rice on the leaf and enveloped it! A fierce hunger now raged within him. His thighs were heavy and there was pain around his hips. He did not notice it, but the sun's rays were coming obliquely from the west, and the birds were on their homeward flight.

When hunger became unbearable, he plucked and ate fruits. There was a clean pond nearby.

He rested for some time and then started to go back home. The only important thing now was home, and all the rest seemed trivial beside it. The Board School affair appeared inconsequential. He marvelled at himself for having taken it seriously and rushed into all this trouble. What a fool he had been! He wished with all his heart that he had held out his hand when the Head Master raised his cane. Even if he had not done it, he wished he had gone home and told his father everything. Father would have scolded him a little (in case he went too far, Granny and Mother could always be depended upon to come to his rescue). All this scolding and frowning would have been worth while, because Father could be depended upon to get him out of any trouble. People were afraid of him. And what foolishness to forgo practice with the match only two days ahead! If the match was lost, there was no knowing what Rajam would do.

Meanwhile, Swaminathan was going back towards the Trunk Road. He thought he would be presently back in it, and then he had only to go straight, and it would take him right into Market Road, and from there he could reach home blindfolded. His parents might get angry with him if he went home so late. But he could tell them that he had lost his way. Or would that be too mild? Suppose he said that he had been kidnapped by Pathans and had to escape from them with great difficulty . . .

He felt he had been walking long enough. He ought to have reached the Trunk Road long ago, but as he stopped and looked about, he found that he was still going along the thick avenue of figs and wood-apple. The ground was strewn with discoloured, disfigured fruits, and leaves. The road seemed to be longer now that he was going back. The fact was that he had unconsciously followed a gentle imperceptible curve, as the road cunningly branched and joined the Mempi Forest Road. Some seventy miles further it split into a number of rough irregular tracks, disappearing into the thick belt of Mempi Forests. If he had just avoided this deceptive curve, he would have reached the Trunk Road long ago.

Night fell suddenly, and his heart beat fast. His throat went dry as he realized that he had not reached the Trunk Road. The trees were still thick and the road was still narrow. The Trunk Road was broader, and there the sky was not screened by branches. But here one could hardly see the sky; the stars gleamed through occasional gaps overhead. He quickened his pace though he was tired. He ran a little distance, his feet falling on the leaf-covered ground with a sharp rustling noise. The birds in the branches overhead started at this noise and fluttered their wings. In that deep darkness and stillness, the noise of fluttering wings had an uncanny ghostly quality. Swaminathan was frightened and stood still. He must reach the Trunk Road and thence find his way home. He would not mind even if it were twelve o'clock when he reached the Trunk Road. There was something reassuring in its spaciousness and in the sparseness of vegetation. But here the closeness of the tree-trunks and their branches intertwining at the top gave the road the appearance of a black bleak cavern with an evil spirit brooding over it.

The noise of the disturbed birds subsided. He started on again. He trod warily so as not to make a noise and disturb the birds again, though he felt an urge to run, run with all his might and reach the Trunk Road and home. The conflict between the impulse to run and the caution that counselled him not to run was fierce. As he walked noiselessly, slowly, suppressing the impulse to run on madly, his nerves quivered with the strain. It was as if he had been ropewalking in a gale.

His ears became abnormally sensitive. They caught every noise his feet made, with the slightest variations. His feet came down on the ground with a light tick or a subdued crackle or a gentle swish, according to the object on the ground: small dry twigs, half-green leaves, or a thick layer of dry withered leaves. There were occasional patches of bare uncovered ground, and there the noise was a light thud, or pit pat; pit pat pit pat in monotonous repetition. Every noise entered Swaminathan's ears. For some time he was conscious of nothing else. His feet said pish—pish—pish—pat—pit—pat—swish and crackled. These noises streamed into his head, monotonously, endlessly. They were like sinister whispers, calling him to a dreadful sacrifice. He clearly heard his name whispered. There was no doubt about it. 'Swami . . . Swami . . . Swami . . . Swami . . . Swami . . .' the voice said, and then the dreadful suggestion of a sacrifice. It was some devil, coming behind him noiselessly, and saying the same thing over and over again, deep into his ears. He stopped and looked about. There the immense monster crouched, with its immense black legs wide apart, and its shadowy arms joined over its head. It now swayed a little. He dared not take his eyes off it for fear that it might pounce upon him. He stood frozen to the ground and stared at this monster. Why did it cease its horrid whispers the moment he turned back? He stood staring. He might have spent about five minutes thus. And when the first thrill of fear subsided, he saw a little more clearly and found that the monster consisted of massive tree-trunks and their top branches.

He continued his journey. He was perhaps within a yard of the Trunk Road, and afterwards he would sing as he sauntered home. He asked himself whether he would rest awhile on the Trunk Road or go, without stopping, home. His legs felt as if they had been made of stone. He decided that he would sit down for some time when he reached the Trunk Road. It did not matter. The Trunk Road was safe and secure even at twelve o'clock. If he took a rest, he would probably be able to run home . . .

He came to a clearing. The stars were visible above. The road wound faintly in front of him. No brooding darkness, no clustering crowded avenue here. He felt a momentary ecstasy as he realized that he had come to the Trunk Road. It bore all the characteristics of the Trunk Road. The sight of the stars above, clear and uninterrupted, revived him. As he paused and watched the million twinkling bodies, he felt like bursting into music, out of sheer relief. He had left behind the horrid, narrow, branch-roofed road. At this realization his strength came back to him. He decided not to waste time in resting. He felt fit to go forward. But presently he felt uneasy. He remembered clearly that the branch road began at right angles to the Trunk Road. But here it continued straight. He stood bewildered for a moment and then told himself that it was probably a continuation of the branch road, a continuation that he had not noticed before. Whatever it was, the Trunk Road must surely cut this at right angles, and if he turned to his right and went forward he would reach home. He looked to his right and left, but there was not the faintest trace of a road anywhere. He soon explained to himself that he was probably not able to see the Trunk Road because of the night. The road must be there all right. He turned to his right, took a step or two, and went knee-deep in quagmire. He waded through it and went forward. Long spiked grass tickled his face and in some places he was lost in undergrowth. He turned back and reached the road.

Presently he realized his position. He was on an unknown distant road at a ghostly hour. Till now the hope that he was moving towards the familiar Trunk Road had sustained him. But now even the false hope being gone, he became faint with fear. When he understood that the Trunk Road was an unreal distant dream, his legs refused to support him. All the same he kept tottering onwards, knowing well that it was a meaningless, aimless, march. He walked like one half stunned. The strangeness of the hour, so silent indeed that even the drop of a leaf resounded through the place, oppressed him with a sense of inhumanity. Its remoteness gave him a feeling that he was walking into a world of horrors, subhuman and supernatural.

He collapsed like an empty bag, and wept bitterly. He called to his father, mother, Granny, Rajam, and Mani. His shrill loud cry went through the night past those half-distinct black shapes looming far ahead, which might be trees or devils or gate-posts of Inferno. Now he prayed to all the gods that he knew to take him out of that place. He promised them offerings: two coconuts every Saturday to the elephant-faced Ganapathi; a vow to roll bare-bodied in dust, beg, and take the alms to the Lord of Thirupathi. He paused as if to give the gods time to consider his offer and descend from their heights to rescue him.

Now his head was full of wild imaginings. He heard heavy footfalls behind, turned and saw a huge lump of darkness coming towards him. It was too late, it had seen him. Its immense tusks showed faintly white. It came roaring, on the way putting its long trunk around a tree and plucking it out by the roots and dashing it on the ground. He could see its small eyes, red with anger, its tusks lowered, and the trunk lifted and poised ready. He just rolled to one side and narrowly escaped. He lay panting for a while, his clothes wet with sweat. He heard stealthy footsteps and a fierce growl, and before he could turn to see what it was, heavy jaws snapped behind his ears, puffing out foul hot breath on his nape. He had the presence of mind to lower his head and lie flat, and the huge yellow-and-black tiger missed him. Now a leopard, now a lion, even a whale, now a huge crowd, a mixed crowd of wild elephants, tigers, lions, and demons, surrounded him. The demons lifted him by his ears, plucked every hair on his head, and peeled off his skin from head to foot. Now what was this, coiling round his legs, cold and slimy? He shrank in horror from a scorpion that was advancing with its sting in the air. No, this was no place for a human being. The cobra and the scorpion were within an inch of him. He shrieked, scrambled to his feet, and ran. He kept looking back, the scorpion was moving as fast as he, there was no escaping it: he held his breath and with the last ounce of strength doubled his pace—

He had touched the other wicket and returned. Two runs. He stood with the bat. The captain of the YMU bowled, and he hit a sixer. The cheers were deafening. Rajam ran round the field in joy, jumped up the wall and down thrice. The next ball was bowled. Instead of hitting it, Swaminathan flung the bat aside and received it on his head. The ball rebounded and speeded back towards the bowler—the Board High School Head Master; but Swaminathan ran after the ball, overtook it halfway, caught it, and raising his arm, let it go with terrific force towards the captain's head, which was presently hit and shattered. The MCC had won, and their victory was marked by chasing the YMU out of the field, with bricks and wickets, bats and balls; and Swaminathan laughed and laughed till he collapsed with exhaustion.

Ranga, the cart-man, was returning to his village, five miles on this side of Mempi Forests, early on Saturday morning. He had left Malgudi at two in the morning so as to be in his village by noon. He had turned the long stretch of the Mempi Forest Road, tied the bullock-rope to the cart, and lain down. The soft tinkling of the bells and the gentle steady pace of the bullock sent him to sleep at once.

Suddenly the bullock stopped with a jerk. Ranga woke up and uttered the series of oaths and driving cries that usually gave the bullock speed, and violently tugged the rope. The bullock merely tossed its head with a tremendous jingle of its bells, but did not move. Ranga, exasperated by its conduct, got down to let the animal know and feel what he thought of it. In the dim morning light, he saw a human form across the way. He shouted, 'Hi! Get up, lazy lubber. A nice place you have found to sleep in! Be up and doing. Do you follow me?' When the sleeper was not awakened by this advice, Ranga went forward to throw him out of the way.

'Ah, a little fellow! Why is he sleeping here?' he said, and bending closer still, exclaimed, 'Oh, Siva, he is dead!' The legs and arms, the exposed portions of the body, were damp with the slight early dew. He tore the boy's shirt and plunged his hand in and was greatly relieved to find the warmth of life still there. His simple mind tortured itself with the mystery of the whole situation. Here was a little boy from the town, his dress and appearance proclaimed, alone in this distant highway, lying nearly dead across the road. Who was he? Where did he come from? Why was he there? Ranga's brain throbbed with these questions. Devils were known to carry away human beings and leave them in distant places. It might be, or might not be. He gave up the attempt to solve the problem himself, feeling that he had better leave such things to learned people like the *sircar* officer who was staying in the Travellers' Bungalow three stones on this side of the forests. His (Ranga's) business would be nothing more than taking the boy to the officer. He gently lifted the boy and carried him to the cart.

He sat in his seat, took the ropes in his hand, raised a foot and kicked the bullock in the stomach, and loosened the rope with the advice to his animal that if it did not for once give up its usual dawdling ways, he would poke a red-hot pike into its side. Intelligently appreciating the spirit of this advice, the bullock shook itself and set off at a trot that it reserved for important occasions.

Swaminathan stared blankly before him. He could not comprehend his situation. At first he had believed he was where he had been day after day for so many years—at home. Then gradually, as his mind cleared, he remembered several remote incidents in a confused jumble. He blinked fast. He put out his arm and fumbled about. He studied the objects before him more keenly. It was an immense struggle to keep the mind alert. He fixed his eyes on a picture on the wall—or was it a calendar?—to find out if it was the same thing that hung before his bed at home. He was understanding its details little by little when all of a sudden his mind collapsed with exhaustion, and confusion began. Was there an object there at all on the wall? He was exasperated by the pranks of the mind . . . He vaguely perceived a human figure in a chair nearby. The figure drew the chair nearer and said, 'That is right, boy. Are you all right now?' . . . These words fell on ears that had not yet awakened to life. Swaminathan was puzzled to see his father there. He wanted to know why he was doing such an extraordinary thing as sitting by his side.

'Father,' he cried, looking at the figure.

'You will see your father presently. Don't worry,' said the figure and put to him a few questions which would occur to any man with normal curiosity. Swaminathan took such a long time to answer each question and then it was all so incoherent and irrelevant that the stranger was first amused, then irritated, and in the end gave up asking questions. Swaminathan was considerably weakened by the number of problems that beset him: Who was this man? Was he Father? If he was not, why was he there? Even if he was, why was he there? Who was he? What was he saying? Why could he not utter his words louder and clearer? This Father-and-not-Father person then left the room. He was Mr M.P.S. Nair, the District Forest Officer, just then camping near Mempi Forests. He had been out in the forest the whole day and returned to the Travellers' Bungalow only at seven in the evening. He had hardly rolled off his puttees and taken off his heavy boots when he was told about the boy. After hours of effort with food and medicine, the boy was revived. But what was the use? He was not in a fit condition to give an account of himself. If the boy's words were to be believed, he seemed to belong to some strange unpronounceable place unknown to geographers.

Early next morning Mr Nair found the boy already up and very active. In the compound, the boy stood a few yards from a tree with a heap of stones at his feet. He stooped, picked up a stone, backed a few yards, took a few quick steps, stopped abruptly, and let the stone go at a particular point on the tree-trunk. He repeated this like clockwork with stone after stone.

'Good morning, young man,' Mr Nair said. 'How are you now?'

'I am grateful to you, sir, you have saved me from great trouble.'

'Oh, yes . . . You are very busy?'

'I am taking practice, sir. We are playing a match against the YMU and Rajam is depending upon me for bowling. They call me Tate. I have not had practice at all—for—for a long time. I did a foolish thing in starting out and missing practice with the match coming off on—What day is this, sir?'

'Why do you want to know?'

'Please tell me, sir. I want to know how many days more we have for the match.'

'This is Sunday.'

'What? What?' Swaminathan stood petrified. Sunday! Sunday! He gazed dully at the heap of stones at his feet.

'What is the matter?'

'The match is on Sunday,' Swaminathan stammered.

'What if it is? You still have a day before you. This is only Saturday.'

'You said it was Sunday, sir.'

'No. No. This is Saturday. See the calendar if you like.'

'But you said it was Sunday.'

'Probably a slip of the tongue.'

'Sir, will you see that I am somehow at the field before Sunday?'

'Certainly, this very evening. But you must tell me which your place is and whose son you are.'

CHAPTER EIGHTEEN

THE RETURN

IT WAS THREE-THIRTY on Sunday afternoon. The match between the MCC and the YMU was still in progress. The YMU had won the toss, and were all out for eighty-six at two o'clock. The captain's was the top score, thirty-two. The MCC had none to bowl him out, and he stood there like an automaton, hitting right and left, tiring out all the bowlers. He kept on for hours, and the next batsman was as formidable, though not a scorer. He exhausted the MCC of the little strength that was left, and Rajam felt keenly the lack of a clever bowler.

After the interval the game started again at two-thirty, and for the hour that the MCC batted the score stood at the unimpressive figure of eight with three out in quick succession. Rajam and Mani had not batted. Rajam watched the game with the blackest heart and heartily cursed everybody concerned. The match would positively close at five-thirty; just two hours more, and would the remaining eight make up at least seventy-eight and draw the match? It was a remote possibility. In his despair he felt that at least six more would follow suit without raising the score even to twenty. And then he and Mani would be left. And he had a wild momentary hope that each might be able to get forty with a few judicious sixers and boundaries.

He was squatting along with his players on the ground in the shade of the compound wall.

'Raju, a minute, come here,' came a voice from above. Rajam looked up and saw his father's head over the wall. 'Father, is it very urgent?'

'It is. I won't detain you for more than a minute.'

When he hopped over the wall and was at his father's side, he was given a letter. He glanced through it, gave it back to his father, and said casually, 'So he is safe and sound. I wonder what he is doing there.' He ruminated for a second and turned to go.

'I am sending this letter to Swaminathan's father. He is sure to get a car and rush to the place. I shall have to go with him. Would you like to come?'

Rajam remained silent for a minute and said emphatically, 'No.'

'Don't you want to see your friend and bring him back?'

'I don't care,' Rajam said briefly, and joined his friends. He went back to his seat in the shade of the wall. The fourth player was promising. Rajam whispered to Mani, 'I say, that boy is not bad. Six runs already! Good, good.'

'If these fellows make at least fifty we can manage the rest.'

Rajam nodded an assent, but an unnoticed corner of his mind began to be busy with something other than the match. His father's news had stirred in him a mixture of feelings. He felt an urgent desire to tell Mani what he had just heard. 'Mani, you know Swami—' he said and stopped short because he remembered that he was not interested in Swaminathan. Mani sprang up and asked, 'What about Swami? What about him? Tell me, Rajam. Has he been found?'

'I don't know.'

'Oh, Rajam, Rajam, you were about to say something about him.'

'Nothing. I don't care.'

Swaminathan had a sense of supreme well-being and security. He was flattered by the number of visitors that were coming to see him. His Granny and mother were hovering round him ceaselessly, and it was with a sneaking satisfaction that he saw his little brother crowing unheeded in the cradle, for once overlooked and abandoned by everybody.

Many of Father's friends came to see him and behaved more or less alike. They stared at him with amusement and said how relieved they were to have him back and asked some stereotyped questions and went away after uttering one or two funny remarks. Father went out with one of his friends. Before going, he said, 'Swami, I hope I shall not have to look for you when I come back.' Swaminathan was hurt by this remark. He felt it to be cruel and inconsiderate.

After his father left, he felt more free, free to lord over a mixed gathering consisting of mother's and Granny's friends and some old men who were known to the family long before Swaminathan's father was born.

Everybody gazed at Swaminathan and uttered loud remarks to his face. Through all this crowd Swaminathan espied the cook and bestowed a smile on him. Over the babble the cook uttered some irrelevant, happy remark, which concluded with the hope that now Father, Mother and Granny might resume the practice of taking food. Swaminathan was about to shout something in reply when his attention was diverted by the statement of a widow, who, rolling her eyes and pointing heavenward, said that He alone had saved the boy, and who could have foreseen that the Forest Officer would be there to save the boy from she jaws of wild beasts? Granny said that she would have to set about fulfilling the great promises of offerings made to the Lord of the Seven Hills to whom alone she owed the safe return of the child.

Mother had meanwhile disappeared into the kitchen and now came out with a tumbler of hot coffee with plenty of sugar in it, and some steaming tiffin in a plate. Swaminathan quickly and with great relish disposed of both. A mixed fragrance, delicate and suggestive, came from the kitchen.

Swaminathan cast his mind back and felt ashamed of himself for his conduct with the Forest Officer, when that harassed gentleman was waiting for a reply from the Deputy Superintendent of Police, which took the form of a taxi drawing up before the Travellers' Bungalow, disgorging Father, Mother, Rajam's father, and an inspector of police. What a scene his mother created when she saw him! He had at first feared that Rajam's father and the inspector were going to handcuff him. What a fine man Rajam's father was! And how extraordinarily kind his own father was! So much so that, five minutes after meeting him, Swaminathan blurted out the whole story, from his evasion of Drill Classes to his disappearance, without concealing a single detail. What was there so funny in his narration? Everybody laughed uproariously, and Mother covered her face with the end of her saree and wiped her eyes at the end of every fit of laughter . . . This retrospect was spoiled by one memory. He had forgotten to take leave of the Forest Officer, though that gentleman opened the door of the car and stood near it. Swaminathan's conscience scorched him at the recollection of it.

A lump came to his throat at the thought of the kindly District Forest Officer, looking after the car speeding away from him, thoroughly broken-hearted by the fact that a person whose life he had saved should be so wicked as to go away without saying 'Good-bye.'

His further reflections on the subject and the quiet discussion among the visitors about the possible dangers that might have befallen Swaminathan, were all disturbed—destroyed, would be more accurate—by a tornado-like personality sweeping into their midst with the tremendous shout, 'What! Oh! Swami!' The visitors were only conscious of some mingled shoutings and brisk movements and after that both Swaminathan and Mani disappeared from the hall.

As they came to a secluded spot in the backyard, Mani said, 'I thought you were dead or some such thing.'

'I was, nearly.'

'What a fool you were to get frightened of that Head Master and run away like that! Rajam told me everything. I wanted to break your shoulders for not calling me when you had come to our school and called Rajam . . .'

'I had no time, Mani.'

'Oh, Swami. I am so glad to see you alive. I was—I was very much troubled about you. Where were you all along?'

'I—I—I really can't say. I don't know where I was. Somewhere—' He recounted in this style his night of terrors and the subsequent events.

'Have I not always said that you were the worst coward I have ever known? You would have got safely back home if you had kept your head cool and followed the straight road. You imagined all sorts of things.'

Swaminathan took this submissively and said, 'But I can't believe that I was picked up by that cart-man. I don't remember it at all.'

Mani advised, 'If he happens to come to your place during Deepavali or Pongal festival, don't behave like a niggard. He deserves a bag of gold. If he had not cared to pick you up, you might have been eaten by a tiger.'

'And I have done another nasty thing,' Swaminathan said, 'I didn't thank and say "Good-bye" to the Forest Officer before I came away. He was standing near the car all the time.'

'If he was so near why did you seal your mouth?'

'I didn't think of it till the car had come half-way.'

'You are a—a very careless fellow. You ought to have thanked him.'

'Now what shall I do? Shall I write to him?'

'Do. But do you know his address?'

'My father probably does.'

'What will you write?'

'Just tell him—I don't know. I shall have to ask Father about it. Some nice letter, you know. I owe him so much for bringing me back in time for the match.'

'What are you saying?' Mani asked.

'Are you deaf? I was saying that I must ask Father to write a nice letter, that is all.'

'Not that. I heard someting about the match. What is it?'

'Yes?'

'Are you mad to think that you are in time for the match?' asked Mani. He then related to Swaminathan the day's encounter with the YMU and the depressing results, liberally explaining what Swaminathan's share was in the collapse of the MCC.

'Why did you have it today?' Swaminathan asked weakly.

'Why not?'

'But this is only Saturday.'

'Who said that?'

'The Forest Officer said that this was only Saturday.'

'You may go and tell him that he is a blockhead,' Mani retorted.

Swaminathan persisted that it could not be Sunday, till Mani threatened to throw him down, sit on his body, and press his entrails out. Swaminathan remained in silence, and then said, 'I won't write him that letter. He has deceived me.'

'Who?'

'The Forest Officer . . . And what does Rajam say about me?'

'Rajam says a lot, which I don't wish to repeat. But I will tell you one thing. Never appear before him. He will never speak to you. He may even shoot you on sight.'

'What have I done?' asked Swaminathan.

'You have ruined the MCC. You need not have promised us, if you had wanted to funk. At least you could have told us you were going away. Why did you hide it from Rajam when you saw him at our school? That is what Rajam wants to know.'

Swaminathan quietly wept, and begged Mani to pacify Rajam and convey to him Swaminathan's love and explanations. Mani refused to interfere. 'You don't know Rajam. He is a gem. But it is difficult to get on with him.'

With a forced optimism in his tone Swaminathan said, 'He will be all right when he sees me. I shall see him tomorrow morning.'

Mani wanted to change the topic, and asked: 'Are you going back to school?'

'Yes, next week. My father has already seen the Head Master, and it seems things will be all right in the school. He seems to have known everything about the Board School business.'

'Yes, I and Rajam told him everything.'

'After all, I shall have to go back to the Board High School. Father says I can't change my school now.'

CHAPTER NINETEEN

PARTING PRESENT

ON TUESDAY MORNING, ten days later, Swaminathan rose from bed with a great effort of will at five o'clock. There was still an hour for the train to arrive at the Malgudi Station and leave it four minutes later, carrying away Rajam, for ever.

Swaminathan had not known that this was to happen till Mani came and told him, on the previous night at about ten, that Rajam's father was transferred to Trichinopoly and the whole family would be leaving Malgudi on the following morning. Mani said that he had known it for about a week, but Rajam had strictly forbidden him to say anything about it to Swaminathan. But at the last moment Mani could not contain himself and had violated Rajam's ban.

A great sense of desolation seized Swaminathan at once. The world seemed to have become blank all of a sudden. The thought of Lawley Extension without Rajam appalled him with its emptiness. He swore that he would never go there again. He raved at Mani. And Mani bore it patiently. Swaminathan could not think of a world without Rajam. What was he to do in the evenings? How was he to spend the holiday afternoons? Whom was he to think of as his friend? At the same time he was filled with a sense of guilt: he had not gone and seen Rajam even once after his return. Fear, shame, a feeling of uncertainty, had made him postpone his visit to Rajam day after day. Twice he had gone up to the gate of Rajam's house, but had turned back, his courage and determination giving way at the last moment. He was in this state, hoping to see Rajam every tomorrow, when Mani came to him with the shattering news. Swaminathan wanted to rush up to Rajam's house that very second and claim him once again. But—but—he felt awkward and shirked. Tomorrow morning at the station. The train was leaving at six. He would go to the station at five.

'Mani, will you call me at five tomorrow morning?'

'No. I am going to sleep in Rajam's house, and go with him to the station.'

For a moment Swaminathan was filled with the darkest jealousy. Mani to sleep in Rajam's house, keep him company till the last moment, talk and laugh till midnight, and he to be excluded! He wanted to cling to Mani desperately and stop his going.

When Mani left, Swaminathan went in, opened his dealwood box, and stood gazing into it. He wanted to pick out something that could be presented to Rajam on the following morning. The contents of the box were a confused heap of odds and ends of all metals and materials. Here a cardboard box that had once touched Swaminathan's fancy, and there a toy watch, a catalogue, some picture books, nuts and bolts, disused insignificant parts of defunct machinery, and so on to the brim. He rummaged in it for half an hour, but there seemed to be nothing in it worth taking to Rajam. The only decent object in it was a green engine given to him over a year ago by Rajam. The sight of it, now dented and chipped in a couple of places and lying between an empty thread-reel and a broken porcelain vase, stirred in him vivid memories. He became maudlin . . . He wondered if he would have to return that engine to Rajam now that they were no longer friends. He picked it up to take it with him to the station and return it to Rajam. On second thoughts, he put it back, partly because he loved the engine very much, partly because he told himself that it might be an insult to reject a present after such a long time . . . Rajam was a good reader, and Swaminathan decided to give him a book. He could not obviously give him any of the text-books. He took out the only book that he respected (as the fact of his separating it from the text-books on his desk and giving it a place in the dealwood box showed). It was a neat tiny volume of Andersen's *Fairy Tales* that his father had bought in Madras years ago for him. He could never get through the book to his satisfaction. There were too many unknown unpronounceable English words in it. He would give this book to Rajam. He went to his desk and wrote on the fly-leaf: 'To my dearest friend Rajam'.

Malgudi Station was half dark when Swaminathan reached it with the tiny volume of Andersen's *Fairy Tales* in his hand. The Station

Master was just out of bed and was working at the table with a kerosene light, not minding in the least the telegraph keys that were tapping away endless messages to the dawn.

A car drew up outside. Swaminathan saw Rajam, his father, mother, someone he did not know, and Mani, getting down. Swaminathan shrank at the sight of Rajam. All his determination oozed out as he saw the captain approach the platform, dressed like a 'European boy'. His very dress and tidiness made Swaminathan feel inferior and small. He shrank back and tried to make himself inconspicuous.

Almost immediately, the platform began to fill with police officers and policemen. Rajam was unapproachable. He was standing with his father in the middle of a cluster of people in uniform. All that Swaminathan could see of Rajam was his left leg, through a gap between two policemen. Even that was obstructed when the policemen drew closer. Swaminathan went round, in search of further gaps.

The train was sighted. There was at once a great bustle. The train hissed and boomed into the platform. The hustle and activity increased. Rajam and his party moved to the edge of the platform. Things were dragged and pushed into a Second Class compartment with desperate haste by a dozen policemen. Rajam's mother got in. Rajam and his father were standing outside the compartment. The police officers now barricaded them completely, bidding them farewell and garlanding them. There was a momentary glimpse of Rajam with a huge rose garland round his neck.

Swaminathan looked for, and found Mani. 'Mani, Rajam is going away.'

'Yes, Swami, he is going away.'

'Mani, will Rajam speak to me?'

'Oh, yes. Why not?' asked Mani.

Now Rajam and his father had got into the compartment. The door was closed and the door-handle turned.

'Mani, this book must be given to Rajam,' Swaminathan said. Mani saw that there was no time to lose. The bell rang. They desperately pushed their way through the crowd and stood under a window. Swaminathan could hardly see anything above. His head hardly came up to the door-handle. The crowd pressed from behind. Mani shouted into the compartment: 'Here is Swami to bid you good-bye.' Swaminathan stood on his toes. A head leaned over the window and said: 'Good-bye, my Mani. Don't forget me. Write to me.'

'Good-bye, friend . . . Here is Swami,' Mani said. Rajam craned his neck. Swaminathan's upturned eyes met his. At the sight of the familiar face Swaminathan lost control of himself and cried: 'Oh, Rajam, Rajam, you are going away, away. When will you come back?' Rajam kept looking at him without a word and then (as it seemed to Swaminathan) opened his mouth to say something, when everything was disturbed by the guard's blast and the hoarse whistle of the engine. There was a slight rattling of chains, a tremendous hissing, and the train began to move. Rajam's face, with the words still unuttered on his lips, receded. Swaminathan became desperate and blurted: 'Oh, Mani! This book must be given to him,' and pressed the book into Mani's hand. Mani ran along the platform with the train and shouted over the noise of the train: 'Good-bye, Rajam. Swami gives you this book.' Rajam held out his hand for the book, and took it, and waved a farewell. Swaminathan waved back frantically.

Swaminathan and Mani stood as if glued, where they were, and watched the train. The small red lamp of the last van could be seen for a long time, it diminished in size every minute, and disappeared around a bend. All the jarring, rattling, clanking, spurting, and hissing of the moving train softened in the distance into something that was half a sob and half a sigh. Swaminathan said: 'Mani, I am glad he has taken the book. Mani, he waved to me. He was about to say something when the train started. Mani, he did wave to me and to me alone. Don't deny it.'

'Yes, yes,' Mani agreed.

Swaminathan broke down and sobbed.

Mani said: 'Don't be foolish, Swami.'

'Does he ever think of me now?' Swaminathan asked hysterically.

'Oh, yes,' said Mani. He paused and added: 'Don't worry. If he has not talked to you, he will write to you.'

'What do you mean?'

'He told me so,' Mani said.

'But he does not know my address.'

'He asked me, and I have given it,' said Mani.

'No. No. It is a lie. Come on, tell me, what is my address?'

'It is—it is—never mind what . . . I have given it to Rajam.'

Swaminathan looked up and gazed on Mani's face to find out whether Mani was joking or was in earnest. But for once Mani's face had become inscrutable.

The Bachelor of Arts

PART ONE

CHAPTER ONE

CHANDRAN WAS JUST climbing the steps of the College Union when Natesan, the secretary, sprang on him and said, 'You are just the person I was looking for. You remember your old promise?'

'No,' said Chandran promptly, to be on the safe side.

'You promised that I could count on you for a debate any time I was hard pressed for a speaker. You must help me now. I can't get a Prime Mover for the debate tomorrow evening. The subject is that in the opinion of this house historians should be slaughtered first. You are the Prime Mover. At five tomorrow evening.' He tried to be off, but Chandran caught his hand and held him: 'I am a history student. I can't move the subject. What a subject! My professor will eat me up.'

'Don't worry. I won't invite your professor.'

'But why not some other subject?'

'We can't change the Union Calendar now.'

Chandran pleaded, 'Any other day, any other subject.'

'Impossible,' said the secretary, and shook himself free.

'At least make me the Prime Opposer,' pleaded Chandran.

'You are a brilliant Mover. The notices will be out in an hour. Tomorrow evening at five . . .'

Chandran went home and all night had dreams of picking up a hatchet and attacking his history professor, Ragavachar. He sat down next morning to prepare for the debate. He took out a piece of paper and wrote:

'Historians to be slaughtered first. Who should come second? Scientists or carpenters? Who will make knife-handles if carpenters are killed first? In any case why kill anybody? Must introduce one or two humorous stories. There was once a historian who dug in his garden and unearthed two ancient coins, which supplied the missing link of some period or other; but they were not ancient coins after all but only two old buttons . . . Oh, a most miserable story. Idiotic. What am I to do? Where can I get a book full of jokes of a historical nature? A query in some newspaper. Sir, will you or any of your numerous readers kindly let me know where I can get historical humours?' It was quite an hour before Chandran woke up and his pen ceased. He looked through the jottings that were supposed to be notes for his evening speech. He suddenly realized that his mind wandered when he held pen over paper, but he could concentrate intensely when he walked about with bent head. He considered this a very important piece of self-realization.

He pushed his chair back, put on his coat, and went out. After about two hours of wandering he returned home, having thought of only one argument for killing historians first, namely, that they might not be there to misrepresent the facts when scientists, poets, and statesmen were being killed in their turn. It appeared to him a very brilliant argument. He could see before him a whole house rocking with laughter . . .

Chandran spent a useful half-hour gazing at the college notice board. He saw his name in a notice announcing the evening's debate. He marched along the corridor, with a preoccupied look, to his class. With difficulty he listened to the lecture and took down notes. When the hour closed and the lecturer left the class, Chandran sat back, put the cap on his pen, and let his mind dwell on the subject of historians. He had just begun a short analysis of the subject when Ramu, sitting three benches down the gallery, shouted to him: 'Shall we go out for a moment till Brown comes in?'

'No.'

'Why not?'

Chandran was irritated. 'You can go if you like.'

'Certainly. And you can just stay there and mope,' said Ramu, and walked down the gallery. Chandran felt relieved at his exit, and was settling down to further meditation on historians when somebody asked him to lend his notes of the lecture in the previous hour; somebody else wanted something else. It went on like that till Professor Brown, principal of the college, entered the class with a pile of books under his arm. This was an important hour, Greek

Drama. Chandran once again had to switch his mind off the debate.

At the end of the hour Chandran went to the library and looked through the catalogue. He opened several shelves and examined the books. He could not get the slightest help or guidance. The subject of the debate seemed to be unique. There was any quantity of literature in support of history, but not one on the extermination of historians.

He went home at three. He still had two hours before the debate. He said to his mother: 'I am speaking in a debate this evening. I am now going to my room to prepare. Nobody must knock on my door or shout near my window.'

He came out of his room at four-thirty, ran up and down the hall, banged his fists on the bathroom door, splashed cold water on his head and ran back to his room. He combed and brushed his hair, put on his chocolate-coloured tweed coat, which was reserved for special occasions, and hurried out of the house.

Natesan, the secretary, who was waiting with a perspiring face on the Union veranda, led Chandran into the hall and pushed him into his seat—the first of the four cushioned chairs arranged below the platform for the main debaters. Chandran mopped his face with his handkerchief and looked about. The gallery, built to accommodate about a thousand members of the Union, was certainly not filled to overflowing. There were about fifty from the junior classes and a score from the final year classes. Natesan bent over Chandran's shoulder and whispered, 'Good house, isn't it?' It was quite a big gathering for a Union debate.

A car stopped outside with a roar. The secretary dashed across the hall and returned in a moment, walking sideways, with a feeble official smile on his face, followed by Professor Brown. He led the professor to the high-backed chair on the platform, and whispered to him that he might open the proceedings. Professor Brown rose and announced, 'I call upon Mr H.V. Chandran to move the proposition . . .' and sat down.

The audience clapped their hands. Chandran rose, looked fixedly at the paperweight on the table, and began, 'Mr Speaker, I am certain that this house, so well known for its sanity and common sense, is going to back me solidly when I say that historians should be slaughtered first. I am a student of History and I ought to know . . .'

He went on thus, for about twenty minutes, inspired by the applause with which the audience received many of his cynicisms.

After that the Prime Opposer held the attention of the audience for about twenty minutes. Chandran noted with slight displeasure that the audience received his speech with equal enthusiasm. And then the seconders of the prime speakers droned on for about ten minutes, each almost repeating what their principals had said. When the speakers in the gallery rose there was an uproar, and Professor Brown had to ring the bell and shout 'Order, order'. Chandran felt very bored. Now that he had delivered his speech he felt that the speeches of the others in the hall were both unnecessary and inferior. His eyes wandered about the hall. He looked at the speaker on the platform. He kept gazing at Professor Brown's pink face. Here he is, Chandran thought, pretending to press the bell and listen to the speeches, but really his thoughts are at the tennis-court and the card-table on the English Club. He is here not out of love for us, but merely to keep up appearances. All Europeans are like this. They will take their thousand or more a month, but won't do the slightest service to Indians with a sincere heart. They must be paid this heavy amount for spending their time in the English Club. Why should not these fellows admit Indians to their clubs? Sheer colour arrogance. If ever I get into power I shall see that Englishmen attend clubs along with Indians and are not so exclusive. Why not give the poor devils—so far away from their home—a chance to club together at least for a few hours at the end of a day's work? Anyway who invited them here?

Into this solo discussion Professor Brown's voice impinged. 'Members from the House having expressed their views, and the Prime Opposer having summed up, I call upon Mr Chandran to speak before putting the proposition to the vote.'

Chandran hurriedly made one or two scratches on a sheet of paper, rose, and began: 'Mr Speaker and the Honourable House, I have followed with keen excitement the views expressed by the honourable members of this House. It has considerably lightened my task as the Prime Mover. I have no doubt what the verdict of this House will be on this proposition . . .' He spun out sentences till the Speaker rang the bell to stop him. Before sitting down he threw in his anecdote about the professor who dug up brass buttons in his garden.

When the division was taken the House, by an overwhelming

majority, voted for an early annihilation of historians. Chandran felt victorious. He dramatically stretched his arm across the table and shook hands with the Prime Opposer.

Professor Brown rose and said that technically he ought not to speak, and then explained for five minutes why historians should be slaughtered and for five minutes why they should be deified. He complimented the movers on their vigorous arguments for the proposition, and the opposers on the able stand they had taken.

As soon as he sat down, the secretary jumped on to the platform and mumbled a vote of thanks. By the time the vote of thanks was over the hall had become empty and silent.

Chandran lingered in the doorway as the lights were dimmed, and the secretary, in a very exhausted condition, supervised the removal of the paperweights and table-cloth to the store-room.

'You are coming my way?' Chandran asked.

'Yes.'

'Well, the meeting is over,' said the secretary as they descended the Union steps. Chandran hoped that the secretary would tell him something about his speech. But the secretary was busy with his own thoughts. 'I am sorry I ever took up this business,' he said. 'Hardly any time is left over for my studies. We are already in the middle of August and I don't know what Political Philosophy is.'

Chandran was not interested in the travails of the secretary. He wanted him to say something about his own speech in the debate. So he said: 'Nobody invited you to become the secretary. You forget that you begged, borrowed, and stole votes at the Union elections.'

'I agree with you,' the secretary said. 'But what is to be done about it now?'

'Resign,' said Chandran. He resented the secretary's superficial interest in Chandran's speech. He had cringed for Chandran's help before the debate, and immediately the thing was over did not trouble to make the slightest reference to the speech.

'I will tell you a secret,' the secretary said. 'If I had kept clear of the Union elections, I should have saved nearly seventy rupees.'

'What do you mean?'

'Every vote was purchased with coffee and tiffin, and, in the election month, the restaurant bill came to seventy. My father wrote to me from the village asking if I thought that rupees lay scattered in our village street.'

Chandran felt sympathy for him, but was still disappointed that he made no reference to his speech. There was no use waiting for him to open the subject. He was a born grumbler. Settle all his debts and give him all the comforts in the world, he would still have something to grumble about.

'I have not paid the restaurant bill yet . . .' began the secretary. Chandran ignored this and asked abruptly:

'What did you think of the Boss's speech?'

'As humorous as ever,' said the secretary.

'It is an idiotic belief you fellows have that every thing he says is humorous. He has only to move his lips for you to hold your sides and laugh.'

'Why are you so cynical?'

'I admit he has genuine flashes of humour, but . . .'

'You can't deny that Brown is a fine principal. He has never turned down any request to preside at meetings.'

'That is all you seem to care for in a man. Presiding over meetings! It proves nothing.'

'No. No. I only mean that he is a very pleasant man.'

'He is a humbug, take it from me,' said Chandran. 'He gets his thousand a month, and no wonder he is pleasant. Remember that he is a scoundrel at heart.'

They had now covered half the length of Market Road. As they passed the fountain in the Square, Chandran realized that he was wasting much time and energy in a futile discussion. A few paces more and they would be at the mouth of Kabir Street. A few more moments of that futile discussion and the other would turn and vanish in the darkness. Chandran resolved to act while there was still time: 'Secretary, how did you like my speech today?'

The secretary stopped, gripped Chandran's hand and said: 'It was a wonderful speech. You should have seen Brown's face as he watched you. He would certainly have clapped his hands, but for the fact that he was the Speaker . . . I say, I really liked your story about the professor and his buttons. Such a thing is quite possible, you know. Fine speech, fine speech. So few are really gifted with eloquence.'

When they came to Kabir Street, Chandran asked, sympathetically, 'You live here?'

'Yes.'

'With your people?'

'They are in the village. I have taken a room in a house where a family lives. I pay a rent of about three rupees. It is a small room.'

'Boarding?'

'I go to a hotel. The whole thing comes to about fifteen rupees. Wretched food, and the room is none too good. But what can I do? After the elections my father cut my allowance, and I had to quit the college hostel. Why don't you come to my room some day?'

'Certainly, with pleasure,' said Chandran.

'Good night.'

The secretary had gone a few yards down Kabir Street, when Chandran called suddenly, 'Here, secretary!' The other came back. Chandran said: 'I did not mean that thing about your resignation seriously. Just for fun.'

'Oh, it is all right,' said the secretary.

'Another thing,' said Chandran. 'Don't for a moment think that I dislike Brown. I agree with you entirely when you say he is a man with a pleasant manner. He has a first-rate sense of humour. He is a great scholar. It is really a treat to be taught Drama by him. I was only trying to suggest that people saw humour even where he was serious. So please don't mistake me.'

'Not at all,' said the secretary, and melted in the darkness of Kabir Street.

Chandran had still a quarter of Market Road to walk. A few dim municipal lamps, and the gas lamps of the roadside shops, lit the way. Chandran walked, thinking of the secretary. The poor idiot! Seemed to be always in trouble and always grumbling. Probably borrowed a lot. Must be taking things on credit everywhere, in addition to living in a dingy room and eating bad food. What with a miserly father in the village and the secretary's work and one thing and another, how was he to pass his examination? Not a bad sort. Seemed to be a sensible fellow.

His feet had mechanically led him to Lawley Extension. His was the last bungalow in the Second Cross Road of the Extension. As he came before the house that was the last but one, he stopped and shouted from the road, 'Ramu!'

'Coming!' a voice answered from inside.

Ramu came out. 'Didn't you come to the debate?' Chandran asked.

'I tried to be there, but my mother wanted me to escort her to the market. How did it go off?'

'Quite well, I think. The proposition was carried.'

'Really!' Ramu exclaimed, and shook Chandran's hand.

They were as excited as if it were the Finance Bill before the Legislative Assembly in Delhi.

'My speech was not bad,' said Chandran. 'Brown presided. I was told that he liked it immensely . . .'

'Good crowd?'

'Fairly good. Two rows of the gallery were full. I am really sorry you were not there.'

'How did the others speak?'

'The voting ought to indicate. Brown really made a splendid speech in the end. It was full of the most uproarious humour.'

Chandran asked: 'Would you care to see a picture tonight?'

'It's nearly nine.'

'It doesn't matter. You've finished your dinner. I won't take even five minutes. Put on your coat and come.'

Ramu asked: 'I hope you are paying for both of us?'

'Of course,' said Chandran.

As Chandran came to his gate, he saw his father in the veranda, pacing up and down. Latecoming was one of the few things that upset him. Chandran hesitated for a moment before lifting the gate chain. He opened the gate a little, slipped in, and put the chain back on its hook noiselessly. His usual move after this would be to slip round to the back door and enter the house without his father's knowledge. But now he had a surge of self-respect. He realized that what he usually did was a piece of evasive cowardice worthy of an adolescent. He was not eighteen but twenty-one. At twenty-one to be afraid of one's parents and adopt sneaky ways! He would be a graduate very soon and he was already a remarkable orator!

This impulse to sneak in was very boyish. He felt sorry for it and remedied it by unnecessarily lifting the gate chain and letting it noisily down. The slightest noise at the gate excited an alert watchfulness in his father. And as his father stood looking towards the gate, Chandran swaggered along the drive with an independent air; but within he had a feeling that he should have chosen some other day for demonstrating his independence. Here he was, later than ever, with a cinema programme before him, and his father would certainly stop him and ask a lot of questions. He mounted the veranda steps. His father said: 'It is nine.'

'I spoke in a debate, Father. It was late when it closed.'

'How did you fare in the debate?'

Chandran gave him an account of it, all the time bothered about the night show. Father never encouraged anyone to attend a night show.

'Very good,' Father said. 'Now get in and have your food. Your mother is waiting.'

Chandran, about to go in, said casually: 'Father, Ramu will be here in a moment; please ask him to wait.'

'All right.'

'We are going to a cinema tonight . . . We are in a rather festive mood after the debate.'

'H'm. But I wouldn't advise you to make it a habit. Late shows are very bad for the health.'

He was in the dining-room in a moment, sitting before his leaf and shouting to the cook to hurry up.

The cook said: 'Please call your mother. She is waiting for you.'

'All right. Bring me first rice and curd.'

He then gave a shout, 'Mother!' which reached her as she sat in the back veranda, turning the prayer beads in her hand, looking at the coconut trees at the far end of the compound. As she turned the beads, her lips uttered the holy name of Sri Rama, part of her mind busied itself with thoughts of her husband, home, children, and relatives, and her eyes took in the delicate beauty of coconut trees waving against a starlit sky.

By the time she reached the dining-room Chandran had finished his dinner. She slowly walked to the *puja* room, hung the string of beads on a nail, prostrated before the gods, and then came to her leaf. By that time Chandran was gone. Mother sat before her leaf and asked the cook, 'Didn't he eat well?'

'No. He took only rice and curd. He bolted it down.'

She called Chandran.

'What, Mother?'

'Why are you in such a hurry?'

'I am going to the cinema.'

'I had that potato sauce prepared specially for you, and you have eaten only curd and rice! Fine boy!'

'Mother, give me a rupee.'

She took out her key bunch and threw it at him. 'Take it from the drawer. Bring the key back.'

They walked to the cinema. Chandran stopped at a shop to buy some betel leaves and a packet of cigarettes. Attending a night show was not an ordinary affair. Chandran was none of your business-like automatons who go to a cinema, sit there, and return home. It was an aesthetic experience to be approached with due preparation. You had to chew the betel leaves and nut, chew gently, until the heart was stimulated and threw out delicate beads of perspiration and caused a fine tingling sensation behind the ears; on top of that you had to light a cigarette, inhale the fumes, and with the night breeze blowing on your perspiring forehead, go to the cinema, smoke more cigarettes there, see the picture, and from there go to a hotel nearby for hot coffee at midnight, take some more betel leaves and cigarettes, and go home and sleep. This was the ideal way to set about a night show. Chandran squeezed the maximum aesthetic delight out of the experience, and Ramu's company was most important to him. It was his presence that gave a sense of completion to things. He too smoked, chewed, drank coffee, laughed (he was the greatest laugher in the world), admired Chandran, ragged him, quarrelled with him, breathed delicious scandal over the names of his professors and friends and unknown people.

The show seemed to have already started, because there was no crowd outside the Select Picture House. It was the only theatre that the town possessed, a long hall roofed with corrugated iron sheets. At the small ticket-window Chandran inquired, 'Has the show begun?'

'Yes, just,' said the ticket man, giving the stock reply. You might be three-quarters of an hour late, yet the man at the ticket window would always say, 'Yes, just.'

'Hurry up, Ramu,' Chandran cried as Ramu slackened his pace to admire a giant poster in the narrow passage leading to the four-annas entrance.

The hall was dark; the ticket collector at the entrance took their tickets and held apart the curtains. Ramu and Chandran looked in, seeking by the glare of the picture on the screen for vacant seats. There were two seats at the farthest end. They pushed their way across the knees of the people already seated. 'Head down!' somebody shouted from a back seat, as two heads obstructed the screen. Ramu and Chandran stooped into their seats.

It was the last five minutes of a comic in which Jas Jim was featured. That fat genius, wearing a ridiculous cap, was just struggling out of a paint barrel.

Chandran clicked his tongue in despair: 'What a pity. I didn't know there was a Jas two-reeler with the picture. We ought to have come earlier.'

Ramu sat rapt. He exploded with laughter. 'What a genius he is!' Chandran murmured as Jas got on his feet, wearing the barrel around his waist like a kilt. He walked away from Chandran, but turned once to throw a wink at the spectators, and, taking a step back, stumbled and fell, and rolled off—and the picture ended. A central light was switched on. Chandran and Ramu raised themselves in their seats, craned their necks, and surveyed the hall.

The light went out again, the projector whirred. Scores of voices read aloud in a chorus: 'Godfrey T. Memel presents Vivian Troilet and Georgie Lomb in *Lightguns of Lauro* . . .' Then came much unwanted information about the people who wrote the story, adapted it, designed the dresses, cut the film to its proper length, and so on. Then the lyrical opening: 'Nestling in the heart of the mid-west, Lauro city owed its tranquillity to the eagle-eyed sheriff—'; then a scene showing a country girl (Vivian Troilet) wearing a check skirt, going up a country lane. Thus started, though with a deceptive quietness, it moved at a breathless pace, supplying love, valour, villainy, intrigue, and battle in enormous quantities for a whole hour. The notice 'Interval' on the screen, and the lights going up, brought Chandran and Ramu down to the ordinary plane. The air was thick with tobacco smoke. Ramu yawned, stood up, and gazed at the people occupying the more expensive seats behind them. 'Chandar, Brown is here with some girl in the First Class.'

'May be his wife,' Chandran commented without turning.

'It is not his wife.'

'Must be some other girl, then. The white fellows are born to enjoy life. Our people really don't know how to live. If a person is seen with a girl by his side, a hundred eyes stare at him and a hundred tongues comment, whereas no European ever goes out without taking a girl with him.'

'This is a wretched country,' Ramu said with feeling.

At this point Chandran had a fit of politeness. He pulled Ramu down, saying that it was very bad manners to stand up and stare at the people in the back seats.

Lights out again. Some slide advertisements, each lasting a second.

'Good fellow, he gets through these inflictions quickly,' said Chandran.

'For each advertisement he gets twenty rupees a month.'

'No, it is only fifteen.'

'But somebody said that it was twenty.'

'It is fifteen rupees. You can take it from me,' Chandran said.

'Even then, what a fraud! Not one stays long enough. I hardly take in the full name of that baby's nourishing food, when they tell me what I ought to smoke. Idiots. I hate advertisements.'

The advertisements ended and the story started again from where it had left off. The hero smelt the ambush ten yards ahead. He took a short cut, climbed a. rock, and scared the ruffians from behind. And so on and on it went, through fire and water, and in the end the good man Lomb always came out triumphant; he was an upright man, a courageous man, a handsome man, and a strong man, and he had to win in the end. Who could not foresee it? And yet every day at every show the happy end was awaited with breathless suspense. Even the old sheriff (all along opposed to the union of Vivian with Georgie) was suddenly transformed, and with tears in his eyes he placed her hands on his. There was a happy moment before the end, when the lovers' heads were shown on an immense scale, their lips welded in a kiss. Good night.

Lights on. People poured out of the exits, sleepy, yawning, rubbing their smarting eyes. This was the worst part of the evening, this trudge back home, all the way from the Select Picture House to Lawley Extension. Two or three cars sounded their horns and started from the theatre.

'Lucky rascals. They will be in their beds in five minutes. When I start earning I shall buy a car first of all. Nothing like it. You can just see the picture and go straight to bed.'

'Coffee?' Chandran asked, when they passed a brightly-lit coffee hotel.

'I don't much care.'

'Nor do I.'

They walked in silence for the most part, occasionally exchanging some very dull, languid jokes.

As soon as his house was reached, Ramu muttered, 'Good night. See you tomorrow,' and slipped through his gate.

Chandran walked on alone, opened the gate silently, woke up his younger brother sleeping in the hall, had the hall door opened, and fumbled his way to his room. He removed his coat in the dark, flung it on a chair, kicked a roll of bedding on the floor, and dropped down on it and closed his eyes even before the bed had spread out.

CHAPTER TWO

JULY, AUGUST, SEPTEMBER and October were months that glided past without touching the conscience. One got up in the morning, studied a bit, attended the classes, promenaded the banks of Sarayu river in the evenings, returned home at about eight-thirty, talked a little about things in general with the people at home, and then went to bed. It did not matter whether all the books were on the table or whether the notes of lectures were up to date. Day after day was squandered thus till one fine morning the younger men opened their eyes and found themselves face to face with November. The first of November was to a young man of normal indifference the first reminder of the final trial—the examination. He now realized that half the college year was already spent. What one ought to do in a full year must now be done in just half the time.

On November the first Chandran left his bed at 5 a.m., bathed in cold water, and sat at his study table, before even his mother, the earliest riser in the house, was up. He sat there strengthening himself with several resolutions. One was that he would get up every day at the same hour, bathe in cold water, and get through three hours of solid work before starting for the college. The second resolution was that he would be back home before eight in the evenings and study till eleven-thirty. He also resolved not to smoke because it was bad for the heart, and a very sound heart was necessary for the examination.

He took out a sheet of paper and noted down all his subjects. He calculated the total number of preparation hours that were available from November the first to March. He had before him over a thousand hours, including the twelve-hour preparations on holidays. Of these thousand hours a just allotment of so many hundred hours was to he made for Modern History, Ancient History,

Political Theories, Greek Drama, Eighteenth-century Prose, and Shakespeare. He then drew up a very complicated timetable, which would enable one to pay equal attention to all subjects. Balance in preparation was everything. What was the use of being able to score a hundred per cent in Modern History if Shakespeare was going to drag you in the mire?

Out of the daily six hours, three were to be devoted to the optional subjects and three to the compulsory. In the morning the compulsory subjects, and Literature at night. European History needed all the freshness and sharpness of the morning brain, while it would be a real pleasure to read Literature in the evenings.

He put down for that day *Othello* and the modern period in Indian history. He would finish these two in about forty-eight hours and then take up Milton and Greek History.

And he settled down to this programme with a scowl on his face.

The modern period in Indian history, which he had to take up immediately, presented innumerable difficulties. The texts on the subject were many, the notes of class lectures very bulky. Moreover, if he went on studying the modern period, what was to happen to the medieval period and the ancient? He could not afford to neglect those two important sections of Indian history. Could he now start at the beginning, with the arrival of the Aryans in India, and at a stretch go on to Lord Curzon's Vice-royalty? That would mean, reckoning on Godstone's three volumes, the mastication of over a thousand pages. It was a noble ambition, no doubt, but hardly a sound one, because the university would not recognize your work and grant you a degree if you got a hundred per cent in History and one per cent in the other subjects? Chandran sat for nearly half an hour lost in this problem.

The household was up by this time. His father was in the garden, minutely examining the plants for evidence of any miracle that might have happened overnight. When he passed before Chandran's window he said: 'You have got up very early today.'

'I shall get up before five every day hereafter,' said Chandran.

'Very good.'

'This is November the first. My examinations are on the eighteenth of March. How many days is it from now?'

'About one hundred and thirty-eight—'

'About that,' said Chandran. 'It must be less because February, which comes before the examination month, has only twenty-eight days unless the leap year gives it a day more. So it must be less than one hundred and twenty-eight by three days. Do you know the total number of pages I have to read? Roughly about five thousand pages, four times over, not to speak of class lecture notes. About twenty thousand pages in one hundred and twenty days. That is the reason why I have to get up so early in the morning. I shall probably have to get up earlier still in course of time. I have drawn up a programme of work. Won't you step in and have a look at it?'

Father came in and gazed at the sheet of paper on Chandran's table. He could not make anything of it. What he saw before him was a very intricate document, as complicated as a railway timetable. He honestly made an attempt to understand it and then said: 'I don't follow this quite clearly.' Chandran took the trouble to explain it to him. He also explained to him the problems that harassed him in studying History, and sought his advice. 'I want to know if it would be safe to read only the modern period in Godstone and study the rest in notes.' His father had studied science. This consultation on an historical point puzzled him. He said: 'I feel you ought not to take such risks.'

Chandran felt disappointed. He had hoped that his father would agree with him in supplementing Godstone with the class notes. This advice irritated him. After all, Father had never been a history student.

'Father, you have no idea what splendid lectures Ragavachar gives in the class. His lectures are the essence of all the books on the subject. If one reads his notes, one can pass even the ICS examination.'

'You know best,' said Father. As he started back for the garden, he said, 'Chandar, if you go to the market will you buy some wire-netting? Somebody is regularly stealing the jasmine from the creeper near the compound wall. I want to put up some kind of obstruction that side.'

'That will spoil the appearance of the house, Father.'

'But what are we to do? Somebody comes in even before dawn and steals the flowers.'

'After all, only flowers,' said Chandran, and Father went out muttering something.

Chandran returned to his work, having definitely made up his mind to study only the modern period in Godstone. He pulled out the book from the shelf, blew off the dust, and began at the Moghul invasion. It was a heavy book with close print and shining pages, interspersed with smudgy pictures of kings dead and gone.

At nine he closed the book, having read five pages. He felt an immense satisfaction at having made a beginning.

While going in to breakfast he saw his younger brother, Seenu, standing in the courtyard and looking at the crows on an arecanut tree far off. He was just eight years old, and was studying in the Third Class in Albert Mission School. Chandran said to him: 'Why do you waste the morning gazing at the sky?'

'I am waiting to bathe. Somebody is in the bathroom.'

'It is only nine. What is the hurry for your bath? Do you want to spend the whole day before the bathroom? Go back to your desk. You will be called when the bathroom is vacant. Let me not catch you like this again!'

Seenu vanished from the spot. Chandran was indignant. In his days in the Albert Mission he had studied for at least two hours every morning. The boys these days had absolutely no sense of responsibility.

His mother appeared from somewhere with the flower-basket in her hand. She was full of grievances: 'Somebody takes away all the flowers in the garden. Is there no way of stopping this nuisance? Nobody seems to care for anything in this house.' She was in a fault-finding mood. Not unusual at this hour. She had a variety of work to do in the mornings—tackling the milkman, the vegetable seller, the oil-monger, and other tradespeople; directing the work of the cook and of the servants; gathering flowers for the daily worship; and attending to all the eccentricities and wants of her husband and children.

Chandran knew that the worst one could do at that time was to argue with her. So he said soothingly: 'We will lock the gate at night, and try to put up some wire-netting on the wall.'

She replied: 'Wire-netting! It will make the house hideous! Has your father been suggesting it again?'

'No, no,' Chandran said, 'he just mentioned it as a last measure if nothing else is possible.'

'I won't have it,' Mother said decisively, 'something else has got to be done.' Chandran said that steps should be taken, and asked himself what could be done short of digging a moat around the house and putting crocodiles in it. Mother, however, was appeased by this assurance. She explained mildly: 'Your father spends nearly twenty-five rupees on the garden and nearly ten rupees on a gardener. What is the use of all this expense if we can't have a handful of flowers in the morning, for throwing on the gods in the *puja* room?'

That afternoon, while crossing the quadrangle, Chandran met Ragavachar, the professor of History. He was about to pass him, paying the usual tribute of a meek salute, when Ragavachar called, 'Chandran!'

'Yes, sir,' answered Chandran, much puzzled, having never been addressed by any professor outside the class. In a big college the professors could know personally only the most sycophantic or the most brilliant. Chandran was neither.

'What hour do you finish your work today?'

'At four-thirty, sir.'

'See me in my room at four-thirty.'

'Yes, sir.'

When told of this meeting Ramu asked: 'Did you try to plant a bomb or anything in his house?' Chandran retorted hotly that he didn't appreciate the joke. Ramu said that he was disappointed to hear this, and asked what Chandran wanted him to do. Chandran said: 'Will you please shut up and try not to explain anything?' They were sitting on the steps outside the lecture hall. Ramu got up and said: 'If you want me, I shall be in the Union reading-room till five.'

'We have *Othello* at three-thirty.'

'I am not attending it,' said Ramu, and was gone. Chandran sat alone, worrying. Why had Ragavachar called him? He hadn't misbehaved; no library book was overdue; there were one or two tests he hadn't attended, but Ragavachar never corrected any test paper. Or could it be that he had suddenly gone through all the test papers and found out that Chandran had not attended some of the tests? If it was only a reprimand, the professor would do it in the open class. Would any professor waive such an opportunity and do it in his room? For that matter, Ramu had not attended a single test in his life. Why was he not called? What did Ramu mean by going away in a temper? 'Not attending it!' Seemed to be taking things easy.

The bell rang. Chandran rose and went in. He climbed the

gallery steps and reached his seat. He opened the pages of *Othello*, placed a sheet of paper on the page, and took out his pen.

It was the assistant professor's subject. The assistant professor of English was Mr Gajapathi, a frail man with a meagre moustache and heavy spectacles. He earned the hatred of the students by his teaching and of his colleagues by his conceit. He said everywhere that not ten persons in the world had understood Shakespeare; he asserted that there were serious errors even in Fowler's *Modern English Usage*; he corrected everybody's English; he said that no Indian could ever write English; this statement hurt all his colleagues, who prepared their lectures in English and wished to think that they wrote well. When he valued test or examination papers, he never gave anybody more than forty per cent; he constituted himself an authority on punctuation, and deducted half a mark per misplaced comma or semicolon in the papers that he corrected.

He entered the hall at a trot, jumped on the platform, opened his book, and began to read a scene in *Othello*. He read Shakespeare in a sing-song fashion, and with a vernacular twang. He stopped now and then to criticize other critics. Though Dowden had said so-and-so, Mr Gajapathi was not prepared to be brow-beaten by a big name. No doubt Bradley and others had done a certain amount of research in Shakespeare, but one couldn't accept all that they said as gospel truth. Gajapathi proved in endless instances how wrong others were.

Chandran attempted to take down notes, but they threatened to shape into something like the Sayings of Gajapathi. Chandran screwed the cap on his pen and sat back. Gajapathi never liked to see people sitting back and looking at him. He probably felt nervous when two hundred pairs of eyes stared at him. It was his habit to say, 'Heads down and pencils busy, gentlemen,' and 'Listen to me with your pencils, gentlemen.'

In due course he said: 'Chandran, I see you taking a rest.'

'Yes, sir.'

'Don't say "yes". Keep your pen busy.'

'Yes, sir.' Chandran, with his head bent, began to scribble on the sheet of paper before him: 'Oh, Gajapathi, Gajapathi! When will you shut up? Do you think that your lecture is very interesting and valuable? In these two lines Shakespeare reveals the innermost core of Iago. *Gaja*, in Sanskrit, means elephant; *pathi* is probably master. A fine name for you, you Elephant Master.' And here followed the sketch of an elephant with spectacles on.

'Chandran, do I understand you are taking down notes?'

'Yes, sir.'

The bell rang. Gajapathi intended to continue the lecture even after the bell; but two hundred copies of Verity's *Othello* shut with a loud report like the cracking of a rifle. The class was on its feet.

When he came down the gallery, Gajapathi said: 'A moment, Chandran.' Chandran stopped near the platform as the others streamed past him. Everybody seemed to want him today.

Gajapathi said: 'I should like to see your lecture notes.'

Chandran was nonplussed for a moment. If he remembered aright he had scribbled an elephant. The other things he did not clearly recollect; but he knew that they were not meant for Gajapathi's scrutiny. He wondered for a moment whether he should escape with a lie, but felt that Gajapathi did not deserve that honour. He said: 'Honestly, I have not taken down anything, sir. If you will excuse me, I must go now. I have to see Professor Ragavchar.'

As he came near the professor's room, Chandran felt very nervous. He adjusted his coat and buttoned it up. He hesitated for a moment before the door. He suddenly pulled himself up. Why this cowardice? Why should he be afraid of Ragavachar or anybody? Human being to human being. Remove those spectacles, the turban, and the long coat, and let Ragavachar appear only in a loincloth, and Mr Ragavachar would lose three-quarters of his appearance. Where was the sense in feeling nervous before a pair of spectacles, a turban, and a black long coat?

'Good evening, sir,' said Chandran, stepping in.

Ragavachar looked up from a bulky red book that he was reading. He took time to switch his mind off his studies and comprehend the present.

'Well,' he said, looking at Chandran.

'You asked me to see you at four-thirty, sir.'

'Yes, yes. Sit down.'

Chandran lowered himself to the edge of a chair. Ragavachar leaned back and spent some time looking at the ceiling. Chandran felt a slight thirsty sensation, but he recollected his vision of Ragavachar in a loincloth, and regained his self-confidence.

'My purpose in calling you now is to ascertain your views on the question of starting an Historical Association in the college.'

Saved! Chandran sat revelling in the sense of relief he now felt.
'What do you think of it?'

'I think it is a good plan, sir,' and he wondered why he was
chosen for this consultation.

'What I want you to do,' went on the commanding voice, 'is to
arrange for an inaugural meeting on the fifteenth instant. We shall
decide the programme afterwards.'

'Very well, sir,' said Chandran.

'You will be the secretary of the association. I shall be its
president. The meeting must be held on the fifteenth.'

'Don't you think, sir . . .' Chandran began.

'What don't I think?' asked the professor.

'Nothing, sir.'

'I hate these sneaky half-syllables,' the professor said. 'You
were about to say something. I won't proceed till I know what you
were saying.'

Chandran cleared his throat and said: 'Nothing, sir. I was only
going to say that some one else might do better as a secretary.'

'I suppose you can leave that to my judgment.'

'Yes, sir.'

'I hope you don't question the need for starting the association.'

'Certainly not, sir.'

'Very good. I for one feel that the amount of ignorance on
historical matters is appalling. The only way in which we can
combat it is to start an association and hold meetings and read
papers.'

'I quite understand, sir.'

'Yet you ask me why we should have this association!'

'No, I did not doubt it.'

'H'm. You talk the matter over with one or two of your friends,
and see me again with some definite programme for the inaugural
meeting.'

Chandran rose.

'You seem to be in a hurry to go,' growled the tiger.

'No, sir,' said Chandran, and sat down again.

'If you are in a hurry to go, I can't stop you because it is past
four-thirty, and you are free to leave the college premises. On the
other hand, if you are not in a hurry, I have some more details to
discuss with you.'

'Yes, sir.'

'There is no use repeating "Yes, sir, yes, sir". You don't come forward with any constructive suggestion.'

'I will talk it over with some friends and come later, sir.'

'Good evening. You may go now.'

Chandran emerged from the professor's room with his head bowed in thought. He felt a slight distaste for himself as a secretary. He felt that he was on the verge of losing his personality. Now he would have to be like Natesan, the Union Secretary. One's head would be full of nothing but meetings to be arranged! He was now condemned to go about with a fixed idea, namely, the inaugural meeting. The inaugural meeting by itself was probably not a bad thing, if it were also the final meeting; but they would expect him to arrange at least half a dozen meetings before March: readings of papers on mock subjects, heavy lectures by paunchy hags, secretary's votes of thanks, and endless other things. He hated the whole business. He would have to sit through the lectures, wait till the lights were put out and the doors locked, and go out into the night with a headache, forgoing the walk by the river with Ramu. Ah, Ramu; that fellow behaved rather queerly in the afternoon, going off in a temper like that.

Chandran went to the reading-room in the Union. None of the half a dozen heads bent over the illustrated journals belonged to Ramu. Chandran had a hope that Ramu might be in the chess room. He was not the sort to play chess, but he occasionally might be found in the company that stood around and watched a game of chess, shutting out light and air from the players. But today the game of chess seemed to be going on without Ramu's supervision; nor was he to be found in the ping-pong room. Chandran descended the Union steps in thorough discontent.

He turned his steps to the river, which was a stone's throw from the college. He walked along the sand. The usual crowd was there—girls with jasmine in their hair, children at play, students loafing about, and elderly persons at their constitutionals. Chandran enjoyed immensely an evening on the river bank: he stared at the girls, pretended to be interested in the children, guffawed at friends, perambulated about twice or thrice, and then walked to the lonely Nallappa's Grove and smoked a cigarette there. Ramu's company and his running commentary lent vitality to the whole experience.

But today his mind was clogged, and Ramu was absent. Chandran was beginning to feel bored. He started homeward.

It was a little past seven when he turned into the Second Cross Road in Lawley Extension. He stood before Ramu's gate and shouted, 'Ramu!' Ramu came out.

'Why were you not in the reading-room?'

'I waited, and thought that you would be late and came away.'

'You were not by the river.'

'I returned home and went for a walk along the Trunk Road.'

'What did you mean by going away like that to the reading-room, so abruptly?'

'I wanted to read the magazines.'

'I don't believe it. You went away in a temper. I wonder why you are so lacking in patience!'

'What about your temper? You meet Ragavachar and are worried, and a fellow says something lightly and you flare up!'

Chandran ignored the charge. He seized upon the subject of Ragavachar. He gave a full account of the amazing interview. They stood on the road, talking the matter over and over again, for nearly two hours.

When Chandran went home his father said: 'Nine o'clock.' Later, when he was about to go to bed, Father asked, 'Your plan of study has not come into force yet?' That question hurt Chandran's conscience. He went to his table and stood looking at the programme he had sketched out in the morning. Not much of it was clear now. He went to bed and his conscience gnawed at him in the dark till about eleven. He had spent the morning in drawing plans and the rest of the day somehow. First of November gone, irrevocably gone, and wasted; six of the forty-eight hours for *Othello* and Godstone thrown on the scrap-heap.

The inaugural meeting troubled Chandran day and night, and he was unable to make any progress in *Othello* and Godstone. His notions as to what one did on the day of the meeting were very vague. He faintly thought that at such a meeting people sat around, drank tea, shook hands with each other, and felt inaugural.

Five mornings before the meeting, in a fit of desperation, he flung aside his Godstone, and started for Natesan's room. If ever there was a man to guide another in these matters, it was Natesan. He had twice been the secretary of the Sanskrit Association, once its vice-president, secretary of the Philosophy Association of a Social Service League, and now of the Union. Heaven knew what other things he was going to be. He must have conducted nearly a hundred meetings in his college life. Though Chandran had sometimes dreaded meeting this man, now he felt happy when he knocked on his door and found him in. It was a very narrow room with a small window opening on the twisting Kabir Street, half-filled with a sleeping cot, and the remaining space given over to the four legs of a very big table, on which books were heaped. One opened the door and stepped on the cot. Natesan was reclining on a roll of bedding and studying. He was very pleased to see Chandran, and invited him to take a seat on the cot.

Chandran poured out his troubles. 'What does one do on the inaugural day?'

'A lengthy address is delivered, and then the chairman thanks the lecturer, and the secretary thanks the lecturer and the chairman, and the audience rises to go home.'

'No tea or anything?'

'Oh, no. Nothing of the sort. Who is to pay for the tea?'

And then hearing of Chandran's vagueness and difficulties, Natesan suggested the Principal for the address, and Professor Ragavachar for the chair. After his interview with Natesan, Chandran realized that a secretary's life was a tormented one. He was now in a position to appreciate the services not only of Natesan, but also of Alam, the secretary of the Literary Association, of Rajan, the Philosophy Association secretary, of Moorty, the secretary of the Economics Association, the people who were responsible for all the meetings in the college. Chandran realized that there was more in these meetings than met the eye or entered the ear. Each meeting was a supreme example of human endeavour, of selfless service. For what did a secretary after all gain by sweating? No special honours from the authorities nor extra marks in the examinations. Far from it. More often ridicule from class-mates and frowns from professors, if something went wrong. The bothers of a secretary were: a clash with other secretaries over the date of a meeting; finding a speaker, finding a subject for the speaker; and getting an audience for the subject.

That day Chandran skipped nearly two periods in order to see the Principal. The peon squatting before the Principal's room would not let him in. Chandran pleaded and begged. The peon spoke in whispers, and commanded Chandran to talk in whispers. Chandran whispered that he had to see the Principal, whispered a threat, whispered an admonition, in whispers cringed and begged, but the peon was adamant.

'I have orders not to let anybody in,' said the peon. He was an old man, grown grey in college service, that is in squatting before the Principal's office door. His name was Aziz.

'Look here, Aziz,' Chandran said in a soothing tone, 'why can't anybody see him now?'

'It is not for me to ask. I won't let anybody in. He is very busy.'

'Busy with what?'

'What do you care?' Aziz asked haughtily.

'Is he given his thousand a month to sit behind that door and refuse to see people?'

At this the servant lost his temper, and asked: 'Who are you to question it?' Chandran gave some stinging answer to this. It was a great strain to carry on the conversation, the whole thing having to be conducted in whispers. Chandran realized that it was no use losing one's temper. He tried strategy now. He said: 'Aziz, I have an old coat at home; not a tear in it. Will you come for it tomorrow morning?'

'What time?'

'Any time you please. I live in Lawley Extension.'

'Yes, I know. I will find out your house.'

'Give me a slip of paper.'

Aziz tore out a slip from a bundle hung on the door. Chandran wrote his name on it and sent it in. Aziz came out of the room in a few minutes and said that Chandran might go in. Chandran adjusted his coat and entered.

'Good morning, sir.'

'Good morning.'

Chandran delivered a short preamble on the Historical Association, and stated his request. The Principal took out a small black diary, turned over its pages, and said: 'The fifteenth evening is free. All right.'

'Thank you, sir,' said Chandran, and remained standing for a few minutes. He himself could not say what he was waiting there for. His business had been completed too rapidly. He didn't know whether he ought to say something more or leave the room abruptly. The Principal took out a cigarette and lighted it. 'Well?'

'We are . . . we are very grateful to you, sir, for your great kindness.'

'Oh, it's all right. Don't mention it.'

'May I take my leave?'

'Yes.'

'Thank you, sir. Good morning.' Chandran marched out of the room. When he passed Aziz he said: 'What a bad fellow you are, you wouldn't let me in!'

'Master, I do my duty and get a bad name. What am I to do? Can I see you tomorrow morning?'

'I shall ask the peon at our gate not to let you in.'

'Oh, master, I am a poor old fellow, always shivering with cold. Don't disappoint me. If you give me a coat, I shall always remember you as my saviour.'

'All right. Come tomorrow,' whispered Chandran, and passed on.

He went to Ragavachar's room and announced that the Principal -had consented to deliver the inaugural address. Ragavachar did not appear excited by the news. He growled, after some rumination: 'I am not sure if his address will be suitable for an Historical Association.'

'I think, sir, he can adjust himself.'

'One hopes so.'

'You must take the chair, sir.'

'I suppose . . . H'm.' Nothing further was said. Having moved with him closely for ten days Chandran understood it to mean consent.

'May I go, sir?'

'Yes.'

CHAPTER THREE

THE FIFTEENTH OF November was a busy day for Chandran. He spent a great part of the morning in making arrangements for the meeting in the evening.

Two days before, he had issued printed notices over his signature to all the members of the staff, and to all the important lawyers, doctors, officials, and teachers in the town. From every board in the college his notices invited every one to be present at the meeting.

As a result of this, on the fifteenth, at five in the evening, while Chandran was still arranging the dais and the chairs in the lecture hall of the college, the audience began to arrive.

The college peon, Aziz, lent him a stout hand in making the arrangements. The old coat had done the trick. Aziz personally attended to the arrangement of the chairs in the front row. He arranged the chairs and the table on the dais. He gave a gorgeous setting to the Historical Association. He spread a red cloth on the dais, and a green baize on the table. He illuminated the hall with petrol lamps.

As the guests arrived, Chandran ran to the veranda and received them and conducted them to their seats. At 5.15 almost all the chairs were occupied; all the seats in the gallery were also filled. Students of the college who came late hung on to the banisters.

The Principal and Professor Ragavachar arrived and stopped in the veranda. Chandran flitted about uncertainly, and invited them in. The Principal looked at his watch and said: 'Five minutes more. We shall stay here till five-thirty.'

Ragavachar adjusted his spectacles and murmured: 'Yes, yes.'

Some more guests arrived. Chandran showed them their seats. Ramu was all the time at his side, running errands, helping him, asking questions, and not always receiving an answer.

'What a crowd!' Ramu said.

'You see . . .' began Chandran, and saw the Head Master of the Albert Mission School arriving and ran forward to meet him. Chandran returned after seating the Head Master in the hall.

Ramu said: 'It looks as if you were giving a dinner-party to the town folk.'

Chandran said, his eyes scanning the drive for visitors, 'Yes, it looks like that. Only flowers, scents, and a dinner missing to complete the picture.'

Ramu asked, 'Shall I wait for you at the end of the lecture?' and was not destined to receive an answer. For, at this moment, Ragavachar looked at his watch and said: 'It is five-thirty, shall we begin?'

'Yes, sir.'

The secretary led the Speaker and the Chairman to their chairs on the dais, and occupied a third chair placed on the edge of the dais.

After the cheering and stamping had subsided Ragavachar rose, put on his spectacles, and began, 'Ladies and gentlemen, I am not going to presume to introduce to you the lecturer of this evening. I do not propose to stand between you and the lecturer. I shall take only a few minutes, perhaps only a few seconds, to enlighten you on a few facts concerning our association . . .' He then filled the hall with his voice for a full forty minutes. The audience gathered from his speech that an Historical Association represented his faith in life; it was a vision which guided him in all his activities. The audience also understood that darkness prevailed in the minds of over ninety per cent of human beings, and that he expected the association to serve the noble end of dispelling this darkness. Great controversial fires were raging over very vital matters in Indian history. And what did they find around them? The public went about their business as if nothing was happening. How could one expect these fires to be extinguished if the great public did not show an intelligent appreciation of the situation and lend a helping hand? To quote an instance: everybody learnt in the secondary school history book that Sirajudowlla locked some of the East Indian Company people in a very small room, and allowed them to die of suffocation. This was the well-known Black Hole of Calcutta. There were super-historians who appeared at a later stage in one's education and said that there had been neither Black nor Hole nor Calcutta. He was not going to indicate his own views on the question. But he only wished to convey to the minds of the audience, to the public at large, to all intelligent humanity in general, what a state of bloody feud existed in the realm of Indian history. True history was neither fiction nor philosophy. It was a hardy science. And to place Indian history there an association was indispensable. If he were asked what the country needed most urgently, he would not say self-government or economic independence, but a clarified, purified Indian history.

After this he repeated that he would not stand between the lecturer and his audience, and, calling upon Professor Brown to deliver the inaugural address, sat down.

As Professor Brown got up there was great applause. He looked about, put his right hand in his trouser pocket, held his temples with his left hand, and began. He looked at Chandran and said that he had not bargained for this, a meeting of this dimension and importance, when he acceded to the secretary's request. Chandran tapped the arms of his chair with his fingers, looked down and smiled, almost feeling that he had played a deep game on the Principal. The lecturer said that he had consented to deliver an address this evening, thinking that he was to be at the opening of a very simple association. From what Ragavachar said, he understood it to be something that was of national importance. If he had known this, his place now would be in one of the chairs that he saw before him, and he would have left the responsible task to better persons. However, it was too late to do anything now. He hoped that he would have an occasion to settle his score with Chandran.

The audience enjoyed every word of this. People who had awaited Brown's humour were fully satisfied.

Professor Brown traced his relations with History from the earliest times when he was in a private school in Somerset to the day on which he entered Oxford, where he shook History off his person, because he found the subject as treacherous as a bog at night. Thereafter, for his degree, he studied Literature, and regularly spent some hours of private study on History. 'I can now give a fairly coherent account of mankind's "doings", if I may borrow an expression from the composition books that I correct. But don't ask me the date of anything. In all History I remember only 1066.'

He held the audience for about an hour thus, with nothing very serious, nothing profound, but with the revelation of a personality, with delicious reminiscences, touched with humour and occasional irony.

He sat down after throwing at his audience this advice: 'Like Art, History must be studied for its own sake; and so, if you are to have an abiding interest in it, take it up after you leave the university. For outside the university you may read your history in any order; from the middle work back to the beginning of things or in any way you like, and nobody will measure how many facts you have rammed into your poor head. Facts are, after all, a secondary matter in real history.'

Ragavachar inwardly fretted and fumed at the speech. If the lecturer had been any one else than Brown, the Principal of the college, he would have taken the speech to bits and thrown it to the four winds, and pulled out the tongue of the lecturer and cut it off. At the end of the lecture, he merely rose and thanked the lecturer on behalf of the audience and sat down. When Chandran rose to propose a hearty vote of thanks to the lecturer and to the chairman for their great kindness in consenting to conduct the meeting, it acted as a signal for the audience to rise and go home. A babble broke out. Chandran's voice could hardly be heard except by a select few in the very first row.

CHAPTER FOUR

CHANDRAN PUT OFF everything till the inaugural meeting was over. He consoled himself with the fact that he had wasted several months so far, and a fortnight more, added to that account, should not matter. He had resolved that the moment the meeting was over he would get up at 4.30 instead of 5 a.m. as decided originally. The time wasted in a fortnight could then be made up by half an hour's earlier rising every day. He would also return home at seven in the evening instead of at seven-thirty. This would give him a clear gain of an hour a day over his previous programme. He hoped to make up the ninety study hours, at six hours a day, lost between the first of November and the fifteenth, in the course of ninety days.

This was a sop to his clamouring conscience. He thought now he would be able to get up at four-thirty on the following morning and begin his whirlwind programme of study. But man can only propose. He was destined to throw away two more mornings. On the night of the big meeting, before going to bed, he spent some time on the carpet in the hall, gossiping with his mother. He announced that he would get up at four-thirty next morning.

Father, who appeared to be reading a newspaper in the veranda, exclaimed: 'So after all!' This remark disturbed Chandran. But he remained silent, hoping that it would discourage his father from uttering further remarks. Father, however, was not to be kept off so easily. The newspaper rustled on the veranda, and five minutes later came the remark: 'Since this is the third time you have made a resolution, it is likely you will stick to it, because every plan must have two trials.' Chandran rose and went on to the veranda. His father was in a puckish, teasing mood. As soon as Chandran came out, he looked at him over his spectacles and asked: 'Don't you agree with me?'

'What, Father?'

'That a plan must have two trials.'

Chandran felt uncomfortable. 'You see, Father, but for this dreadful meeting, I should have done ninety hours of study, according to my timetable. I shall still make it up. I shall not be available to anyone from tomorrow.' He gave a glowing account of what he was going to do from the next morning onwards.

Father said that he was quite pleased to hear it. He said: 'If you get up at four-thirty, do wake me up also. I want to wait and catch the scoundrel who steals the flowers in the morning.'

Mother's voice came from the hall: 'So, after all, you are doing something!'

'Hardly my fault that,' Father shouted back. 'I offered to put up wire-fencing over the wall.'

'Why, do you want to give the thief some wire in addition to the flowers?'

Father was greatly affected by this taunt.

Mother added fuel to it by remarking, 'Twenty-five rupees on the garden and not a single petal of any flower for the gods in the *puja* room.'

Father was very indignant. He behaved like a medieval warrior goaded by his lady love into slaying a dragon. Father dropped a hint that the flower thief would be placed at her feet next day, alive or dead.

Next morning Chandran was awakened by his alarm clock. He went to his father's room and woke him up. After that he went to the bathroom for a cold bath.

In ten minutes Chandran was at his table. He adjusted the light, drew the chair into position, and pondered over the piece of paper on which he had written a timetable.

His father entered the room, carrying a stout bamboo staff in his hand. Behind him came Seenu, armed with another stick. There was the light of a hunter in Father's eyes, and Seenu was bubbling over with enthusiasm. Chandran was slightly annoyed at this intrusion. But Father whispered an apology, and requested, 'Put out that light. If it is seen in your room, the thief will not come near the house.'

'So much the better. Mother can take the flowers in the morning,' said Chandran.

'He will come some other day.'

'From now on, at least till March, there is no fear of this room ever being without a light at this hour. So the flower thief will be away till March. Let us catch him after that.'

'Oh, that is all far-fetched. I must get him today. It doesn't matter if you lose about an hour. You can make it up later.'

Chandran blew out the lamp and sat in the dark. Father and Seenu went out into the garden. Chandran sat in his chair for some time. He rose and stood looking out of the window. It was very dark in the garden.

Chandran began to wonder what his father and brother were doing, and how far they had progressed with the thief. His curiosity increased. He went into the garden, and moved cautiously along the shadows, and heard hoarse whispers coming from behind a big sprawling croton.

'Oh, it is Chandran,' said a voice.

Father and Seenu were crouching behind the croton.

'Don't make any noise,' Father whispered to Chandran.

Chandran found the tactics weak. He took command. It seemed to him a waste to concentrate all the forces in one place. He ordered his father to go a little forward and conceal himself behind a rose bush; and his younger brother to prowl around the back yard, while he himself would be here and there and everywhere, moving with panther-like steps from cover to cover.

There was a slight hitch in the campaign. Seenu objected to the post he was allotted. It was still dark, and the back yard had a mysterious air. Chandran called him a coward and several other things, and asked him why he had left his bed at all if he could not be of some use to people.

In about an hour the sun came out and revealed the jasmine and other plants bare of flowers. Father merely looked at them and said: 'We must get up at four o'clock, not at four-thirty.'

Next day Chandran was out of bed at four, and with his father hunting in the garden. Nothing happened for about ten minutes. Then a slight noise was heard near the gate. Father was behind the rose bush, and Chandran had pressed himself close to the compound wall. A figure heaved itself on to the portion of the wall next to the gate, and jumped into the garden. The stranger looked about for a fraction of a second and went towards the jasmine creeper in a business-like way.

Hardly had he plucked half a dozen flowers when father and

son threw themselves on him with war cries. It was quite a surprise for Chandran to see his father so violent. They dragged the thief into the house, held him down, and shouted to Mother to wake up and light the lamp.

The light showed the thief to be a middle-aged man, bare-bodied, with matted hair, wearing only a loincloth. The loincloth was ochre-coloured, indicating that he was a *sanyasi*, an ascetic. Father relaxed his hold on noticing this.

Mother screamed, 'Oh, hold him, hold him.' She was shaking with excitement. 'Take him away and give him to the police.'

Chandran said to the thief, 'You wear the garb of a *sanyasi*, and yet you do this sort of thing!'

'Is he a *sanyasi*?' Mother asked, and noticed the colour of the thief's loincloth. 'Ah, leave him alone, let him go.' She was seized with fear now. The curse of a holy man might fall on the family. 'You can go, sir,' she said respectfully.

Chandran was cynical. 'What, Mother, you are frightened of every long hair and ochre dress you see. If you are really a holy man, why should you do this?'

'What have I done?' asked the thief.

'Jumping in and stealing flowers.'

'If you lock the gate, how else can I get in than by jumping over the wall? As for stealing flowers, flowers are there, God-given. What matters is whether you throw the flowers on the gods, or I do it. It is all the same.'

'But you should ask our permission.'

'You are all asleep at that hour, and I don't wish to disturb you. I can't wait until you get up because my worship is over before sunrise.'

Mother interposed and said: 'You can go now, sir. If you want flowers you can take them. There couldn't be a better way of worship than giving flowers to those who really worship.'

'Truly said, Mother,' said the holy man. 'I should certainly have asked your permission but for the fact that none of you are awake at that hour.'

'I shall be awake,' said Chandran, 'from tomorrow.'

'Do you use these flowers for your worship, Mother?' asked the stranger.

'Certainly, every day. I never let a day go without worship.'

'Ah, I did not know that. I had thought that here, as in many other bungalows, flowers were kept only for ornament. I am happy to hear that they are put to holy use. Hereafter I shall take only a handful and leave the rest for your worship. May I take leave of you now?' He crossed the hall and descended the veranda steps.

Father said to Chandran: 'Take the gate key and open the gate. How can he get out?'

'If you leave him alone, he will jump over the wall and go,' mumbled Chandran sourly as he took the gate key from the nail on the veranda wall.

CHAPTER FIVE

NOVEMBER TO MARCH was a very busy period for Chandran. He got up every day at four-thirty in the morning, and did not get to bed until eleven. He practised his iron scheme of study to the letter. By the beginning of March he was well up in every subject. There were still a few inevitable dark corners in his mind: a few hopeless controversies among Shakespearian scholars, a few impossible periods in History like the muddle that was called the medieval south Indian history, early Christianity with warring Popes and kings, and feudalism. He allowed the muddle to remain undisturbed in his mind; he got into the habit of postponing the mighty task of clarifying these issues to a distant favourable day. He usually encouraged himself in all this vagueness by saying that even if he lost thirty marks in each paper owing to these doubts he would still be well within the reach of seventy in each, and, out of this, allowing twenty for defective presentation and examiners' eccentricities, he would still get fifty marks in each paper, which would be ten more than necessary for a pass degree.

He had a few other achievements to his credit. Before March he conducted about eight meetings of the Historical Association. He himself read a paper on 'The Lesser-known Aspects of Mauryan Polity'.

The Historical Association was responsible for two interesting contacts. He came to know Veeraswami, the revolutionary, and Mohan, the poet.

Veeraswami was a dark, stocky person, about twenty-two years old. One day he came to Chandran and offered to read a paper on 'The Aids to British Expansion in India'. Chandran was delighted. He had never met anyone who volunteered to address the association. On a fateful day, to an audience of thirty-five, Veeraswami read his paper. It was the most violent paper ever read before an association. It pilloried Great Britain before the action, and ended by hoping that the British would he ousted from India by force. Ragavachar, who was present at the meeting, felt very uncomfortable. Next day he received a note from Brown, the custodian of British prestige, suggesting that in future papers meant to be read before the association should be first sent to him. This infuriated Chandran so much that he thought of resigning till Ragavachar assured him that he would not get his degree if he tried these antics. Chandran sought Veeraswami and told him of the turmoil that his paper had caused, and consulted him on the ways and means to put an end to Brown's autocracy. Veeraswami suggested that he should be allowed to read a paper on 'The Subtleties of Imperialism', without sending the paper to Brown for his approval. Chandran declined this offer, explaining that he did not wish to be expelled from the college. Veeraswami asked why not, and called Chandran a coward. Chandran had a feeling that he had got into bed with a porcupine. Veeraswami bristled with prejudices and violence. Imperialism was his favourite demon. He believed in smuggling arms into the country, and, on a given day, shooting all the Englishmen. He assured Chandran that he was even then preparing for that great work. His education, sleep, contacts and everything, were a preparation. He was even then gathering followers. He seemed to have considered this plan in all its aspects. Indians were hopelessly underfed and sickly. He proposed to cure hunger by encouraging the use of coconuts and the fruits of cactus for food. He was shortly going to issue pamphlets in Tamil, Telugu, and English on the subject. In regard to sickness he believed that the British encouraged it in order to provide a permanent market for the British drug manufacturers. He was going to defeat that plan by propagating the nature-cure idea. After thus improving the physique of the masses he would take charge of their minds. He would assume the garb of a village worker, a rural reconstruction maniac, but secretly prepare the mind of the peasantry for revolution.

After that Veeraswami never gave Chandran a moment's peace. In all leisure hours Chandran lived in terror of being caught by Veeraswami, which invariably happened. If Chandran went to the reading-room, Veeraswami was sure to hunt him down; if he went into the ping-pong room, he would be chased even there. So Chandran took to slinking out and going to a secluded spot on the river bank. This almost led to a misunderstanding with Ramu, who thought that Chandran was avoiding him. In the evenings, too, Veeraswami would catch Chandran and follow him everywhere. Veeraswami would talk all the evening as Ramu and Chandran followed him with the look of a sacrificial goat in their eyes.

The other person whom the Historical Association brought in, Mohan, was less troublesome. He sidled up to Chandran one afternoon as the latter sat over his coffee in the Union Restaurant, and asked if a meeting could be arranged where some poems might be read. Chandran felt quite thrilled to meet a poet in the flesh. He never read poetry for pleasure, but he had a great admiration for poets. Chandran asked the other to take a seat and offered him a cup of coffee.

'Have your poems anything to do with history?'

'I don't understand you.'

'I want to know if they deal with historical facts. Something like a poem on the Moghul Emperors and things of that type. Otherwise it would not be easy to get them read before the Historical Association.'

'I am sorry you are so narrow-minded. You want everything to stay in watertight compartments. When will you get a synthetic view of things? Why should you think that poetry is different from history?'

Chandran felt that he was being dragged into dangerous zones. He said: 'Please let me know what your subjects are.'

'Why should a poem have any subject? Is it not enough that there it is in itself?'

Chandran was thoroughly mystified. He asked: 'You write in English or in Tamil?'

'Of course in English. It is the language of the world.'

'Why don't you read your poems before the Literary Association?'

'Ah, do you think any such thing is possible with Grandmother Brown as its president? As long as he is in this college no original work will ever be possible. He is very jealous, won't tolerate a pinch of original work. Go and read before the Literary Association, for the two-hundredth time, a rehash of his lecture notes on Wordsworth or eighteenth-century prose, and he will permit it. He won't stand anything else.'

'I should certainly like to read your poems myself, but I don't see how it will be possible before the association.'

'If you have properly understood history as a record of human culture and development, you can't fail to see poetry as an integral part of it. If poems are to be read anywhere, it must be before an Historical Association.'

When Chandran asked for permission to arrange this meeting, Ragavachar ruled it out. He said that he did not care to have all sorts of versifiers come and contaminate the association with their stuff. As he conveyed the refusal to Mohan, Chandran felt a great pity for the poet. He liked the poet. He was fascinated by his obscure statements. He desired to cultivate his friendship. He expressed his willingness to have some of the poems read to him. The only time he could spare was the evening, after the college was over. So the next evening he cancelled his walk and listened to verse. Ramu told Chandran not to expect him to sit down and enjoy that kind of entertainment, and went away before Mohan arrived.

Chandran hated his room in the evenings, but now he resigned himself to suffer in the cause of poetry.

Mohan came, with a bundle of typed sheets under his arm. After giving him a seat, Chandran asked: 'How many poems have you brought?'

'A selection of about twenty-five, that is all.'

'I hope we can finish them before seven,' said Chandran, 'because at seven-thirty I have to sit down to my studies.'

'Oh, yes,' said the poet, and began. He read far into the evening. The poems were on a wide variety of subjects—from A Roadside Grass-seller to The Planet in Its Orbit; from Lines Suggested by an Ant to The Dying Musician. All conceivable things seemed to have incited Mohan to anger, gloom, despair, and defiance. Some had rhymes, some had not; some had a beginning, some had no end, some had no middle. But most of the poems mystified Chandran. After a time he gave up all attempt to understand them. He sat passively, listening, as the poet read by the twilight. He sighed with relief when the poet put down the twenty-fifth poem. The clock showed seven-fifteen. Chandran suggested a short stroll.

Chandran had a slight headache. The poet was hoarse with reading. During the stroll Chandran suggested, 'Why don't you try to get some of the poems published in a paper?'

'By every post I receive my poems back,' said the poet. 'For the last five years I have been trying to get my poems accepted. I have tried almost all the papers and magazines in the world— England, America, Canada, South Africa, Australia, and our own country. I must have spent a fortune in postage.'

Chandran expressed his admiration for the other for still writing so much.

'I can no more help writing than I can help breathing,' said the poet. 'I shall go on writing till my fingers are paralysed. Every day I write. I hardly read any of the class texts, I know I shall fail. I don't care. I hope some day I shall come across an editor or publisher who is not stupid.'

'Oh, you will very soon be a famous man,' said Chandran with conviction.

In March Chandran lost about six pounds in weight. He hardly thought of anything, saw anybody, or did anything, except study. The college now existed only for the classroom, and the classroom only for the lectures. Everybody in the college was very serious and purposeful. Even Gajapathi now devoted less of his time to attacks on critics than to lectures that would be useful in the examination.

On the last day of the term there was an air of conclusion about everything. Every professor and lecturer came to the end of his subject and closed his book. Brown shut Sophocles and ended the year with the hope that his pupils' interest in literature would long survive the examination. He left the class amid great cheering and clapping of hands. Gajapathi put away his copy of *Othello*, and hoped that he had presented Shakespeare's mind clearly to his class; he also hoped that after the examination they would all be in a position to form independent judgments of their own. The professor of European History closed the year with the League of Nations. The last period on the last day was Indian History. Ragavachar growled out the full stop with a summary of the Montagu-Chelmsford Reforms, and left the class after warning them not to disturb the other classes by cheering and clapping.

They had their Class Socials that evening. A group photo, with the Principal sitting in the centre, was taken. A large lunch was eaten, and coffee drunk. Songs were sung, speeches were made, everybody wished everybody else success in the examination; professors shook hands with the students, and students shook hands with each other. Everybody was soft and sentimental. They did everything short of shedding tears at the parting.

As they dispersed and went home, Chandran was aware that he had passed the very last moments in his college life, which had filled the major portion of his waking hours for the last four years. There would be no more college for him from tomorrow. He would return to it a fortnight hence for the examination and (hoping for the best) pass it, and pass out into the world, for ever out of Albert College. He felt very tender and depressed.

PART TWO

CHAPTER SIX

WITHIN SIX MONTHS of becoming a graduate Chandran began
to receive suggestions from relatives and elderly friends of the
family as to what he should do with himself. Till this time it had
never occurred to him that he ought to be doing anything at all. But
now, wherever he went, he was pestered with the question, 'Now
what do you propose to do?'

'I have not thought of anything yet.'

'Why don't you go to Madras and study Law?'

There was his uncle in Nellore who wrote to him that he ought
to do something and try to settle in life. There was his mother's
cousin who advised him to study Law. There was his Madras uncle
who said that staying in Malgudi would not lead him anywhere, but
that he ought to go to a big city and see people. He had immense
faith in seeing people. He himself volunteered to give a letter of
introduction to some big man, an auditor in the railways, who in his
turn would give a further introduction to someone else, and finally
fix up Chandran in the railways. This uncle seemed to live in an
endless dream of introductory letters. Several relatives, chiefly
women, asked him why he did not sit for the Indian Civil Service
or the Indian Audit Service examination. Chandran felt flattered by
their faith in him. There were others who said that there was
nothing like a business occupation; start on a small capital and open
a shop; independence and profit. All sorts of persons advised him to
apply for a clerk's post in some Government office. Nothing like
Government service, they said; on the first of the month you were
sure of your money; security. Chandran had a feeling of persecution.
He opened his heart to his father when the latter was trimming the

roses early one morning.

'I am sorry, Father, that I ever passed the BA.'

'Why?'

'Why should everybody talk about my career? Why can't they mind their business?'

'It is the way of the world. You must not let that upset you. It is just a form of courtesy, you see.'

Then they began to talk of Chandran's future. His father gathered that Chandran had a vague desire to go to England and do something there. He did not consider the plan absurd himself.

'What do you propose to do in England?'

'I want to get a doctorate or something and come back, and then some quiet lectureship in some college will suit me wonderfully. Plenty of independence and leisure.'

After that Chandran went about with a freer mind. To his persecutors he would say: 'I am going to England next year.' Some demanded why he was not starting immediately. Chandran told them: 'We can't go to England on an impulse, can we?'

And now, without college or studies to fetter him, Chandran was enjoying a freedom he had never experienced in his life before. From his infant class up to BA, a period of over sixteen years, he had known nothing like this holiday, which stretched over six months. He would have enjoyed his freedom still more if Ramu had been there with him. After the results were announced Ramu disappeared. He went away to Bombay in search of employment, and drifted all over northern India without securing any. Chandran received only one card informing hint that Ramu had joined the law course in Poona.

So Chandran was compelled to organize his life without Ramu. He became a member of the Town Public Library, and read an enormous quantity of fiction and general literature. He discovered Carlyle. He found that after all Shakespeare had written some stirring dramas, and that several poets were not as dull as they were made out to be. There was no scheme or order in his study. He read books just as they came. He read a light humorist and switched on to Carlyle, and from there pounced on Shakespeare, and then wandered to Shaw and Wells. The thing that mattered most to him was that the book should be enjoyable, and he ruthlessly shut books that threatened to bore him.

After spending a large part of the day with books he went out in the evening for long walks, necessarily alone, since most of his friends had gone away. He went on long rambles by the river, returned home late, and sat up for an hour or two chatting with his parents, and then read a little in bed. As he settled down to this routine he got used to it and enjoyed this quiet life. Every day as he went through one item he eagerly looked forward to the next, and then the next, till he looked forward to the delicious surge of sleep as he put away his book for the night.

CHAPTER SEVEN

IT WAS ON one of his river ramblings that he met Malathi and thought that he would not have room for anything else in his mind. No one can explain the attraction between two human beings. It happens.

One evening he came to the river, and was loafing along it, when he saw a girl, about fifteen years old, playing with her younger sister on the sands. Chandran had been in the habit of staring at every girl who sat on the sand, but he had never felt before the acute interest he felt in this girl now. He liked the way she sat; he liked the way she played with her sister; he liked the way she dug her hands into the sand and threw it in the air. He paused only for a moment to observe the girl. He would have willingly settled there and spent the rest of his life watching her dig her hands into the sand. But that could not be done. There were a lot of people about.

He passed on. He went forward a few paces and wanted to turn back and take another look at the girl. But that could not be done. He felt that the scores of persons squatting on the sand were all watching him.

He went on his usual walk down to Nallappa's Grove, crossed the river, went up the opposite bank, and away into the fields there; but he caught himself more than once thinking of the girl. How old was she? Probably fourteen. Might be even fifteen or sixteen. If she was more than fourteen she must be married. There was a touch of despair in this thought. What was the use of thinking of a married girl? It would be very improper. He tried to force his mind to think of other things. He tried to engage it in his favourite subject—his trip to England in the coming year. If he was going to England how was he to dress himself? He had better get used to tie and shoes and coat and hat and knife and fork. He would get a first-class degree in England and come back and marry. What was the use of thinking of a married girl? Probably she was not married. Her parents were very likely rational and modern, people who abhorred the custom of rushing a young child into marriage. He tried to analyse why he was thinking of her. Why did he think of her so much? Was it her looks? Was she so good-looking as all that? Who could say? He hadn't noticed her before. Then how could he say that she was the most beautiful girl in the world? When did he say that? Didn't he? If not, why was he thinking of her so much? Chandran was puzzled, greatly puzzled by the whole thing.

He wondered next what her name might be. She looked like one with the name of Lakshmi. Quite a beautiful name, the name of the goddess of wealth, the spouse of god Vishnu, who was the protector of creatures.

That night he went home very preoccupied. It was at five o'clock that he had met her, and at nine he was still thinking of her.

After dinner he did not squat on the carpet in the hall, but preferred to go to his room and remain there alone. He tried to read a little; he was in the middle of Wells's *Tono Bungay*. He had found the book gripping, but now he felt it was obtrusive. He was irritated. He put away the book and sat staring at the wall. He presently realized that darkness would be more soothing. He blew out the lamp and sat in his chair. Suppose, though unmarried, she belonged to some other caste? A marriage would not be tolerated even between subsects of the same caste. If India was to attain salvation these watertight divisions must go—community, caste, sects, subsects, and still further divisions. He felt very indignant. He would set an example himself by marrying this girl whatever her caste or sect might be.

The next day he shaved with great care and paid a great deal of attention to his hair, and awaited the evening. When evening came he put on his chocolate-coloured tweed coat and started out. At five he was on the river bank, squatting on the sand near the spot where he had seen the girl the previous day. He sat there for over two hours. The girl did not come. Dozens of other townspeople came to the river and sprawled all over the place, but not that girl. Chandran rose and walked along, peering furtively at every group. It was a very keen search, but it brought forth nothing. Why wasn't she there? His heart beat fast at the sight of every figure that approached the river clad in a saree. It was seven-forty-five when he set his face homeward, feeling that his brilliantine, shave, ironed tweed coat were all wasted.

The next day he again went to the river and again waited till seven-forty-five in the evening, and went home dispirited. He tossed in bed all night. In moments he whispered the word 'Lakshmi', 'Lakshmi'. He suddenly pulled himself up and laughed at himself: it looked as if the girl had paid a first and last visit to the river, and it seemed more than likely that she belonged to another caste, and was married. What a fool he was to go on thinking of her night and day for three whole days. It was a ridiculous obsession. His sobriety ought to assert itself now. An idle brain was the devil's workshop. Too true. A brain given rest for over nine months brought one to this state.

He rose in the morning with a haggard face. His mother asked him if he was not well. Chandran felt that some explanation was due and said he had a terrible headache. His mother, standing two inches shorter than he, put out her hands, stroked his temples, gave him special coffee, and advised him to stay at home the whole day. Chandran felt that nothing could be better than that. He decided not to shave or comb his hair or wear a coat and go out. For he feared that if he went out he might be tempted to go on the foolish quest.

He stayed in his room all day. His father came in at midday and kept him company. He sat in the chair and talked of this and that. Chandran realized all of a sudden that he had better leave Malgudi. That would solve the problem.

'Father, will you let me go to Madras?'

'By all means, if you'd like a change.'

'I suppose it will be very hot there?'

'Must be. The saying is that Madras is hot for ten months in the year and hotter for two.'

'Then I don't want to go and fry myself there,' said Chandran.

'Try some other place. You can go to your aunt at Bangalore.'

'No, no. She will keep telling me what jewels she has got for her daughter. I can't stand her.' He decided that he would stay in the best place on earth, home.

Mother came in at about three o'clock to ask how he was feeling. Seenu came in at four-thirty, as soon as school was over, and stood near Chandran's bed, staring at him silently.

'What is it?' Chandran asked.

'Nothing. Why are you in bed?'

'Never mind why. What is the news in the school?'

'We are playing against the YMU on Saturday. After that we are meeting the Board School Eleven. What we can't understand is why the captain has left out Mohideen. He is bound to have a lot of trouble over that. People are prepared to take it up to the Head Master.'

He could not stay in bed beyond six-thirty. He got up, opened all the windows, washed his face, combed his hair, put on a coat (not the tweed one), and went out. What he needed, he told himself, was plenty of fresh air and exercise and things to think about. Since he wanted exercise he decided to avoid the riverside. The place, he persuaded himself, was stale and crowded. He wished today to take a walk at the very opposite end of the town, the Trunk Road. He walked a mile along the Trunk Road and turned back. He hurried back across Lawley Extension, Market Road and the North Street, and reached the river. It was dark and most people had gone home.

Chandran saw her at the river bank next evening. She was wearing a green saree, and playing with her little companion. Chandran saw her from a distance and went towards her as if drawn by a rope. But, on approaching her, his courage failed him, and he walked away in the opposite direction. Presently he stopped and blamed himself for wasting a good opportunity of making his person familiar to her; he turned once again with the intention of passing before her closely, slowly, and deliberately. At a distance he could look at her, but when he came close he felt self-conscious and awkward, and while passing actually in front of her he bent his head, fixed his gaze on the ground, and walked fast. He was away, many yards away, from her in a moment. He checked his pace once again and looked back for a fraction of a second, and was quite thrilled at the sight of the green saree in the distance. He did not dare to look longer; for he was obsessed with the feeling that he was being observed by the whole crowd on the river bank . . . He hoped that she had observed him. He hoped that she had noted his ironed coat. He stood there and debated with himself whether she had seen him or not. One part of him said that she could not have observed him, because he had walked very fast and because there were a lot of people passing and repassing on the sand. Chandran steadily discouraged this sceptical half of his mind, and lent his wholehearted support to the other half, which was saying that just as he had noticed her in a crowd she was sure to have noticed him. Destiny always worked that way. His well-ironed chocolate tweed was sure to invite notice. He hoped that he didn't walk clumsily in front of her. He again told himself she must have noticed that he was not like the rest of the crowd. And so why should he not now go and occupy a place that would be close to her and in the direct line of her vision? Starting was half the victory in love. His sceptical half now said that by this procedure he might scare her off the river for ever; but, said the other half, tomorrow she may not come to the river at all, and if you don't start an eye friendship immediately, you may not get the opportunity again for a million years . . . He was engaged in this internal controversy when he received a slap on the back and saw Veeraswami and Mohan, his old classmates, behind him.

'How are you, Chandran? It seems years since we met.'

'We met only last March, less than a year, you know,' said Chandran.

Mohan asked: 'Chandran, do you remember the evening we spent in your room, reading poetry?'

'Yes, yes. What have you done with your poems?'

'They are still with me.'

Chandran felt all his courtesy exhausted. He was not keen on reunions just then. He tried to get away. But Veeraswami would not let him go: 'A year since we met. I have been dying to see an old classmate, and you want to cut me! Won't you come and have a little coffee with us in some restaurant?' He hooked his arm in Chandran's and dragged him along. Chandran tried to resist, and then said: 'Let us go this way. I promised to meet somebody. I must see if he is there . . .' He pointed down the river, past the spot of green saree. They went in that direction. Mohan inquired three times what Chandran was doing and received no reply; Veeraswami was talking without a pause. Chandran pretended to listen to him, but constantly turned his head to his left and stole glances at something there; he had to do this without being noticed by his friends. Finally, when he passed before her, he looked at her for so short a space of time that she appeared only as a passing green blur . . . Before leaving the river bank he looked back only twice. He heartily disliked his companions.

'What are you doing now, Chandran?' Mohan asked, undefeated.

'Nothing at present. I am going to England in a few months.'

At this Veeraswami started a heated discourse on the value of going to England. 'What have we to learn from the English? I don't know when this craze for going to England will stop. It is a drain on the country's resources. What have we to learn from the English?'

'I may be going there to teach them something,' said Chandran. Even granted that she had not noticed him the first time, she couldn't have helped noticing him when he passed before her again; that was why he didn't look at her fully; he didn't want to embarrass her by meeting her gaze.

'Shall we go to the Welcome?' Veeraswami asked.

They had now left the river and were in North Street.

'Anywhere,' Chandran said mechanically.

'You seem to be worried over something,' Veeraswami said.

'Oh, nothing. I am sorry.' Chandran pulled himself up resolutely. Here were two fellows eager for his company, and he had no business to be absorbed in distant thoughts.

'Forgive me,' he said again.

They were now before the Welcome Restaurant, a small, smoky building, from which the smell of sweets and burning ghee assailed the nostrils of passers-by in the street.

They sat round an oily table in the dark hall. Serving boys were shouting menus and bills and were dashing hither and thither. A server came and asked: 'What will you have, sir?'

'What shall we have?'

'What will you have?'

'I want only coffee.'

'Have something with it.'

'Impossible. Only coffee.'

'Bring three cups of coffee, good, strong.'

Chandran asked: 'What are you doing, Mohan? Did you get through?'

'No. I failed, and my uncle cut me. I am now the Malgudi correspondent of the *Daily Messenger* of Madras. They have given me the whole district. They pay me three-eight per column of twenty-one inches.'

'Are you making much money?'

'Sometimes fifty, sometimes ten. It all depends on those rascals, mad fellows. Sometimes they cut everything that I send.'

'It is a moderate paper,' Veeraswami said jeeringly.

'I am not concerned with their policy,' Mohan said.

'What are you doing?' Chandran asked, turning to Veeraswami.

'It will take a whole day for me to tell you. I am starting a movement called the Resurrection Brigade. I am touring about a lot on that business.'

'What is the brigade?'

'It is only an attempt to prepare the country for revolution. Montagu-Chelmsford reforms, Simon Report, and what not, are all a fraud. Our politicians, including the Congressmen, are playing into the hands of the Imperialists. The Civil Disobedience Movement is a childish business. Our brigade will gain the salvation of our country by an original method. Will you join it? Mohan is already a member.'

Chandran promised to think it over, and asked what they expected Mohan to do for the movement.

'Everything. We want everybody there, poets, philosophers, musicians, sculptors, and swordsmen.'

'What is its strength now?'

'About twenty-five have so far signed the brigade pledge. I expect that in two years we shall have a membership of fifty thousand in south India alone.'

They finished their coffee and rose. They went back to the river, smoked cigarettes, and talked all the evening. Before parting, Chandran promised to see them again and asked them where they lived.

'I am staying with Mohan,' said Veeraswami.

'Where do you live, Mohan?'

'Room 14, Modern Indian Lodge, Mill Street.'

'Right. I shall drop in sometime,' said Chandran.

'I won't be in town after Tuesday. I am going into the country for six months,' said Veeraswami.

Chandran realized that friends and acquaintances were likely to prove a nuisance to him by the river. He decided to cut everyone hereafter. With this resolution he went to the Sarayu bank next evening. He also decided to be very bold, and indifferent to the public's observation and criticism.

She was there with her little companion.

Chandran went straight to a spot just thirty yards from where she sat, and settled down there. He had determined to stare at her this evening. He might even throw in an elegant wink or smile. He was going to stare at her and take in a lot of details regarding her features. He had not made out yet whether she was fair or light brown; whether she had long hair or short, and whether her eyes were round or almond-shaped; and he had also some doubts about her nose.

He sat at this thirty yards range and kept throwing at her a side glance every fifth second. He noticed that she played a great deal with her little companion. He wanted to go to her and ask whether the little companion was her sister or cousin and how old she was. But he abandoned the idea. A man of twenty-two going up and conversing with a grown-up girl, a perfect stranger, would be affording a very uncommon sight to the public.

This optical communion became a daily habit. His powers of observation and deduction increased tremendously. He gathered several facts about the girl. She wore a dark saree and a green saree alternately. She came to the river chiefly for the sake of her little companion. She was invariably absent on Fridays and came late on Wednesdays. Chandran concluded from this that the girl went to the temple on Friday evenings, and was delayed by a music master or a stitching master on Wednesdays. He further gathered that she was of a religious disposition, and was accomplished in the art of music or embroidery. From her regularity he concluded that she was a person of very systematic habits. The fact that she played with her young companion showed that she had a loving disposition. He concluded that she had no brothers, since not a single soul escorted her on any evening. Encouraged by this conclusion, he wondered if he should not stop her and talk to her when she rose to go home. He might even accompany her to her house. That might become a beautiful habit. What wonderful things he would have to say to her. When the traffic of the town had died, they could walk together under the moon or in magic starlight. He would stop a few yards from her house. What a parting of sweetness and pain! . . . It must be noted that in this dream the young companion did not exist, or, if she did, she came to the river and went home all by herself.

An evening of this optical fulfilment filled him with tranquillity. He left the river and went home late in the evening, meditating on

God, and praying to Him with concentration that He would bless this romance with success. All night he repeated her name, 'Lakshmi', and fervently hoped that her soul heard his call through the night.

He had lived for over a month in a state of bliss, notwithstanding his ignorance. He began to feel now that he ought to be up and doing and get a little more practical. He could not go on staring at her on the sands all his life. He must know all about her.

He followed her at a distance of about half a furlong on a dark evening when she returned home from the river. He saw her enter a house in Mill Street. He paced before the house slowly, twice, slowing up to see if there was any board before the house. There was none.

He remembered suddenly that Mohan lived in Mill Street. Room number 14, Modern Indian Lodge, he had said. He went up and down the street in search of the hotel. At last he found it was the building opposite the girl's house. There was a signboard, but that could not be seen in the dark. Room number 14 was half a cubicle on the staircase landing. The cubicle was divided by a high wooden partition into Room 14 and Room 15.

Mohan was delighted to receive Chandran.

'Is Veeraswami gone?' Chandran asked.

'Weeks ago,' replied Mohan.

There was not a single table or chair in the room. Mohan lived on a striped carpet spread on the floor. He sat on it reclining against the wooden partition. There was a yellow trunk in a corner of the room, on which a shining nickel flower-vase was kept with some paper flowers in it. The room received its light and ventilation from the single window in Room 15, over the wooden partition. A bright gas lamp hung over the wooden partition and shed its greenish glare impartially on Room 14 and Room 15.

'Would you believe it? I have never been in this street before,' said Chandran.

'Indeed! But why should you come here? You live at the south end while this is the east end of the town.'

'I like this street,' Chandran said. 'I wonder why this is called Mill Street. Are all the people that live here millowners?'

'Nothing of the kind. Years ago there were two weaving mills at the end of the street. There are all sorts of people here.'

'Oh. Any particularly important person?'

'None that I can think of.'

It was on Chandran's lips, at this point, to ask who lived in the opposite house. But he merely said that he wished to meet his friend oftener in his room.

'I go out news-hunting at ten in the morning and return at about four, after posting my letters. I do not usually go out after that. You can come any time you please,' said Mohan.

'Have you no holidays?'

'On Sundays we have no paper. And so on Saturday I have a holiday. I spend the whole day in the room. Please do come any time you like, and as often as you like.'

'Thanks, thanks. I have absolutely no company. I shall be delighted to come here frequently.'

CHAPTER EIGHT

THROUGH MOHAN'S COOPERATION Chandran learnt that his sweetheart's name was Malathi, that she was unmarried, and that she was the daughter of Mr D.W. Krishna Iyer, head clerk in the Executive Engineer's office.

The suffix to the name of the girl's father was a comforting indication that he was of the same caste and subcaste. Chandran shuddered at the thought of all the complications that he would have had to face if the gentleman had been Krishna Iyengar, or Krishna Rao, or Krishna Mudaliar. His father would certainly cast him off if he tried to marry out of caste.

Chandran took it all as a favourable sign, as an answer to his prayers, which were growing intenser every day. In each fact, that Mohan lived in the hotel opposite her house, that she was unmarried, that her father was an 'Iyer', Chandran felt that God was revealing Himself.

Chandran prayed to God to give him courage, and went to his father to talk to him about his marriage. His courage failed him at the last moment, and he went away after discussing some fatuous subject. The next day he again went to his father with the same resolution and again lapsed into fatuity. He went back to his room and regretted his cowardice. He would be unworthy of Malathi if he was going to be such a spineless worm. Afraid of a father! He was not a baby asking for a toy, but a full-grown adult out on serious business, very serious business. It was very doubtful if a squirming coward would be any good to Malathi as a husband.

He went back to his father, who was on the veranda reading something. Mother had gone out to see some friends; Seenu had gone to school. This was the best time to talk to Father confidentially.

Father put down the book on seeing Chandran, and pulled the

spectacles from over his nose. Chandran drew a chair close to Father's easy chair.

'Have you read this book, Chandran?'

Chandran looked at it—some old novel, Dickens. 'No.' At another time he would have added, 'I hate Dickens's laborious humour,' and involved himself in a debate. But now he merely said, 'I will try to read it later.' He did not want to throw away precious time in literary discussions.

'Father, please don't mistake me. I want to marry D.W. Krishna Iyer's daughter.'

Father put on his spectacles and looked at his son with a frown. He sat up and asked: 'Who is he?'

'Head clerk in the Executive Engineer's office.'

'Why do you want to marry his daughter?'

'I like her.'

'Do you know the girl?'

'Yes. I have seen her often.'

'Where?'

Chandran told him.

'Have you spoken to each other?'

'No . . .'

'Does she know you?'

'I don't know.'

Father laughed, and it cut into Chandran's soul.

Father asked: 'In that case why this girl alone and not any other?'

Chandran said: 'I like her,' and left Father's company abruptly as Father said: 'I don't know anything about these things. I must speak to your mother.'

Later Mother came into Chandran's room and asked, 'What is all this?' Chandran answered with an insolent silence.

'Who is this girl?' There was great anxiety in her voice. Chandran told her. She was very disappointed. A head clerk's daughter was not what she had hoped to get for her son. 'Chandar, why won't you consider any of the dozens of girls that have been proposed to you?'

Chandran rejected this suggestion indignantly.

'But suppose those girls are richer and more beautiful?'

'I don't care. I shall marry this girl and no one else.'

'But how are you sure they are prepared to give their daughter to you?'

'They will have to.'

'Extraordinary! Do you think marriage is a child's game? We don't know anything about them, who they are, what they are, what they are worth, if the stars and the other things about the girl are all right, and above all, whether they are prepared to marry their girl at all . . .'

'They will have to. I hear that this season she will be married because she is getting on for sixteen.'

'Sixteen!' Mother screamed. 'They can't be all right if they have kept the girl unmarried till sixteen. She must have attained puberty ages ago. They can't be all right. We have a face to keep in this town. Do you think it is all child's play?' She left the room in a temper.

In a few days this hostility had to be abandoned, because Chandran's parents could not bear for long the sight of an unhappy Chandran. For his sake they were prepared to compromise to this extent: they were prepared to consider the proposal if it came from the other side. Whatever happened they would not take the initiative in the matter; for they belonged to the bridegroom's side, and according to time-honoured practice it was the bride's people who proposed first. Anything done contrary to this would make them the laughing stock of the community.

Chandran raved: 'To the dust-pot with your silly customs.'

But his mother replied that she at any rate belonged to a generation which was in no way worse than the present one for all its observances; and as long as she lived she would insist on respecting the old customs. Ordinary talk at home was becoming rarer every day. It was always a debate on Custom and Reason. His father usually remained quiet during these debates. One of the major mysteries in life for Chandran at this period was the question as to which side his father favoured. He did not appear to place active obstacles in Chandran's way, but he did little else. He appeared to distrust his own wisdom in these matters and to have handed the full rein to his wife. Chandran once or twice tried to sound him and gain him to his side; but he was evasive and non-committal.

Chandran's only support and consolation at this juncture was Mohan. To his room he went every night after dinner. This visit was not entirely from an unmixed motive. While on his way he could tarry for a while before her house and gladden his heart with a sight of her under the hall lamp as she passed from one part of the house to another. Probably she was going to bed; blessed be those pillows. Or probably she went in and read; ah, blessed books with the touch of her hands on them. He would often speculate what hour she would go to bed, what hour she would rise, and how she lay down and slept and how her bed looked. Could he not just dash into the house, hide in the passage, steal up to her bed at night, crush her in his arms, and carry her away?

If it happened to be late, and the lights in the house were put out, he would walk distractedly up and down before the house, and then go to Room 14 of the Modern Indian Lodge.

Mohan would put away whatever poem he was writing. But for him Chandran would have been shrivelled up by the heat of a hopeless love. Mohan would put away his pad, and clear a space on the carpet for Chandran.

Chandran would give him the latest bulletin from the battle front, and then pass on to a discussion of theories.

'If the girl's father were called something other than a head clerk, and given a hundred more to his pay, I am sure your parents would move heaven and earth to secure his alliance,' said the poet.

'Why should we be cudgelled and nose-led by our elders?' Chandran asked indignantly. 'Why can't we be allowed to arrange our lives as we please? Why can't they leave us to rise or sink on our own ideals?'

These were mighty questions; and the poet tackled them in his own way. 'Money is the greatest God in life. Father and mother and brother do not care for anything but your money. Give them money and they will leave you alone. I am just writing a few lines entitled "Moneylove". It is free verse. You must hear it. I have dedicated it to you.' Mohan picked up the pad and read:

'The parents love you, you thought.
No, no, not you, my dear.
They've loved nothing less for its own sake.
They fed you and petted you and pampered you
Because some day they hope you will bring them money;
Much money, so much and more and still more;
Because some day, they hope, you'll earn a
Bride who'll bring much money, so much and
More and still more . . .'

There were two more stanzas in the same strain. It brought tears to Chandran's eyes. He hated his father and mother. He took this poem with him when he went home.

He gave it to his father next day. Father read through it twice and asked with a dry smile: 'Did you write this?'

'Never mind the authorship,' Chandran said.

'Do you believe what these lines say?'

'I do,' said Chandran, and did not stay there for further talk.

When he was gone Father explained the poem to Mother, who began to cry. Father calmed her and said: 'This is what he seems to feel. I don't know what to do.'

'We have promised to consider it if it is made from that side. What more can we do?'

'I don't know.'

'They seem to be thorough rogues. The marriage season has already begun. Why can't they approach us? They expect Chandran to go to them, touch their feet, and beg them for their girl.'

'They probably do not know that Chandran is available,' said Father.

'Why do you defend them? They can't be ignorant of the existence of a possible bridegroom like Chandran. That man, the girl's father, seems to be a deep man. He is playing a deep game. He is waiting for our boy to go to him, when he can get a good husband for his daughter without giving a dowry and without an expensive wedding . . . This boy Chandran is talking nonsense. This is what we get from our children for all our troubles . . . I am in a mood to let him do anything he likes . . . But what more can we do? I shall drown myself in Sarayu before I allow any proposal to go from here.'

CHAPTER NINE

CHANDRAN'S PARENTS SENT for Ganapathi Sastrigal, who was match-maker in general to a few important families in Malgudi. He had a small income from his lands in the village; he was once a third clerk in a Collector's office, which also gave him now a two-digit pension. After retiring from Government service he settled down as a general adviser, officiating priest at rituals, and a match-maker. He confined his activities to a few rich families in the town.

He came next day in the hot sun, and went straight into the kitchen, where Chandran's mother was preparing some sweets.

'Oh, come in, come in,' Chandran's mother exclaimed on seeing him. 'Why have you been neglecting us so long? It is over a year since you came to our house.'

'I had to spend some months in the village. There was some dispute about the lands; and also some arrears had to be collected from the tenants. I tell you lands are a curse . . .'

'Oh, you are standing,' she cried, and said to the cook, 'take a sitting-board and give it to him.'

'No, no, no. Don't trouble yourself. I can sit on the floor,' said the old man. He received the proffered sitting-board, but gently put it away and sat on the floor.

'Won't you take a little tiffin and coffee?' Chandran's mother asked.

'Oh, no. Don't trouble yourself. I have just had it all in my house. Don't trouble yourself.'

'Absolutely no trouble,' she said, and set before him a plate of sweets and a tumbler of coffee.

He ate the sweets slowly, and poured the coffee down his throat, holding the tumbler high over his lips. He said: 'I have taken this because you have put it before me, and I don't like to see anything wasted. My digestion is not as good as it was before I had the jaundice. I recently showed myself to a doctor, Doctor Kesavan. I wonder if you know him? He is the son-in-law of Raju of Trichinopoly, whom I have known since his boyhood. The doctor said that I must give up tamarind and use only lemon in its place . . .'

Afterwards he followed her out of the kitchen to the back veranda of the house. Chandran's mother spread a mat before him and requested him to sit on it, and opened the subject.

'Do you know D.W. Krishna Iyer's family?'

The old man sat thinking for a while, and then said: 'D.W. Krishnan; you mean Coimbatore Appayi's nephew, the fellow who is in the Executive Engineer's office? I have known their family for three generations.'

'I am told that he has a daughter ready for marriage.'

The old man remained vey thoughtful and said: 'Yes, it is true. He has a daughter old enough to have a son, but not yet married.'

'Why is it so? Anything wrong with the family?'

'Absolutely nothing,' replied the old man. He now saw he ought not to be critical in his remaks. He tried to mend his previous statement. 'Absolutely nothing. Anyone that says such a thing will have a rotting tongue. The girl is only well-grown, and I don't think she is as old as she looks. She can't be more than fifteen. This has become the standard age for girls nowadays. Everybody holds advanced views in these days. Even in an ancient and orthodox family like Sadasiva Iyer's they married a girl recently at fifteen!'

This was very comforting to Chandran's mother. She asked: 'Do you think that it is a good family?'

'D.W. Krishnan comes of a very noble family. His father was . . .' The Sastrigal went on giving an impressive history of the family, ranging over three generations. 'If Krishnan is now only a head clerk it is because when he came into the property his elder brothers had squandered . all of it and left only debts and encumbrances. Krishanan was rocked in a golden cradle when he was young, but became the foster-son of misfortune after his father died. It is all fate. Who can foresee what is going to happen?'

After two hours of talk he left the house on a mission; that was to go to D.W. Krishna Iyer's house and ascertain if they were going to marry their girl this season, and to move them to take the initiative in a proposal for an alliance with Chandran's family. The old man was to give out that he was acting independently, and on his own initiative.

Next day Ganapathi Sastrigal came with good news. As soon as Chandran's mother saw him at the gate she cried: 'Sastrigal has come!'

As soon as he climbed the veranda steps Chandran's father said: 'Ah, come in, come in, Sastriar,' and pushed a chair towards him. The Sastrigal sat on the edge of the chair, wiped the sweat off his nape with his upper cloth, and said to Mother, 'Summer has started very early this year . . . Do you cool water in a mud jug?'

'Certainly, otherwise it is impossible to quench our thirst in summer. It is indispensable.'

'If that is so, please ask your cook to bring me a tumbler of jug water.'

'You must drink some coffee.'

'Don't trouble yourself. Water will do.'

'Will you take a little tiffin?'

'No, no. Give me only water. Don't trouble yourself about coffee or tiffin.'

'Absolutely no trouble,' said Mother, and went in and returned with a tumbler of coffee.

'You are putting yourself to great trouble bringing me this coffee,' said the old man, taking the tumbler.

'Have you any news for us?' she asked.

'Plenty, plenty,' said the old man. 'I went to D.W. Krishnan's house this morning; as you may already know, we have known each other for three generations. He was not at home when I went. He had gone to see his officer or on some such work, but his wife was there. She asked her daughter to spread a mat for me, and then sent her in to bring me coffee. I am simply filled with coffee everywhere. I drank the coffee and gave the tumbler back to the girl . . . She is a smart girl; stands very tall, and has a good figure. Her skin is fair; may be called fair, though not as fair as that of our lady here; but she is by no means to be classed as a dark girl. Her mother says that the girl has just completed her fourteenth year.' Chandran's mother felt a great load off her mind now. She wouldn't have to marry her son to a girl over sixteen, and incur the comments of the community.

'I knew all along that there couldn't be truth in what people said . . .' she said.

'And then we talked of one thing and another,' said the
Sastrigal, 'and the subject came to marriage. You can take it from
me that they are going to marry their girl this season. She will
certainly be married in *Panguni* month. Just as I was thinking of
going, Krishnan came in. He is a very good fellow. He showed me
the regard due to my age, and due to me for my friendship with his
father and uncles. He is very eager to complete the marriage this
season. He asked me to help him to secure a bridegroom. I
suggested two or three others and then your son. I may tell you that
he thinks he will be extraordinarily blessed if he can secure an
alliance with your family. He feels you may not stoop to his status.'

'Status! Status!' Chandran's mother exclaimed. 'We have seen
with these very eyes people who were rich once, but are in the
streets now, and such pranks of fate. What a foolish notion to
measure status with money. It is here today and gone tomorrow.
What I would personally care for most in any alliance would be
character and integrity.'

'That I can guarantee,' said the Sastrigal. 'When I mentioned
this family, the lady was greatly elated. She seems to know you all
very well. She even said that she and you were related. It seems
that your maternal grandfather's first wife and her paternal
grandfather were sister and brother, not cousins, but direct sister
and brother.'

'Ah, I did not know that. I am so happy to hear it.' She then
asked: 'Have you any idea how much they are prepared to spend?'

'Yes. I got it out in a manner; very broadly, of course; but that
will do for the present. I think they are prepared to give a cash
dowry of about two thousand rupees, silver vessels, and spend
about a thousand on the wedding celebrations. These will be in
addition to about a thousand worth of diamond and gold on the
girl.'

Chandran's mother was slightly disappointed at the figures.
'We can settle all that later.'

'Quite right,' said the old man. 'Tomorrow, if everything is
auspicious, they will send you the girl's horoscope. We shall proceed
with the other matters after comparing the horoscopes. I am certain
that this marriage will take place very soon. Even as I started for
their house a man came bearing pots of foaming toddy; it is an
excellent omen. I am certain that this alliance will he completed.'

'Why bother with horoscopes?' asked Chandran's father. 'Personally, I have no faith in them.'

'You must not say that,' said the Sastrigal. 'How are we to know whether two persons brought together will have health, happiness, harmony, and long life, if we do not study their horoscopes individually and together?'

Chandran felt very happy that her horoscope was coming. He imagined that the very next thing after the horoscope would be marriage. The very fact that they were willing to send the girl's horoscope for comparison proved that they were not averse to this alliance. They were probably goaded on by the girl. He had every reason to believe that the girl had told her parents she would marry Chandran and no one else. But how could she know him or his name? Girls had a knack of learning of these things by a sort of sixth sense. How splendid of her to speak out her mind like this, brave girl. If her mind matched her form, it must be one of the grandest things in the world . . .

The thought of her melted him. He clutched his pillow and cried in the darkness: 'Darling, what are you doing? Do you hear me?'

In these days he met her less often at the river, but he made it up by going to Mill Street and wandering in front of her house until her form passed under the hall light. He put down her absence at the river to her desire to save Chandran's reputation. She felt, Chandran thought, that seeing him every day at the river would give rise to gossip. Such a selfless creature. Would rather sacrifice her evening's outing than subject Chandran to gossip. Chandran had no doubt that she was going to be the most perfect wife a man could ever hope to get.

As he sauntered in front of her house, Chandran would often ask God when His grace would bend low so that Chandran might cease to be a man in the street and stride into the house as a son-in-law. After they were married, he would tell her everything. They would sit in their creeper-covered villa on the hill-slope, just those two, and watch the sun set. In the afterglow of the evening he would tell her of his travails, and they would both laugh.

The next day Ganapathi Sastrigal did not come, and Chandran began to think wild things. What was the matter? Had they suddenly backed out?

The horoscope was not sent on the next day either. Chandran asked his mother every half-hour if it had come, and finally suggested that some one should be sent to bring it. When this suggestion reached Father's ears, he asked: 'Why don't you yourself go and ask them for a copy of the girl's horoscope?'

Chandran's mind being in a state of lowered efficiency, he asked eagerly: 'Shall I? I thought I shouldn't do it.'

Father laughed and told it to Mother, who became scared and said: 'Chandra, please don't do it. It would be a very curious procedure. They will send the horoscope themselves.'

Father said to Chandran: 'Look here, you will never be qualified to marry unless you cultivate a lot of patience. It is the only power that you will be allowed to exercise when you are married.'

Mother looked at Father suspiciously and said: 'Will you kindly make your meaning clearer?'

Chandran went to his room in a very distracted state. He tried to read a novel, but his mind kept wandering. Seenu, his younger brother, came in and asked: 'Brother, are you not well?' He could not understand what was wrong with Chandran. He very much missed Chandran's company in the after-dinner chatting group; he very much missed his supervision, though it had always been aggressive. Chandran looked at him without giving any answer. Seenu wanted to ask if his brother was about to be married, but he was too shy to mention a thing like marriage. So he asked if Chandran was unwell. Chandran answered, after the question was repeated: 'I am quite well; why?'

'You don't look well.'

'Quite likely.'

'That is all I wanted to know. Because Mother said that you were going to be married.'

There was no obvious connection between the two, but Seenu felt he had led on to the delicate topic with cunning diplomacy.

Chandran asked: 'Boy, would you like to have a sister-in-law?'

Seenu slunk behind the chair with shame at this question.

Chandran made it worse by asking: 'Would you like a sister-in-law to be called Malathi?'

At this Seenu was so abashed that he ran out of the room, leaving Chandran to the torture of his thoughts and worries.

When the horoscope did not come on the next day, Chandran went to Mohan and asked: 'Why should I not go to Mr Krishna Iyer and ask for it?'

Mohan replied: 'Why have you not done it already?'

'I thought that it might be irregular.'

'Would it be different now?'

Chandran remained silent. His special pride in the conducting of his romance so far was that he had not committed the slightest irregularity at any time. He felt that he could easily have talked to her when she was alone on the sands; he could have tried to write to her; he could have befriended Mr Krishna Iyer and asked him for the hand of his daughter; and he could have done a number of other things, but he didn't, for the sake of his parents; he wanted everything to be done in the correct, orthodox manner.

Mohan said: 'I don't care for orthodoxy and correctness myself. But since you care for those things, at least for the sake of your parents keep it up and don't do anything rashly now.'

But Chandran wailed that they had not sent the horoscope. What could it mean except coldness on their part?

Mohan said: 'Till they show some more solid proof of their coldness we ought not to do anything.'

Chandran rested in gloom for a while and then came out with a bright idea: 'I have got to know the girl's father, and you must help me.'

'How?'

'You are a newspaper correspondent, and you have access everywhere. Why don't you go to his house on some work; say that you want some news connected with the Engineering department. People are awfully nice to newspaper correspondents.'

'They are. But where do you come in?'

'You can take me along with you and introduce me to him. You may even say that I am your assistant.'

'How is that going to help you?'

'You had better leave that to me.'

'There is absolutely no excuse for me to go and see him.'

'There is a rumour of a bridge over the Sarayu, near Nallappa's Grove. You must know if it is true. Engineering department.' Mohan realized that love sharpened the wits extraordinarily.

While walking home Chandran formulated a perfect scheme for interviewing Mr D.W. Krishna Iyer. He would do it without Mohan's help. The scheme that he had suggested to Mohan fired his imagination. Chandran decided to go and knock on the door of Krishna Iyer's house. Malathi would open the door. He would ask her if her father was in, and tell her he was there in order to know if it was a fact that there was going to he a bridge over the Sarayu; he could tell her he would call in again and go away. This would help him to see her at close quarters, and to decide once and for all whether her eyes were round or almond-shaped, and whether her complexion was light brown or dusky translucence. He might even carry a small camera with him and take a snapshot of her. For one of the major exercises for his mind at that time was trying to recollect the features of Malathi, which constantly dissolved and tormented him. His latest hobby was scanning the faces of passers-by in the streets to see if any one resembled her. She had no double in the world. There was a boy in a wayside shop whose arched, dark eyebrows seemed to Chandran to resemble Malathi's; Chandran often went to that shop and bought three-pies' worth of peppermint and gazed at the boy's eyebrows.

There was good news for him at home. Ganapathi Sastrigal came in the evening with the girl's horoscope. He explained that the delay was due to the fact that the preceding days were inauspicious. He took Chandran's horoscope with him, to give to the girl's people.

So the first courtesies were exchanged between the families. As Chandran looked at the small piece of paper on which the horoscope was drawn, his heart bubbled over with joy. He noticed that the corners of the paper were touched with saffron—a mark of auspiciousness. So they had fully realized that it was an auspicious undertaking. Did not that fact indicate that they approved of this bridegroom and were anxious to secure him? If they were anxious to secure him, did not that mean that she would soon be his? Chandran read the horoscope a number of times, though he understood very little of it. It dissipated his accumulated gloom in a moment.

Chandran was very happy the whole of the next day; but his mother constantly checked his exuberance: 'Chandra, you must not think that the only thing now to be settled is the date of the marriage. God helping, all the difficulties will be solved, but there are yet a number of preliminaries to be settled. First, our astrologer must tell us if your horoscope can be matched with the girl's; and then I don't know what their astrologer will say. Let us hope for the best. After that, they must come and invite us to see the girl.'

'I have seen the girl, Mother, and I like her.'

'All the same they must invite us, and we must go there formally. After that they must come and ask us if you like the girl. And the terms of the marriage must be discussed and settled . . . I don't mean to discourage you, but you must be patient till all this is settled.'

Chandran sat biting his nails: 'But, Mother, you won't create difficulties over the dowry?'

'We shall see. We must not be too exacting, nor can we cheapen ourselves.'

'But suppose you haggle too much?'

'Don't you worry about anything, boy. If they won't give you the girl on reasonable conditions, I shall get you other girls a thousand times more suitable.'

'Don't talk like that, Mother. I shall never forgive you if this marriage does not take place through your bickerings over the dowry and the presents.'

'We have a status and a prestige to keep. We can't lower ourselves unduly.'

'You care more for your status than for the happiness of your son.'

'It doesn't seem proper for you to be speaking like this, Chandra.'

Chandran argued and tried to prove that demanding a cash dowry amounted to extortion. He said that the bridegroom's parents exploited the anxiety of the parents of a girl, who must be married before she attained puberty. This kind of talk always irritated Chandran's mother. She said: 'My father gave seven thousand in cash to your father, and over two thousand in silver vessels, and spent nearly five thousand on wedding celebrations. What was wrong in it? How are we any the worse for it? It is the duty of every father to set some money apart for securing a son-in-law. We can't disregard custom.'

Chandran said that it was all irrational extravagance and that the total expenses for a marriage ought not to exceed a hundred rupees.

'You may go and tell your girl's father that, and finish your marriage and come home. I shall gladly receive you and your wife, but don't expect any of us to attend the wedding. If you want us there, everything must be done in the proper manner.'

'But, Mother,' Chandran pleaded, 'you will be reasonable in your demands, won't you? They are not well-to-do.'

'We shall see; but don't try to play their lawyer already. Time enough for that.'

Father was dressing to go out. Chandran went to him and reported his mother's attitude. Father said: 'Don't be frightened. She doesn't mean you any harm.'

'But suppose she holds to a big dowry and they can't pay. What is to happen?'

'Well, well, there is time to think of that yet. They have taken your horoscope. Let them come and tell us what they think of the horoscopes.'

He took his walking-stick and started out. Chandran followed him to the gate, pleading. He wanted his father to stop and assure him of his support against Mother.

But Father merely said: 'Don't worry,' and went out.

CHAPTER TEN

THREE DAYS LATER a peon from the Engineering department came with a letter for Father. Father, who was on the veranda, took it, and after reading it, passed it on to Chandran, who was sitting in a chair with a book. The letter read:

> Dear and respected sir—I am returning herewith the copy of your son's horoscope, which you so kindly sent to me for comparison with my daughter's. Our family astrologer, after careful study and comparison, says that the horoscopes cannot be matched. Since I have great faith in horoscopy, and since I have known from experience that the marriage of couples ill-matched in the stars often leads to misfortune and even tragedy, I have to seek a bridegroom elsewhere. I hope that your honoured self, your wife, and your son will forgive me for the unnecessary trouble I have caused you. No one can have a greater regret at missing an alliance with your family than I. However, we can only propose. He on the Thirupathi Hills alone knows what is best for us.
>
> With regards,
> Yours sincerely,
> D.W. Krishnan.

Chandran gave the letter back to his father, rose without a word, and went to his room. Father sat tapping the envelope on his left hand, and called his wife.

'Here they have written that the horoscopes don't match.'

'Have they? . . . H'm. I knew all along that they were up to some such trick. If there is any flaw in the horoscope it must be in the girl's, not in the boy's. His is a first-class horoscope. They want a cheap bridegroom, somebody who will be content with a dowry

of one hundred rupees and a day's celebration of the wedding, and
they know that they cannot get Chandra on those terms. They want
some excuse to back out now.' She remained silent for a while, and
said: 'So much the better. I have always disliked this proposal to
tack Chandran on to a hefty, middle-aged girl. There are fifty girls
waiting to be married to him.'

Just when Father was dressed and ready to go out, Chandran
came out of his room and said in a voice that was thick: 'Father, will
you still try and find out if something can't be done?'

Father was about to answer: 'Don't worry about this girl, I shall
get you another girl,' but he looked up and saw that Chandran's
eyes were red. So he said: 'Don't worry. I shall find out what is
wrong and try to set it right.' He went out and Chandran went back
to his room and bolted the door. Chandran's father wrote next day:

> Dear Mr Krishnan—I shall be very glad if you will kindly
> come and see me this evening. I meant to call on you, but
> I did not know what hour would suit you. Since I am
> always free, I shall be at your service and await the pleasure
> of meeting you.

Mr Krishna Iyer came that evening. After the courtesies of coffee
and inane inquiries were over, Chandran's father asked: 'Now, sir,
please tell me why the horoscopes don't match.'

'I ought not to be saying it, sir, but there is a flaw in your son's
horoscope. Our astrologer has found that the horoscopes cannot be
matched. If my girl's horoscope had Moon or Mars in the seventh
house, there couldn't be a better match than your son for her. But
as it is . . .'

'Are you sure?'

'I know a little astrology myself. I am prepared to overlook
many things in a horoscope. I don't usually concern myself with the
factors that indicate prosperity, wealth, progeny, and all that. I
usually overlook them. But I can't ignore the question of longevity.
I know hundreds of cases where the presence of Mars in this house
. . . I can tell you that . . .' He hesitated to say it. 'It kills the wife
soon after the marriage,' he said, when pressed by Chandran's
father.

Chandran's father was for dropping the question at this point,
but when he remembered that Chandran had shut himself in his
room, he sent for one Srouthigal, an eminent astrologer and almanac-

compiler in the town.

The next day there was a conference over the question of the stars and their potency. After four hours of intricate calculations and the filling of several sheets of paper with figures, Srouthigal said that there was nothing wrong with Chandran's horoscope. D.W. Krishna Iyer was sent for, and he came. Srouthigal looked at Krishna Iyer and said: 'These two horoscopes are well matched.'

'Did you notice the Mars?'

'Yes, but it is powerless now. It is now under the sway of the Sun, which looks at it from the fifth house.'

'But I doubt it, sir,' Krishna Iyer said.

Srouthigal thrust the papers into Krishna Iyer's hands, and asked: 'How old is the boy?'

'Nearly twenty-three.'

'What is twelve and eight?'

'Twenty.'

'How can the boy be affected by it at twenty-three? If he had married at twenty, he might have had to marry again, but not now. Mars became powerless when the boy was twenty years, three months, and five days old.'

'But I get it differently in my calculations,' said Krishna Iyer. 'The power of Mars lasts till the boy reaches twenty-five years and eight months.'

'Which almanac do you follow?' asked Srouthigal, with a fiery look.

'The *Vakya*,' said Krishna Iyer.

'There you are,' said Srouthigal. 'Why don't you base your calculations on the *Drig* almanac?'

'From time immemorial we have followed only the *Vakya*, and nothing has gone wrong so far. I think it is the only true almanac.'

'You are making a very strange statement,' said the Srouthigal, with a sneer.

When he went home Krishna Iyer took the papers with him, promising to calculate again and reconsider. He wrote to Chandran's father next day:

I worked all night, till about 4 a.m., on the horoscopes. Our astrologer was also with me. We have not arrived at any substantially different results now. The only change we find is that the Sun's sway comes in the boy's twenty-fifth

year and fourth month and not in the eighth month as I
stated previously.

Anyone who is not a fanatic of the *Drig* system will see
that the potency of Mars lasts very nearly till the boy's
twenty-fifth year. This is not a matter in which we can take
risks. It is a question of life and death to a girl. Mars has
never been known to spare. He kills.

I seek your forgiveness for all the trouble I may have
caused you in this business. I cannot find adequate words
to express how unhappy I am to miss the opportunity of an
alliance with your great house. I hope God will bless Mr
Chandran with a suitable bride soon . . .

Chandran's mother raved: 'Why can't you leave these creatures
alone? A black dot on Chandran's horoscope is what we get for
associating with them. If they go on spreading the rumour that
Chandran has Mars, a nice chance he will have of ever getting a girl.
This is what we get for trying to pick up something from the
gutter.'

When she was gone, Chandran suggested to his father: 'Let us
grant that Mars lasts till my twenty-fifth year. I am nearly twenty-
three now. I shall be twenty-five very soon. Why don't you tell
them that I will wait till my twenty-fifth year; let them also wait for
two years. Let us come to an understanding with them.'

Chandran's father knew that it would be perfectly useless to
reason things with Chandran. Hence he said that he would try to
meet Krishna Iyer and suggest this to him.

Thereafter every day Chandran privately asked his father if he
had met Krishna Iyer, and Father gave the stock reply that Krishna
Iyer could not be found either at home or in his office.

After waiting for a few days Chandran wrote a letter to Malathi. He
guarded against making it a love letter. It was, according to
Chandran's belief, a simple, matter-of-fact piece of writing. It only
contained an account of his love for her. It explained to her the
difficulty in the horoscope, and asked her if she was prepared to
wait for him for two years. Let her write the single word 'Yes' or
'No' on a piece of paper and post it to him. He enclosed a stamped
addressed envelope for a reply.

He took the letter to Mohan and said: 'This is my last chance.'

'What is this?'

'It is a letter to her.'

'Oh, God! You can't do that!'

'It is not a love letter. It is a dry, business letter. You must see that it is somehow delivered to her.'

'Have I to wait for a reply?'

'No. She can post a reply. I have arranged for it.'

'They will shoo me out if they see me delivering a letter to a grown-up girl.'

'But you must somehow manage it for my sake. This is my last attempt. I shall wait till I receive a reply . . .' said Chandran, and completed the sentence in sobs.

Next morning he went to the post office and asked the Lawley Extension postman if there was any letter for him. This became a daily routine. Day followed day thus. He rarely went to the river now. He avoided going to the Modern Indian Lodge because it was opposite her house.

On an evening, a fortnight later, Chandran started for the Modern Indian Lodge. 'I must grit my teeth and pass before her house, go to the hotel, see Mohan, and ask him why there is no letter yet,' he told himself.

When he came to Mill Street he heard a drum and pipe music. His heart beat fast. When he reached the Modern Indian Lodge he saw that the entrance of the opposite house was decorated with plantain stems and festoons of mango leaves. These were marks of an auspicious event. Chandran's body trembled. The drummer, sitting on the *pyol* in front of the house, beat the drum with all the vigour in his arms; the piper was working a crescendo in Kalyani raga. The music scalded Chandran's ears. He ran up the steps to Mohan's room.

'What are they doing in the opposite house?'

Mohan sprang up, put his arms around Chandran, and soothed him: 'Calm yourself. This won't do.'

Chandran shouted: 'What are they doing in the opposite house? Tell me! Why this pipe, why the mango leaves, who is going to be married in that house?'

'Nobody yet, but presently. They are celebrating the wedding notice. I learn that she is to marry her cousin next week.'

'What has happened to my letter?'

'I don't know.'

'Will nobody choke that piper? He is murdering the tune.'

'Sit down, Chandran.'

'Did you deliver that letter?'

'I couldn't get a chance, and I destroyed it this morning when I learnt that she is to be married.'

Chandran threw him an angry look. He said: 'Good bye,' turned round and fled down the stairs.

The opposite house shone in the greenish brilliance of two Kitson lamps. People were coming to the house, women wearing lace-bordered sarees, and men in well-ironed shirts and upper cloths—guests to the wedding notice ceremony. Chandran ran down the street, chased by the Kalyani raga, and the doom-doom of the drummer.

Chandran had fever that night. He had a high temperature and he raved. In about ten days, when he was well again, he insisted on being sent to Madras for a change. His father gave him fifty rupees, sent a wire to his brother at Madras to meet Chandran at the Egmore station, and put Chandran in a train going to Madras. Chandran's mother said at the station that he must return to Malgudi very plump and fat, and without any kind of worry in his head; Father said that he could write for more money if he needed it; Seenu, who had also come to the station, asked: 'Brother, do you know Messrs. Binns in Madras?'

'No,' said Chandran.

'It is in Mount Road,' said Seenu, and explained that it was the most magnificent sports goods firm in the country. 'Please go there and ask them to send me their fat catalogue; there are a lot of cricket pictures in it. Please buy a Junior Willard bat for me. Note it down, you may forget the name, it is Binns, Junior Willard,' he cried as the engine lurched, and Mother wiped her eyes, and Father stood looking after the train.

PART THREE

CHAPTER ELEVEN

NEXT MORNING AS the train steamed into the Madras Egmore station, Chandran, watching through the window of his compartment, saw in the crowd on the platform his uncle's son. Chandran understood that the other was there to receive him, and quickly withdrew his head into the compartment. The moment the train halted, Chandran pushed his bag and hold-all into the hands of a porter, and hurried off the platform. Outside a *jutka* driver greeted him and invited him to get into his carriage. Chandran got in and said: 'Drive to the hotel.'

'Which hotel, master?'

'Any hotel you like.'

'Would you like the one opposite the People's Park?'

'Yes,' said Chandran.

The *jutka* driver whipped his horse and shouted to the pedestrians to keep out of the way.

The *jutka* stopped in front of a red smoky building. Chandran jumped out of the carriage and walked into the hotel, the *jutka* driver following him, carrying the bag and the hold-all.

A man was sitting before a table making entries in a ledger. Chandran stood before him and asked: 'Have you rooms?'

'Yes,' said the man without looking up.

'My fare, sir,' reminded the *jutka* driver at this point.

'How much?' Chandran asked.

'A rupee, master. I have brought you here all the way from the station.'

Chandran took out his purse and gave him a rupee, and the *jutka* driver went away gasping with astonishment. Invariably if he asked for a rupee he would be given only a quarter of it, after endless haggling and argument. Now this fare had flung out a rupee without any question. It was a good beginning for the day; he always regretted afterwards that it hadn't occurred to him to ask for two rupees at the first shot.

The man at the table pressed a bell; a servant appeared. The man said: 'Room Three, upstairs,' and gave him a key. The servant lifted the hold-all and the bag and disappeared. Chandran stood hesitating, not knowing what he was expected to do.

'The advance,' said the man at the table.

'How much?' Chandran asked, wishing that the people of Madras were more human; they were so mechanical and impersonal; the porter at the station had behaved as if he were blind, deaf, and mute; now this hotel man would not even look at his guest; these fellows simply did not care what happened to you after they had received your money; the *jutka* man had departed promptly after he received the rupee, not uttering a single word . . . Chandran had a feeling of being neglected. 'How many days are you staying?' asked the man at the table. Chandran realized that he had not thought of this question; but he was afraid to say so; the other might put his hand on his neck and push him out; anything was possible in this impersonal place.

'Three days,' Chandran said.

'Then a day's advance will do now,' the man said, looking at Chandran for the first time.

'How much?'

'Four rupees. Upstairs room four rupees a day, and downstairs two-eight a day. I have sent your things to Three upstairs.'

'Thank you very much,' Chandran said, and gave him the advance.

His room was up a winding staircase. It was a small room containing a chair, a table, and an iron bedstead.

Chandran sat on the bedstead and rubbed his eyes. He felt weary. He got up and stood looking out of the window: tramcars were grinding the road; motor-cars, cycles, rickshaws, buses, *jutkas*, and all kinds of vehicles were going up and down in a tremendous hurry in the General Hospital Road below. Electric trains roared behind the hotel building. Chandran could not bear the noise of traffic. He returned to his bedstead and sat on it, holding his head between his hands. Somebody was humming a tune in the next room. The humming faded and then seemed to come nearer. Chandran looked up and saw a stranger carrying a towel and a soap box, standing in the doorway. He was a dark, whiskered person. He stood for a while there, looking at Chandran unconcernedly and humming a tune.

'Not coming to bathe, friend?' he asked.

'No. I shall bathe later,' replied Chandran.

'When? You won't have water in the tap after nine. Come with me. I will show you the bathroom.'

From that moment the whiskered man, who announced that his name was Kailas, took charge of Chandran. He acted as his guide and adviser in every minute detail of personal existence.

They went out together after breakfast. Chandran had absolutely no courage to oppose the other in anything. Kailas had an aggressive hospitality. He never showed the slightest toleration for any amendment or suggestion that Chandran made. Chandran was taken out and was whirled about in all sorts of tramcars and buses all day. They had tiffin in at least four hotels before the evening. Kailas paid for everything, and talked without a pause. Chandran learnt that Kailas had married two wives and loved both of them; had years ago made plenty of money in Malaya, and had now settled down in his old village, which was about a night's journey from Madras, and that he occasionally descended on Madras in order to have a good time. 'I have brought two hundred rupees with me. I shall stay here till this is spent, and then return to my village and sleep between the two wives for the next three months, and then come here again. I don't know how long it is going to last. What do you think my age is?'

'About thirty,' Chandran said, giving out the first number that came to his head.

'Ah, ah, ah! Do you think my hair is dyed?'

'No, no,' Chandran assured him.

'In these days fellows get greying hairs before they are twenty-five. I am fifty-one. I shall be good enough for this kind of life for another twenty years at least. After that it doesn't matter what happens; I shall have lived a man's life. A man must spend forty years in making money and forty years in spending it.'

By the evening Chandran felt very exhausted. To Kailas's inquiry Chandran replied that he was a student in Tanjore come out to Madras on a holiday tour.

At about five o'clock Kailas took Chandran into a building where ferns were kept in pots in the hall.

'What is this?' Chandran asked.

'Hotel Merton. I am going to have a little drink, if you don't mind.'

Kailas led Chandran up a flight of stairs, and selected a table in the upstairs veranda. A waiter appeared behind them.

'Have you Tenets?' Kailas asked.

'Yes, master.'

'Bring a bottle and two glasses. You will have a small drink with me?' he asked, turning to Chandran.

'Beer? No, sorry. I don't drink.'

'Come on, be a sport. You must keep me company.'

Chandran's heart palpitated. 'I never take alcohol.'

'Who said that there was alcohol in beer? Less than five per cent. There is less alcohol in beer than in some of the tonics your doctors advise you to take.'

The waiter came with a bottle of beer and two glasses. Kailas argued and debated till some persons sitting at other tables looked at them. Chandran was firm. In his opinion he was being asked to commit the darkest crime.

Kailas said to the waiter: 'Take the beer away, boy. That young master won't drink. Get me a gin and soda. You will have lime juice?'

'Yes.'

'Give that master lime juice.' The waiter departed. 'Why don't you have a little port or something?'

'No, no,' said Chandran.

'Why not even a port?'

'Excuse me. I made a vow never to touch alcohol in my life, before my mother,' said Chandran. This affected Kailas profoundly. He remained solemn for a moment and said: 'Then don't. Mother is a sacred object. It is a commodity whose value we don't realize as long as it is with us. One must lose it to know what a precious possession it is. If I had my mother I should have studied in a college and become a respectable person. You wouldn't find me here. After this, where do you think I am going?'

'I don't know.'

'To the house of a prostitute.' He remained reflective for a moment and said with a sigh: 'As long as my mother lived she said every minute, "Do this. Don't do that." And I remained a good son to her. The moment she died I changed. It is a rare commodity, sir.

Mother is a rare commodity.'

The spree went on till about eight-thirty in the evening, whisky following gin, and gin following whisky. There was a steady traffic between the table and the bar. At about eight-thirty Kailas belched loudly, hiccuped thrice, looked at Chandran with red eyes, and asked if Chandran thought he was drunk; he smiled with great satisfaction when Chandran said that he did not think so.

'There are fellows,' said Kailas in a very heavy voice, 'who will get drunk on two pegs of brandy. I throw out a challenge to any one. Put fifteen pegs of neat whisky, neat, mind you, into this soul'—he tapped his chest—'and I will tell you my name, do any multiplication or addition, and repeat numbers from a hundred backwards.'

They left the hotel. Kailas put his arm on Chandran's shoulder for support. They walked down Broadway, this strange pair. Kailas often stopped to roll his eyes foolishly and scratch his whiskers. He was discoursing on a variety of topics. He stopped suddenly in the road and asked: 'Did you have anything to eat?'

'Thanks. Plenty of cakes.'

'Did you drink anything?'

'Gallons of lime juice.'

'Why not a little beer or something? What a selfish rascal I am!'

'No, no,' said Chandran with anxiety. 'I have made a vow to my mother never to touch alcohol.'

'Ah!' said Kailas. He blew his nose and wiped his eyes with his kerchief. 'Mother! Mother!' He remained moody for some time, and said with an air of contentment: 'I know that my mother will be happy to know that I am happy.' He drew in a sharp breath and moved on again resolutely, as if determined not to let his feelings overcome him.

They walked in silence to the end of the road, and Kailas said: 'Why won't you call a taxi?'

'Where am I to find it?'

Kailas gave a short, bitter laugh. 'You ask me! Go and ask that electric post. Has God made you so blind that you can't see that I can't walk owing to a vile corn on the left foot?'

Chandran stood puzzled. He was afraid to cross the road, though the traffic was light now. Kailas appealed to him:

'Don't stand there, gaping open-mouthed at the wonders of the world, my boy. Get brisk and be helpful. Be a true friend. A friend in need is a friend indeed. Haven't you learnt it at school? I wonder what they teach you in schools nowadays!'

A passer-by helped Chandran to find a taxi. Kailas gave Chandran a hug when the taxi came. He got into the taxi and asked the driver: 'Do you know Kokilam's house?'

'No,' replied the driver.

Kailas threw at Chandran an accusing look and said: 'This is the kind of taxi you are pleased to call! Let us get down.'

'Where does she live?' asked the taxi driver.

'Roundabout Mint Street.'

'Ah!' said the taxi driver. 'Don't I know Kokilam's house?' He started the car, drove about for half an hour and stopped before a house in a narrow congested road. 'Here it is,' he said.

'Get down,' said Kailas to Chandran. 'How much?'

'The meter shows fifteen rupees, eight annas,' said the driver.

'Take seventeen-eight,' said Kailas, and gave him the money. The taxi drove away.

'Whose house is this?' asked Chandran.

'My girl's house,' said Kailas. He surveyed the house up and down and said doubtfully: 'It looks different today. Never mind.' He climbed the steps and asked somebody at the door: 'Is this Kokilam's house?'

'What does a name matter? You are welcome to my poor abode, sir.' It was a middle-aged woman.

'You are right,' said Kailas, greatly pleased. He suddenly asked Chandran: 'Did you take the taxi number?'

'No.'

'Funny man! Do you want me to be telling you every moment what you must do? Have you no common sense?'

'I am sorry,' said Chandran. 'The taxi is over there. I will note the number and come back.' He turned round, feeling happy at this brilliant piece of strategy, and jumped down the steps of the house. Kailas muttered: 'Good boy. You are a good friend in need is a friend inde-e-e-ed.'

Chandran fled from Mint Street. He had escaped from Kailas. This was the first time he had been so close to a man in drink; this was the first time he had stood at the portals of a prostitute's house. He was thoroughly terrified.

After leaving Kailas several streets behind, Chandran felt exhausted and sat down on a pavement. He felt very homesick. He wondered if there was any train which would take him back to Malgudi that very night. He felt that he had left home years ago, and not on the previous evening. The thought of Malgudi was very sweet. He would walk to Lawley Extension, to his house, to his room, and sleep on his cot snugly. He lulled his mind with this vision for some time. It was not long before his searching mind put to him the question why he was wandering about the streets of a strange city, leaving his delightful heaven? The answer brought a medley of memories: piper shrieking through his pipe Kalyani raga, glare of Kitson lamps, astrologers, horoscopes, and unsympathetic Mother. Ah, even at this moment Malathi was probably crying into her pillow at having to marry a person she did not like. What sort of a person was he? Would he be able to support her, and would he treat her well? Somebody else to be her husband, and he having dreamed for weeks on the evening sands of the Sarayu.

Chandran decided never to return to Malgudi. He hated the place. Everything there would remind him of Malathi—the sands on the Sarayu bank, the cobbles in Market Road, Mill Street, the little shopkeeper with Malathi's eyebrows. It would be impossible for him to live again in that hell. It was a horrible town, with its preparation for Malathi's wedding . . . Suppose even now some epidemic caught her future husband? Such things never happened in real life.

Chandran realized that he had definitely left his home. Now what did it matter where he lived? He was like a *sanyasi*. Why 'like'? He *was* a sanyasi; the simplest solution. Shave the head, dye the clothes in ochre, and you were dead for aught the world cared. The only thing possible; short of committing suicide, there was no other way out. He had done with the gamble of life. He was beaten. He could not go on living, probably for sixty years more, with people and friends and parents, with Malathi married and gone.

He got up. He wandered a little in search of his hotel, and then suddenly realized that it was quite an unnecessary search. What was he going to do after finding the hotel? Pay the bill, take the bag, and clear out somewhere? Why should a *sanyasi* carry a bag? Cast the bag and the hold-all aside, he told himself. As for payment, the hotel man had already been paid an advance, and if he wanted he could take the bag and the hold-all also into possession.

He slept that night on a pavement, rolling close to some wall. A board hung on the wall. He looked at it to make out what place it was; but the board only said 'Bill Stickers Will Be Prosecuted', which its Tamil translation elaborated in meaning, 'Those Who Stick Notices Will Be Handed Over To The Police'. 'Don't worry, I won't stick notices here,' he told the wall, and lay down. The fatigue of the day brought on sleep. Bill Stickers . . . He dreamt a number of times that while sleeping close to the wall he was mistaken for a poster, peeled off the wall by policemen, and placed under arrest.

Next morning he was awakened by a sweeper. Chandran sat rubbing his eyes. When his mind emerged from sleep, he resolved to get out of Madras immediately. There was no use remaining in the city any longer. It was so big and confusing that one didn't know even the way out of it. There was, moreover, the danger of being caught again by Kailas.

He found his way to the Central station, went to a ticket counter, and asked: 'When is the next train leaving?'

'For?'

'For—for,' repeated Chandran, 'wait a minute, please.' He glanced at a big railway map hanging on the wall and said: 'Bezwada.'

'Grand Trunk Express at seven-forty.'

'One third-class, please, for Bezwada.'

He got into the train. The compartment was not crowded. He suddenly felt very unhappy at having to go to Bezwada. He looked at the yellow ticket in his hand, and turned it between his fingers . . . He was not going to be tyrannized by that piece of yellow cardboard into taking a trip to Bezwada. He didn't like the place, a place with the letter 'z' in its name. He was not going to be driven to that place by anything. The first bell rang. He flung the ticket out of the window and jumped out of the train. He was soon out of the station.

He crossed the road, got into a tram, and settled down comfortably in a seat. The conductor came and said: 'Ticket, please.'

'Where does this go?'

'Mylapore.'

'One ticket, Mylapore. How much?'

For the next half-hour his problems as to where to go were set at rest. When the tram halted at the terminus he got down and walked till he saw the magnificent grey spire of Kapaleeswarar temple against the morning sky.

He entered the temple, went round the holy corridor, and prostrated before every image and sanctuary that he saw.

He saw a barber sitting on the steps of the temple tank waiting for customers. Chandran went to him and asked, 'Will you shave me?'

'Yes, master.' The barber was rather surprised. Young students with hair never showed any trust in him. His only customers were widows who shaved their heads completely and orthodox Brahmins who shaved their heads almost completely. Now here was a man willing to abandon his hair into his hands. Chandran said: 'I will give you a lot of money if you will do me a little service.'

'I can also crop well, master.'

'It is not only that. You must buy a cheap loincloth and an upper covering for me, dye them in ochre, and bring them to me. After that you can shave my head, and take these clothes I am wearing and also the purse in my pocket.' He held the purse open before him. The barber saw in it rupees and some notes, wages for six months' work in these days of safety razors and self-shaving.

'But not a word about it to any one, mind you,' said Chandran.

'Are you becoming a *sanyasi*?'

'Don't ask questions,' commanded Chandran.

'Master, at your age!'

'Will you stop asking questions or shall I get into a bus and go away? I want your help because I don't know where to get these things in this wretched place. What is your name?'

'Ragavan.'

'Ragavan, help me. You will gain my eternal gratitude. You will also profit yourself. My heart is dead, Ragavan. I have lost everybody I love in this world, Ragavan. I will be waiting for you here. Come soon.'

'Master, if you don't mind, why should you not come and wait in my poor hut?'

Chandran went with him to his house, beyond a network of stifling lanes and by-lanes. It was a one-roomed house, with a small bunk attached to it, full of heat and smoke, serving as kitchen. A very tall, stout woman came out of it and asked the barber: 'Why have you come back so soon?' He went near her and whispered something.

He unrolled a mat for Chandran, requested him to make

himself comfortable, and went out.

Chandran's mind and spirit had become so deadened that it did not matter to him where he waited, and how long. So, though he had to spend nearly half the day alone in the barber's house, seeing nothing but the barber's oily pillow and a red rug, and a calendar picture, without month or date sheets, showing Brahma, the creator of the universe, and an iron-banded teakwood box, Chandran did not feel the passing of the time.

The barber returned at three o'clock in the afternoon. He brought with him two pieces of cloth dyed in ochre. He brought also a few plantains and a green coconut.

Chandran was hungry, and did not refuse the coconut and fruits. He sent the barber out again for a postcard.

When the postcard was brought, Chandran borrowed a short pencil from the barber, and wrote to his father: 'Reached this place safely. I am staying with a friend I met at the station, and not with Uncle. I am leaving this for . . . I won't tell you where. I am going to wander about a lot. I am quite happy and cheerful. Don't fear that I am still worried about the marriage. Not at all. I am going to wander a good deal, and so don't run to the police station if you don't hear from me for a long time. You must promise not to make a fuss. My respects to Mother. I shall be all right.' He added a postscript: 'Am going with some friends, old class-mates, whom I met here.'

CHAPTER TWELVE

HIS DRESS AND appearance, the shaven pate and the ochre loincloth, declared him now and henceforth to be a *sanyasi* one who had renounced the world and was untouched by its joys and sorrows.

He travelled several districts on foot. When he felt tired he stopped a passing country cart and begged for a lift. No one easily refused an obligation to a *sanyasi*. Occasionally he stopped even buses on the highway.

He never cared to know where he was going or where he was staying (except that it was not in the direction of Malgudi). For what did it matter to a *sanyasi* where he was going? One town was very much like another: the same bazaar street, hair-cutting saloons, coffee hotels, tailors squatting before sewing-machines, grocers, Government officials, cycles, cars, and cattle. The difference was only in the name, and why should a *sanyasi* learn a name?

When he felt hungry he tapped at the nearest house and begged for food; or he begged in the bazaar street for a coconut or plantain.

For the first few days his system craved for coffee, to which he was addicted since his childhood. While one part of him suffered acutely, another part derived a satisfaction in watching it writhe and in saying to it: 'Go on: suffer and be miserable. You were not sent into this world to enjoy. Go on: be miserable and perish. You won't get coffee.' Circumstances gradually wore this craving out.

If anybody invited him to sleep under a roof he did it; if not, he slept in the open, or in a public rest-house, where were gathered scores like him. When he was hungry and found none to feed him, he usually dragged himself about in a weak state, and enjoyed the pain of hunger. He said to his stomach: 'Rage as much as you like. ·

Why don't you kill me?'

His cheekbones stood out; the dust of the highway was on him; his limbs had become horny; his complexion had turned from brown to a dark tan. His looks said nothing; they did not even seem to conceal a mystery; they looked dead. His lips rarely smiled.

He shaved once or twice and found that it was easier to allow the hair to grow as it pleased than to keep it down. His hair grew unhindered; in course of time a very young beard and moustache encircled his mouth.

He was different from the usual *sanyasi*. Others may renounce with a spiritual motive or purpose. Renunciation may be to them a means to attain peace or may be peace itself. They are perhaps dead in time, but they do live in eternity. But Chandran's renunciation was not of that kind. It was an alternative to suicide. Suicide he would have committed but for its social stigma. Perhaps he lacked the barest physical courage that was necessary for it. He was a *sanyasi* because it pleased him to mortify his flesh. His renunciation was a revenge on society, circumstances, and perhaps also on destiny.

After about eight months of wandering he reached Koopal village in Sainad district. It was a small village nestling at the foot of the range of mountains that connected the Eastern and the Western Ghats.

On a hot afternoon Chandran arrived in this village, and drank water from the channel that fed the paddy fields. He then went and sat in the shade of a banyan tree. He had been walking since dawn, and he felt tired. He reclined on a stout root of the banyan and closed his eyes.

When he opened his eyes again he saw some villagers standing around him.

'May we know where our master is coming from?' somebody asked.

Chandran was tired of inverting an answer to this question. On the flash of an idea he touched his mouth and shook his head.

'He is dumb.'

'No, he can hear us. Can you hear us?'

Chandran shook his head in assent.

'Can you talk?'

Chandran shook his head in assent, held up his ten fingers, touched his lips, looked heavenward, and shook his head. They understood. 'He is under a vow of silence of ten years or ten months or ten days.'

A number of villagers stood around Chandran and gaped at him. Chandran felt rather embarrassed at being the target of the stare of a crowd. He closed his eyes. This was taken by the others for meditation.

An important man of the village came forward and asked: 'Won't you come and reside in my poor abode?'

Chandran declined the offer with a gesture, and spent the night under the tree.

Next day, as the villagers passed him on their way to the fields, they saluted him with joined palms. Somebody brought a few plantains and placed them before him; somebody else offered him milk. Chandran accepted the gifts, consumed them, and then rose to go.

Somebody asked him: 'Master, where are you going?'

With a sweep of his hands Chandran indicated a faraway destination.

At this they begged him to stay. 'Master, our village is so unlucky that few come this way. Bless us with your holy presence for some more days, we beg of you.' Chandran shook his head, but they would not let him go. 'Master, your very presence will bless our village. We rarely see holy men here. We beg of you to stay for some days more.'

Chandran was touched by this request. No one had valued his presence so highly till now. He was treated with consideration everywhere, but not with so much of it as he saw here. He felt: 'Poor fellows. Probably no interesting person comes this way, which is God knows how far from everywhere. Why not stay if it is going to give them any pleasure? This is as good a place as another.'

He went back to the banyan seat. There was great rejoicing when he consented to stay. Men, women and children followed him to the banyan tree.

Soon the news spread from hamlet to hamlet and village to village that a holy man under a vow of silence for ten years had arrived, and that he spent his time in rigorous meditation under a banyan tree.

Next day scores of visitors came from all the surrounding villages, and gathered under the banyan tree. Chandran sat in the correct pose of a man in meditation, cross-legged and with his eyes shut.

It never occurred to them to doubt. They were innocent and unsophisticated in most matters (excepting their factions and fights), and took an ascetic's make-up at its face value.

Late in the evening Chandran opened his eyes and saw only a few villagers standing around him. He signed to them to leave him alone. After this request was repeated twice they left him.

The night had fallen. Somebody had brought and left a lighted lantern beside him. He looked about. They had all brought gifts for him, milk and fruits and food. The sight of the gifts sent a spear through his heart. He felt a cad, a fraud, and a confidence trickster. These were gifts for a counterfeit exchange. He wished that he deserved their faith in him. The sight of the gifts made him unhappy. He ate some fruit and drank a little milk with the greatest self-deprecation.

He moved away from the gifts; still the light shone on them. He even blew out the lantern—he did not deserve the light.

Sitting in the dark, he subjected his soul to a remorseless vivisection. From the moment he had donned the ochre cloth to the present, he had been living on charity, charity given in mistake, given on the face value of a counterfeit. He had been humbugging through life. He told himself that if he were such an ascetic he ought to do without food or perish of starvation. He ought not to feed his miserable stomach with food which he had neither earned nor, by virtue of spiritual worth, deserved.

He sought an answer to the question why he had come to this degradation. He was in no mood for self-deception, and so he found the answer in the words 'Malathi' and 'Love'. The former had brought him to this state. He had deserted his parents, who had spent on him all their love, care, and savings. He told himself that he had surely done this to spite his parents, who probably had died of anxiety by now. This was all his return for their love and for all that they had done for him. The more he reflected on this, the greater became his anger with Malathi. It was a silly infatuation. Little sign did she show of caring for a fellow; she couldn't say that she had no chance. She had plenty of opportunities to show that she noticed him. Where there was a will there was a way. She had only been playing with him, the devil. Women were like that, they enjoyed torturing people. And for the sake of her memory he had come to this. He railed against that memory, against love. There was no such thing; a foolish literary notion. If people didn't read stories they wouldn't know there was such a thing as love. It was a scorching madness. There was no such thing. And driven by a non-existent thing he had become a deserter and a counterfeit.

He wondered if he ought not to stand in the village street, call everybody, and announce to them what he was. They might not believe, or they might think he had gone mad, or they might believe and feel that they were fooled and mob him and beat him to a pulp. He toyed with this vision, a punishment that he would surely deserve.

He rose. He decided to leave the village, as the most decent and practical thing that he could do. He moved out of the banyan shade.

Chandran walked all night, and early in the morning sighted a bus. He stopped it.

'Will you please take me in?'

'Where are you going?'

'In your direction.'

The conductor looked at the seats and grumbled.

'I will get down anywhere you like, any time you get passengers for the full bus.'

The bus was still empty, and the request came from one who wore the ochre garb, so the conductor said: 'Come on.'

The *sanyasi* climbed the bus and said: 'I have walked all night. Put me down in a place where there is a telegraph office.'

The bus conductor thought for a moment and said: 'There is one at Maduram.'

'How far is it from here?'

'About ten miles, but we do not go there. We branch off about two miles from Maduram. This bus goes to Kalki.'

Chandran got down from the bus at the crossroads and walked to Maduram. It was a small town on the banks of the Samari river. In the central street there was a post and telegraph office. Chandran tapped on the post office window and said to the postmaster: 'I want to have a word with you. Can I come in?'

After a severe scrutiny of the visitor the postmaster said: 'Yes.'

Chandran went into the small post office. The postmaster looked at Chandran suspiciously. Too many English-speaking *sanyasis* were about the place now, offering to tell the future, and leaving their hosts minus a rupee or two at the end.

'You want to tell me my future, I suppose,' said the postmaster.

'No, sir. I don't know any astrology.'

'Too many *sanyasis* come here nowadays. We simply can't afford to pay for all the astrology that is available.'

'I wish I had at least that to give in exchange,' said Chandran, and then opened his heart to the postmaster. He gave a clear account of his life and troubles.

After hearing his story the postmaster agreed to lend him a rupee and eight annas for sending a telegram to his father for money.

Chandran expressed a desire for a shave and a change of clothing. The postmaster sent for a barber and gave Chandran an old shirt and a white *dhoti*.

Chandran requested the barber to pay special attention to his head, and to use the scissors carefully there. He also requested the barber to shave his face thrice over.

After that he went in for a bath, and came out of the bathroom feeling resurrected. He was dressed in the postmaster's *dhoti* and shirt. He had in his hand his *sanyasi* robes in a bundle. After inviting the postmaster to witness the sight, he flung the bundle over the wall into the adjoining lane.

He asked for a little hair oil and a comb. He rubbed the oil on his head and tried to comb his hair before a mirror.

The feel of a shirt on his body and of a smooth chin, after months of shirtless and prickly existence, gave him an ecstatic sensation.

At about four in the afternoon a message arrived endowing Chandran with fifty rupees, though he had wired for only twenty-five.

The mail train towards Madras passed Maduram station at one o'clock at night. Chandran bought a ticket for Malgudi, changed trains at two junctions, and finally got down at Malgudi station in the morning two days later.

PART FOUR

CHAPTER THIRTEEN

HIS PARENTS WERE amazed to see him so transformed.

'I should have come to the station, Chandar,' said his father, 'but I was not sure when you were coming.'

Mother said: 'You are looking like a corpse. How your bones stick out! What sunken cheeks! What were you at all these days?'

Seenu said: 'What about the cricket bat? Where is your coat? Your shirt is a bit loose. You have also spoilt your hair. It is very short. Where is your bag?'

Father and Mother looked very careworn.

Mother asked: 'Why couldn't you write to us at least a card?'

'I did,' said Chandran.

'Only one. You should have written to us at least once after that.'

Father asked: 'Did you travel much? What were the places you visited?'

'Lots of places. Rolled about a great deal,' said Chandran, and stopped at that. His father could never get more than that from him.

'Why didn't you go to your uncle's?'

'I didn't fancy him,' said Chandran. 'Were you all very greatly worried about me?'

'Your mother was. She thought that something terrible had happened to you. Every morning she troubled me to go and inform the police.' He turned to his wife and added: 'Have I not been telling you that you were merely imagining things?'

'Ah,' she said, 'as if you weren't anxious! How many times did you say that an announcement must be made in the papers?'

Father looked abashed.

Chandran asked: 'I hope you haven't told the police or advertised in the papers?'

'No, no,' said Father. 'But I should certainly have done something if I hadn't heard from you for some weeks more. It was only your mother who was very, very worried.'

'As if you weren't,' Mother retorted. 'Why did you go thrice to Madras, and then to Trichinopoly, and write to all sorts of people?'

Seenu said: 'Father and Mother were worried about you, Brother. Nobody would talk to me in this house. They were all very ill-tempered and morose all these months. I didn't like our house, Brother. No one to talk to in the house except the cook. You ought to have written to us at least once or twice. I hoped that you would go to Binns' and bring at least their catalogue.'

Chandran went to his room and found everything there just as he had left it. The books that had been kept on the table were there; the cot in the same position, the bookshelf in the same old place, his old grey coat on the same hook on the coat stand; the table near the window with even the writing pad in the same position. There was not a speck of dust on anything, nor a single spider's web. In fact the room and all the objects in it were tidier than they had ever been. The sight of things spick and span excited him. Everything excited him now. He ran to his mother and asked, panting: 'Mother, how is it everything is so neat in my room?'

Father replied: 'She swept and cleaned it with great care every day.'

'Why did you take so much trouble, Mother?'

She became red and was embarrassed. 'What better business did I have?'

'How did you manage to keep Seenu out of my room, Mother?'

'Mother used to lock up the room, and never left it open even for an hour,' Seenu replied.

Chandran suddenly asked: 'What has happened to Ramu? Did anybody hear from him?'

'No.'

'No letters from him for me?'

'None,' his mother replied.

'Where are his people? Are they not in the next house?'

'His father was transferred to some Telugu district, and they have cleared out of this place, bag and baggage.'

Chandran realized that this was the last he would hear of Ramu. Ramu was dead as far as Chandran was concerned. Ramu was never in the habit of writing. Except one card he had not written for nearly two years now. His people till now were in the next house, and there was some hope of hearing about him. Now that too was gone. Chandran reflected gloomily: 'I and he are parted now. He won't bother about me any more. Very frivolous-minded. Won't bother about a thing that is out of sight.'

Mother said: 'They came here to take leave of us, and they said that Ramu had found an appointment at seventy-five rupees a month in the Bombay Railways.'

Chandran felt very hurt on hearing this. Here was a person who didn't care to communicate to a friend such happy news as the securing of a job. That was like Ramu. Friendship was another illusion like love, though it did not reach the same mad heights. People pretended that they were friends, when the fact was they were brought together by force of circumstances. The classroom or the club or the office created friendships. When the circumstances changed the relations, too, snapped. What did Ramu care for him now, after all the rambles on the river, cigarettes, cinema, and confidences? Friendship—what meaningless expressions had come into use!

'What is the matter, Chandra, you are suddenly moody?' asked Chandran's father.

'Nothing, nothing,' said Chandran. 'I was only thinking of something. Father, have you any idea where your old college friends are now?'

Father tried to recollect. He gave up the attempt. 'I don't know. If I look at the old college group photo I may be able to tell you something.' He turned to his wife and asked: 'Where is that group photo?'

'How should I know?' she replied.

Seenu said: 'I don't know if it is the one you want. I found a large group photo in the junk room, and I have hung it over my table, but the glass is broken.'

Chandran said: 'I don't mean the whole class. Just some particular friends you had in the college.'

'For the four years I spent in the Christian College I had about three or four intimate friends. We were room-mates and neighbours in the hostel. We were always together . . . Sivaraman, he entered the Imperial Service and was in Bihar for some time. It is over thirty years since we wrote to each other. I recently saw in the papers that he retired as Chief something-or-other in the Railway Board. Gopal Menon, he was in the Civil Service. He died some time ago of heart failure. This, too, I saw only in the papers, and then wrote a condolence letter to his wife. The other, we used to call him Kutti, his full name was something or other. I don't know where he is now. The only old friend who is still in this town is Madhava Rao.'

'You mean the old man who lives near the college?'

'No, that is another person. I am referring to K.T. Madhava Rao, the retired Postal Superintendent. He and I were very intimate friends.'

'Do you meet often now?'

'Once in a way. He doesn't come to the club. Now that you ask me, I remember I went to his house about four years ago, when he was laid up with blood pressure.'

'And you used to spend all your time together in the college?'

'Yes, yes. But you see . . . We can't afford to be together always, you know. Each of us has to go his own way.'

To Chandran it was a depressing revelation. Well, probably ages hence he would be saying to his grandson: 'I had a friend called Ramu. It is fifty years since we have written to each other. I don't know if he is still living.' His father at least had a group photo in the junk room; he hadn't even that—he had simply forgotten to buy his class group. '. . . This too I saw only in the papers . . .' The callousness of time!

He stepped down into the garden. He found the garden paths overgrown with grass, and plants in various stages of decay. Thick weeds had sprung up everywhere, and were choking a few crotons and roses that were still struggling for life. He had never seen the garden in this state. Ever since he could remember his father had worked morning and evening in the garden. Now what had happened to the gardener? What had happened to Father?

He went in and asked: 'What has happened to the plants?'

Father looked awkward and said: 'I don't know . . .'

'What, have you not been gardening?'

'I couldn't attend to the plants,' he said.

'What were you busy with, then?'

'I don't know what account to give of myself.'

Mother said mischievously: 'He was busy searching for a missing son.'

'But I wrote to you, Father, that you wouldn't hear from me for a long time and not to worry.'

'Oh, yes, you did. It wasn't that. Your mother is only joking. Don't take her seriously.'

Chandran went to Mohan's hotel in the evening. Before starting, he said to his mother: 'I may not come back tonight. I shall sleep in Mohan's hotel.'

As he approached Mohan's hotel he could not help recollecting with a grim detachment the state of mind he was in the last time he was here. The detachment was forced, his heart beat fast as he came in front of the Modern Indian Lodge. Suppose she was standing at that very moment at the entrance of the opposite house? Before slipping into the hotel, in spite of his resolve, he turned his head once; but there was no one at the entrance. As he climbed the staircase he reproached himself severely for this. Still a prey to illusions! Was he making for another bout of asceticism and wandering?

He stopped at the landing and found Room 14 locked. On the door some other name was scrawled in pencil. Chandran descended the stairs and asked the manager if Mohan was still in the hotel.

'Room 14,' said the manager.

'But it is locked. Some other name on the door.'

'That is the old Fourteen. The new Fourteen is on the topmost floor.'

Chandran went up and found Mohan in a newly-built small room at the topmost part of the building. It was airy and bright, a thorough contrast to the wooden-partitioned cell on the landing. There were a table and a chair, a few pictures on the wall. Everything tidy.

Mohan was speechless for five minutes, and then he opened his mouth and let out a volley of questions: 'What did you do with yourself? Where were you? Why . . .'

'This is really a splendid room!' Chandran said. 'How did you manage to leave the old one?'

'I am prosperous now, you see,' Mohan said happily. 'Tell me about yourself.'

'Mine is a long story. It is like *Ramayanam*. You will hear it presently. Tell me how you are prospering.'

'Quite well, as I told you. The *Daily Messenger* now sells a total of thirty thousand copies a day. They now pay me five rupees a column, and don't cut much because they want to establish a good circulation in these districts. New company running it now. They are very regular in payment. I am making nearly twenty columns a month. Besides this, they publish my poems once a week in their magazine page, and pay me four annas a line.' Mohan looked very healthy and cheerful.

'This is great news,' said Chandran. 'I am glad you have left that old cell.'

'I am paying five rupees more for this room. I insisted on this room being called Fourteen. It is a lucky number. So this is known as the New Fourteen, and the other as the Old Fourteen. This room was built very recently. The hotel proprietor is very prosperous now; he has purchased this building, and has added many rooms. The poor fellow was down in luck for a number of years; but now lots of guests come here, and he is doing very well. I thought of shifting to another hotel, but hadn't the heart to do it. The old man and I have been friends since our bad days. In those days sometimes he would not have a measure of rice in the whole hotel; and I have several times borrowed a rupee or two and given it to him for running the hotel.'

After attempting to smother the question a dozen times Chandran asked: 'Are they still in the opposite house?'

Mohan smiled a little and paused before answering: 'Soon after the marriage they left that house. I don't know where they are now.'

'Who is living in the house now?'

'Some marwari, a moneylender, has acquired it.'

Everywhere there seemed to be change. Change, change, everywhere. Chandran hated it. 'Have I been away for only eight months or eighteen years?' Chandran asked himself. 'Mohan, let us go and spend the whole evening and night on the Sarayu bank. I have a lot of things to tell you. I want you. Let us eat something at a hotel and go to the river.'

Mohan demurred. His presence was urgently needed at an adjourned meeting of the Municipality.

Chandran turned a deaf ear to the call of duty, and insisted on seducing Mohan away from the meeting. Mohan yielded, saying: 'I shall take it from the *Gazette* man tomorrow. I have got to report it to my paper.'

They went to a coffee hotel, and then to the river bank. Long after the babble of the crowd on the sands had died, and darkness had fallen on the earth, Chandran's voice was heard, in tune with the rumble of the flowing river, narrating to Mohan his wanderings. He then explained his new philosophy, which followed the devastating discovery that love and friendship were the veriest illusions. He explained that people married because their sexual appetite had to be satisfied and there must be somebody to manage the house. There was nothing deeper than that in any man-and-woman relationship.

The Taluk Office gong sounded eleven at night when Chandran said: 'Remember, I have not told any one that I was a *sanyasi* for eight months. You must keep it all to yourself. I don't want any one to talk about me.'

They rose and walked back to the hotel through the silent streets.

CHAPTER FOURTEEN

CHANDRAN SETTLED DOWN to a life of quiet and sobriety. He felt that his greatest striving ought to be for a life freed from distracting illusions and hysterics.

He tended the garden a great deal now. Every morning he spent over two hours in the garden. He divided his time between plants and books. In the evening he took his bicycle (a second-hand one that he had bought recently) and went out for long rides on the Trunk Road. Late in the evening he went to Mohan's hotel.

This kind of life was conducive to quiet and, possibly, sobriety. With an iron will he chased away distracting illusions, and conscientiously avoided hysterics, with the care of one walking on a tightrope. He decided not to give his mind a moment of freedom. All the mischief started there. Whatever he did, he did it with a desperate concentration now. If he dug the garden, the mind was allowed to play about only the soil and the pick. If he read a book, he tried to make the print a complete drug for the mind. The training of the mind was done feverishly and unsparingly.

There were still sights and sounds and hours which breathed, through some association or other, memories of Malathi. But he avoided them. He rarely went to the river before sundown; and never to the old spot. He was glad that the house opposite the Modern Indian Lodge was now occupied by a moneylender. The sound of pipe music, especially when Kalyani raga was played on it, disturbed his equanimity; when going to Mohan's hotel, he carefully avoided the route that took him by the Shiva temple, where there was pipe music every evening. He never looked at the shop in Market Road for fear of encountering the eyebrows of the boy in the shop. Even then something or other was sure to remind him of Malathi and trouble him. At such moments he fumigated his mind with reflections: this is a mischievous disturbance; this is false; these thoughts of Malathi are unreal because love is only a brain affection; it led me to beg and cheat; to desert my parents; it is responsible for my mother's extra wrinkles and grey hairs, for my father's neglect of the garden; and a poor postmaster is a shirt and a *dhoti* less on account of my love.

However, there was another matter that troubled him, which could not be forced off the mind. It was the question of occupation. He often told himself that he was making arrangements to go to England in the coming year, and that he ought to come back from there with some distinction, and then search for employment. Sometimes this quietened his mind, sometimes not. He was getting on for twenty-four. It was nearly two years since he left college, and he was still leeching on his father. He was so much bothered by this thought one day that he went to his father in the garden and asked: 'Why should I not apply for a Government post?'

Father looked up from the bed of annuals that he was digging. 'Why do you want to do it?'

Chandran mumbled something.

Father understood that something was troubling him and said: 'Well, there is no hurry.'

'But I have wasted a lot of time already, Father. It is nearly two years since I became a graduate, and I have neither studied further nor done anything else.'

'It is no waste,' Father said. 'You have been reading and getting to know people and life and so on. Don't worry. Time enough to apply for jobs after you return from England. It will be really worthwhile, you see. There is no use in getting a bare forty or fifty as a clerk, though even that would be difficult to secure in these days.'

'But I am nearly twenty-four, Father, not a baby. There are fellows who support a family at my age.'

'Well, you too could have done it if it was necessary. You could have finished your college before you were twenty if I hadn't put you to school late, and if you hadn't been held up by typhoid for a year.'

Chandran admired his father for admitting as causes of wasted time late schooling and typhoid, and leaving out of account the vagrant eight months, but for which he would have been in England already. Chandran comforted himself by saying that he would compensate for all this by doing something really great in England and getting into some really high post in the Education service. His father was constantly writing to his brother at Madras for a lot of preliminary information connected with Chandran's trip to England. These letters gave Chandran a feeling of progress towards an earning life. But there were times when he doubted this too. He wondered if he really ought to put his father to that expense. He wondered if his comfort from the thought of going to England soon was not another illusion, and if it would not be super-parasitic of him. He could not decide the issue himself. He consulted Mohan. Mohan asked why, if he felt so, he should not do something else. Chandran asked what, and Mohan explained, 'Why not the chief agency of our paper? They are not satisfied with the present agent, and have given him notice. They have advertised for an agent in this and in a few other districts.'

'What is it likely to bring?'

'It all depends. If you canvass a large circulation, you will make a lot of money.'

Chandran was sceptical. 'Where am I to go and canvass?'

'That is what an agent gets his income for. In six months the daily circulation of the *Messenger* has gone up to thirty thousand, quite a good figure, and it circulates all over the Presidency. It ought to find a sale in this place also. But for the agent the circulation would not have gone above a bare twenty-five. All the same they are publishing my news because they hope that it will ultimately pull up the circulation.'

Chandran was not quite convinced that it was a very useful line to take.

Next day Mohan came out with further information. 'I saw the present agent. He gets a quarter of an anna per paper sold.' Mohan wrote to the office for information, and in due course, when it arrived, passed it on to Chandran. After some more talk and thought, Chandran became quite enthusiastic. He asked his father: 'Will you be disappointed if I don't go to England?'

'What is the matter? I have already written for official information.'

'I feel that going to England will only mean a lot of expense.'

'You need not worry about that.'

'Getting a distinction and coming back and securing a suitable appointment, all these seem to be a gamble.'

Father was silent. He felt nervous when Chandran came and proposed anything. But Chandran went on developing exquisitely the theme of the *Messenger* agency. He saw in it a beautiful vision of an independent life full of profit and leisure. He quoted facts and figures. A quarter of an anna per day per paper sold. With a miserly circulation of 1,000 for the whole district, he would be making 250 annas a day. He would get at that rate about 480 rupees a month, which one couldn't dream of getting in the Government service even after fifteen years of slavery. And there was always the possibility of expanding the business. He gave the area of Malgudi, its population, out of which the English-knowing persons were at least 10,000; out of that number at least 5,000 would be able to spend an anna a day on a newspaper; and it was these who were going to support the *Daily Messenger*.

'For the agency we must give a security of 2,000 rupees, for which they later pay interest. Somebody has written from the office that a number of people have already applied and that there is a keen fight for the agency. They are selecting the agent only on the first. It is a good chance, Father. I think it is better than going to England.'

Father listened in silence.

Mother, who was twisting small cotton bits into wicks for the lamps in the gods' room, said: 'I think so. Why should he go to England?'

Father replied that the question could not be so easily settled. He was very ignorant of the newspaper business. He wrote a letter to his brother in Madras for enlightenment on the subject. That evening, in the club, he took aside Nanjundiah, a barrister of the town, a public figure, and his particular friend, and asked him: 'Do you read the *Daily Messenger*?'

'Yes.'

'What sort of a paper is it? I saw a copy, but I should like to have your opinion.'

'I don't subscribe for it but get it from a neighbour. It is quite a good paper, non-party and independent.'

'You see,' said Chandran's father, 'my son wants to take up the agency, giving a security of 2,000 rupees. I have absolutely no idea what it is all about, but he seems to think that it will be a good investment.'

'What about his going to England?'

'Seems to be more keen on this. I don't know, that boy gets a new notion every day; but I don't like to stand in his way if it is really a sound proposition.'

He said to Chandran that night: 'I spoke to Nanjundiah about the paper. He thinks well of it, but doesn't know anything else. However, he has promised to find out and tell me.'

Chandran said: 'We can't be wasting time over all these inquiries. There is a rush for the agency. We must look sharp.'

After Chandran had gone to his room his mother said: 'Why are you tormenting the boy?' Father did not vouchsafe an answer but merely rustled his paper. She repeated the question, and he said: 'Why don't you leave it to me?'

'If the boy wishes to stay here, why won't you let him stay? What is the use of sending him to England? Waste of a lot of money. What do our boys, who go to England, specially achieve? They only learn to smoke cigarettes, drink wine, and dance with white girls.'

'It is my hope that our boy will do something more than that.'

'If there is as much money in the paper as he says, why shouldn't he do that work?'

'If there is; that is what I must know before I let him do it. I can't very well give him a cheque for 2,000 rupees and ask him to invest it, without knowing something about the persons that are running the paper, how long it will last, and other things. There is hardly any sense in letting him in for work which may not last even a year! I have written to my brother. Let me see what he writes.'

'You have to write to your brother about everything,' she said, rising to go in. 'Only I don't want you to drive the boy to desperation.'

Father looked after her for a long time, shifted in his easy chair a little, and rustled the paper.

Chandran said to himself: 'I have no business to hustle and harass my father. He has every right to wait and delay. If I am destined to get the agency, I shall get it; if not, I shall not get it for all the hustling.'

There was a delay of four or five days before a reply arrived from his uncle. Till then Father went about his business without mentioning the paper, and Chandran too conducted himself as if there was no such thing as the *Daily Messenger*. But every morning he went out at about nine o'clock, met the Lawley Extension postman on the way and asked if there was any letter for Father. At last, one morning, the postman carried a letter in his hand for Father. It bore the Madras postmark. At other times Chandran would have snatched the letter from the postman, taken it to his father, and demanded to be told of its contents. But now he curbed that impulse, asked the postman to carry the letter himself, went to the town reading-room, and returned home at midday. He did not go before Father at all, but confined his movements between the kitchen and the dining-hall, till Father himself called Chandran and gave him the letter. Chandran opened the letter and read 'There is an influential directorate at the head of the paper. J.W. Prabhu, Sir N.M. Rao, and others are on it. An agency would really be worthwhile, but would not be easy to secure. If you send Chandran over here immediately I shall see if anything can be done through a friend of mine who knows the Managing Director . . .'

Chandran read the letter twice, gave it back to his father, and asked as casually as possible: 'What do you think of it?'

'You can go to Madras today. I shall send a wire to your uncle.'

'All right.'

He went to his mother and said: 'I am starting for Madras today.'

She asked anxiously: 'When will you be back?'

'In two or three days, as soon as my work is finished.'

'Are you sure?'

'Oh, don't worry, Mother. I shall positively come back.'

He immediately started packing his trunk. As he sat in his room, with all his clothes lying scattered about, his father frequently came in with something or other for Chandran in hand. He brought half a dozen handkerchiefs.

'You may want these in Madras.' He came next with a pair of new *dhotis*. 'I have a lot more in the chest of drawers.' He then brought a woolen scarf and requested Chandran to hand it over to his brother in Madras. Mother came in and asked if Chandran would like to carry anything to eat on the way. She then expressed a desire to send a small basket of vegetables to her sister-in-law. Chandran said that he would not take it with him. But she argued that she wasn't asking him to carry the load on his head. He threatened that if he were given any basket he would throw it out of the train.

At five o'clock he had finished his dinner and was ready to

start. His steel trunk and a roll of bedding were brought to the hall.
Mother added a small basket to Chandran's luggage. Chandran
protested at the sight of the basket. Mother lifted the basket and
said: 'See, it is very light; contains only some vegetables for your
aunt. You mustn't go with empty hands.'

His father, mother, and Seenu saw Chandran off at the station.
Seenu said: 'Don't stay away long. Don't forget Binns this time.'

Next morning as the train steamed into the Madras Egmore station,
Chandran, peeping out of the window, saw his uncle on the
platform.

His uncle was about forty years old, a cheerful plump man with
a greying crop, and wearing thick-rimmed spectacles. He was a
businessman and a general broker, doing a lot of work, and knowing
all possible persons in the city.

As Chandran got down from the train, his uncle said: 'I came
here myself in order that you might not slip away this time.'

Chandran blushed and said: 'Father has sent you a scarf.'

'So after all he has the strength to part with it. Is it the same
or a different one?'

'Deep blue wool.'

'It is the same. He wouldn't give it to me for years.'

A porter carried the things to a car outside. Chandran sat with
his uncle in the front seat.

'How do you like this car?' his uncle asked.

'It is quite good.'

'I bought it recently, giving away my old Essex in exchange.'

'Oh,' said Chandran. He felt quite happy that his uncle was
speaking to him like an equal, and was not teasing him as he used
to do before. Chandran had always avoided his uncle if he could,
but now he found him quite tolerable.

His uncle asked why Chandran had dropped the idea of going
to England. He chatted incessantly as he drove along, cutting across
tramcars, hooting behind pedestrians, and taking turns recklessly.

He lived in a bungalow in the Luz Church Road. Chandran's
aunt and cousins (one of his own age, a youngster, and a girl) were
standing on the veranda to receive Chandran.

'Ah, how tall Chandra has grown!' said his aunt; and Chandran
felt very tall and proud.

'Mother has sent a basket of vegetables for you, Aunt,' he said, and surveyed his cousins. The one of his own age smiled and said: 'I came to the station last time.'

'Oh,' said Chandran, and blushed. When were people going to forget his last trip?

'Raju, take Chandra's things to your room, and then show him the bathroom,' Uncle said to this cousin.

His cousin took him to his room. Chandran removed his coat, and Raju said again: 'I came to the station last time, and searched for you on the platform.'

Chandran paid no attention, but opened his trunk, took out a towel and soap, and sternly said: 'Show me the bathroom.'

When Chandran was combing his hair, his aunt brought in a very small child with curly hair and large eyes, and said: 'Have you seen this girl? She is just up from bed. She simply wouldn't stay in it, but wanted to be taken to you immediately.'

Chandran tapped its cheeks with his fingers. 'What is her name?'

'Kamala,' replied his aunt.

'Ah, Kamal. What, Kamala?' Chandran asked, staring at the child, and raising his hand once again to tap its cheeks. The child looked at him fixedly for a moment and began to cry. Chandran stood still, not knowing what he was expected to do. Aunt took away the child, saying: 'She can't stand new faces. She will be all right when she gets to know you a little more.'

At eleven o'clock, after food, his uncle took him out in the car. The car stopped before a four-storied building in Linga Chetty Street.

He followed his uncle up three flights of stairs, past a corridor and a glass door, into an office. Before a table littered with files a man was sitting.

His uncle said: 'Good morning, Murugesam.'

'Hello, hello, come in,' said the man at the table, pushing aside a file that he was reading.

Uncle said: 'This is my nephew whom I spoke to you about. This is Mr S.T. Murugesam, General Manager of Engladia Limited.'

Chandran stretched his hand across the table and said: 'I am glad to meet you, sir.'

'Take a chair,' said Murugesam.

Uncle and Murugesam talked for a while, and then Uncle got up. 'I shall have to be going now. Some railway people are coming to my office at twelve. So you will take this boy and fix him up?'

'I will do my best.'

'That is not enough,' said Uncle. 'You have got to fix him up. He is a graduate, son of a big Government pensioner; he will give any security you want. You must fix him up. He has even cancelled his trip to England for the sake of this paper . . . You can keep him here. I shall pick him up on my way back.' He went out.

Murugesam looked at the time and said: 'We shall go out at two o'clock. I hope you won't mind half an hour's wait.'

'Not at all. You can take your own time, sir,' said Chandran, and leant back in his chair. Murugesam signed a heap of papers, pushed them away, gripped the telephone on the table, and said into it: 'Shipping.' He waited for a moment and said, 'Inform Damodars that we can't load *Waterway* before Thursday midnight. Thursday midnight. Bags are still arriving. She is not sailing before Saturday evening . . . Right. Thank you.'

Chandran watched him, fascinated. For the first time he was witnessing a businessman at work. Chandran felt a great admiration for Murugesam, a slight man, keeping in his hands the strings of mighty activities; probably ships were waiting to sail at a word from him. How did he pick up so much business knowledge? What did he earn? Ten thousand? What did he do with so much money? When would he find time to spend the money and enjoy life with so many demands on his attention? The telephone bell rang. Murugesam took it up and said: 'That is right. Tell them they will get the notice in due course. Thank you,' and put down the receiver. An assistant brought in some letters and put them before him. Murugesam wrote something on them, gave them back to the assistant, and said: 'I am going out, and shall not be back for about half an hour. If there are any urgent calls, you can ring me up at the *Daily Messenger*.'

'Yes, sir.'

'But remember, don't send anyone there. Only very urgent calls.' He rose and picked up his fur cap. Chandran was impressed with the other's simplicity of dress. He was wearing only a *dhoti*, a long silk coat, and a black fur cap.

He led Chandran out of the building, and got into a sedan. They drove in the car for about a quarter of an hour through whirling traffic, and got down before a new, white building in Mount Road, before which stood in huge letters the sign '*Daily*

Messenger'. They went up in a lift, through several halls filled with tables and men bent in work, past shining counters and twisting passages. Murugesam pushed a red-curtained door. A man was sitting at a table littered with files. 'Hello, Murugesam,' he said. He was a pink, bald man, wearing rimless glasses. A fan was whirring over his head.

'I have brought this young man to see you,' Murugesam said.

The bald man looked at Chandran coldly, and said to Murugesam: 'You were not at the club yesterday.'

'I couldn't come. Had to go to the wharf.'

A servant brought in a visiting-card. The bald man looked at it critically and said: 'No more interviews today. Tomorrow at one-thirty.'

Murugesam went over to the other side of the table and spoke in whispers to the bald man. Murugesam almost sat on the arm of the bald man's revolving chair. Chandran was not asked to sit, and so he stood, uncertainly, looking at the walls, with his arms locked behind him. The bald man suddenly looked at Chandran and asked: 'Your father is . . . ?'

'H.C. Venkatachala Iyer.'

'He was . . . ?'

'A District Judge.'

'I see,' said the bald man. He turned to Murugesam and said: 'I have no idea what they are doing in regard to the agencies. I must ask Sankaran. I will let you know afterwards.'

Murugesam made some deprecating noises and said: 'That won't do. Call up Sankaran and tell him what to do. Surely you can dictate.' He left the arm of the chair and went to another chair, saying: 'He is a graduate, comes from a big family, prepared to give any security. He has cancelled his tour to England for the sake of your paper.'

'Why did you want to go to England?' asked the bald man, turning to Chandran.

'Wanted to get a doctorate.'

'At?'

'The London University.'

'In?'

'Economics or Politics,' said Chandran, choosing his subject for the first time.

'Why do you want to work for our paper?'

'Because I like it, sir.'

'Which? The paper or the agency?'

'Both,' said Chandran.

'Are you confident of sending up the circulation if you are given a district?'

'Yes, sir.'

'By how much?'

Chandran quoted 5,000, and explained the figures with reference to the area of Malgudi, its literate population, and the number of people who could spend an anna a day.

'That is a fair offer,' said Murugesam.

The bald man said with a dry smile: 'It is good to be optimistic.'

'Optimistic or not, you must give him a fair trial,' said Murugesam.

The bald man said: 'The trouble is that I don't usually interfere in these details. The managers concerned look to it. I have no idea what they are doing.'

'Well, well, well,' said Murugesam impatiently. 'There is no harm in it. You can break the rule occasionally and dictate. Just for my sake. I have to go back to the office. Hurry up. Send for Sankaran.' Murugesam pressed a bell. A servant came. Murugesam said: 'Tell Mr Sankaran to come up.'

A man with a scowling face came in, nodded, went straight to a chair, sat down, and leaned forward.

The bald man asked: 'Have you any vacancies in the Southern Districts?'

'For correspondents? No.'

'I mean agencies.'

'Yes, a few where we want to change the present agents.'

'Yours is Malgudi, is it not?' asked the bald man, turning to Chandran.

'Yes, sir.'

'I think that is one of the places,' said Sankaran.

The bald man said: 'Please give me some details of the place.'

Sankaran pressed a bell, scribbled something on a bit of paper, and gave it to the servant. 'Take it to Sastri.'

The servant went out and returned in a few minutes followed by an old man, who was carrying a register with him. He placed the register on the table before Sankaran, opened a page, and stood away respectfully.

Murugesam said at this point: 'Sit down, Mr Chandran.'

'Yes, yes, why are you standing?' asked the bald man.

Chandran sat in a chair and looked at the bald man, Sankaran, the turban-wearing Sastri, and Murugesam, and thought: 'My life is in these fellows' hands! Absolute strangers. Decision of my fate in their hands, absolutely! Why is it so?'

Sankaran said, looking at the register: 'Here are the facts, sir. Malgudi agency: the present man has been there since the old regime. The top circulation 35 till two years ago; since then steady at 25! Eleven applications for the agency up to date; one from the old agent himself promising to turn over a new leaf. Potential circulation in the district, 7,000.'

'Thank you,' said the bald man. 'When are you settling it?'

'I want to wait till the first.'

'Why should there be any delay? If you have no particular objection, give the agency to this gentleman. He promises to give the security immediately and work for the paper.'

Sankaran looked at Chandran and said to the bald man: 'Some more applications may be coming in, sir.'

'File them.'

'Very well, sir,' said Sankaran, and rose. 'Come with me,' he said to Chandran.

Sankaran took Chandran into a hall, where a number of persons were seated at tables, from the edges of which galley proofs streamed down to the floor. They went to the farthest end of the hall and sat down. Sankaran began a short speech on the *Daily Messenger*: 'The *Daily Messenger* is not the old paper that it was a year or two ago. The circulation has gone up from 8,000 to 30,000 in less than a year. That is due both to the circulation and the editorial departments. They both have work to do, just as you need both legs for walking.' He spoke over the din of the office and of the press below for half an hour, winding up with the threat that if Chandran did not show real progress within six months from the date of appointment, the agency would be immediately transferred to another.

CHAPTER FIFTEEN

CHANDRAN RETURNED TO Malgudi and plunged himself in work. He took a small room in Market Road for a rent of seven rupees a month, and hung on the doorway an immense sign: 'THE DAILY MESSENGER (Local Offices)'. He furnished his office with a table, a chair, and a long bench.

He sat in his office from eleven till five, preparing a list of possible subscribers in the town. At the lowest estimate there were five hundred. After enlisting them, he would go out into the district and enlist another five hundred; and for six months he would be quite content to stay at a thousand. He took out a sheet of paper and noted on it the procedure to be followed in canvassing. He often bit the pen and looked at the traffic in Market Road, steeped in thought. After four days of intense thinking and watching of traffic, he was able to sketch out a complete plan of attack. He wrote: 'Bulletin; Specimen; Interview; Advance.' He would first send his bulletin to the persons on his list, then supply free specimen copies for two days, then go and see them in person, and finally take a month's subscription in advance.

Next he planned the bulletin. It approached a client in four stages: Information; Illumination; Appeal; and Force.

Bulletin One said: 'Mr H.V. Chandran, BA, requests the pleasure of your company with family and friends at C-96 Market Road, where he has just opened the local offices of the *Daily Messenger* of Madras.' Bulletin Two said: 'Five reasons why you should immediately subscribe to the *Daily Messenger*: Its daily circulation is 30,000 in the Presidency, and 30,000 persons cannot be making a mistake every day. It is auspicious to wake to the thud of a paper dropped on the floor; and we are prepared to provide you with this auspicious start every morning by bringing the DM to your house and pushing it in through your front window. It has at its command all the news services in the world, so that you will find in it a Municipal Council resolution in Malgudi as well as a political assassination in Iceland, reported accurately and quickly. The mark of culture is wide information; and the DM will give you politics, economics, sports, literature; and its magazine supplement covers all the other branches of human knowledge. Even in mere bulk you will be getting your anna's worth; if you find the contents uninteresting you can sell away your copy to the grocer at a rupee per *maund*.' Bulletin Three said: 'As a son of the Motherland it is your duty to subscribe to the DM. With every anna that you pay, you support the anaemic child, Indian Industry. You must contribute your mite for the economic and political salvation of our country.' Bulletin Four merely stated: 'To the hesitant. It is never too late. Come at once to C-96 Market Road and take your paper, or shall we send it to your house? Never postpone to a tomorrow what you can do today.'

He gave these for printing to the Truth Printing Works, which was situated in another room like his, four doors off. The Truth Works consisted of a treadle, a typeboard, and a compositor, besides the proprietor.

The printer delivered the bulletins in about a week. Chandran put them in envelopes and addressed them according to the list he had prepared. He had now in his service three small boys for distributing the paper, and he had purchased for them three cheap cycles. He divided the town into three sections and allotted each of them a section, and gave them the envelopes for distribution. He sent the bulletins out in their order, one on each day.

After that he engaged a small party of brass band and street boys, and sent them through the principal streets of the town in a noisy procession, in which huge placards, shrieking out the virtues of the *Daily Messenger*, were carried.

He then distributed a hundred copies of the *Messenger* every day as specimens to the persons to whom he had sent the bulletins.

After all this preparation, he set out every morning on his cycle, neatly shaved and groomed, and dressed in an impeccable check suit, and interviewed his prospects. He took the town ward by ward. He calculated that if he worked from eight in the morning till eight in the evening he would be able to see about thirty-six prospects a day, giving about twenty minutes to each prospect.

He sent his card into every house and said as soon as his prospect appeared: 'Good morning, sir. How do you like our paper?' Soon he became an adept salesman, and in ten minutes could classify and label the person before him. He now realized that humanity fell into four types: (1) Persons who cared for the latest news and could afford an anna a day, (2) Persons who were satisfied with stale news in old papers which could be borrowed from neighbours, (3) Persons who read newspapers in reading-rooms, (4) Persons who could be coerced by repeated visits.

Chandran talked a great deal to 1 and 4, and never wasted more than a few seconds on 2 and 3.

He visited club secretaries, reading-room secretaries, head masters of schools, lawyers, doctors, businessmen, and landowners, and every literate person in the town, at home, office, and club. To some places, when he was hard-pressed for time, he sent Mohan.

In a few weeks he settled down to a routine. Every morning he left his bed at five o'clock and went to the station to meet the train from Madras at five-thirty. He took the bundles of papers and sent them in various directions with the cycle boys. After that he returned home, and went to his office only at eleven o'clock, and stayed there till five in the evening, when Mohan would drop in after posting his news for the day. Often Mohan would set him on the track of new clients: 'I have reported an interesting criminal case today. Full details will appear in tomorrow's paper.' As soon as the report appeared Chandran would go to the parties concerned and show them the news in print and induce them to part with a month's subscription, or if that was not possible, at least manage to sell them some loose copies containing their names. Some persons would be so pleased to see their names in print that they would buy even a dozen copies at a time. These stray sales accounted for, on an average, half a dozen copies every day. Mohan reported a wide variety of topics: excise raids, football matches, accidents, 'smart' arrests by police sub-inspectors, suicides, murders, thefts, lectures in Albert College Union, and social events like anniversaries, tea-parties, and farewell dinners.

The DM was responsible for taking him back to his old college after two years. Mohan had secured the Union and college orders. One of the boys came and told Chandran one day, suddenly: 'Sir, the college clerk says that they don't want the paper from tomorrow.'

'Why?'

'I don't know, sir. They said the same thing in the Union too.'

Chandran went to the college in person. The Union clerk recognized him and asked: 'How are you, Mr Chandran?'

'I say, my boy tells me that you have stopped the paper. Have you any idea why?'

'I don't know, sir. It is the President's order.'

'Who is the President this year?'

'History Ragavachar,' said the clerk.

He left the Union and went to the college, to the good old right wing, in which his Professor's room was situated. Ragavachar was holding a small class in his room, and Chandran went back to the Union to wait till the end of the hour. He sat in the gallery of the debating hall, and nobody took any notice of him. One or two boys stared at him and passed. He had been the Prime Mover in this very hall on a score of occasions; he had been the focus of attention. In those days, when he sat like this in the interim periods, how many people would gather round him, how they would all swagger about and shout as if they owned the place, and how they would throw pitying looks at strangers who sometimes came to look at the Union and moved about the place timidly. 'Not one here that belonged to my set, all new faces, all absolute strangers. Probably these were High School boys when we were in the college . . . Ramu, Ramu. How often have I come here looking for Ramu. If any class or lecture threatened to be boring Ramu would prefer to come away and spend his time reading a novel here or up in the reading-room. He had been quite a warm friend, but probably people changed. Time passed swiftly in Ramu's company. He would have some comment or other to make on every blessed thing on earth . . . If he had real affection for a friend he should have written letters, especially when there was happy news like the securing of a job. Out of sight, out of mind, but that is not a quality of friendship. There is no such thing as friendship . . .'

Chandran rose from the gallery and stood looking at some group photos hanging on the wall. All your interests, joys, sorrows, hopes, contacts, and experience boiled down to group photos, Chandran thought. You lived in the college, thinking that you were the first and the last of your kind the college would ever see, and you ended as a group photo; the laughing, giggling fellows one saw

about the Union now little knew that they would shortly be frozen
into group photos . . . He stopped before the group representing the
1931 set. He stood on tiptoe to see the faces. Many faces were
familiar, but he could not recollect all their names. Where were all
these now? He met so few of his classmates, though they had been
two hundred strong for four years. Where were they? Scattered like
spray. They were probably merchants, advocates, murderers, police
inspectors, clerks, officers, and what not. Some must have gone to
England, some married and had children, some turned agriculturists,
dead and starving and unemployed, all at grips with life, like a
buffalo caught in the coils of a python . . .

There was Veeraswami, the revolutionary. He had appeared
only once on the sands of the Sarayu, like a dead man come to life
for an instant. He had talked of some brigade and a revolution and
Nature Cure. Where was he? What had he done with himself? . . .
Among the people seated in the front row there was Natesan, the
old Union secretary, always in complications, always grumbling and
arranging meetings. Chandran realized that he hadn't heard of
Natesan after the examination; didn't know to which part of the
country he belonged. He had been a good friend, very helpful and
accommodating; but for his help the Historical Association could
not have done any work. Where was he? Had he committed
suicide? Could an advertisement be inserted in the papers: 'Oh,
Natesa, my friend, where are you?'

The bell rang. Chandran hurried out to meet Ragavachar. He
saw several students walking in the corridors of the college. Scores
of new faces. 'At any rate they were better built in our days. All
these fellows are puny.' He recognized a few that had been the
rawest juniors in his days, but were senior students now. They
greeted him with smiles, and he felt greatly pleased. He strode into
Ragavachar's room. Ragavachar sat in his chair and was just returning
his spectacles to their case.

'Good morning, sir,' said Chandran. The professor appeared to
be slightly loose in the joints now. How he had been terrified of
him in those days, Chandran reflected, as the professor opened his
case, put on the spectacles, and surveyed his visitor. There was no
recognition in his manner.

'Please sit down,' said the professor, still trying to place his
visitor.

'Don't you recognize me, sir?'

'Were you in this college at any time?'

'Yes, sir, in 1931. I was the first secretary of the Historical Association. My name is H.V. Chandran.'

'H.V. Chandran,' the professor repeated reflectively. 'Yes, yes. I remember. How are you? What are you doing now? You see, about two hundred persons pass out of the college every year; sometimes it is difficult to recollect, you see.'

Chandran had never thought that Ragavachar could talk so mildly. In those days how his voice silenced whole classes!

'What are you doing, Chandran?'

Chandran told him, and then stated his business.

'Send for the Union clerk,' said the professor. When the clerk came, he asked: 'Why have you stopped the *Daily Messenger*?'

'There was a President's order to stop some of the papers,' replied the clerk.

'And you chose the *Daily Messenger*, I suppose?' growled Ragavachar. His voice had lost none of its tigerishness. 'Which daily are you getting in the Union?'

'The *Everyday Post*, sir.'

This name set up a slight agitation in Chandran. The *Post* was his deadliest enemy; but for it he would have enlisted a thousand subscribers in a fortnight. He said: 'The *Post*! It isn't served by the Planet News Service, sir.'

'Isn't it?' asked Ragavachar.

'No, sir. It gets only the "C" grade of B.K. Press Agency.'

'Is there much difference?'

'Absolutely, sir. I am not saying it because I am the agent of the *Messenger*. You can compare the telegrams in the *Messenger* with those in the *Post*, and you will see the difference, sir. B.K. Agency is not half as wide an organization as the Planet, and its "C" grade is its very lowest service, and supplies the minimum news; the "A" and "B" grades are better. Our paper gets the "A" and "B" grades of the B.K. Agency in addition to the First Grade of the Planet Service; so that our paper gives all the news available.'

'Still, a lot of people buy the *Post*,' said Ragavachar.

'No, sir. Quite a lot of people are now buying only the *Messenger*. The circulation of the *Post* has steadily gone down to 2,000. Once upon a time it reigned supreme, when it was the only paper in the south.'

Ragavachar turned to the clerk and commanded: 'Get the

Messenger from tomorrow. Stop the *Post*.'

When Chandran rose to go, the professor said: 'I wish you luck. Please keep in touch with us. It ought to be easier for our students to remember us than for us to remember them. So don't forget.'

'Certainly not, sir,' Chandran said, resolving at that moment to visit his professor at least once a week.

The college library clerk told him that Gajapathi was in charge of the college reading-room. Chandran went to the Common Room and sent his card in and waited, wondering if Gajapathi was going to resume his attacks on Dowden and Bradley.

'Hello, hello, Chandran. It is ages since I saw you. What are you doing now?' Gajapathi put his arm round Chandran's shoulders and patted him. Chandran was taken aback by this affability, something they had not thought him capable of. Except for this Gajapathi had not changed. He still wore his discoloured frame spectacles and the drooping moustache.

When Chandran stated his business, Gajapathi said: 'If they are getting the *Messenger* in the Union we can't get it in the college reading-room, because the Principal has passed an order that papers and magazines should not be duplicated in the two reading-rooms.'

'But it is a waste of money to get the *Post*, sir. There is absolutely no news in it. It has a very inadequate service for telegrams, and it hasn't half as many correspondents as the *Messenger* has.'

'Whatever it is, that is the Principal's order.'

'Why don't you subscribe to my paper, sir?'

'Me! I never read any newspaper.'

Chandran was horrified to hear it. 'What do you do for news, sir?'

'I am not interested in any news.'

Evidently this man read only Shakespeare and his critics.

'Well, sir, if you won't consider it a piece of impertinence, I think you ought to get into the newspaper habit. I am sure you will like it. I am sure you wouldn't like to be without it even for a day.'

'Very well then, send it along. What is the subscription?'

'Two-eight a month and the paper is delivered at your door.'

'Here it is, for a month.' Gajapathi took out his purse and gave a month's subscription. 'You can ask your boy to deliver it to me at—'

'Thank you, sir. I shall send the receipt tomorrow.'

'Don't you trouble yourself about it. I only want my old students to do well in life. I am happy when I see it.'

Chandran had never known this fact, and now he was profoundly moved by it.

'You must visit my office some time, sir,' he said.

'Certainly, certainly. Where is it?'

Before parting, Chandran tried to gratify him by saying: 'I have been reading a lot since I left the college, sir.'

'Really very glad to hear it. What have you been reading?'

'A little of Shakespeare; some Victorian essayists. But in fiction I think the present-day writers are really the masters. Don't you think, sir, that Wells, Galsworthy, and Hardy are superior to the old novelists?'

Gajapathi paused before pronouncing an opinion. 'I honestly think that there has not been anything worth reading after the eighteenth century, and for anyone who cares for the real flavour of literature nothing to equal the Elizabethans. All the rest is trash.'

'Galsworthy, sir?'

'I find him tiresome.'

'Wells and Hardy?' gasped Chandran.

'Wells is a social thinker, hardly a literary figure. He is a bit cranky too. Hardy? Much overrated; some parts of *Tess* are good.'

Chandran realized that time had not touched his fanaticisms. What an unknown, unsuspected enemy Wells, Galsworthy, Hardy, and a host of critics had in Gajapathi, Chandran thought.

'Don't forget to visit my office, sir, some time,' Chandran pleaded before taking his leave.

CHAPTER SIXTEEN

ONE EVENING AT five o'clock, as Chandran sat in his office signing receipts and putting them in envelopes for distribution next morning, his father walked in. Chandran pushed his chair back and rose, quite surprised, for Father seldom came to the office; he had dropped in on the opening day, and again at another time with a friend, explaining apologetically that the friend wanted to see Chandran. Now this was his third visit.

'Sit down, Chandar, don't disturb yourself,' said Father, and tried to sit on the bench. Chandran pushed the chair towards him, entreating him to be seated on it.

Father looked about and asked: 'How is your business?'

'Quite steady, Father. The only trouble is in collection. If I go in person they pay the subscription; if I send the boys they put them off with some excuse or other. I can't be visiting the 350 subscribers in person every morning. I must engage a bill collector. I can just afford one now.'

'Are they pleased with your work in the Head Office?'

'They must be. For six months I have shown a monthly average of over fifty new subscriptions; but they have not written anything, which is a good sign. I don't expect anything better. If work is unsatisfactory our bosses will bark at us; if it is satisfactory they won't say so, but merely keep quiet.'

'You are right. In Government service, too, it is the same; the best that we can expect from those above us is a very passive appreciation.'

And then the conversation lagged for some time. Father suddenly said: 'I have come on a mission. I was sent by your mother.'

'Mother?'

'Yes. She wants this thing to be made known to you. She is

rather nervous to talk to you about it herself. So she has sent me.'

'What is it, Father?'

'But I wish you to understand clearly that I have not done anything behind your back. I have had no hand in this. It is entirely your mother's work.'

'What is it, Father?'

'You see, Mr Jayarama Iyer, who is a leading lawyer in Talapur, sent his daughter's horoscope to us some time ago; and for courtesy's sake yours was sent to them in return. Yesterday they have written to say that the horoscopes match very well, and asking if we have any objection to this alliance. I was for dropping the whole matter there, but your mother is very eager to make it known to you and to leave it to your decision. They have got in touch with us through our Ganapathi Sastrigal.'

Chandran sat looking at the floor. His father paused for a moment and said: 'I hear that the girl is about fifteen. They have sent a photo. She is good-looking. You can have a look at the photo if you like. They have written that she is very fair. They are prepared to give a cash dowry of 3,000 and other presents.'

He waited for Chandran's answer. Chandran looked at him. There were drops of sweat on Father's brow, and his voice quivered slightly. Chandran felt a great pity for his father. What a strain this talk and the preparation for it must have been to him! Father sat silent for a moment and then said, rising: 'I will be going now. I have to go to the club.'

Chandran saw his father off at the door and watched his back as he swung his cane and walked down the road. Chandran suddenly realized that he hadn't said anything in reply, and that his father might interpret silence for consent and live on false hopes. What a dreadful thing. He called his office boy, who was squatting on the steps of a neighbouring shop, asked him to remain in the office, took out his cycle, and pedalled in the direction his father had taken. Father hadn't gone far. Chandran caught up with him.

'You want me?'

'Yes, Father.'

Father slowed down, and Chandran followed him, looking at the ground. 'You have taken the trouble to come so far, Father, but I must tell you that I can't marry, Father.'

'It is all right, Chandar. Don't let that bother you.'

Chandran followed him for a few yards, and said: 'Shall I go back to the office?'

'Yes.'

As Chandran was about to mount his cycle, Father stopped him and said: 'I saw in your office some papers and letters lying loose on your table. They are likely to be blown away by a wind. Remind me, I will give you some paperweights tomorrow.'

He came back to his table and tried to sign a few more receipts. His father's visit opened a lid that had smothered raging flames. It started once again all the old controversies that racked one's soul. It violently shook a poise that was delicate and attained with infinite trouble and discipline.

He could not sign any more receipts. He pushed away the envelopes and the receipt books in order to make room for his elbows, which he rested on the table, and sat with his face in his hands, staring at the opposite wall.

Mohan came at six o'clock. He flung his cap on the table and sat down on the bench before the table, obstructing Chandran's view of the opposite wall.

Chandran asked mechanically, 'What is the latest news?'

'Nothing special. The usual drab nonsense; lectures and sports and suicides. I am seriously thinking of resigning.'

He was very sullen.

'What is wrong now?' asked Chandran.

'Everything. I took up this work as a stop-gap till I should get a footing in the literary world. And now what has. happened? Reporting has swallowed me up. From morning to night I roam about town, noting other people's business, and then go back to the hotel and sleep. I hardly have any inclination to write a single line of poetry. It is four months since I wrote a single line. The stuff you see in the magazine page are my old bits. When I take my pen I can't write anything more soul-stirring than "Judgment was delivered today in a case in which somebody or other stood charged with something or other . . ." '

'I am very hungry,' said Chandran. 'Shall we go to a hotel?'

'Yes.'

When they came out of the hotel, Mohan's mood had changed. He now condemned .his previous mood. 'If I have not written anything, it is hardly anybody's fault. I ought to plan my time to include it.'

They smoked a few cigarettes and walked along the river.

They walked to Nallappa's Grove, crossed over to the opposite bank, walked some distance there, turned back, and sat down on the sands. Mohan went on talking and solacing himself by planning. He even stretched the definition of poetry; he said that there ought to be no special thing called poetry, and that if one was properly constituted one ought to get a poetic thrill out of the composing of even news paragraphs. There ought to be no narrow boundaries. There ought to be a proper synthesis of life.

When Mohan had exhausted his poetic theories, Chandran quietly said: 'My father came to the office at five o'clock with an offer of marriage.' The troubles of a poet instantly ceased or were forgotten. He listened in silence to Chandran's narration of his father's visit. And Mohan dared not comment. From the manner in which Chandran spoke Mohan couldn't tell which way he was inclined; there was the usual denunciation of Love, Marriage, and Woman, but at the same time there was a lack of fire in the denunciation. Mohan could not decide whether it was the beginning of a change of attitude or whether it was a state of atrophy, so complete than even fury and fire were dead. Chandran concluded: '. . . And I ran after my father and told him that it was unthinkable.'

Chandran stopped. Mohan did not offer any comment. For some moments there was only the rustle of the banyan branches on the water's edge.

'I am very sorry for my poor mother, for her wild hope and her fears. I curse myself for having brought her to this state. But what can I do? What other answer could I give to my father?'

'How did he take it?'

'Quite indifferently. He talked of paperweights. My trouble is, I don't know, I don't know. I can't get angry with my mother for busying herself with my marriage again. I have had enough of it once.'

'Then leave it alone. You are under no compulsion to worry about it.'

'But I pity my father and mother. What a frantic attempt. There is something in the whole business that looks very pathetic to me.'

'What I can't understand is,' said Mohan, 'why you are still worrying about it, seeing that you have very politely told your father that it is unthinkable. I can't understand why you still talk about it.'

'You are right. That question is settled. Let us talk of something else.'

'Something else' was not easy to find. There was another interlude of silence.

'Shall we be starting back?' asked Mohan.

'Yes,' said Chandran, but again sat in silence, not making any effort to get up. For nearly a quarter of an hour Mohan sat listening to the voice of the river, and Chandran drew circles in the sand.

'What would you do in my place?' asked Chandran abruptly.

'How can I say? What would you do in mine?' asked Mohan.

Chandran asked directly: 'What would you honestly advise me to do?'

'If the girl is not bad-looking, and if you are getting some money into the bargain, why don't you marry? You will have some money and the benefits of a permanent helpmate.'

Chandran remarked that Mohan had grown very coarse and prosaic. No wonder he could not write any more poetry.

Stung by this, Mohan said: 'If one has to marry one must do it for love, if there is such a thing, or for the money and comforts. There is no sense in shutting your eyes to the reality of things. I am beginning to believe in a callous realism.' He liked immensely the expression he had invented. He loved it. He delivered a short speech on Callous Realism. He had not thought of it till now. Now that he had coined the expression he began to believe in it fully. He raised it to the status of a personal philosophy. Before he had expatiated for five minutes on it, he became a fanatic. He challenged all other philosophies, and pleaded for more Callous Realism in all human thought. When he reached the height of intoxication he said with a great deal of callous realism: 'I don't see why you shouldn't consider this offer with the greatest care and attention. You get a fat three thousand, and get a good-looking companion, who will sew on your buttons, mend your clothes, and dust your furniture while you are out distributing newspapers, and who will bring the coffee to your room. In addition to all this, it is always pleasant to have a soft companion near at hand.'

'And on top of it pleasing one's parents,' added Chandran.

'Quite right. Three cheers for Her Majesty the Soft Companion,' cried Mohan.

'Hip, hip, hooray!'

The callous realist now asked: 'Will you kindly answer a few questions I am going to ask?'

'Yes.'

'You must answer my questions honestly and truthfully. They are to search your heart.'

'Right, go on,' said Chandran.

'Are you still thinking of Malathi?'

'I have trained my mind not to. She is another man's wife now.'

'Do you love the memory of her still?'

'I don't believe in love. It doesn't exist in my philosophy. There is no such thing as love. If I am not unkind to my parents it is because of gratitude, and nothing else. If I get a wife I shall not wrench her hand or swear at her, because it would be indecent. That is all the motive for a lot of habitual decent behaviour we see, which we call love. There is no such thing as love.'

'Then it ought not to make any difference to you whether you marry or not; and so why don't you marry when you know that it will please your parents, when you are getting a lot of money, and when you are earning so well?'

There was no answer to this. Chandran chewed on these thoughts in silence, and then said: 'Mohan, let us toss and decide.' They rose and walked across the sand to a dim municipal lantern at the end of North Street. The lantern threw a pale yellow circle of light around a central shadow. Chandran took a copper coin from his pocket. Mohan held Chandran's hand and said: 'Put that back. Let us toss a silver coin. Marriage, you know.' Mohan took out a four anna silver coin, balanced it on the forefinger of his right hand, and asked: 'Shall I toss?'

'Yes. Heads, marriage.'

'Right.'

Mohan tossed the silver coin. It fell down in the dim circumference of light. Both stooped. Mohan shouted: 'You must keep your word. Heads. Ha! Ha!'

'Is it?' There was a tremor in Chandran's voice. 'Very well, if the girl is good-looking; only if she is good-looking,' said Chandran.

'That goes without saying,' said Mohan, picking up the coin and putting it in his pocket.

EARLY IN THE morning, five days later, Chandran, with his mother, was in a train going to Talapur. He was to look at the girl who had been proposed to him, and then give his final word.

He said to his mother for the dozenth time: 'If I don't like the girl, I hope they won't mind.'

'Not at all. Before I married your father, some three or four persons came and looked at me and went away.'

'Why did they not approve of you?' Chandran asked, looking at her.

'It is all a matter of fate,' said Mother. 'You can marry only the person whom you are destined to marry and at the appointed time. When the time comes, let her be the ugliest girl, she will look all right to the destined eye.'

'None of that, Mother,' Chandran protested. 'I won't marry an ugly girl.'

'Ugliness and beauty is all as it strikes one's eye. Everyone has his own vision. How do all the ugly girls in the world get married?'

Chandran became apprehensive. 'Mother, are you suggesting that this girl is ugly?'

'Not at all. Not at all. See her for yourself and decide. You have the photo.'

'She is all right in the photo, but that may be only a trick of the camera.'

'You will have to wait for only a few hours more. You can see her and then give your decision.'

'But, Mother, to go all the way to their house and see the girl, and then to say we can't marry her. That won't be nice.'

'What is there in it? It is the custom. When a girl is ready for marriage her horoscope will be sent in ten directions, and ten different persons will see her and approve or disapprove, or they might be disapproved by the girl herself; and after all only one will marry her. A year before my marriage a certain doctor was eager for an alliance with our family; the horoscopes, too, matched; and his son came to look at me, but I didn't like his appearance, and told my father that I wouldn't marry him. It was after that that your father was proposed, and he liked my appearance, and when my father asked me if I would marry him I didn't say "no". It is all settled already, the husband of every girl and the wife of every man. It is in nobody's choice.'

They reached Talapur at 4 p.m. A boy of about eighteen came and peeped into the compartment and asked: 'Are you from Malgudi?'

'Yes,' said Chandran.

'I am Mr Jayarama Iyer's son. Shall I ask my servant to carry your baggage?'

'We have brought nothing. We are going back by the seven o'clock train, you see,' said Chandran. Chandran and his mother exchanged a brief look. 'This is the girl's brother,' the look said. Chandran took another look at the boy and tried to guess the appearance of the girl. If the girl looked anything like her brother...! The boy was dark and rugged. Probably this was not her own brother; he might be her first cousin. Chandran opened his mouth, and was about to ask if Jayarama Iyer was his own father, but he checked himself and asked instead: 'Are you Mr Jayarama Iyer's eldest son?'

'I am his second son,' replied the boy. This answer did not throw any light on the appearance of the girl, as, in some absurd manner, Chandran had imagined that it would.

The boy took them to a car outside. They were soon in the Extensions.

They were welcomed into the house by Mr Jayarama Iyer and his wife, both of whom subjected Chandran to a covert examination just as he tried to make out something of his future relatives-in-law. He found Mr Jayarama Iyer to be a middle-aged person with a greying crop and a sensitive face. He was rather dark, but Chandran noted that the mother looked quite fair, and hoped that the girl would have a judicious mixture of the father's sensitive appearance and the mother's complexion.

And to his immense satisfaction he found that it was so, when, about an hour later, she appeared before him. She had to be coaxed and cajoled by her parents to come to the hall. With her eyes fixed on the ground she stepped from an inner room, a few inches into the hall, trembling and uncertain, ready to vanish in a moment.

Chandran's first impulse was to look away from the girl. He spent a few seconds looking at a picture on the wall; but suddenly remembered that he simply could not afford to look at anything else now. With a sudden decision, he turned his head and stared at her. She was dressed in a blue saree. A few diamonds glittered in her earlobes and neck. His heart gave a wild beat and, as he thought, stopped. 'Her figure is wonderful,' some corner of his mind murmured. 'Her face must also be wonderful, but I can't see it very well, she is looking at the ground.' Could he shriek out to Mr Jayarama Iyer, sitting in the chair on his right and uttering inanities at this holy moment: 'Please ask your daughter to look up, sir, I can't see her face'?

Mr Jayarama Iyer said to his daughter: 'You mustn't be so shy, my girl. Come here. Come here.'

The girl was still hesitating and very nervous. Chandran felt a great sympathy for her. He pleaded: 'Sir, please don't trouble her. Let her stay there.'

'As you please,' said Jayarama Iyer.

At this moment the girl slightly raised her head and stole a glance at Chandran. He saw her face now. It was divine; there was no doubt about it. He secretly compared it with Malathi's, and wondered what he had seen in the latter to drive him so mad . . .

Jayarama Iyer said to his daughter: 'Will you play a little song on the veena?' Chandran saw that she was still nervous, and once again rushed to her succour. 'Please don't trouble her, sir. I don't mind. She seems to be nervous.'

'She is not nervous,' said her father. 'She plays very well, and also sings.'

'I am happy to hear that, sir, but it must be very difficult for her to sing now. I hope to hear her music some other day.'

Jayarama Iyer looked at him with amusement and said: 'All right.'

It was with a very heavy heart that Chandran allowed himself to be carried away in the car from the bungalow. He could have cried when he said 'Good-bye' to his future brother-in-law, and the train moved out of Talapur station.

His mother asked him in the train: 'Do you like the girl?'

'Yes, Mother,' said Chandran with fervour. 'Did you tell them that?'

'We can't tell them anything till they come and ask us.'

Chandran made a gesture of despair and said: 'Oh, these formalities. I loathe them. All this means unnecessary delay. Why shouldn't we send them a wire tomorrow?'

'Be patient. Be patient. All in its time, Chandra.'

'But supposing they don't ask us?'

'They will. In two or three days they will come to us or write.'

'I ought to have told Mr Jayarama Iyer that I liked his girl,' Chandran said regretfully.

Mother asked apprehensively: 'I hope you have not done any such thing?'

'No, Mother.'

'Patience, Chandra. You must allow things to be done in proper order.'

Chandran leaned back, resigned himself to his fate, and sat looking out of the window sulkily.

He asked: 'Mother, do you like the girl?'

'Yes, she is good-looking.'

'Is her voice all right? Does she talk all right?'

'She talks quite well.'

'Does she talk intelligently?'

'Oh, yes. But she spoke very little before me. She was shy before her future mother-in-law.'

'What class is she reading in, Mother?'

'Sixth Form.'

'Is she a good student?'

'Her mother says that she is very good in her class.'

'Her father says that she plays very well on the veena. It seems she can also sing very well . . . Mother, her name is . . . ?' He knew it very well, but loved to hear it again.

'Susila,' Mother said.

'I know it,' Chandran said, fearing that his Mother might understand him. 'I want to know if she has any other name at home.'

'Her mother called her once or twice before me, and she called her Susila.'

For the rest of the journey the music of the word 'Susila' rang in his cars. Susila, Susila, Susila. Her name, music, figure, face, and everything about her was divine. Susila, Susila—Malathi, not a spot beside Susila; it was a tongue-twister; he wondered why people liked that name.

CHAPTER EIGHTEEN

A FORTNIGHT LATER the ceremony of the wedding notice was celebrated. Jayarama Iyer and a party came to Malgudi for that purpose. It was a day of feast and reception in Chandran's house. A large number of guests were invited, and at the auspicious moment Jayarama Iyer stood up and read the saffron-touched paper which announced that, by the blessing of God, Chandran, son of so-and-so, was to marry Susila, daughter of so-and-so, on a particular auspicious date, ten days hence.

The days that followed were days of intense activity. They were days of preparation for the wedding, a period in which Chandran felt the *Daily Messenger* a great nuisance. Chandran had an endless round of visits to make every day, to the tailor, to the jewellers, to the silk shops, and to the printer.

The invitation cards, gold-edged and elegantly printed, were sent to over a thousand in Malgudi and outside. It was while sitting in his office and writing down the addresses that Chandran realized once again how far time had removed him from old class-mates and friends. He was very anxious not to miss anyone. But with the utmost difficulty he could remember only a dozen or so that he occasionally met in the town; he could recollect a few more, but couldn't trace their whereabouts. It rent his heart when he realized his helplessness in regard to even Ramu, Veeraswami, and Natesan. While he knew that Ramu was somewhere in Bombay, there was no one who could give him his address. Heaven knew where Natesan was. And Veeraswami? 'Probably he is a political prisoner somewhere, or he may be in Russia now.'

'Or it is more likely that he is a tame clerk in some Government office,' said Mohan.

'What has happened to his Brigade?'

'I have no idea; he came to my hotel once or twice some years ago. I didn't see him after that.'

'Probably his brigade has a strength of a million members now, all of whom may be waiting to overthrow the Government,' said Chandran.

'It is more likely that he has a lucrative job as a police informer,' said the cynical poet. He repeated: 'I have no idea where he is. He came and stayed in my hotel twice several months or years ago.'

This started a train of memories in Chandran. Evenings and evenings ago; Chandran, Mohan, and Veeraswami; Malathi evenings; mad days . . . There was a radiance about Susila that was lacking in Malathi . . . No, no. He checked himself this time; he told himself that it was very unfair to compare and decry; it was a very vile thing to do. He told himself that he was doing it only out of spite . . . Poor Malathi! For the first time he was able to view her as a sister in a distant town. Poor girl, she had her points. Of course Susila was different.

'What are you thinking?' asked Mohan.

'That postmaster, the Maduram postmaster, we must send him a card. I don't know if he still remembers me.'

While Chandran was away at Talapur for his wedding, Mohan looked after the newspaper.

Chandran returned a new man, his mind full of Susila, the fragrance of jasmine and sandal paste, the smokiness of the sacred fire, of brilliant lights, music, gaiety, and laughter.

For nearly a month after that Mohan had to endure monologues from Chandran: 'On the first day she was too shy to talk to me. It was only on the third day that she uttered a few syllables. Before I came away she spoke quite a lot. Shy at first, you know. She is a very sensible girl; talks very intelligently. I asked her what she thought of me; she merely threw at me a mischievous side-glance. She has a very mischievous look. She has promised to write to me on alternate days; she writes beautiful English . . .'

Thereafter, every day, Chandran spent a large portion of his waking hours in writing letters to her or in reading her letters. He would have to live on them for nearly a year more. His talks to Mohan were usually on the subject of these letters. 'She has written a wonderful letter to me today, has addressed me as "My Own

Darling" for the first time; she has sent me twenty thousand kisses though I sent her only fifteen thousand in my last letter . . .' Or, 'She likes very much the silk pieces that I sent to her. She says that they are wonderful.' Or, touching his inner pocket, in which more than one of her letters always rested, 'Poor girl! She writes asking me to take very great care of my health. Says that I ought not to get up so early every morning. She has inquired about the business and wishes me more subscribers. She wishes the *Daily Messenger* long life and health. She has a very great sense of humour.'

Two months later, one evening, Chandran was sitting in his office in a very depressed state. Mohan came, sat on the bench, and asked: 'What is wrong?'

Chandran lifted a careworn face to him, and said: 'No letter even today. This is the sixth day. I don't know what the matter is.'

'Probably she is studying for the examination or something. She will probably write to you tomorrow.'

'I don't think so,' said Chandran. He was in complete despair. 'This is the first time she has not written for so many days.'

Mohan was baffled. He had never been face to face with such a problem before.

Chandran said: 'I shouldn't worry but for the fact that she is unwell. She wrote in her last letter that she had a bad cold. She is probably down with high fever now. Who knows what fever it might be.'

'It may be just malaria,' hazarded Mohan.

'For six days, unintermittently!' Chandran laughed gloomily. 'I dare not name anything now. I don't know if her people will attend to her properly . . . I must go in person and see. I shall go home now, and then catch the six o'clock train. I shall be in Talapur tomorrow morning. Till I come back, please look after the office, will you?'

'Yes,' said Mohan to the afflicted man.

'Many thanks. I shall try to be back soon,' said Chandran and rose. He stepped into the road, took out his cycle from its stand, and said to Mohan: 'I have marked two addresses on the tablet. If they don't give the subscription tell the boys not to deliver them the papers tomorrow.'

As he was ready to get on the cycle, Mohan ran to the door, and said: 'Look here, not that I shirk work and don't want to look after the office or anything, but why do you suppose all these terrible things? On the authority of absent letters and the mention of a slight cold?'

Chandran scorned this question, jumped on his cycle without a word, and pedalled away. Mohan stood looking after the cycle for some time, and turned in, throwing up his arms in despair. But then, it is a poet's business only to ask questions; he cannot always expect an answer.

The Vendor of Sweets

CHAPTER ONE

'CONQUER TASTE, AND you will have conquered the self,' said Jagan to his listener, who asked, 'Why conquer the self?' Jagan said, 'I do not know, but all our sages advise us so.'

The listener lost interest in the question; his aim was only to stimulate conversation, while he occupied a low wooden stool next to Jagan's chair. Jagan sat under the framed picture of the Goddess Lakshmi hanging on the wall, and offered prayers first thing in the day by reverently placing a string of jasmine on top of the frame; he also lit an incense stick and stuck it in a crevice in the wall. The air was charged with the scent of jasmine and incense and imperceptibly blended with the fragrance of sweetmeats frying in ghee, in the kitchen across the hall.

The listener was a cousin, though how he came to be called so could not be explained, since he claimed cousin-hood with many others in the town (total incompatibles, at times); but if challenged he could always overwhelm the sceptic with genealogy. He was a man-about-town and visited many places and houses from morning till night, and invariably every day at about four-thirty he arrived, threw a brief glance and a nod at Jagan, passed straight into the kitchen, and came out ten minutes later wiping his mouth with the end of a towel on his shoulder, commenting, 'The sugar situation may need watching. I hear the Government is going to raise the price. Wheat flour is all right today. I gave that supplier a bit of my mind yesterday when I passed Godown Street. Don't ask me what took me there. I have friends and relations all over this city and everyone wants me to attend to this or that. I do not grudge serving others. What is life worth unless we serve and help each other?'

Jagan asked, 'Did you try the new sweet the cook experimented with today?'

'Yes, of course. It is tasty.'

'Oh, I think it is only an old recipe in a new shape. All sweetmeats after all are the same. Don't you agree?'

'No, sir,' said the cousin, 'I still see a lot of difference between one sweet and another. I hope I shall not become a *yogi* and lose the taste for all.'

It was then that Jagan pronounced his philosophy: 'Conquer taste and you will have conquered the self.' They chattered thus for half an hour more, and then Jagan asked, 'Do you know what I eat nowadays?'

'Anything new?' asked the cousin.

'I have given up salt since this morning.' Jagan said it with a glow of triumph. He felt satisfied with the effect produced and expanded his theory. 'One must eat only natural salt.'

'What is natural salt?' asked the cousin, and added, 'The salt that dries on one's back when one has run a mile in the sun?'

Jagan made a wry face at the coarse reference. He had the outlook of a soul disembodied, floating above the grime of this earth. At fifty-five his appearance was slight and elfish, his brown skin was translucent, his brow receded gently into a walnut-shade of baldness, and beyond the fringe his hair fell in a couple of speckled waves on his nape. His chin was covered with whitening bristles as he shaved only at certain intervals, feeling that to view oneself daily in a mirror was an intolerable European habit. He wore a loose *jibba* over his *dhoti*, both made of material spun with his own hand; every day he spun for an hour, and produced enough yarn for his sartorial requirements. He never possessed more than two sets of clothes at any one time and he delivered all the excess yarn in neat bundles to the local handloom committee in exchange for cash; although the cash he thus earned was less than five rupees a month, he felt a sentimental thrill in receiving it, as he had begun the habit when Gandhi visited the town over twenty years ago and had been commended for it. He wore a narrow almond-shaped pair of glasses set in a yellowish frame, and peeped at the world over their pale rim. He draped his shoulders in a *khaddar* shawl with gaudy, yellow patterns on it, and he shod his feet with thick sandals made out of the leather of an animal which had died of old age. Being a follower of Gandhi, he explained, 'I do not like to think that a living creature should have its throat cut for the comfort of my feet,' and this occasionally involved him in excursions to remote villages where a cow or calf was reported to be dying. When he secured the hide he soaked it in some solution, and then turned it over to an old cobbler he knew, who had his little repair shop under a tree in the Albert Mission compound.

When his son was six years old he was a happy supporter of Jagan's tanning activities in the back veranda of the house, but as he grew older he began to complain of the stench whenever his father brought home leather. Jagan's wife proved even less tolerant than the son; she shut herself in a room and refused to come out until the tanning ended. Since it was a prolonged process, carried on over several days, one can understand the dislocation into which the household was thrown whenever Jagan attempted to renew his footwear. It was a difficult and hazardous operation. The presence of the leather at home threatened to blast his domestic life; he had to preserve it, in the early stages of tanning, out of his wife's reach in the fuel shed, where there was danger of rats nibbling it. When she lay dying, she summoned Jagan to come closer to her and mumbled something. He could not make out her words, but was harrowed by the thought that probably she was saying, 'Throw away the leather.' In deference to what was possibly her last wish, he did give away the last bit of leather at home to a mission and felt happy that he was enabling someone else to take to non-violent footwear. Afterwards he just trusted the cobbler at the Albert Mission to supply his rather complicated footwear.

Now his cousin's reference to natural salt upset his delicate balance and he reddened in the face. The cousin, satisfied with the effect he had produced, tried to restore his mood with a pleasing remark, 'You have simplified your life so completely, and made yourself absolutely self-dependent, as I was saying to the Cooperative Registrar the other day . . .' This had the desired effect and Jagan said, 'I have discontinued sugar, as you know. I find twenty drops of honey in hot water quite adequate, and this is the natural way of taking in the sugar we need.'

'You have perfected the art of living on nothing,' said the cousin.

Encouraged, Jagan added, 'I have given up rice too. I cook a little stone-ground wheat and take it with honey and greens.'

'And yet,' said the cousin, 'I cannot understand why you go on working and earning, taking all this trouble!' He waved his hands in the direction of the sweets displayed on trays at the window, but stopped short of asking why Jagan should expect others to eat sweets and keep him flourishing. He felt he had said enough, and stirred in his seat. Jagan's counting hour was approaching, and the cousin knew he should move, as Jagan did not like his cash to be watched.

The time was six, the peak sales were over and the front-stall boy would be bringing in the main collection for the day. At this moment Jagan almost fancied himself a monarch on a throne surveying his people (consisting of the four cooks in the kitchen and the front-stall boy) and accepting their tributes. The throne was a flat-bottomed wooden chair covered with a thin cushion, hoisted on a platform, strategically placed so that he could keep an eye on all sides of his world of confections. The chair was nearly a century old, with shining brass strips on the arms and back and carved legs, especially made by his father when he built his house behind the Lawley statue. Normally he would not have bothered to design a piece of furniture, as the family always sat on the polished floor, but he had frequent visits from a Mr Noble, an Englishman, the District Collector, who came for lessons in astrology, and found it painful to sit on the floor, and even more painful to extricate himself from the sitting posture at the end of the lessons. A signed portrait ripening yellow with time was among the prized possessions dumped in the loft; but at some point in the history of the family the photograph was brought down, the children played with it for a while, and then substituted in its glassed frame the picture of a god and hung it up, while the photograph in the bare mount was tossed about as the children gazed on Mr Noble's side whiskers and giggled all the afternoon. They fanned themselves with it, too, when the summer became too hot; finally it disappeared back to the loft amidst old account books and other obscure family junk.

Sitting there, Jagan was filled with a sense of fulfilment. On one side he could hear, see and smell whatever was happening in the kitchen whence a constant traffic of trays laden with colourful sweetmeats passed to the front counter. As long as the frying and sizzling noise in the kitchen continued and the trays passed, Jagan noticed nothing, his gaze unflinchingly fixed on the Sanskrit lines in a red bound copy of the *Bhagavad Gita*, but if there was the slightest pause in the sizzling, he cried out, without lifting his eyes from the sacred text, 'What is happening?' The head cook would give a routine reply, 'Nothing,' and that would quieten Jagan's mind and enable it to return to the Lord's sayings until again some slackness was noticed at the front stall and he would shout, 'Captain!—That little girl in the yellow skirt, ask her what she wants. She has been standing there so long!' His shout would alert the counter-attendant as well as the watchman at the door, an ex-army man in khaki, who had a tendency to doze off on his dealwood seat. Or Jagan would cry, 'Captain, that beggar should not be seen here except on Fridays. This is not a charity home.'

The surroundings were hushed when the master counted his earnings for the day. Although the boy at the front stall received all the cash, he was not supposed to know the total. He just dropped every paisa he received into a long-necked bronze jug, and brought it in at six o'clock, returned to his seat and brought in another instalment in a smaller container at seven, when the shutters were drawn. Jagan would not count the cash yet, but continued to read the Lord's sayings. Without looking up he was aware that the frying had stopped, he noticed the hissing of the oven when the fire died out, the clinking of pans and ladles being washed, and then the footsteps approaching him, four pairs of feet from the kitchen, and one pair from the front stall, as trays of leftovers were brought in as the last act for the day. Then, when he knew that all of them were assembled at his desk, he addressed in a general way a routine question, 'How much is left over?'

'Not much.'

'Be exact.'

'Two seers of *Mysore pak*.'

'That we can sell tomorrow.'

'*Jilebi*, half a seer.'

'Won't be so good tomorrow. All right, go.'

The front-stall boy carried in the leftover trays and unobtrusively made his exit. The cooks still awaited his permission to leave. Jagan asked, 'Are all the windows shut?'

'Yes.'

Jagan now addressed himself to the head cook, 'Tomorrow no *jilebi*. What is wrong with it?' It bothered him to think of the leftovers. They rankled in his mind as if he had a splinter in his skull. He loved to see clean shining trays return to the kitchen at the end of a day. A babble of argument followed. Jagan asked, 'What do we do with the leftovers?'

The head cook said soothingly as usual, 'We will try a new

sweet tomorrow, if you will let me do it. There will be no problem of leftovers. We can always pulp everything back and fry them afresh in a new shape.'

Jagan said philosophically, 'After all, everything consists of flour, sugar and flavours . . .' trying to come to a decision which he had been resisting all along; but, after all, one had to take a practical view, with the price of foodstuff going up.

When his staff was gone he put away his scripture book and pulled the drawer of his table half out; it was padded with a folded towel in order to muffle the sound of coin being emptied from the bronze jug. His fingers quickly sorted out the denominations, the fives, tens, and quarters, with the flourish of a virtuoso running his fingers over a keyboard; his eyes swept the collection at a glance and arrived at the final count within fifteen minutes. He made an entry in a small notebook, and then more elaborate entries in a ledger which could be inspected by anyone. In his small notebook he entered only the cash that came in after six o'clock, out of the smaller jug. This cash was in an independent category; he viewed it as free cash, whatever that might mean, a sort of immaculate conception, self-generated, arising out of itself and entitled to survive without reference to any tax. It was converted into crisp currency at the earliest moment, tied into a bundle and put away to keep company with the portrait of Mr Noble in the loft at home.

Jagan gave a final look at the cash in the drawer, locked it carefully, tugged the handle four times, and pushed his chair back with a lot of noise. He put a huge brass lock on the door, turned the key and put it in his pocket, and said, 'Captain! See if the lock is all right.' The captain seized the lock in a martial grip, as if it were a hand grenade, and gave it a final jerk. 'This is a very strong lock, sir, can't get it nowadays. I know about locks; this must have been made in a village foundry.' He expatiated on the world of locks and locksmiths. Jagan cut him short with, 'Well, be watchful.' The captain gave him a military salute, and that was the end of the day.

CHAPTER TWO

A LULL HAD fallen on Market Road when he walked back home at a little past seven-thirty. An enormous shaft of blue light fell on the road from the Krishna Dispensary. He noticed Dr Krishna at his table peering at the throat of a patient. A street dog lay snoring on a heap of stones on the roadside, kept there since the first municipal body was elected in Free India in 1947 and meant for paving the road. A light was still seen under the door of Truth Printing although it was shut in deference to the Shopping Hours Act. Jagan knew that if he knocked, Nataraj would open the door, and he could always have the excuse of asking if the book was ready. The book had been in the press for years out of count, his magnum opus on Nature Cure and Natural Diet. Jagan knew that Nataraj would say again that he was waiting for types, but he could always sit down in one of his chairs and discuss politics. He overcame the temptation and passed on. 'Must be home, the boy will be lonely. Not today.' He fell into a brooding and introspective state as he walked on the edge of the road and was alone with himself. *Jutkas* drove past him with the drivers urging their horses with shrill cries, and then a few cycles, a scooter and a couple of cars loudly honking their horns. The traffic thinned and disappeared and he knew that he had come past Kabir Lane, as no more light fell in the street from the shops. At the junction of Market Road and Lawley Extension there was a short parapet over a culvert. As usual the vagrant was sitting on it, staring at passers-by and spitting into the gutter, and the donkey stood beside the wall as if it were offering itself for target practice. Jagan knew what the vagrant was waiting for: for the dining leaves to be cast out of the homes in Kabir Street: he would collect them, scour them with his hands and fill his belly with any vegetables and rice that might be left on them. 'The remedy would be for our nation to change its habits, for people to eat off plates and not use leaves for the purpose: the plates could be washed and kept, unlike the leaves which are thrown out after ·dinner for vagrants to pick,' Jagan reflected. He was for a moment racked with the problem of national improvement in various directions. 'If everyone discarded dining leaves, those engaged in the leaf trade would be thrown out of their profession and an alternative engagement would have to be found for them. But first statistics should be taken of the percentage of the population eating off leaves (and those eating off plates: what kind of plate? Silver, aluminium or what metal?). How many were engaged in gathering the dry leaves from the forests of Mempi and stitching them with little splinters, and how many in cultivating special banana leaves used for dining?' Till all this was done on a national scale this vagrant would continue to remain here. Late in the night he emerged from this culvert and went down the streets crying at every door, 'O good mother, give a handful of rice for this hungry one . . .' He had a deep voice which penetrated the door and reached the kitchen beyond; his tone also quietened troublesome children as he was described to be a man with three eyes. 'He is a disgrace to the nation,' Jagan commented within himself and by the time he reached the statue of Lawley, a furlong off, his head throbbed with several national and human problems and their ramifications. Sir Frederick Lawley faced the city; his back was supposed to be the back of beyond at one time, the limit of the city's expansion, but this prophecy was confounded when Lawley Extension, South Extension, and the New Extension all stretched out beyond the statue, and Jagan's ancestral home which had been the last house outskirting the city became the first one for all the newer colonies.

As Jagan approached the statue, he felt a thrill, not at the spectacle of the enormous gentleman standing in a Napoleonic attitude, benignly surveying the history and fortunes of Malgudi in a grand sweep (Jagan had ceased to notice the statue for over forty years now), but because he anticipated a glimpse of his son Mali on the other side of the statue. The pedestal had broad steps all around, and served as a park bench for the young and the old of the neighbourhood. Pensioners, idlers, tired workmen, sickly citizens advised by their doctors to inhale fresh air, sat facing east, west, north and south on the steps. Students leaning on their cycles formed a group on the southern steps, all dressed in tight trousers and colourful shirts, hotly discussing film stars and cricket and fashions in dress and deportment. Jagan passed the statue on its north side so that he might not embarrass his son, but he liked to make sure that he was there; with a swift glance at the group, he spotted Mali by the deep yellow of his shirt, and the brief glimpse filled him with joy. He tiptoed away looking elsewhere, muttering to himself irrelevantly, 'Poor boy, poor boy, let him be.' He was very proud of his son's height, weight and growth. 'There are others, but he stands out among them. I wonder what God has in store for him,' he reflected, 'must give him more time.' He reached home, his thoughts still hovering about his son.

He let himself into his house, switched on the light in the front room, took off his upper cloth and hung it on a nail in the wall, took off his *jibba* and thrust it into a basket for tomorrow's wash. He passed through the ancient house, through its triple series of open courtyards and corridors, and reached the back door, lifted the crossbar, and let it down gently. He stood for a moment gazing at the stars, enthralled at the spectacle of the firmament. 'One still wonders,' he told himself, 'but the problem remains. Who lives in those? We are probably glimpsing the real Heaven and don't know it. Probably all our ancient sages are looking down at us. What are those constellations?' He couldn't be clear about them. His astronomy was limited to the location of the Pole Star from Orion's Belt or Sword or some such point, for which knowledge he had been awarded a second-class badge many years ago when he was a scout. His astronomy did not progress beyond that. For all the million stellar bodies sparkling, as far as Jagan was concerned they might not be more than the two he had been taught to identify. In addition to Orion and the Pole Star he often noticed an extraordinary lively firework in the sky, which sometimes stood poised over the earth in the westerly direction. He sometimes called it Venus, sometimes Jupiter, never being sure, but admiring it unreservedly and feeling proud that he was also a part of the same creation. All this was a habitual second of contemplation whenever he passed into the bathroom in the backyard.

The bathroom was a shack, roofed with corrugated sheets; beaten-out tin was fixed anyhow to a wooden frame to serve as a door on rusty hinges; the wooden frame was warped and the door never shut flush, but always left a gap through which one obtained a partial glimpse of anyone bathing. But it had been a house practice, for generations, for its members not to look through. This bathroom remained very much what it had been in the days of his father, who had resisted all suggestions for improvement, declaring, 'After all, no one is expected to live in a bathroom; one had better come out of it soon so that the rest may have a chance of tidying themselves.' A very tall coconut tree loomed over the bath, shedding enormous withered fronds and other horticultural odds and ends on the corrugated roof with a resounding thud. Everything in this home had the sanctity of usage, which was the reason why no improvement was possible. Jagan's father, as everyone knew, had lived at first in a thatched hut at the very back of this ground. Jagan remembered playing in a sand heap outside the hut; the floor of the hut was paved with cool clay and one could put one's cheek to it on a warm day and feel heavenly. His father had also trained up a beanstalk on to the thatch and watched its development with anxiety. When he found some money, he put up the walls of the bathroom, laying the bricks with his own hands, and that became practically the starting point of the house. They fetched water from a well across the road and stored it in old kerosene tins and drums. His father expanded the house from the backyard to the front (although stubbornly refusing to improve the bath). As a child, Jagan had no notion how his father's fortune improved, although he heard vague words such as 'appeal', 'lawyers', 'lower court' and 'upper court'. By the time he became an adult, capable of understanding these affairs, they were over and he never could explain what the litigations were about and against whom. There came a time when the hut was finally pulled down, its thatches were used for heating a cauldron of water for the bath, and the cool mud floor was torn up and dug into pits for planting coconut seedlings. His father spent a whole week in these operations. Jagan and his brothers carried off baskets of shovelled earth, screaming with delight, 'Let us build a mountain.' Father had his theories of coconut-rearing and filled the pits with great quantities of salt. 'Salt is the only thing that can make a coconut tree grow,' he remarked every day. 'Show me the man who can grow a coconut tree properly and I will show you one with a practical head on his shoulders.'

Regularly at five in the morning Jagan got up from bed, broke a twig from a margosa tree in the backyard, chewed its tip, and brushed his teeth. He was opposed to the use of a toothbrush. 'The bristles are made of the hair from the pig's tail,' he declared. 'It's unthinkable that anyone should bite a pig's tail first thing in the morning.' It was impossible to disentangle the sources of his theories and say what he owed to Mahatmaji and how much he had imbibed from his father, who had also spent a lifetime perfecting his theories of sound living and trying them on himself, his coconut trees, children and wife. Even after the advent of nylon bristles Jagan never changed his views, maintaining that nylon had an adverse effect on the enamel. 'You disbelieve me. Remember my father who died at ninety without a single tooth loose in his jaw.' Jagan had immense faith in the properties of margosa, and in spite of its bitterness he called it 'Amrita'—the ambrosia which kept the gods alive; and sometimes he called it 'Sanjeevini', the rare herb, mentioned in the epics, which held at the nostrils could bring the dead to life. He never ceased to feel grateful to his father for planting a seedling in his time and providing him with a perennial source of twigs—enough for his generation and the next, considering the dimensions of the tree. He chewed its bitter leaves once a month, as it destroyed all bacteria in the system, and he felt elated when the breeze blew—the air passing through the margosa boughs became an anti-typhoid agent, and during the summer rains the place became fragrant as the little yellow flowers drifted down like floss. He collected them, fried them in ghee, and consumed the ambrosia for all his worth once a week. His wife refused to associate herself with any of his health-giving activities. She hated his theories and lived her own life. Their first clash occurred when he forbade her to swallow aspirin and suggested that she should fry a little margosa flower in ghee and swallow it for relief from headache. Seated beside the ancient pillar in their courtyard, she had knotted a towel around her temples and swayed madly back and forth, desperately begging for aspirin. Jagan was very sympathetic, no doubt, but was convinced that aspirin would do her no good. She had just looked up at him and said, 'Oh, this headache is not half as unbearable as your talk. You would sooner see me dead, I suppose.'

'Your headache has made you crazy,' he said, his temper rising. He hated her appearance with that silly towel knotted around her head and her dishevelled hair. She looked ghoulish and no wonder she suffered inexplicable headaches! He suddenly realized the trend of his thinking and suppressed it with a deliberate effort. 'You may do what you like. Only don't suffer.'

'Leave me alone,' she said in reply.

Jagan wanted to ask, 'Why are you disgusted with me?' but passed on into Mali's room. Mali had insisted upon having a room of his own, and in that vast house it was not difficult to find him one. Mali got a long hall without a ventilator or window, known as the 'cool room' in those days, which had a stone-topped round table at the centre and a stool, and seemed delighted to be assigned this room as it was near the kitchen and the main hall and he could enjoy privacy without losing sight of all the goings-on of the house—such as the arguments between his father and mother or their conversation with visitors. He had a few books heaped on the round table and some house-building blocks.

Jagan had asked him, 'Boy, do you know where your mother keeps her headache pills?'

'I know, but she will not let me touch them.'

'Why?'

'Because I may eat them. That's all. They look so nice.'

Jagan was scared. 'Boy, don't you go near them; they are poison.'

'What's poison?' asked the boy innocently, looking up from a paper kite he was fiddling with.

'Oh,' Jagan said rather desperately. He tried to avoid uttering inauspicious words, but there seemed to be no other way. He said, 'People die when they eat poison.'

Mali listened with interest and asked, 'And then what?' as if listening to a story.

Matters seemed to be proceeding in an unexpected direction. 'Where are the pills?' Jagan asked.

The boy indicated the cupboard in the hall and cried, 'On the very top, so high that you all think I cannot reach them.'

Jagan found his son's attraction to aspirin ominous. He merely replied, 'I'll get you better things to eat than this pill. Forget it, you understand?'

Then he had gone to the cupboard and found the pills for his wife. But that was some years ago, and Mali had grown.

CHAPTER THREE

MALI SAID ONE morning, 'I have an idea.'

Jagan felt slightly nervous and asked, 'What may it be?'

The boy paused while swallowing his breakfast. 'I can't study any more.'

The father was aghast. 'Has anyone been rude to you in the college?'

'Let them try!' said the boy.

'Tell me what's happened.'

'Nothing,' said the boy, 'I do not find it interesting, that's all,' and he went on munching his food with his eyes down.

Jagan had never seen him so serious. The boy seemed to have suddenly grown up. He had never spoken before in this tone to his father. Jagan merely repeated, 'If it's something I can do, tell me.'

'I don't want to study, that's all,' repeated the boy.

The morning sun came through a glass tile and touched with radiance the little heap of *uppumav* on his plate—a piece of green chilli and some globules of oil made the stuff sparkle, catching Jagan's eye insistently for a moment, making him wonder if he had made some strange edible gem-set for his son rather than merely frying semolina and spicing it. Shaking himself out of this fantasy, he said, 'All right, I'll come to your college and speak to those people.' The boy looked up angrily. In his anxiety to communicate a new idea to his father, he had become brusque and aggressive. His face was flushed. 'So early in the morning, and the boy showing such a temper!' Jagan reflected as if temper had an approved timetable. 'All right, get on with your eating. We'll talk of these things later,' he mumbled when he should have said, 'Swallow your food and run off to your class.' He was a cowardly father and felt afraid to mention class or college. The boy might scream at their mention or kick away his breakfast. Jagan had an almost maternal obsession about the boy feeding properly. At home he spent all his time cooking for his son; it had started when his wife had her first attack of brain fever and was taken to the hospital. When he was old enough to notice things, Mali had asked, 'Father, why don't you engage a cook?'

'I don't believe in engaging a cook.'

'Why not?'

'Do we engage a servant to do the breathing for us? Food is similar.'

'Oh, Father, Father,' the boy cried, 'don't you engage cooks in your sweetmeat shop?'

'Oh, that's different. It's like a factory and they are specialists and technicians,' said Jagan, giving full rein to his imagination.

The boy failed to grasp the distinction and cried desperately, 'I do not want you to cook for me. We have our college canteen. I can look after myself.' He had stuck to it, relaxing his resolution only to the extent of accepting the breakfast made by Jagan. The practice had continued. Particularly after his wife's death, Jagan became obsessed with his son's diet, and brooded over the question night and day. At night before retiring, he held a long conference with his son on not only what he had eaten during the day but what he would prefer to eat next day. The son, cornered at this hour, answered in his usual manner of half-syllables and clipped sentences, and the day would conclude with Jagan's exposition of his usual theories of nutrition, halfway through which Mali would turn away and bolt the door of his room, leaving Jagan with his unfinished sentence. He would spend a few moments staring at the door, then rise and unroll his mat in the open veranda in the second block and fall asleep before the gong at the Taluk office sounded nine.

Now he felt desperate to know what his son would do if he left the college or rather the college canteen. He asked idiotically, 'Where will you eat?'

His son smiled grimly and replied, 'Why do you bother when you keep saying one need not eat?' He put on his yellow shirt, picked up his bicycle and was off.

Jagan had to bottle up his confusions until the arrival of his cousin in the evening. 'Come here,' he cried the moment he sighted him, much to the bewilderment of the cousin who wanted first of all to go through and try the sweets as they came out of the frying pan. He flourished his arms as if to say, 'Your banalities can wait,' and passed on. Jagan saw him disappear into the kitchen with resignation. 'He is bound to come out sooner or later. No one can stay long in all that heat and smoke. Moreover, he will reach satiety soon with those sweets . . .' Market Road suddenly became alive with the shouts of schoolchildren just let off. A few of them, satchels slung on their shoulders, stood as usual in front of the Sweet Mart gaping at the display beyond the glass. Jagan watched them from his seat without emotion. 'It's up to their parents to provide them with the money for sweets. I can't be handing out charity packets.' He felt apologetic sitting there and collecting the cash—a vestige of conscience from his days of public service. If the public could have joined and subscribed, he'd have given away a portion of his profits in order to provide sweets for every child that gazed at his counter. 'But this is a poor country, sir. Per capita income is three annas.' He still stuck to the figure that he had got out of a book called *Poverty and un-British Rule in India* in his college days, but this figure restrained him from demanding of every parent in town that he spend eight annas a day at his shop. 'Poor country! Most people cannot afford even rice for two meals a day. When I cease to be a merchant, I'll . . . But sugar costs one and thirty per kilogram and flour and butter, real or fake, cost thrice as much, and what about the seasoning? Nutmegs seventy paise each—mark it, each! They used to be got in handfuls for the smallest coin and what *halva* would be worth its name if you did not crush a little nutmeg into it?'

When the cousin emerged from the kitchen wiping his mouth with the towel, Jagan said, as a continuation of his thoughts on social problems which for the moment swamped his private sorrows, 'Do you realize how few ever really understand how fortunate they are in their circumstances?'

The cousin nodded a general approval, secretly puzzled as to what this profound thinker might be driving at. 'They all forget or get used to things; that's the way of the world,' he said, smacking his lips and stating a philosophy that could fit any circumstance.

'Especially young men,' said Jagan; 'they are a problem everywhere. I was reading a little while ago somewhere,' and he tried to quote from some sort of a report on the youth of today, although he could not remember where he had read it or what it said.

'It takes one nowhere,' said the cousin sympathetically, his mind gloating over the memory of the sweets he had eaten.

The conversation was proceeding smoothly thus, when Jagan said abruptly, 'Mali is displaying strange notions.'

The cousin opened his eyes widely to register the appropriate reaction, not being certain how critical he could sound of Mali. Jagan explained. The cousin suddenly assumed a definite stand and said, 'It'd be best to know what the boy is thinking, our educational methods being what they are today.' You could always hit education if you had no other target.

'I was always hoping that he'd be a graduate and that's the basic qualification one should have, don't you think so?' Jagan added with a sigh, 'If I had passed the BA, I could have done so many other things.'

'But it was not to be, and yet what's lacking in your present state?'

'I had to leave the college when Gandhi ordered us to non-cooperate. I spent the best of my student years in prison,' said Jagan, feeling heroic, his reminiscential mood slurring over the fact that he had failed several times in the BA, ceased to attend the college and had begun to take his examinations as a private candidate long before the call of Gandhi. 'But what excuse can these boys have for refusing to study?' he asked.

The cousin, ever a man of caution, repeated, 'It's worth finding out from the boy himself. Why didn't you have a talk with him?'

'Why don't you?' asked Jagan in a tone of pointless challenge and added sentimentally, 'He has called you Uncle ever since he could lisp the syllables.'

'The only person to whom I'm not a cousin,' said the gentleman, and both of them laughed. The serious burden of life returning to Jagan presently, he said, 'You must do something about it and tell me tonight.'

At ten that night the cousin came up and knocked on the door softly. Jagan, for once, was awake after nine. The boy had retired and shut himself in his room without giving his father a chance to refer to the day's events. Jagan had noticed the light burning in his room, and resisted an impulse to peep through the keyhole. 'I wish you had peeped in—you'd have seen what he was doing,' said the cousin, when they had stolen on tiptoe from Jagan's house, strolled down the road to the foot of the Lawley statue and settled comfortably on the granite platform there. The cool night air was blowing on their faces. Sir Frederick loomed over them aggressively with his head amidst the stars.

'What do you mean?' said Jagan, leaning back in the shadow of Sir Frederick's spurs. All kinds of morbid and terrifying speculations arose in Jagan's mind. Was the boy counterfeiting money or murdering someone? A hundred evil possibilities occurred to him. He gripped the other's wrist and commanded, 'Tell me everything without concealing anything.'

The cousin shook off the hold contemptuously. 'He is writing, that's all. Wants to be a writer.'

'Writer' meant in Jagan's dictionary only one thing, a 'clerk'— an Anglo-Indian, colonial term from the days when Macaulay had devised a system of education to provide a constant supply of clerical staff for the East India Company. Jagan felt aghast. Here was he trying to shape the boy into an aristocrat with a bicycle, college life, striped shirts and everything, and he wanted to be a 'writer'! Strange!

'Why does he want to be a writer?' he asked.

'I don't know. You will have to ask him.'

'Where does he want to work? It's degrading,' he cried. 'After all the trouble I have taken to build up a reputation and a status!' He beat his brow in despair.

It never occurred to the cousin that Jagan had misunderstood the word 'writer'. He said, 'I lost no time after you told me this evening to go out in search of the boy. I waited at the college gate . . .'

'Oh, did he go to his college after all?' cried Jagan ecstatically, concluding that he must have eaten in the canteen.

'Yes,' replied the cousin. 'It was only a farewell visit. I saw him come out with a gang of friends, who patted his back and shook his hand and did all sorts of things. A couple of teachers came out, looked at him, and said something. I heard him say, "My father has other plans—probably he is sending me to America." '

'Ah!' Jagan exclaimed. 'What'll he do in America? America indeed!'

'Don't be hasty,' said the cousin slowly. 'He had to tell them something before leaving. Until he demands to be sent to America, don't take any notice of it.'

'All sorts of ideas! All sorts of ideas!' Jagan cried helplessly, tapping his fingers on the granite.

'Well, he may become a second Bharati or Tagore or Shakespeare some day. How can you judge now?' the cousin said.

The truth finally dawned on Jagan. 'Oh, how stupid am I? Yes, of course, "writer", I know. I've become illiterate, I think,' he cried happily. It was a great relief that the son was not attempting to be the other sort.

'What else did you think?' the cousin asked and added, 'I have heard that writers earn a lot of money nowadays. They become famous.'

'What does he want to write?'

'I don't know. Poetry, perhaps, easiest to start with, or stories. What else do people write?' said the cousin, not wanting to flounder in unknown seas. 'Actually, it was difficult to get even that out of him. I met him at his school . . .'

'College,' corrected Jagan, feeling somewhat piqued.

'Yes, yes, I meant college. I always think of Mali as a little fellow and it's very difficult to remember that he is no longer a mere schoolboy. At his college gate, when the teachers left him, he saw me and stopped to ask what had brought me there. I didn't want to seem officious and so said something and then asked if he would come for a cup of coffee somewhere. "Not just coffee," he said, "I want a lot to eat as well." '

'Poor boy, he must have been starving,' cried Jagan, feeling anguished.

'Not necessarily,' said the cousin. 'Young men eat and still wish to eat a lot more, you know.'

'Certainly,' cried Jagan. 'What is there to prevent his eating as much as he likes and at all hours of the day?'

'Do you leave enough cash with him?'

'Of course I do,' said Jagan. 'Did he say anything about it?'

'Oh, no, oh, no,' cried the cousin. 'He is not that sort of young man. Even if you starved him and denied him everything he'd never complain.'

Jagan felt proud at these encomiums heaped on his son. He remained thoughtful, while the stars in the sky paused in their courses. A couple of dogs trotted in a chase. The vagrant stirred in his sleep, muttering to himself on the other side of the statue. Jagan peeped around and said, 'Disgraceful that our nation cannot attack this problem of vagrants. Must do something about it, when I find the time.'

The cousin ignored this larger social problem and continued, 'I took him to Ananda Bhavan; you know that place, the loudspeaker deafening you all the time.'

Jagan implored, 'I want to hear nothing about the Ananda Bhavan restaurant. Tell me about the boy, please.'

'Yes, yes, be patient. I know you don't like the Ananda Bhavan people. I know they tried to blackmail you with the sales tax.'

'Oh, please stick to the point. I don't care what they do or did. Tell me what the boy said. Was he unhappy?'

'Yes and no. Happy that he was going to be free to be a writer, unhappy that you should expect him to study at . . .'

'The college,' completed Jagan, almost afraid lest the man should blunder into saying 'school' again.

The cousin took the hint and said, 'College, college and of course college. The very word drives him crazy, although you like it so much. He hates his lessons; he hates his syllabus and all his books. The very thought infuriates him. Do you know what he did? He had his class books in his hand. I had ordered *dosais* for him and we were waiting. He suddenly tore up the pages of his books savagely, beckoned an attendant and said, 'Put these in the fire in the kitchen.'

'Could you not stop him? Didn't you tell him that books must be treated respectfully, being a form of the Goddess Saraswathi? How could this boy ever pass his BA?'

'I don't know,' said the cousin reflectively. 'It didn't occur to me to argue with him, that's all; what use would it be anyway?'

'Are you also mad?' cried Jagan. 'Don't you see . . .'

The cousin said, 'No. When he tore the books it seemed very appropriate, our education being what it is . . .'

'Oh, stop it. I hope you have not been telling him things.'

The cousin ignored this insinuation and said, 'Do you know what he said after sending his books to the fire? He made up a verse on the spot: "Let us show gratitude to the Great Fire that consumes our horrid books—" or something like it. It sounded very smart and sensible. He ate *dosais* and a number of things, the total bill being three rupees.'

'Great boy!' said Jagan, gratified by his son's verse as well as his gluttony. 'I'll reimburse you. Remind me at the shop tomorrow.'

'No hurry, no hurry. You can take your own time to return it to me,' said the cousin.

It seemed difficult to keep to the point, there being no precise point to keep to, no main subject to return to. They went on rambling thus until the Taluk office gong sounded twelve o'clock. It boomed through the silent town and Jagan said, 'Even burglars will have gone home to sleep, but still I have got nowhere. I don't know why he cannot write and also read his college books.'

'He said that the one interfered with the other,' explained the cousin.

After a brief pause, Jagan suddenly asked, 'Was Shakespeare a BA?'—a question that no one could answer in that place.

The cousin said, 'Why go so far? I know Kalidasa never went to a college.'

'Because there were no colleges three thousand years ago,' said Jagan.

'How can you know whether there were colleges or not?'

'College or no college, I know Kalidasa was a village idiot and a shepherd until the Goddess Saraswathi made a scratch on his tongue and then he burst into that song "*Syamaladandakam*", and wrote *Sakuntala* and so on. I know the story. I have heard it often enough,' said Jagan.

'If you know the story, you must believe in it and hope that some day Mali will be another Kalidasa,' said the cousin soothingly.

Jagan, at the earliest opportunity, applied his eye to the keyhole of Mali's door, which remained shut most hours of the day. The boy seemed to be avoiding him. Jagan prepared the breakfast and left it on the hall table, and also tucked a five-rupee note under the plate so that the boy might eat wherever he liked the rest of the day. Mali would go out and return home at some hour of the night and shut himself in. Jagan went about his sweet-making without any outward sign of agitation, but inside he was all torn up. He could not understand where his son spent the day, or what he ate. He had never suspected that his zeal for education was going to ruin their relationship. He wanted to make it up with his son.

Through the keyhole he saw the light burning in Mali's room. He saw Mali sitting on a stool with his elbow on the table, just brooding. He felt disappointed that the boy was not writing. He had imagined the writer burning the midnight oil and littering the table with sheets of paper in a delirium of inspiration: Kalidasa suddenly bursting into inspired song, the walls of the ancient house reverberating with a new song to be on everybody's lips for a thousand years to come. But the picture that presented itself to him was different. The boy seemed to be moping in dejection and boredom. It was time to pull him out of it.

Jagan realized the time had come for him to forget college education and get completely identified with Mali's fantasies, at least until he came out of his gloom. Jagan beat upon the door with both fists, stooping and squinting at the keyhole having proved irksome.

'What's happened? Why are you bringing down the house?' asked the boy, opening the door.

Jagan pushed his way in, announcing, 'Boy, I like your idea. Come on, let us talk about it.' He breezily paced around and sat on a stool. The boy followed him mutely, his misgivings not totally forgotten. Jagan smoothed his own brow and the corners of his face so that there should be not the slightest trace of a frown and managed to give his face an affable grin, exuding an impression of total approval. They stared at each other uncomfortably for a second, and then the son came over and sat on the circular table with a marble top.

Jagan asked soothingly, 'Do you want a good table?'

'What for?' asked the boy, poised between doubt and trust.

The slightest pressure at the wrong place could topple him over to the wrong side. And so Jagan said, 'A writer needs a lot of space for his manuscripts—they are precious, you know.'

The boy was evidently pleased that the new table was not being planned for college books and notes. 'Who has told you about me?'

'These things become known. A writer has to come out!' He was amazed at his own fluency.

'Oh! I don't care either way!'

Jagan looked about. There was no sign of a book in the making. The marble top was clean, all the college books having been swept out of view. He felt a moment's curiosity about their fate, but checked himself. Not his business, anyway.

'Do you want me to buy you white paper? Have you got a good pen? I think I had better get you a new desk with a lot of drawers.' Peace and understanding were returning after all, and they could grope their way through the world of letters now, each thinking that the other might know better. 'What are you writing now?' asked Jagan with the humility of a junior reporter interviewing a celebrity.

'A novel,' the boy said condescendingly.

'Oh, wonderful. Where did you learn to write novels?'

Mali did not answer the question; Jagan repeated it.

'Are you examining me?' Mali asked.

'Oh, no, I'm just interested, that's all. What story are you writing?'

'I can't tell you now. It may turn out to be a poem after all. I don't know.'

'But don't you know what you are going to write when you sit down to write?'

'No,' said the boy haughtily. 'It's not like frying sweets in your shop.'

This was completely mystifying to the junior reporter. He said pathetically, 'Tell me if you want my help in any matter.'

The boy received that in sullen silence.

'Are your friends also writers?'

'How can they be? They are only readers and want to get their degrees. That's all.' Jagan rigorously suppressed his approval of those friends' attitude. The boy added, 'They are all ordinary fellows who are no good for anything else.'

'I thought you were fond of your friends,' Jagan said, seizing every opportunity to acquire a better understanding of his son's mind. He had thought that the friends were dear to the boy, the way they stood beside the statue leaning on their bicycles and talking loudly. It was also a slight matter of relief, for Jagan had had a fear that his friends might be misleading the boy; now it was some satisfaction to know that he was going astray entirely through his own individual effort. 'For twenty years,' Jagan reflected, 'he has grown up with me, under the same roof, but how little I have known him! But the boy has been up to something. He will count for something sooner or later.'

'I saw in *Ananda Vikatan* a competition for novels,' Mali explained. 'They will pay twenty-five thousand rupees for the best.'

'On what conditions?'

'It must be sent before September 30th, that's all, and a coupon in the magazine must be filled in.'

Jagan leaned over to study the dates on a calendar on the wall. 'This is just May.'

'I know,' snapped the boy. 'I have five months.'

'Have you begun to write?' Jagan asked timidly.

'I am not the sort to show my story to anyone before I finish it.'

'What's the story?' asked Jagan, persisting.

The boy shrank away from him and repeated, 'Are you examining me?' in an ominous manner.

'Oh, no, it's not that.'

'You don't believe me, I know,' said the boy half-despairingly.

Jagan was confused for a moment. He reaffirmed his faith in his son in the loudest terms possible. Secretly his mind was bothered as to why there was always an invisible barrier between them. He had never been harsh to the boy so long as he could remember, he had always got him whatever he wanted these twenty years; during the last ten particularly he had become excessively considerate, after the boy lost his mother. The scene remained for ever fresh in Jagan's memory—that terrible Friday when their doctor, Krishna, had observed her breathing and just said, 'No doctor could do more; a very rare type of brain tumour; if one knew why it came, one would also know how to get rid of it.' It was nearing midnight and the doctor had been in continuous attendance for forty-eight hours with needle, oxygen and ice-bag, sparing no apparatus in order to save a life: he was physically worn out by the effort and driven nearly mad by Jagan's hints that a nature-cure might have benefited her. 'Nature!' he snapped irritably, turning his head from the bed. 'Nature would sooner see us dead. She has no use for a brain affected by malignant growth, that's all . . .' Jagan had shut his mouth, feeling that the moment was inappropriate for his theories. But when the doctor took his final leave and moved off to his car, Jagan, following him out, could not help putting in a word on the subject: 'You'll see for yourself, Doctor, when I publish my book. I have all the material for it.'

The doctor made an impatient gesture, and said, 'Go back, go back to your wife for the few hours left. Your son is watching us. Protect him.' Turning back from the car, Jagan saw Mali at the door with bewilderment in his eyes. It was harrowing to look at his thin, scraggy frame (he developed and grew tall and broad suddenly after his eighteenth birthday). The boy asked, 'What did the doctor say?' He had been attending on his mother for many weeks now. In her rare moments of lucidity she beckoned to him, and accepted the diet if he fed her. He came running home from school in order to feed her, rarely going out to play with his friends. At the boy's question Jagan had lost his nerve completely, held his son's hands and broken into a loud wail. Mali had shaken himself off and watched his father from a distance with a look of dismay and puzzlement.

Even with the passage of time, Jagan never got over the memory of that moment; the coarse, raw pain he had felt at the sight of Mali on that fateful day remained petrified in some vital centre of his being. From that day, the barrier had come into being. The boy had ceased to speak to him normally.

'Oh, no!' apologized Jagan. 'I'm sure you are going to write something good, my boy. I do not in the least doubt it. I just wanted to know the story, that's all. You know how much I like stories. Do you remember the stories I used to tell you at nights? The one about a black monkey which you used to like so much!' After taking complete charge of his son, he used to divert his mind by telling him stories from the *Panchatantra*. The boy showed no sign that he remembered those days or wanted to be reminded of them. He showed no reaction. Jagan said, 'You know, I'm also a kind of writer. You will know more about it when Truth Printing lets it out of the press.' And he laughed in a hollow manner.

The boy said simply, 'Father, you do not understand. I want to write something different.'

'Of course, of course . . . Tell me if you need my help.'

It seemed a very simple way of earning twenty-five thousand rupees without frying or baking anything. They sat talking until one in the morning, while Jagan was subjected to a revelation every other minute. He learnt that the boy had cut the coupon from the magazine of his college library, risking punishment and humiliation if caught. 'I did it with a blade, under the very nose of the librarian,' the boy said with a hint of laughter.

'Would that be the right thing to do?' Jagan asked, puzzled.

'Of course, how else could I get the coupon?' the boy asked, producing it from within the pages of a small pocket diary.

Jagan said, looking at it, 'If this is from *Vikatan* you could have bought a copy for four annas, or as many copies as you needed.'

'That anyone could do,' the boy said, and added mysteriously, 'I have always wanted to teach that librarian a lesson; he always thought he was too clever.'

Jagan derived a peculiar thrill in speaking of his son as a writer.

Next day, on the way to his Sweet Mart, he stopped at least three acquaintances on the road and spoke to them of his son. The fourth person to be told was the head cook. As soon as he arrived, Jagan summoned him to his throne and said, 'My son is writing a book.' The head cook, between thoughts of the frying for the day, said it was a grand piece of news and evinced interest in the literary progress of Mali.

'He is going to earn twenty-five thousand rupees out of it, and he says he is going to finish it before September, wonderful boy! I never knew that my son was such a genius. Actually, you know, he need not do all this to get twenty-five thousand, that's always there. But I don't want to give it to him to handle. It's not like my generation; we came under the spell of Gandhi and could do no wrong.'

'For all your wealth, you are such a simple man, eating nothing.'

'Eating to live, that's all,' corrected Jagan. 'You will know when my book is printed. I'm also a sort of writer, you understand?'

'No wonder your son takes to it so happily,' said the cook.

The cousin came at the usual hour and heard the story. Jagan repeated himself and concluded, 'I hope he will also emulate my philosophy of living. Simple living and high thinking, as Gandhi has taught us.'

'True, true. But what I don't understand is why you should run a trade, make money and accumulate it.'

'I do not accumulate, it just grows naturally,' said Jagan. 'What can I do? Moreover, I work, because it's one's duty to work.' He pulled the drawer, took out his *Bhagavad Gita*, and read: "It's my duty to go on doing something." Moreover'—he raised his voice— 'that man, and the other one, and the one here, it supports them. What would our head cook do if it weren't for this establishment?'

'He'd probably be frying stuff in some other kitchen. He is a master fryer, who'll get a job anywhere.'

'It's not that, my dear fellow. Mine is the biggest sweet shop in the country. Have you any doubt about it?'

'None whatever; and your fry master makes unadulterated good stuff.'

Jagan felt soothed by this flattery. All the same he said, 'No wonder Mali wants to try a new line. There are bound to be changes of outlook from generation to generation. Otherwise there will be no progress,' he added in a sudden outburst of theorizing, once again a vestige of his *Satyagraha* days. It was all as agreeable as the fragrance of the ghee, nutmeg and saffron which emanated from the kitchen. He suddenly said, without any provocation, 'I have always resisted the use of essences for flavouring or colouring. You can get any flavour from Germany; it is easy to deceive even the most fastidious nowadays.'

'How false and illusory!' commented the cousin, in a philosophical strain.

'But I'll never use them as long as I am a master of this establishment,' asserted Jagan. The cousin, as a sampler flourishing on absolute purity every afternoon, expressed unqualified approval of this statement.

CHAPTER FOUR

PEACE REIGNED AT home, with speech reduced to a minimum between father and son. Mali seemed to have brightened up at the fact that he wouldn't be expected to study. Jagan continued to feel gratified that his son was pursuing a fresh course, all his own. 'Instead of reading other people's books, he is providing reading for others,' he often reflected with a lot of pride. 'He is doing a service in his own way.' When he remembered the word 'service', any activity became touched with significance. 'Service' intoxicated him, sent a thrill through his whole being and explained everything. The first time he had heard the word was in 1937 when Mahatma Gandhi visited Malgudi and had addressed a vast gathering on the sands of the river. He spoke of 'service', explaining how every human action acquired a meaning when it was performed as a service. Inspired by this definition, Jagan joined the movement for freeing India from foreign rule, gave up his studies, home and normal life, and violated the British laws of the time. Neither the beatings from the police nor the successive periods of prison life ever touched him when he remembered that he was performing a 'service'. 'Everyone should be free to serve humanity in his own way,' he told himself, and, 'Mali is really helping mankind with his writing.' What does he really write, he often wondered. Stories? What sort of stories? Poems? Or did he write philosophy? He had a passing misgiving about his son's experience of life, his equipment to be a writer. He had uneasy thoughts sometimes when he sat on his throne in the shop looking at the pages of the *Bhagavad Gita*. However profound the lines before him, his own thoughts seemed to be stronger and capable of pushing aside all philosophy, while revolving round the subject of Mali's manuscript. He wanted to know which language his son's Muses accepted, whether Tamil or

English. If he wrote in Tamil he would be recognized at home; if in English, he would be known in other countries too. But did he know enough English, Tamil or any language? He felt worried, his mind was racked with questions. The simplest solution of questioning Mali directly seemed impracticable. What could they discuss? Mali seemed to have become detached, more detached than ever. The only link between them was the five-rupee currency note that he left on the hall table every morning and checked later to find out if it had been accepted. Perhaps the boy lunched and dined at Ananda Bhavan; it was galling to think that his money should find its way into that cash-desk. It could not be helped; it was supposed to be the best restaurant in the town; but Jagan knew that they did not use pure ghee but hydrogenated vegetable oil in unlabelled tins—they were naïve enough to think that if the tins were unlabelled the public would take them to be real butter!

It was long past the thirtieth of September and Jagan would have given anything to know if the manuscript had gone off. But there had been no sign of it anywhere. The boy's movements were so finely adjusted out of his own orbit that, though they lived under one roof, they might be in two different worlds. When he saw the light through the chink in the door, Jagan knew that the boy was in his room. He dared not knock on it. Rarely did they ever reach home at the same time so that there was no chance of their meeting in the hall. Jagan felt harrowed by the lack of information. When the cousin arrived at his appointed time, he found Jagan looking so restless that he felt constrained to remark as he emerged from the kitchen, 'You are blessed with every gift of life: with what ninety out of a hundred people crave for—money, and with what a hundred out of a hundred do not attain—contentment. Yet you have not mastered one thing, that's the art of looking happy. You are always looking careworn.'

'If one looks worn out by cares, God knows one must have sufficient cause. Do you see Mali at all?'

'Not much. No. No. Long ago, I saw him on a cycle one afternoon in Vinayak Street. Don't ask me what I was doing there. I generally go even farther than that when I have some work—always in the service of someone else, you may be sure. I do nothing for myself.'

'Did he speak to you?'

'Of course not. He was riding a bicycle, I told you.'

'What was he doing so far away?'

'Why not ask him?' asked the cousin.

'He won't answer, that's all,' said Jagan.

'Have you tried?'

'No.'

'Then try.'

'He may resent the question and think I'm interfering.'

'If I meet him, I'll find out, if you like.'

'Please don't. He'll think I have sent you to him.'

'Of course, I'll tell him that I'm talking for you.'

Jagan looked scared on hearing this. Sweat broke out on his brow. The cousin could not help remarking, 'You puzzle me. Why are you frightened?'

'I hate to upset him, that's all. I have never upset him in all my life.'

'That means you have carried things to a point where you cannot speak to him at all.'

'It's not that,' said Jagan, not willing to accept this view.

'Can you tell me when you had your last conversation with him?'

There was a pause while Jagan threw his mind back. The cousin watched him ruthlessly, gently sucking the sweet on his tongue. Jagan remembered that their last speech had been three and a half months ago. He had been reading the paper in the hall, and his son had come out of his room.

'Ready to go out?'

'H'm.'

That had terrified Jagan and at once he had covered up any hint of inquisitiveness. 'Did you see today's paper?'

'No.'

'Don't you want to?'

'Nothing in it for me.' The boy had walked across the hall. Jagan could hear the cycle being taken off its spring stand, and the front door slamming. He sat still with his eyes glued to the newspaper. 'God be thanked that there is no direct exit from his room to the street as my father once foolishly planned; otherwise I'd have lost the memory of my son's identity long ago.'

Reporting this meeting to the cousin was out of the question, so he said, 'The trouble is our hours are so different. By the time

I open my eyes from prayer, he's gone; it's been a time-honoured custom in our house not to disturb me when I am praying. But that's all beside the point. We are straying away from the subject. I want you to help me. Please find out, as if you were doing it on your own, where he goes every day and what happened to the story. Did he finish it? Try to meet him and give me some information, please. I'll be grateful for your help.'

'No, no; it's my duty to be of service to you. Don't thank me. I'll see what I can do in my humble way.' He swelled with the importance and the weight of the undertaking. Jagan felt relieved.

The cousin came back four days later, took his seat beside the throne and said, 'New things are coming your way; your son wants to go to America. Didn't I hint to you long ago that it was coming?'

The first shock of the impact blanked out Jagan's mind for a time, and he caught his breath as he had a momentary panic at the thought of his son removing himself so far geographically. He inanely repeated, 'America! Why America? What has happened to his book? Has he written it? Hasn't he written it?'

'He thinks he will have to learn the art in America.'

Jagan was furious at this notion; it was outrageous and hurt his national pride.

'Going there to learn storytelling! He should rather go to a village granny,' he said, all his patriotic sentiments surging.

'Exactly what I told him,' echoed the cousin.

'Did Valmiki go to America or Germany in order to learn to write his *Ramayana*?' asked Jagan with pugnacity. 'Strange notions these boys get nowadays!' he said, avoiding gently any specific reference to his son. The head cook interrupted at this point, bringing in the flavour of kitchen-smoke, in order to announce, 'Saffron stock out. Will last only another day.' Jagan looked at him bemusedly, not able to grasp the subject clearly. The cousin answered for him and promised to arrange for a fresh supply. When the cook retreated into the kitchen, Jagan asked, 'Have you found out where he spends his day?'

'At the Town Public Library.'

'Where is it?' asked Jagan, never having dreamt that his town possessed a library. The cousin himself was not sure and flourished his arms vaguely in the direction of the river. 'Must be one of those things for which a foundation stone is laid, whenever a minister visits this town.'

'I'd have known about it if it had been a thing of any importance. Anyway, do they let him live there?'

'He seems to like it, and does some amount of work there.'

'What sort of work?' asked Jagan, appalled at the notion that Mali should have become a library assistant of all things! 'What has happened to his book?' he asked desperately.

'He will write it in America,' said the cousin.

Jagan felt completely crushed; adverse forces seemed to hem him in on all sides. 'What has America to do with writing his book?'

'He has read in one of the magazines at the library about a college where they teach novel writing.'

Jagan once again felt like bursting out about Valmiki or a village granny, but restrained himself. 'What happened to the prize?'

'Perhaps it's gone. He hasn't written the book yet,' said the cousin. 'Anyway, a book cannot be rushed.'

'True, true,' said Jagan, suddenly remembering his son's words the other night; but added as his own contribution to the theory of writing, 'Still, I suppose, a book has to be written.'

They spent a little time brooding over the mechanics of book production. 'Why America?' asked Jagan, ignoring the instalment of cash that was brought in, while the cousin made no effort to leave.

'Because, perhaps, it's the only country where they teach such things.'

'They eat only beef and pork in that country. I used to know a man from America and he told me . . .'

'They also drink a lot of intoxicating drinks, never water or milk,' said the cousin, contributing his own bit of information. 'And the women are free,' he added. 'I have seen some of their magazines about films; their women mix freely with men and snap off marriages without ado, and bask in the sun without clothes.'

'Where did you see all this?' asked Jagan, and did not note the answer from the cousin, who flourished his arms vaguely. Jagan went on, 'It may not all be true,' not wishing to think a country to which Mali was going was one to corrupt his body with wine, women and meat, and his soul with other things. He said with a sudden determination, 'But it's unthinkable. Mali shall stay here.'

The cousin smiled cynically. Jagan had a momentary stab of suspicion that this man was at the back of it all, but the doubt passed.

The cousin said, 'He has made all kinds of preparations.'

'Without my permission or help!' cried Jagan.

'They have a typewriter at the library and he has been using it.'

Partly filled with admiration, and partly enraged at the library, Jagan shouted suddenly without thinking of what he was saying, 'If they are going to make use of the library for such nefarious activities . . .!'

The cousin said, 'Did you know that he had gone to Madras for a few days?'

'No? Without my permission or help, without telling me anything? I thought he was in his room.' He remembered that the five-rupee notes left by him had not been picked up on certain days. Thinking that the boy had been saving, he had withheld the allowance, hoping to be asked.

'He has fixed his passport and other such things.'

'How is he going to find the fare?'

'He says he has got it; he said he always knew where to find the money in the house.'

Jagan felt shocked for a moment, but he also felt a sneaking admiration. 'The boy is very practical,' he said with feeling. He sat brooding for some time and then said, trying to put on a happy look, 'See, how self-reliant he has grown! I have always believed in leaving the entity to develop by itself, without relying on extraneous support. As they say in the *Gita*, 'Every soul is God . . .''

'And God can always look after himself,' added the cousin.

'That's the whole point,' said Jagan. 'That's why I never wished to interfere when he suddenly decided to end his education. I said to myself, "Perhaps he wants to educate himself in the school of life," and left him free'—echoing various tit-bits of banality he had picked up in the course of his life and haphazard reading.

The cousin said, 'Exactly my principle in life. I know much about people and their problems and the world. Did I go to a college to learn the art of living?'

'But I am surprised that he still thinks he can learn the art of writing from an American college!' Jagan sniggered gently at the thought. 'As my good cousin, please try and stop him. I don't know how I can live in that house without him. The very thought depresses me.'

'Yes, I will,' said the cousin mechanically, without conviction. 'But do you know that he has worked out the details minutely? He is getting his American clothes made in Madras.'

'I have always told him to buy a lot of clothes; especially in foreign countries one must always wear tie and shoes and such things, morning till night. Does he want any sort of help from me?' Jagan asked pathetically, almost appealing to the cousin to intercede and do something about it.

'What can you do?' asked the cousin brutally.

'I have a friend in Madras, a deputy minister, who was my prison mate in those days in Bellary jail.'

'No harm in trying your friend, but Mali needs no help from us. The librarian has a brother in the aeroplane company and he has done everything for Mali.'

'Is he going to fly?' asked Jagan, panic-stricken.

'Who does not nowadays?' Jagan almost wept as he said, 'Please tell him to go by steamer. It's safer. Let him be safe. I don't like aeroplanes.'

'He has almost paid for the air ticket,' said the cousin, enjoying Jagan's predicament.

'It must be very costly,' said Jagan like a prattling baby.

'But he has doubtless found the cash for it,' said the cousin.

'Naturally. What is the cash worth to me? It's all for him. He can have everything he wants,' said Jagan, making a note mentally to count at the earliest moment his cash hoarded in the loft. He also considered transferring it all, in due course, to a casket behind the family gods in the *puja* room.

In the dead of night, he put up the ladder and climbed to the loft. About ten thousand rupees had been extracted from the bundled currency. He made a rough and ready calculation. 'About four or five thousand rupees for passage; and the balance for clothes and other things. He should ask for more if he wants it, and, of course, a monthly remittance later. Why should he not?' He heard the front door opening, put out the torch and sat still until he felt sure that Mali had safely locked himself in, feeling like a burglar himself, instead of one whose cash had been extracted.

CHAPTER FIVE

HE HAD NEVER thought that he could feel so superior about it. Now it seemed to him worth all the money and the pangs of separation. 'My son is in America,' he said to a dozen persons every day, puffing with pride on each occasion. It delayed his daily routine. On his way to the shop he had only to detect the slightest acquaintance on the road, and he would block his path, and instead of discussing weather or politics, as was his custom, would lead the talk on gently to the topic of America and of his son's presence there. After days and days of hopeless waiting, when a colourful air letter had arrived by post, he had almost felt the same joy as if Mali had come back. He hardly had the patience to read the printed instruction 'To open, cut here', but thrust his finger in desperately and gashed the air letter until it split longitudinally, forcing him to piece it together like a jigsaw puzzle for deciphering. The message simply said, 'Arrived. New York is big. The buildings are very tall, not like ours. Thousands of motor cars in the street. Food is difficult. I am in a hostel. Next week I go to school.' Jagan read it with pleasure, although he was somewhat disturbed at the boy's mention of 'school' rather than 'college'. It had arrived by the first post, and he sat on the hall bench and pored over it for nearly an hour, scanning every word and visualizing Mali in that enormous background. He could not keep the good news to himself. The first entrance open to him was the Truth Printing Works. Nataraj was at his desk, ever affable and welcoming visitors. The door was only half open, and when the light was blocked Nataraj looked up from his proofs and smiled, and immediately Jagan made the announcement: 'Mali has reached . . .'

'Have you received a telegram?'

'Oh, no, he's prudent. Won't waste ten rupees when ten

cents—any idea how much a cent is worth in our money?'

Nataraj made a rapid calculation. A dollar was equivalent to five rupees, seven rupees on the black market as one of his customers had told him, four rupees odd according to the Government, a hundred cents to a dollar . . . He gave up the attempt at multiplication and division and thought it best to change the subject. 'You will be getting your proofs very soon.'

'Oh, yes, I know once you take it up, you will get on with it. As you know, it's a contribution and a service, and not written for profit.' After this statement, he switched over to America. 'It's a place of enormous buildings and lots of motor cars. I hope the boy will have a room on the ground floor and not too high up.'

'Our boys are very clever,' said Nataraj, 'and can take care of themselves anywhere in the world.'

Accepting this agreeable statement, Jagan withdrew from the doorway and proceeded towards his shop. On the way he caught a glimpse of the adjournment lawyer at the turning of Kabir Lane. He clapped his hands and stopped him. He could take that liberty with him as they had been class-mates at the Albert Mission more than a generation ago and had been together in the National Movement (although the lawyer elegantly avoided going to prison). The lawyer, a one-toothed man with a sprinkling of silver dust on his unshaven cheeks, smiled, exposing his bare gums. 'I've got to go home; some parties are waiting for me.'

'I won't take more than a minute,' said Jagan. 'I felt you'd be happy to know that Mali has written.'

'Have you received a telegram?'

What was the matter with everybody? Jagan felt annoyance at the tendency of people to get obsessed with telegrams.

'After all, why spend ten rupees when ten cents bring over a letter in four days?'

'Four days!' said the lawyer. 'No, no, you must be mistaken. It takes longer than that. It takes at least fifteen days.'

That was the limit. How presumptuous of the man to talk of America, while he was there to provide first-hand information! People's notions were fixed. Stupid fellows! Frogs in the well!

Ahead of him, he saw the chemist at his door, looking down at the street. He greeted Jagan warmly. 'Rather late today?' he said with a lot of friendliness.

'Yes, I know, I know,' Jagan said, approaching him eagerly.

'The postman was rather late today. Well, when one has a son living so far away . . .'

'Has he reached America safely?'

'Yes, I was somewhat anxious for two or three days! Other boys would have wasted money on a telegram, but a letter at a tenth of the cost takes only a couple of days more. He's prudent, you know.'

'What's the postage? I want to send for a free catalogue from Sears Roebuck. You know, it is an interesting book. It'll give us wonderful ideas on all sorts of things.' Jagan almost groaned when the other asked, 'What's the equivalent of fifty cents, which is the postage for the catalogue?'

He passed on. None so good as the cousin, who deserved all the sweets he ate for his listening capacity: all the others in the town were obsessed with their own notions, were ignorant and resisted enlightenment on the subject of America. When he was sitting in his seat, the head cook came to ask for the day's programme. Jagan repeated the formula and then added a postscript as a favour to the cook: 'Mali has safely reached the other end, and that's a big relief to me. It's a huge country with a lot of motor cars. Everyone has a car there.' The cook listened respectfully and turned away without comment. Jagan felt relieved that the fellow had not stopped to ask about telegrams or the equivalent of a cent.

He had to hold his soul in peace until four-thirty when the cousin arrived, passed straight in to savour, and came out of the kitchen. Jagan said with a quiet firmness, 'The boy has reached the other end safely.' He flourished a fragment of the air letter as a special favour, affording the cousin a glimpse of the letter while he had only mentioned it to others.

'Excellent news! I knew he'd be all right,' he said, smacking his lips.

'He didn't send a telegram.'

'Yes, yes, why should he? Letters arrive so quickly nowadays. You must offer a couple of coconuts to Ganesha at the corner temple.'

'Surely, it goes without saying,' said Jagan as if there were a specific contract between himself and the god in the matter of his son's safety. 'It shall be done this very evening.'

'I'll buy the coconut on my way,' said the cousin, and immediately Jagan snatched up a coin from his drawer and handed it to the other.

'I feel a great burden off my head today. When someone goes on such a long pilgrimage, especially if he is flying, it's always a worry, although one doesn't talk about it.'

'I know, I know,' said the cousin. 'What does he say about himself?'

'He likes the new experience, of course. Lots of tall buildings and cars everywhere. I hope he will walk carefully in the streets . . . He says the food is good. I'm relieved. You know it's a country of millionaires. Everyone is so rich.'

Mali proved unusually communicative from across the seas, and although at times he sounded brusque, disconnected or impersonal, he generalized a good deal about the civilization in which he found himself. The blue air mail letters grew into a file. If only Mali had taken the precaution of leaving a proper margin to his epistles, Jagan would have bound them into a neat little volume at Truth Printing; surely Nataraj would have realized its importance and obliged him with speedy execution. Jagan stuffed his *jibba* pocket with the letters, and pulled them out for choice reading of passages to all and sundry, mostly to his cousin who, as ever, remained an uncomplaining listener. Gradually his reading of the *Bhagavad Gita* was replaced by the blue air mail letters. From their study he formed a picture of America and was able to speak with authority on the subject of American landscape, culture and civilization. He hardly noticed to whom he spoke; anyone on the road seemed good enough. His acquaintances feared that he was afflicted with the Talking Disease.

From the minute he stepped out of his house, he scanned the landscape for a familiar face, pounced hawklike on the unwary victim and held him in thrall; he even stopped the vagrant on the culvert one day in order to describe the Grand Canyon. 'Actually, there is nothing like it anywhere in the world,' he concluded and gave him five paise for listening. It was a matter of luck for another, whether he could slip away in time or got entangled in American lore. Jagan found everyone restless when he spoke, but he rushed through his narration breathlessly. He had the feeling of having to bottle up his ideas until the blessed hour that brought his cousin in, who displayed such an enthusiasm for American information that Jagan could hardly tell him enough.

The cousin often wanted to see the letters himself, but Jagan resisted the idea: he held them in sacred trust and would not allow a third person to touch them.

Day after day, the cousin collected information on American life and manners and passed them on to his own circle of listeners. Very soon most people in Malgudi knew that fifty thousand human lives were lost in road accidents, every year, in America; and how people broke down on hearing of the death of Kennedy at street corners and crowded round anyone with a transistor radio. Jagan felt quite competent to describe, as if he had watched it himself, the route of Kennedy's motorcade on that fateful day, and he felt choked when he recounted how on that very morning, in Dallas, Kennedy had mingled in enormous crowds which grabbed and tore at his clothes and hair in sheer affection; nor did he spare his listener any detail of Oswald's death later.

The only letter Jagan rigorously suppressed was the one in which Mali had written after three years' experience of America, 'I've taken to eating beef, and I don't think I'm any the worse for it. Steak is something quite tasty and juicy. Now I want to suggest, why don't you people start eating beef? It'll solve the problem of useless cattle in our country and we won't have to beg food from America. I sometimes feel ashamed when India asks for American aid. Instead of that, why not slaughter useless cows which wander in the streets and block the traffic?' Jagan felt outraged. The *Shastras* defined the five deadly sins and the killing of a cow headed the list.

While he was cogitating on how to make his feelings felt on the subject and collecting quotations from the *Shastras* and Gandhi's writings on the cow, to be incorporated in his letter to Mali, there came a cable one morning: 'Arriving home: another person with me.' Jagan was puzzled. What sort of a person? He had terrible misgivings and the added trouble of not being able to talk about it to the cousin, as he might spread the news of 'another person' all over the town. His worst misgivings were confirmed on an afternoon when the train dumped Mali, 'another person' and an enormous quantity of baggage onto the railway platform and puffed away. The very sight of the streamlined trunks, suitcases and corded cartons filled Jagan with uneasiness and a feeling of inferiority. The old porter at the railway station could hardly handle this quantity of baggage, although normally he would seize and carry scores of boxes and baskets without a thought. Now he had to call in the boy at the cigarette shop for assistance. Mali kept muttering without moving his head or lips much, 'Be careful, awful lot of things that might break. Have spent a fortune in air freight.' Jagan slipped into the background, pushing his cousin to the fore to do all the talking and receiving. He was overwhelmed by the spectacle of his son, who seemed to have grown taller, broader and fairer and carried himself in long strides. He wore a dark suit, with an overcoat, an airbag, a camera, an umbrella and whatnot on his person.

Jagan felt that he was following a stranger. When Mali approached him, extending his hand, he tried to shrink away and shield himself behind the cousin. When he had to speak to his son, with great difficulty he restrained himself from calling him 'sir' and employing the honorific plural.

Matters became worse when Mali indicated the girl at his side and said, 'This is Grace. We are married. Grace, my dad.' Complete confusion. Married? When were you married? You didn't tell me. Don't you have to tell your father? Who is she? Anyway she looks like a Chinese. Don't you know that one can't marry a Chinese nowadays? They have invaded our borders . . . Or perhaps she is a Japanese. How was one to find out? Any indiscreet question might upset the gentleman with the camera. Jagan threw a panicky look at his cousin and fled on the pretext of supervising the loading of the baggage into Gaffur's taxi outside. A small gaping crowd followed them to the car murmuring, 'He's come from America.' Mali took notice of Gaffur by saying, 'Jalopy going strong?' Gaffur did not understand the word (which sounded to everyone like the *jilebi* prepared in Jagan's shop). Jagan and the cousin sat with Gaffur in the front seat, leaving the back for Grace and Mali. Gaffur said without turning his head, 'Why didn't you bring a car for me?' Jagan feared that Gaffur's familiarity might upset Mali, but the young man, fresh from democratic surroundings, said, 'I wish you had told me; oh, I sold my Pontiac before coming.' Gaffur, driving the car, entered into a description of the state of the nation with reference to automobiles, how you had to wait for five years to get a Fiat, three for an Ambassador, and so forth, how no importation was allowed and how a brand-new Plymouth was seized and destroyed at the customs, all of which upset the young man, freshly come home.

Mali occasionally peeped out to say, 'Nothing has changed.' Grace gazed with fascination at the streets and bazaars and cooed,

'Oh, charming! Charming! Charming!'

'Honey, live in it and see what it is like,' said Mali, on hearing which Jagan wondered whether he should address her as Honey or Grace. Time enough to settle that question. When they approached the statue, she asked, 'Who is that?' No one answered her. Jagan became tense at the approach of the house beyond the statue. When they stopped, he jumped out of the car and panted up the steps in order to open the main door. He had spent the fortnight in rigging up his house to suit his son's requirements. Under the guidance of the doctor's wife known to the cousin, he had spent a fortune in building a modern toilet and bathroom adjoining Mali's bedroom and had scrubbed and colour-washed the walls and put up new tables and chairs. Mali went straight to his room to wash and change. Gaffur and the cousin left after piling the boxes in the passage. Grace was left alone, standing uncertainly in the hall. 'Sit in that chair,' Jagan said, unable to find anything else to say. He added, 'Tell me what you want. I will get it. I do not know exactly what you will like to have.'

'Oh, how kind you are!' she said, genuinely pleased with his attention. She drew a chair for him and said, 'Please be seated yourself, you must be tired.'

'Oh, no,' Jagan said. 'I am a very active man. The whole secret of human energy . . .' he began and cut short his sentence when he noticed the bewilderment in the girl's face. 'I must really be off, you know, must go back to my shop, otherwise . . .'

'Oh, please do go and attend to your work.'

'Make yourself comfortable,' he cried, and hurried out while Mali was still in the bathroom.

He began to avoid people. His anxiety was lest the lawyer or the printer or anyone else should stop him in the street to inquire about his daughter-in-law. He walked hurriedly to his shop with downcast eyes. Even his cousin found great stretches of silence when they met. Jagan had grown unwilling to talk about his son. Everything about him had become an inconvenient question. The cousin wanted to know what Mali had qualified himself for, what he proposed to do, and, above all, who was that casteless girl at home. He was dying to know what dietary arrangements were made at home and if they cooked meat. He inquired indirectly, 'Does Mali still like our coffee or does he ask for tea as some of these foreign-returned people do?'

Jagan understood the purpose of this question and said in order to put an end once and for all to inquisitiveness, 'What another person eats or drinks never interests me; why should I pry into it? The kitchen is there and they should know what to do with themselves.'

'It'd be all right for Mali. But it's the girl I'm thinking of . . .'

'Oh, she is all right. She was cooking for him and feeding him before, and she is able to do it now, I suppose.' Feeling suddenly that after all the cousin did deserve some enlightenment, he added, 'I can only provide what I'm used to. If they don't like it, they can go and eat where they please.'

'The Palace Hotel in the New Extension, I hear, provides European food.'

'Whatever it is, one can only do one's duty up to a point. Even in the *Gita* you find it mentioned. The limit of one's duty is well defined.'

The cousin changed the subject: he'd agreed with so much of the *Gita* day after day that he felt weary of it. As long as Mali's blue air mail letters had been the theme, the *Gita* had receded into the background. Now it was coming back, which showed that Jagan was becoming mentally disturbed again.

Occasionally one of Mali's old friends came to meet him. He seated the friend in the hall and conversed in low tones, as became a gentleman, and Jagan had no means of knowing what they talked about. Perhaps Mali was describing the Grand Canyon and Niagara and the Statue of Liberty and the traffic jams in New York; he knew all about such things and could have joined in if they'd let him, but he felt it might seem presumptuous unless he was invited. In that hope he sometimes let his feet lag crossing the hall while Mali was playing a gramophone or a tape-recorder or displaying to his friend a polaroid camera or one or other of the hundred things he had brought with him, which had included a wrapped package for Jagan. Grace had pressed it into his hands with: 'Father, this is for you.' It was a pale yellow casket with compartments containing spoons, forks and knives. He had examined it, turned it round in his hand and said, 'Beautiful! But what is it?'

Grace replied, 'It's a picnic hamper. Mali thought you would appreciate it.'

'Of course, it's welcome,' Jagan had said, wondering how one used it, and locked it up in his almirah.

Mali never wore a *dhoti* at home, but a pair of dark trousers over a white shirt, and always had his feet in slippers. He hardly ever left his room or visited any part of the house. He seldom went out: if he did, he waited for darkness to descend on the town and then, dressed elaborately in socks, shoes, jacket and tie, stepped out in the company of Grace and strolled up a deserted part of New Extension Road, but never in the direction of the statue or Market Road. He carried himself like a celebrity avoiding the attention of the rabble.

One morning, Grace parted the mustard-coloured curtain which divided the house into two sections, came into Jagan's quarters, and tidied them up. He was not used to being helped and felt uneasy while his roll of mat was shaken and put away, and his pillow of hard cotton patted. She washed the vessels in his kitchen and arranged them neatly on a shelf. His protests went unheeded. She clutched the broom and raked every corner of the floor, saying, 'Father, you think I mind it? I don't. I must not forget that I am an Indian daughter-in-law.'

Jagan did not know what to say in reply and mumbled, 'That's true indeed.' She was stooping and scrubbing the ancient granite sink in the kitchen at floor level, tucking up her saree (which she had learnt to wear), exposing her ivory hued kneecap. Jagan could not take his eyes off that ivory patch as he protested, 'Oh, Grace, Grace, you must not. I'm not used to it. Don't you bother yourself. I believe in doing all my work myself.'

'And I believe in not letting you do it, that's all,' she said. 'I like to work. What else should I be doing all day?'

Jagan, who had been in the *puja* room before the gods, was now following Grace about, turning the rosary between his fingers. He said, 'What will people think if they see a modern girl, brought up in New York, doing all this drudgery? Mali may not like it.'

'It's not his business anyway,' she said. 'He is writing letters, and I'm doing the house, that's all. This is the loveliest house I have ever seen in my life.'

'Don't you find it musty and old?'

'No, it's lovely. I've always dreamt of living in a house like this.'

Nowadays he left home late, as he had got into the habit of waiting for Grace. He was getting used to the extreme air of orderliness that the feminine touch imparted to one's surroundings.

One day Grace said, 'I wish you would let me cook for you.'

'Oh, that is impossible. I'm under a vow about that.'

He explained how he ate to live only on what he could cook with his own hands.

Grace cried, 'Oh, you sound thrilling!' This was the first time someone had had a good word to say about his habits. Encouraged by her enthusiasm, he expatiated on his own creations of salt-free and sugar-free food, and concluded by saying that she should really look forward to reading his book when Truth Printing let it out of the press. She said ecstatically, 'I'm sure it's going to be a best-seller.'

At the earliest chance he inquired, feeling very awkward, 'What did Mali . . . ? I mean, what I want to ask is, has he finished his studies and acquired a degree in America?'

Grace looked up from a vessel she was scrubbing, and asked, 'Why, didn't you know?'

Jagan, feeling that he must cover up his relationship with his son and not betray the actual state of affairs, said, 'I've had no time actually to talk to Mali about all these matters, and so . . .'

'Yes, yes, I understand,' Grace said. 'Still, he ought to have told you.'

'Oh, no,' cried Jagan. 'Don't take it that way. I am not complaining . . .'

'Of course not,' she agreed. 'I still say that Mali should have told you. Suppose I tell him to speak to you about it; it is pretty important, you know. Unless he talks to you, what can he plan, really?'

'Yes, I was also thinking that. I'd like to know his plans.'

'You will, you will . . .' she said.

Jagan said, 'I thought he would mention something in his letters, but, you know, I only learnt a great deal about your country from them.'

At this she rose to her feet with a peal of laughter, and said, 'Oh, oh, Father, Father, get me one of the letters and I will tell you . . .'

'What?' Jagan asked, rather puzzled. 'What do you mean?'

'Have you any of those letters? I will explain . . .'

He went to his favourite cupboard and took out a cardboard box in which all the blue letters had been neatly treasured, and riffled through the lot. 'Here they are; I do not know which one you want to see.' He was still hesitant, being averse to letting anyone touch these valuable documents, but he could not say so to Grace.

'Wow! What a lot!' she exclaimed, and pulled out a letter at random. 'Ah, here it is!' She pointed to the signature at the end. 'Can you read this?'

Jagan fumbled for his glasses, put them on, and read aloud. ' "GM", is it?'

'Surely, didn't you notice it before? I thought you knew. "GM" is Grace and Mali, that's me and him, after we . . . we . . .' She tailed off. 'I composed all those letters, though both of us signed them.'

'You wrote them?' Jagan said, gulping down the saliva in his awkwardness. 'How should I know? I never even knew that you were there.'

'Didn't Mali ever write to you himself?'

Jagan remained silent. This was not going to do anyone any good; he silently prayed to Gandhi's spirit to forgive the lie he was about to utter. 'Yes, yes, but I did not know these letters were yours.'

'What did Mali have to say about me? Were you shocked?'

'He didn't describe you. How can one write about a person fully? Words after all convey so little; that's why I thought he was taking up a very difficult line when he said he wanted to be a writer . . .' He was rambling on thus when Grace put away her mop and brooms, came up, and sat down by his side, dangling her legs down the steps of the courtyard. 'I didn't gather much about you from him.' He let his clumsy imagination soar. 'He only wrote that he was going to marry. I didn't know much about you; even now I don't know much about you except that you are a good girl.'

'That is all one should bother about, don't you think? Why should we ask or know more?'

Jagan did not like to let this opportunity slip and said, 'It is a custom in this country to inquire where one was born and bred and who is who generally, and then we go on to other things.'

'Only the passport and income tax people ask for such details in other countries. However, since I am an Indian now, I might as well get used to things and tell you something. My mother was a Korean and my father was an American soldier serving in the Far East after the Second World War. I was born in New Jersey when my father went on home leave and took my mother along; he was recalled while my mother was still confined, and . . .' She remained silent for a moment and said, 'He never came home again. My mother decided to stay in America and I studied at Margaret's. Have you heard of it?'

'No,' Jagan said. 'What is it?'

'A girls' school. How I adore the memory of it!'

'Must be a good place,' Jagan said. It was his habit to pick up tit-bits of American information and build on them.

'I studied Domestic Science at Michigan and met Mo when he came there for his Creative Writing course. We sat side by side at a football game. Oh, you must see the football matches in Michigan; have you such things here?'

'Yes, yes, we have football too. All the schoolboys play it.'

'I thought he must have written to you all about it.'

'Yes, yes, but you know sometimes letters get lost. The other day I heard a friend complaining to the postmaster that his letters never reach him properly . . .'

'You are happy, aren't you?' she asked suddenly. Jagan nodded.

She said, 'I had heard so much about the caste system in this country, I was afraid to come here, and when I first saw you all at the railway station I shook with fear. I thought I might not be accepted. Mo has really been wonderful, you know. It was very courageous of him to bring me here.'

'Well, we don't believe in caste these days, you know,' Jagan said generously. 'Gandhi fought for its abolition.'

'Is it gone now?' she asked innocently.

'It's going,' Jagan said, sounding like a politician, 'we don't think of it nowadays,' hoping that the girl would not cross-examine him further.

Mali suddenly dashed into Jagan's presence one day to ask, 'Can't you get a telephone for the house?'

Jagan said, 'I've not thought of it.'

'Yes, that's it. This is awkward and backward. How can we do any business without a telephone?'

Jagan wanted to say, 'After all, Malgudi is a small town; everyone is within shouting distance.'

'Even in your business,' Mali went on, 'if you had a telephone, more business would flow in. People might order by telephone.'

Jagan merely said, 'I've not thought of it,' while he wanted to reply, 'My daily sale is such and such even without a telephone, which shows that when one wants to eat sweets one doesn't wait for a telephone.'

The boy said, 'I felt embarrassed because I could not give my associates a telephone number.'

'Who are your associates? What's the association?'

'Grace!' Mali called. 'Will you join us? We are discussing business now.'

Jagan was seized with a cold dread at the prospect of a business discussion with Mali, although pleased that after all Mali was going to talk to him. He was in one of his rare moods of communication. Jagan could see by the deliberate manner in which Grace kept herself in the background that she must have been responsible for this meeting. Mali suggested, 'Father, let us adjourn to the hall. We have chairs there.' Jagan was getting ready to leave for his shop, but thought it worthwhile to postpone his routine. Nowadays, with one thing and another, his timetable was getting slightly upset.

Jagan obediently trooped behind his son and took his seat in the hall, where he had not stepped for many weeks now. He noticed that Grace had transformed the place with curtains, mats, tablecloth. A couple of modern paintings hung on the walls: Jagan found them bewildering, but said 'Yes' when Grace asked, 'Aren't they marvellous?' The bamboo chairs were piled with coloured cushions. A little vase on a table held a sprig of margosa leaves. Jagan's heart throbbed at the sight. He said, 'Margosa is the ambrosia mentioned in our *Vedas*, did you know that, Grace?'

She almost hugged the flower vase and cried, 'How grand! How did they know? They know all about everything in the *Vedas*, don't they?'

'Of course they do, all the *Vedas* have emanated from God's feet.'

'Ah, what a conception!' Grace cried. She found everything thrilling. Everything stirred in her some poetic feeling, deep within.

Mali cautioned her, 'Don't start swallowing margosa leaves, my dear.'

Jagan said, 'No harm in it. It is a natural antiseptic, purifies the blood, supplies iron . . .' His eyes lit up when he spoke of margosa leaves. 'I've explained it in detail in my book. When you read it, you will understand better . . .' Grace was now readjusting the flowers in the vase with a deliberate interest, as if she were privileged to handle ambrosia as a result of marrying an Indian.

It was a long time since Jagan had observed his son's face at close quarters. Now he noticed that the freshness and the glow of foreignness that he had possessed when he arrived was gone; he looked even a shade below par. He had not re-acquired the taste for South Indian food, but seemed to be eating his meals out of hermetically sealed tins. Jagan repressed his remarks on this subject, although he sadly noted that Mali's eyes were dark-ringed. What was he worrying about? Jagan patiently waited for the other to speak. He noticed that Mali wore socks under his sandals, and wanted to cry out, 'Socks should never be worn, because they are certain to heat the blood through interference with the natural radiation which occurs through one's soles, and also because you insulate yourself against beneficial magnetic charges of the earth's surface. I have argued in my book that this is one of the reasons, a possible reason, for heart attacks in European countries . . .' While he was busy with these thoughts, he was also dimly aware that Mali had been talking. He had been aware of the sound, but he had missed the substance of the words. He had anticipated this meeting for a long time and he realized now with a shudder that he had probably missed the opportunity of a lifetime. He woke up with a start and became extra-attentive, bending to the task all his powers of concentration, as Mali was concluding his passage with, 'You get it?' Jagan was at a loss whether to say 'yes' or 'no', but sat staring ahead and making non-committal sounds in his throat.

'Well, think over it; you have all the data,' said Mali. Then he glanced at his watch and rose muttering, 'I must check at the rail. station about my unaccompanied baggage, expected today; if only we had a telephone . . .' He went to the door, turned to Grace and said, 'Don't wait for lunch.' They heard his scooter palpitating away.

Jagan sat still, quietly enjoying the thought that his son had spoken to him at such length. When he rose to go, Grace held the door open for him and asked, 'Did you have any questions for Mali? Was everything clear?'

Jagan replied, 'I can always go back to the subject, can't I?' with a significant smile, and Grace said, 'Of course.'

CHAPTER SIX

THE COUSIN NOWADAYS found Jagan rather hesitant about speaking of his son, but on the theory that conversation must go on he said, 'Did you hear that there was a fight at the market? The jaggery merchant as usual was cornering the stock, and . . .'

Jagan, seated on his throne, with the flavour of frying ghee filling the hall, said, 'Our merchants are becoming heartless.'

'You just wait and see what's going to happen to the rice dealers; they are playing with fire.'

'Even when one wants to make profits, one should retain some sense of service. I have not raised the price here, in spite of the sugar crisis.'

'Oh, everybody is not you,' the cousin flattered, giving a soft back-stroke to his tuft. Flattery was his accredited business in life; even when he joked and disparaged it was all a part of his flattery. He said, 'You are not one who knows how to make money. If you were unscrupulous, you could have built many mansions, who knows?'

'And what would one do with many mansions?' asked Jagan and quoted a Tamil verse which said that even if eighty million ideas float across your mind, you cannot wear more than four cubits of cloth or eat more than a little measure of rice at a time.

'Ah!' jeered the cousin genially, stuffing a piece of tobacco into his mouth, 'that's why I say that you do not know the art of living and flourishing, and yet the goddess of wealth chooses you for her favours!'

Jagan laughed happily, and, feeling that now the other deserved a little dose of information about Mali, said, 'I came late this morning because Mali wanted to discuss his plans.' He was very proud of being able to mention something so concrete about his son. The cousin became alert and sat up attentively in order not to miss a word. Jagan paused after the announcement and the cousin filled the momentary gap with: 'I had a glimpse of him this morning on a scooter. Has he bought one?'

'It's a friend's, I hear. He must have a conveyance.'

'Who could that friend be?' the cousin speculated. 'Scooter-riding boys—one is that kerosene agent's son; another is the man who has come from the Punjab to establish a button factory. Another scooter belongs to the District Judge's nephew—you know, that young man in the Public Works Department in charge of the new roads in the hills.'

'Boys must have their own vehicles nowadays; they don't like to walk,' generalized Jagan. 'I always like to move on my feet, but these are days of speed; people must go from place to place quickly. They have more to do than we had, don't you think so? Mali has never fancied walking. He has always cycled. I bought him his first cycle when he was seven years old, and he could go wherever he pleased. I sometimes found that he would cycle up to Ellaman Street, not in the least minding the crowd on Market Road.'

'Even adults shy away from Market Road in the evenings.'

'But that boy grew up fearlessly, full of self-reliance at an age when other boys were being mollycoddled.'

'But poor boy, his mother was so ailing.'

'That's another reason why I tried to keep his mind diverted.'

The dialogue was rambling off into a series of side issues. The cousin tried to pull it back to the main theme. 'You were starting to tell me about Mali's plans. You must be feeling relieved now.'

'Yes, yes, but I always knew that everything must be going well, with nothing to bother about.'

'Now, have you any idea of his plans?'

'Yes. He was in a hurry to go to the railway station this morning, and he could give me only a general idea. Of course, he'll tell us the details later.' This was the utmost Jagan could essay without betraying his ignorance.

The cousin asked abruptly, 'Are you in favour of his scheme?'

'Which scheme?' Jagan asked, looking surprised. He hadn't suspected any scheme. The cousin paused for a second, while the noise of school breaking up next door enlivened the air. A group of children as usual hung about the front stall gazing at the sweets arranged on trays. 'Captain, don't allow crowds to stand there; they obstruct the traffic.' Traffic was not Jagan's real concern—there were many obstructions on Market Road: a couple of cows belonging to a milk-seller always stood in the centre of the road in their off-hours, not to speak of a rogue bull, belonging to no one in particular, which sometimes chased the cows amorously, scattering the pedestrians, *jutkas* and cycles alike on to the steps of the shops; there were groups from villages, bringing in grain and fruit to the market, who sat on the edge of Market Road in a circle, overflowing onto the middle; cycles and bullock carts and automobiles threaded their way through without damage to themselves or to others. No one protested or bothered, but Jagan always mentioned the word 'obstruction' because the sight of the children at the counter made him uneasy, even guilty at times. He preferred them to go away without looking at the sweets so hungrily. It was his habit to call out to the captain and issue an order whenever he felt any sort of mental strain.

The cousin now realized that the word 'scheme' had set up an agitation in Jagan's mind; he watched Jagan's face with satisfaction. Jagan's studied avoidance of the subject of his son had not been to the cousin's liking. It made him feel that he had been suddenly converted into an outsider; he didn't like the status, and so here he found an opportunity to bring himself back into the fold. 'I didn't want to speak to you unnecessarily about it, but I'm so happy that the boy still calls me "Uncle" whenever he meets me; although he has travelled to the other end of the earth, he has not forgotten his uncle. You see, I didn't like to thrust myself on him after his return home. People change, you know, especially when they go abroad. I know of a foreign-returned ICS officer who disowned his parents when they came to meet him at the railway station.'

'Horrible fellow, he must have been mad! Mali could not be in the least like him.'

'I know, I know; that's what I am telling you. I went to the Registrar's house last week, and Mali was talking to his son. You know their house in the New Extension? I had gone there because I had promised to find a suitable cook for them; the lady is not in good health. I have to do various things for various persons.'

'The Registrar's son and Mali are friends, I suppose?'

'Oh, yes, they were conversing on the front veranda. As I passed in, Mali himself addressed me. "Give me a few minutes before you go." "Yes, Mali," I said, "I'm at your service." After finishing my business inside, I came out and Mali said, "I'll walk with you." '

'Did he want to walk? I thought he never cared to walk.'

'Only up to the gate, because he did not like to let his friends overhear what he wanted to say.'

'What did he say?' Jagan asked, now completely at the mercy of the cousin.

'He wants to manufacture story-writing machines,' said the cousin.

Jagan felt so baffled by this statement that he couldn't phrase his surprise properly. He blurted out a couple of questions incoherently and lapsed into silence.

The cousin watched his face, relishing the bewilderment he saw in it, and said with an innocent look, 'Haven't you heard of story-writing machines?' as if they were an article of daily use. This was a minor victory for him in the matter of American knowledge. Jagan felt it best to acknowledge defeat and give up all pretence. The cousin rubbed it in by saying, 'I thought he would have told you everything. What else was he telling you this morning?'

Jagan said loftily, 'We had other things to talk about. He was telling me of other matters.'

'But this proposition is uppermost in his mind; he is thinking of it night and day.'

'Yes, yes,' said Jagan. 'I knew of course that he was speaking about a machine, but something else came up before I could ask him to explain.'

'This is not just an ordinary machine,' said the cousin.

At this moment Jagan let out his periodic shout: 'Captain! Why is there a crowd?' but the cousin continued in a tone of authority, 'Now listen carefully. This story-writing machine, as you might have guessed, is a story-writing machine.'

'How does it do that?' asked Jagan, genuinely surprised.

'Don't ask me,' said the cousin. 'I am not an engineer. Mali constantly used the word "electronic" or "electric" or something like that, and explained it at length. It sounds very interesting; why don't you ask him? I am sure he will be able to explain it to you satisfactorily.'

Jagan bided his time and the next morning when Grace came in to clean his kitchen, applied for an interview. 'I want to talk to Mali; is he free?'

'Of course,' she said. 'If he isn't, he will free himself for your sake.' She paused and then heard the clatter of a typewriter from Mali's room. 'He is busy, I think,' she added. 'I will tell him.' She went up and came out a few minutes later with an air of importance. 'He will see you in fifteen minutes.'

For a moment Jagan felt as if he were a petitioner in his own house, and there flashed across his mind those far-off days when Mali used to stand at his door, cringing for some concession or for cash, and for a brief second he was aghast at the transformations that had come with time. 'I have to be off myself,' he said to redress the balance of importance, but Grace went back to her work in the kitchen without a reply. Unable to make up his mind, he idly opened a cupboard and stood gazing at the old bottles and packing paper that he had preserved on the theory of keeping a thing for seven years.

Grace said from the kitchen, 'Another day I will clean up that cupboard for you. We need to do some spring-cleaning in this house.'

Jagan, aghast at the implications, said with some intensity, 'Don't do anything yet.' Meanwhile the typewriter ceased and a bell sounded, and Grace said, 'He is ready for you. You want to go in?' She seemed to have built Mali up into a celebrity. She led him forward. 'He is very methodical, you know.'

Jagan was pleased and baffled at the same time. He gritted himself for the interview. He glanced at the clock on the wall and muttered, 'Must be going in fifteen minutes.'

Jagan took the visitor's chair, looked for a moment at his son and plunged into the subject straight away. 'How exactly does the story-machine operate?'

'I explained it to you yesterday,' said Mali.

'There were some points which I did not quite grasp, but I was in a hurry.'

The son looked pityingly at him, rose, opened a packing case, pushed aside a lot of brown paper and thread and lifted out a small object which looked like a radio cabinet and placed it on the table. 'I was only waiting for this to arrive; yesterday I had to clear it from the railway office. What a lot of time is wasted here! I have never seen a more wasteful country than this.' Jagan refrained from retorting, 'We find it quite adequate for our purpose.' Now Mali stood beside the cabinet in the attitude of a lecturer; he patted it fondly and said, 'With this machine anyone can write a story. Come nearer, and you will see it working.' Jagan obediently pushed his chair back, rose and stood beside his son, who seemed to tower above him. He felt proud of him. 'God knows what he eats out of those tins; he looks tired, no doubt, but how well grown he is!' he reflected as Mali explained, 'You see these four knobs? One is for characters, one for plot situations, one for climax, and the fourth is built on the basis that a story is made up of characters, situations, emotions and climax, and by the right combination . . .' He interrupted his oration for a moment to pull a drawer out and glance at a cyclostyled sheet of paper; he shut the drawer and came back to say, 'You can work on it like a typewriter. You make up your mind about the number of characters. It works on a transistor and ordinary valves. Absolutely foolproof. Ultimately we are going to add a little fixture, by which any existing story could be split up into components and analysed; the next model will incorporate it.'

Jagan asked, 'Do you want to use this for writing stories?'

'Yes, I am also going to manufacture and sell it in this country. An American company is offering to collaborate. In course of time, every home in the country will possess one and we will produce more stories than any other nation in the world. Now we are a little backward. Except for *Ramayana* and *Mahabharata*, those old stories, there is no modern writing, whereas in America alone every publishing season ten thousand books are published.' He rushed back to his desk-drawer and gazed on the cyclostyled sheet again before repeating, 'Yes, ten thousand titles. It is a "must" for every home; all a writer will have to do is to own one and press the keys, and he will get the formula in a moment, on a roll of paper, from which he can build up the rest . . .'

Jagan left his seat and went over to examine the machine as if it were something from another planet. He approached it so cautiously that Mali said, 'Touch it and see for yourself.' Jagan peered at the apparatus closely and read the headings: 'Characters: good, bad, neutral. Emotions: love, hate, revenge, devotion, pity. Complexities: characters, incidents, accidents. Climax: placement and disposal and conclusion.' It looked pretty, its mahogany veneer was grained; its keys were green, red and yellow to indicate the different categories. 'How can one write a story with it?' Jagan asked.

'Exactly as one does with a typewriter,' Mali answered, and

Jagan admired him for the fund of information he had gathered on the subject.

Just at this moment, Grace came in, stood beside them and said, 'Isn't he clever?' in a jocular manner. Jagan could not answer her immediately, his mind was too full of confusion and questions. He felt hemmed in: the room had lost its original appearance and looked like an office in a foreign country. What was Mali trying to do? What was his own part in all this activity? What was going to be the nature of his involvement? He said with some trepidation, 'Grace, do you know that our ancestors never even wrote the epics? They composed the epics and recited them, and the great books lived thus from generation to generation, by the breath of people . . .'

Before he could proceed further, Mali said with a gesture of disgust, 'Oh, these are not the days of your ancestors. Today we have to compete with advanced countries not only in economics and industry, but also in culture.' While on the one hand Jagan felt delighted at the way his son seemed to be blossoming after years of sullen silence, he was at the same time saddened by the kind of development he noticed in him now. The boy went on, 'If you have the time, I'd like to explain to you one or two other points.' Jagan helplessly glanced at a travelling clock on Mali's table, and jingled the keys of his shop in the depths of his *jibba* pocket. 'Ultimately, you may have to give up your sweet-making and work in our business. I'll give you a nice air-conditioned room with a couple of secretaries.'

Jagan had never known his son talk so fluently; he wished secretly that he would speak differently. He felt the time had come for him to ask his questions. 'Do they write all their stories with this machine in America?' he asked, as if he wished to fill a lacuna in his knowledge of that land and its civilization.

'Mostly, mostly,' said Mali.

'Most magazines,' added Grace, 'are nowadays switching over to the machine in their fiction departments, and out of the best-sellers last year at least three were a product. The proposition is that we get American collaboration worth two hundred thousand dollars, provided we find fifty-one thousand to start the business.'

'Fifty-one thousand dollars would be the equivalent of . . .' began Jagan, starting the age-old calculation.

'Work it out yourself,' said Mali with a touch of irritation in his voice. 'Let me first finish my sentence. They will be responsible for the knowhow and technical personnel, help us set up the plant, run it for six months and then quit; they will also provide us with promotional material.' What a lot of new expressions the boy had learnt, Jagan reflected with admiration, while Mali added, 'We shall have to collect forty-nine thousand dollars by public subscription, and then the controlling stock will be in our hands.'

Jagan had thought till then that his son was a moron. He looked for a brief second at Grace and asked, 'What was your subject in college?'

She answered, 'I've told you I post-graduated in Domestic Science at Michigan.'

'Why go into all that now?' asked Mali.

Jagan said, rising, 'I was wondering if Grace had also studied business subjects.' And now it was Mali's turn to wonder why his father said that.

Jagan left without further comment. At four-thirty when the cousin arrived, he told him, 'Have you any idea what fifty thousand dollars is in rupees?'

The cousin said, 'A little over two lakhs of rupees.'

'How do you know?'

'By a simple calculation and I also verified it yesterday when I met Dodhaji, our banker, after I left Mali.'

'Two lakhs!' mused Jagan. 'Where does one find it?'

'In your bank book,' said the cousin promptly in a jocular way.

'Are people under the impression that I have amassed wealth?'

'Yes, of course, although everyone admires your simple living and high-thinking habits.'

'How can wealth accumulate with the price of foodstuff standing where it is? I just keep up the business so that these poor fellows may not be thrown out of employment, that's all.'

'That everybody knows,' said the cousin. 'Are you interested in buying raisins? I saw a fresh stock arrive at the *sait*'s shop, handpicked quality.'

'Have you asked the cook?'

'He told me that he needed them because I found the *sohan papdi* rather tame without raisins today.'

Jagan cried furiously, 'Is that so? Why didn't he tell me?'

The cousin said, 'You didn't come in time, that's all, and he couldn't wait for the stuff. Why do you get upset?'

'It's because I do not like the idea of cheating my customers.

Do you realize that the price for the customer remains the same with or without raisins?'

'And your own margin of profit is improved,' said the cousin. Jagan glared at him. The cousin added, 'You are a rare being, but that would be the line of thought of some of your compatriots in this city.'

Mollified, Jagan said, with a touch of pride, 'I was held up by Mali, poor boy. I have to give him the time he needs now and then; otherwise there is bound to be a lot of misunderstanding. His ideas turn on big figures nowadays. He seems to have learnt many things in America.'

'He wants me to use my influence to sell the shares of the company.'

This was a relief to Jagan. 'I'm sure many people will be interested in the proposal.'

'Including your good self.'

'No harm in finding five or ten along with the rest.'

'Mali's idea is different. He has reserved five or ten for people outside, and counts on you for the fifty-one thousand dollars for a start.'

'And you have found its rupee equivalent?'

'About two and a half lakhs.'

'Where does one find it?'

'I've already indicated.'

'Does Mali think so?'

'Of course, and he also says he knows where you keep cash not sent to the bank.'

'He says so, does he?' said Jagan, laughing within himself at the fact that he had changed the venue of the immaculate cash. 'Money is an evil,' he added with great feeling.

The cousin said, 'Shall I ask the front-stall boy to throw away that bronze jug?'

They both laughed at the joke, but the relaxation was short-lived for Jagan. He became very serious suddenly and said, 'I hope you will find an occasion to tell my son that I have not got all that money.'

'Now you are both on speaking terms, why don't you tell him yourself?

Jagan sighed and said, 'I do not wish to spoil his mood.'

The tempo of Mali's demand increased. Though at one time

Jagan had sighed for a word from his son, he now wished that the thaw had not occurred.

He was being hunted. When he passed in and out of the house he felt his steps were being watched, his face being secretly studied for a yes or no. Grace gazed at his face meaningfully. Mali, if he was at home, kept on coming into his quarters on some excuse or other. After the first day's demonstration Jagan had studiously avoided all literary topics. 'Here is a scheme to make me bankrupt,' he said to himself whenever he heard footfalls approaching his room. 'Fifty-one thousand dollars! I am not growing over-fond of money, but I'm not prepared to squander it. Why should we want stories or machines for writing them?'

One morning Mali stood at the doorway of the *puja* room after breakfast, in blue pants, with his hands resting on the top of the threshold as Jagan sat before his gods. 'They do everything with machines nowadays. Washing machines, have you seen one?'

'No,' said Jagan, trying to cut all mechanical references to a minimum.

'Grinding, powdering or calculating—nowadays one uses electricity for everything.' Behind him stood Grace, adding, 'Even for mending pencils we have machines.'

'We should have brought one with us,' Mali said, turning to her. Mali, who never used to seek him before, was now intruding even into the privacy of his *puja* room, interrupting his prayers. Jagan met this disturbance passively by shutting his eyes and muttering some incantations until Grace said, 'We should not disturb his prayers.' Prayer was a sound way of isolating oneself—but sooner or later it ended: one could not go on praying eternally, though one ought to.

He had become rather sneaky nowadays. Soon after his prayers, he tiptoed to the kitchen to prepare his salt-free food, bolt it down, put on his *khadi jibba* and slip away with the least noise, but he always found Grace at the passage ready to open the door for him with some remark about the weather or politics, gazing on his face with an unmistakable inquiry about his views on the machine. He was amazed at the intensity of her interest in Mali's fortunes. As ever, he had two opposite feelings: appreciation of her interest in Mali and resentment at her effort to involve him in their business. Mali never thrust himself forward more than a minimum; he seemed to have left the task to Grace; even his visitation at the threshold of the *puja* room in the morning seemed to have been

dictated by Grace. An occasional misgiving tainted Jagan's thoughts—
might not Grace's interest, friendliness and attentiveness be a
calculated effort to win his dollars? Walking to his shop with head
lowered in thought, as the vagrant at the statue corner greeted him
and begged for money, Jagan paused to ask, for the hundredth time
in a year, 'You are sturdy; why don't you seek work?'

'When have I the time, master? By the time I have gone round
begging and returned here the day is over . . .'

Jagan tossed a five-paise coin at him as he remembered an
ancient injunction: 'Perform thy charity without question.'

In appreciation the beggar said, 'Master does not tell me much
about America nowadays. Why?'

'Because I have told you all you should know.'

'What's the little master doing?' asked the beggar.

'Well, he'll be starting a factory soon,' replied Jagan, without
conviction.

'What'll he make?'

'Some machinery,' Jagan said, not wishing to elaborate and
wishing the beggar would leave him alone. Fortunately he slipped
off to pester some other person coming in the opposite direction,
and Jagan quickened his pace. Passing Truth Printing, he spied
Nataraj alone at his desk and on an impulse stopped to ask, 'I hope
you have not forgotten my work?'

'How could I?' said Nataraj. 'As soon as the pressure of the
seasonal printing lessens, yours will be the first. I'm your family
printer, you know. Your son has given me an urgent work which he
wants in three days, the prospectus for his new enterprise.'

'Ah!' cried Jagan. The 'scheme' seemed to dog his steps.

'Your name is in it!' said Nataraj.

'Ah! Ah!' exclaimed Jagan.

Nataraj pushed up his roll-top and produced a proof sheet and
Jagan saw his name in print as one of the principal promoters of
Mali Enterprises. The others in the list were Grace and a few of
Mali's scooter-riding friends. Nataraj studied his face and said,
'Why, aren't you pleased?'

Jagan replied in a hollow tone, 'Yes, yes, no doubt.'

'Seems to be an interesting new kind of enterprise . . .'

'Yes, yes, no doubt.'

He hurriedly left for his shop. As the cook stood before him
taking instructions for the day, he feared he too might begin to

speak of the story-writing machine, but luckily this man's universe of kitchen smoke and frying oil had not lost its insularity yet. Occupying his throne, with the scent of incense and frying, Jagan recovered a little bit of his sense of security. He opened the drawer and let his eyes rest on the copy of the *Bhagavad Gita* for a while, opened a page at random and tried to get absorbed in its eternal message, but part of his mind was deeply injured by the sight of his own name in print on the prospectus. How could Mali perpetrate such a deed, take so much for granted? But the poor boy probably had complete confidence in his father's support, and there was nothing heinous in that. It was natural. Still, he should at least have had the courtesy to mention it to him. Neither Grace nor Mali . . . But perhaps they had only been hanging about his *puja* room to inform him of that rather than ask for capital; and he blamed himself for not giving them a chance.

Whoever was the American associate, he had done his coaching perfectly; and Nataraj proved extraordinarily prompt. The city was soon flooded with the prospectus of Mali's company. The first one came by post to Jagan himself at his shop. It went into the cultural shortcomings of the country, and the need for it to take its place in the comity of nations, and how this machine was going to cut time and distance, and lift the country out of its rut, and then followed many facts and figures. One thing Jagan noted was that the jungles on Mempi Hills would provide the soft wood required for some part of the machine, and so it could be had for a song. Then they went into details of production and marketing and location. Jagan now realized that the son of the kerosene agent was actually the economic brain behind the whole show—a young fellow in jeans and striped shirt, who rode a scooter and carried Mali on the pillion.

Very soon they abandoned the scooter and were seen moving about in an old automobile. Grace explained to Jagan one morning, 'The company have now made a start with an automobile. Although it's an old one, it is useful. One has to move about so much on business nowadays.'

'What car is it? It looks green,' said Jagan, out of the polite need to say something, and not wishing to ask, 'What is its price? Who has paid for it?'

Grace replied, 'It's pretty, isn't it?' and Jagan lapsed into meditation before the gods, and remained in meditation until she moved away from the threshold and he could hear her talking to Mali in the front portion of the house.

'Gandhi has taught me peaceful methods, and that's how I'm going to meet their demand. These two are bent upon involving me in all sorts of things,' he reflected. He was bewildered by his son's scheme and distrusted it totally. He was aware that pressure was being subtly exercised on him to make him part with his cash. He was going to meet the situation by ignoring the whole business; a sort of non-violent non-cooperation.

But he found his domestic life irksome. He had lost the quiet joy of anticipation he used to experience whenever he turned the Statue Corner. He felt nervous as he approached the ancient house. The expectant stare of Grace when she opened the door and the significant side-glances of Mali got on his nerves. He was aware of a silent tension growing. He felt happy if nobody came when he turned the key in the door, at the times when both were away, Grace shopping and Mali with his local associates in his green car. 'Thank God,' Jagan thought, 'for the green car.' When he was in, if he heard them open the front door, he retreated far into the backyard of the house or sometimes even locked himself in the bathing shack.

But the state of non-cooperation could not last for ever. Grace asked him one morning point-blank, 'Have you thought over the proposition?'

Jagan felt cornered—if he had just picked up his upper cloth a minute earlier, he could have reached the street by now. Grace had studied his movements and timed her interception perfectly. He had dodged this encounter for two weeks by sheer manoeuvring of arrival and departure. Now he felt trapped. He wanted to say, 'Leave these questions for menfolk to settle; keep away, charmer from Outer Mongolia or somewhere.' She had stuck a flower with a pin in her bobbed hair and he longed to tell her, 'Take off that flower, it's ridiculous.' He merely remarked, 'I see you have jasmine in your hair this morning.'

'As it's a Friday, I have remembered my duties as a Hindu wife. I have also washed the doorsteps and decorated the threshold with white flour. I went to a shop yesterday to get it. See what I have done!' She was so importunate that he had to look cheerful and follow her out. She pointed at a floral design on the ground and cried, 'Don't you believe now that I could have been a Hindu in my last life? I am able to bend down and draw the design on the floor as I see a lot of others do.'

Jagan wanted to say, 'An orthodox Hindu woman would never clip her hair as you have done,' but actually remarked, 'It's a long time since anyone attended to these things in this house. How did you know that Friday is auspicious?'

'I have friends who tell me what is proper,' she said.

Just as Jagan was thinking of slipping away, a window opened, and Mali peeped out and commanded, 'Father, come in for a moment. I must talk to you.' Jagan felt that Grace had only been holding him in a trap and scowled at her accusingly, but she merely said as though she were the usherette at a Presidential interview,' 'Certainly, go in,' suggesting that he should feel honoured at the summons.

Muttering, 'I have to go and open the shop,' Jagan went in.

Mali was at his desk and flourished a finger towards the visitor's chair. Jagan lowered himself into it gingerly, still muttering, 'I must go and open the shop.'

Mali ignored his plea and asked, 'Have you thought it over?'

'What?' asked Jagan, trying to look absent-minded, but he knew he was not bringing it off successfully, for Mali, with Grace sneaking up behind, as if to complete the trapping operation, held him in a pincer movement. Mali tossed a prospectus at him. 'I mailed you one, didn't you get it?'

Jagan said neither yes nor no; there was danger in either statement. His mind wandered off in another direction: how could Nataraj have managed to issue this piece of work so quickly from his press, while his own book had remained untouched for so many years? What charm did Mali exercise? As he sat brooding on it, Mali suddenly said, 'You don't even care to look at it.'

Jagan feared that the season of sweet temper was coming to a close, and replied mildly, 'I have looked at it, and I have also noticed that you have put my name in without even telling me.'

'What is happening to you? On the very first day I spoke to you, I spent over thirty minutes in explanations; I asked if I might print your name and didn't you say "Go ahead"?'

Jagan cast his mind back. 'What day was that?'

Mali's temper had now risen. Grace saw the symptoms and stepped in to say, 'On the very first day when he told you about his scheme.'

'Oh, yes, yes,' said Jagan, realizing that he might have said anything at any time. He added mildly, 'Yes, but I naturally thought you would tell me again before actually going to the press, you know.'

'I really do not know what you mean. You expect everything to be said ten times; no wonder nothing gets done in this country.'

'Why do you blame the country for everything? It has been good enough for four hundred millions,' Jagan said, remembering the heritage of *Ramayana* and *Bhagavad Gita* and all the trials and sufferings he had undergone to win independence. He muttered, 'You were not born in those days.'

Mali made a gesture of despair. 'I do not know what you are talking about. I want to get on with the business. We had two long sessions, and I told you everything, and now . . .'

Grace interposed to say, 'Father, if you have any questions, I am sure Mali will answer them.'

Jagan felt, like a man in a witness box, that anything he uttered might be used as evidence against him and so he said, 'I must be going now, I have to open the shop.'

Mali said, 'We have to make a beginning, our associates are waiting on us. We will lose everything unless we act at once. I have explained to you the basis of our participation.'

Fifty thousand dollars! Whatever its equivalent might be, it was a staggering sum. 'I am a poor man,' Jagan wailed, and immediately noticed the shock on Mali's face and the embarrassment he had created in the presence of Grace. It was as if he had uttered a bad word. Seeing this, Jagan said, 'Gandhi always advocated poverty and not riches.'

'And yet you earn your thousand rupees a day,' said Mali with a vicious smile.

'If you feel you can take up the business and run it, do so; it is yours if you want it.'

'You expect me to do that? I have better plans than to be a vendor of sweetmeats.'

Jagan did not wait to hear more. He pushed the chair back very slowly and gently, pausing for a second to study the faces of the other two. For once he saw Grace's eyes unlit with a smile. It was impassive. 'Is she a good girl or a bad one?' Jagan asked within himself. 'I wish I could decide.' Mali was biting his thumbnail and kicking the footrest below the table. Jagan did not have the courage to stay and face him. Without another word he took his upper cloth off the hook and was out of the room in a moment. When he passed the culvert at the confluence, the vagrant said, 'My master does not even look at me nowadays.'

'I gave you five paise only . . .' He couldn't remember when, but he concluded, 'I am a poor man like you. Do you think I have inexhaustible cash?'

'Master should not say such a thing.'

At least this fellow spoke better than Mali in similar circumstances, who didn't want him if he did not claim to be a wealthy father!

He remained morose throughout the day. At four-thirty the cousin entered, went into the kitchen and came out. He knew that Jagan was waiting to spring some terrible information on him. Wiping his lips with the towel, he sat down on his stool, remarking, '*Chandra kala* (digit of the moon) tastes absolutely divine today, and if the reputation of this shop is going to shoot sky-high in this town, it will be on account of it.' As always, flattery helped; a few webs spread around Jagan's eyes and he said, 'It is purity that is important. Yesterday I came early to see that pure cow's butter was melted for frying. I won't touch buffalo butter, though it may be cheaper: Gandhi was opposed to buffalo products. I had sent one of the cooks to collect cow's butter from Koppal, he came back at five in the morning, and I came straight in before eight in order to melt it right. A fortune had been spent on it, and I didn't want to risk over-boiling it.'

'You pay attention to every detail. I have often wanted to ask you, why did you choose this business? Rather a specialized job, isn't it?'

'When I was in jail, I was given kitchen duties, and after coming out this seemed to me as good a business as any other.' He was slipping into a reminiscential mood, much to the relief of the cousin. 'But the reputation of the shop is all due to Sivaraman; but for him I don't know where I would be. I wanted to serve the public in my own way by making available pure sweets, particularly for poor children.'

'An excellent ideal,' said the cousin, deliberately refraining from the reminder that poor children were just the ones who could not afford to buy sweets. He said it another way: 'If the stuff is to be pure a price has to be paid for it.'

'That's true,' said Jagan. He sat brooding for a while and then announced, 'From tomorrow the price of everything will be reduced. I have made up my mind about it.'

'Why?' asked the cousin in consternation.

Jagan spurned an explanation. He just said, 'We buy provisions for, let us say, a hundred rupees a day, and the salaries of our staff and the rent amount to, let us say, a hundred.' He lowered his voice, 'And the stuff produced need not earn more than, let us say, two hundred in all. Now, the truth is . . .' he began but slurred over the details at the last minute, not wishing to reveal the actual figures. 'More people will benefit by a reduction.'

'But you are opposed to the eating of sugar, aren't you?'

Jagan took time to digest this contradiction before saying, 'I see no connection. If others want to eat sweets, they must have the purest ones, that is all. I am thinking particularly of children and poor people.'

'What about your share?' the other asked testily.

'I have had enough,' Jagan said.

The cousin sought further explanation, like someone scrutinizing and assaying a tricky diplomatic statement. 'Enough of what?' he asked.

'Of everything,' Jagan said. The cousin looked appropriately serious and gloomy. 'If you are thinking of retiring from the business I am sure someone will be willing to take it over and run it.'

'Oh, it is not so easy,' Jagan said. 'I told Mali so this morning and he said . . .' He remained silent. The recollection of the scene, he felt, would overwhelm him; he might break down and it would be silly to be seen in tears while he was occupying the throne. He had a mental picture of himself standing, like a ragged petitioner in the presence of Mali and the Chinese girl, being sneered at for his business of a lifetime, a business that had provided the money for Mali to fly to America and do all sorts of things there. 'Vendor of sweetmeats', indeed! Jagan became aware of the cousin waiting for his reply and said quickly, 'He was not interested in vending sweets.'

The cousin felt that this was the time to sound sympathetic and said, 'What better income could one have? But, you see, his ideas are different, as you know.'

'Money is an evil,' Jagan said, uttering an oft-repeated sentiment.

'We should all be happier without it. It is enough if an activity goes on self-supported; no need to earn money, no need to earn money. Captain!' he shouted, 'Who are those boys? What do they want?'

'I will send them away, sir.'

'No, no, tell that boy at the counter to give them each a packet and then send them away.'

'They may not have the money.'

'Who cares? I can afford to give away. Boy,' he shouted from his throne, 'treat those children.' The children got their sweets and went away greatly surprised.

'If those boys go out and tell others, you will be mobbed and unable to leave the place.'

'We will manage, don't worry,' said Jagan. 'In a day or two some changes are coming.'

The cousin looked scared and said, 'Don't be hasty; go on a pilgrimage to the temples and bathe in the sacred rivers. I will mind the shop, if you like, while you are away.'

'I will tell you when I am ready.'

The boy from the front stall now brought in the bronze jug. The cousin, who usually timed his departure at this point, got up but did not leave, curious to know whether Jagan would accept the cash or just throw it out. Jagan pulled out the drawer, spread the folded towel to deaden the noise of the coins cascading down, looked up at the cousin and said, 'Tonight and tomorrow I will have to do a lot of reckoning with concentration. I have left things to drift too long.'

The cousin, worrying where these hints were leading, said, like the peacemaker he was, 'I will speak to Mali; I know I can talk to him. Even to that girl Grace; she is so trusting!'

'By all means, speak to him on any matter you like,' Jagan said and added with firmness, 'but not on my behalf.'

CHAPTER SEVEN

TWO DAYS LATER, coming at the usual time, the cousin found the shop entrance crowded. A placard hung from the counter: 'Any packet 25 paise'. There was such a clamour for the packets that the boy at the counter looked harried and exhausted. Old men, young men, children, beggars and labourers, everyone fell over each other with outstretched arms, and the trays were emptied as fast as they were filled from the kitchen. By five o'clock the entire stock of sweets for the day was exhausted. Sivaraman and the other cooks came out of the kitchen, stood before Jagan and asked, 'What do we do now?'

'Go home,' said Jagan. 'If the sweets have been sold, our work for the day is over.'

'I do not understand,' said Sivaraman, turning the golden bead at his throat. 'What has happened? What is all this for?'

'Let more people eat sweets, that is all. Aren't they happy?'

'Do you plan to close down?' asked Sivaraman, and his assistant said, 'At this rate, we will be swamped.'

'It will make no difference to you,' said Jagan. 'We shall reduce nothing, either in quantity or quality.'

'How? How can we?' asked Sivaraman.

Jagan could not easily explain what he was doing or why. The cousin, sitting on the stool, came to his rescue: 'We are only trying some new measures to meet the competition. I will explain it all to you tomorrow.' The cooks went away, and the shop emptied itself at six o'clock, the boy bringing in the bronze jug earlier than usual, saying, 'Still a crowd outside waiting, sir. They are angry that they are not getting anything today.'

'Tell them to come tomorrow.' They could hear the shouts of the crowd outside and the captain swearing at them.

'Our people must learn to be disciplined,' Jagan observed.

He felt light at heart after this arrangement, but it took time for his staff to get adjusted to the idea, as they were afraid that stagnant business might limit prospects and promotions. Jagan had not thought of that, but he pretended to have taken into consideration all aspects of the question and just brushed off comments. They returned to the subject again and again. They had more time to stand around the throne and discuss things now that the frying operations lasted only three hours from midday and the sales only an hour; but for the crowd at the counter vainly clamouring for more, the place became free from all activity. This was a cause of great concern for Sivaraman, who felt that the crowd might turn unruly. Jagan replied, 'Be patient and watch; our people have to learn discipline and will certainly learn soon. Don't worry.' To everyone else in that little hall it sounded irrelevant, but they were too polite to say so. 'Maybe we shall have to prepare more,' said Sivaraman, chewing a piece of tobacco in a most leisurely manner.

'No harm in trying it, but what for?' asked Jagan.

They merely mumbled, 'So that no one is turned back.'

'What for?' asked Jagan again.

Sivaraman and his four assistants were pure technicians in the matter of confectionery; they floundered over questions of economics, marketing and politics. Sivaraman had a sudden inspiration and answered, 'Because more people are asking for our sweets now that the price has been so much reduced.'

'Oh, that is a brilliant explanation,' Jagan felt, but he did not think it politic to say so, he merely remarked, 'Well, that is a point of view; we will consider it after we see how it all goes for at least fifteen days.' He knew that his staff viewed him as an astute businessman; although his decision was baffling, doubtless, they thought he must have some sound reason for taking this step; they credited him with some canny purpose, and he could not bring himself to disillusion them. He felt curiously flattered and gratified, and, although a lover of truth generally, in this instance he enjoyed shining in a false light.

Sivaraman finally said, 'Is it possible that you have found a way to draw all the business in the town to your door?'

He had just enough tact and vanity to permit himself a meaningful smile and they felt pleased and smiled meaningfully too. He then held before them greater treasures than mere profit.

He said, 'You have leisure now and do not know how to use it. Let me help you. Sit down and learn how best to utilize the precious hours that come to us, not by lounging in the marketplace or discussing money matters. Sit down, all of you. I will read to you from the *Bhagavad Gita* every day for an hour. You will benefit by it. Call in the captain also, if he likes to join us.' He commanded them to be seated again, looked on them with benign pity from his throne, took out his *Bhagavad Gita*, opened it on the first page and began: 'On the field of Kurukshetra two armies arrayed and ready for battle faced each other. Do you know why they were there?'

Sivaraman, now completely relaxed, sitting cross-legged and bolt upright on the floor, said, 'Of course, we all know why they were there. I am sure all these boys know too.' They murmured an assent; the captain, standing respectfully apart with arms folded and his short stick under his right arm, nodded appreciatively.

Not minding what the head cook said, Jagan began again from the first line in a singsong, and felt a thrill at the sound of Sanskrit. 'At this moment the great warrior Arjuna had a misgiving as to how he could fight his own uncles and cousins; his knees shook at the thought. Then God himself, who had chosen to be his charioteer, explained to him the need to fight for a cause even if you had to face your brothers, cousins, uncles or even sons. No good has been achieved without a fight at the proper time. Do you understand?' All their heads nodded an assent although their minds were wandering a little: they were anxious lest he should inflict on them a repetition of the same stanza. After further explanation Jagan said, 'There is no such thing as reading this book finally; it is something to be read all one's life. Mahatma Gandhi read it to us every day; was it because he did not know it or thought we did not?'

'True, true,' all of them chorused.

'Mahatmaji placed his fight against Britain in the same category.' The place was beginning to take on the look of a schoolroom, and that the pupils were not quite enjoying it became evident by the number of times Sivaraman got up to spit out tobacco and the others went out to blow noses or take snuff. Even the captain, the very picture of good manners, at one point pretended to notice some intruders at the door and slipped away. It was doubtful how long this could have gone on, for these men, after all, flourished in kitchen smoke and preferred frying to enlightenment, but to everyone's relief three visitors burst in. The captain strutted up, saluted and ushered the visitors before the throne, as was his duty, and withdrew. The cooks lounging on the floor presented an odd spectacle at this hour when business should be at its peak and the kitchen belching fire. Jagan became incoherent and effusive when he recognized his visitors; one was the *sait* from Ananda Bhavan, the man who had built an enormous business on eating within a span of fifteen years although he hailed from a province a thousand miles away; the second ran a canteen at the law-courts, and the third man, who had a white beard, was a stranger. 'Perhaps someone's brother,' Jagan reflected. 'Ah, what an hour,' he kept repeating, and almost embraced them. His audience for the *Bhagavad Gita* melted away unobtrusively. There were not enough seats for all the visitors, but luckily the cousin's stool was available today and Jagan fussily offered it to the bulky *sait*. The captain brought in an iron chair from the soda shop next door which Jagan allotted to the law-court canteen man, leaving 'someone's brother' to fend for himself, and resumed his seat on the throne; it was impossible for him to occupy any other position within this hall. 'Someone's brother' stood about uncertainly while they talked of politics, the weather and general market conditions for half an hour, before coming to the point. Then the *sait* asked, 'What is it that you have been trying to do during the last . . .'

'Four days,' said the 'brother'.

The *sait* added, 'He is our friend.'

Jagan threw a smile at him and, encouraged, the bearded man edged nearer and sat on the platform at Jagan's feet.

The *sait* said, 'You are making a drastic reduction in the price of your sweets?'

'Yes.'

'May we know why?'

'So that more people may enjoy the eating of sweets,' replied Jagan with a beatific smile.

The others looked shocked at this heresy. 'What prevents more people from eating at the right price?'

'The price of the stuff itself,' said Jagan, hitting upon a lucid explanation.

'It is bad business,' said the canteen owner.

In answer Jagan said, 'I am unhappy, my distinguished guests, that I have nothing to offer you, all our trays having become empty an hour ago.'

'Then that is good business,' said the *sait* with a twinkle in his eyes. Jagan accepted the compliment with a knowing nod, looking gratified at his own cuteness. 'But why should you upset all our business?' asked the *sait*.

'I will ask the customers who clamour here to go to your shop, provided you promise them pure quality.'

'Do you mean to say that we don't use pure stuff?'

'I don't know. I use the purest butter for frying and the best flour and spices.'

'And yet you say you are able to sell a packet for twenty-five paise?' They all laughed at the joke. The *sait* went on, 'In 1956 I used to do that myself, but now where can we get pure stuff at the right price?'

'I can help you to get the supplies if you like. As Lord Krishna says in the *Gita*, it is all in one's hand. Make up your mind and you will find the object of your search.'

The bearded man sitting on the platform butted in to remark, 'Ah, the *Gita* is a treasure, truly a treasurehouse of wisdom.'

'I never spend a moment without reading it.'

'One can go on reading it all one's life,' agreed the *sait* himself, and the canteen man said, 'We all know it. The *Gita* also says every man must perform his duty in the right spirit and the right measure. Do you think you are doing that?' he assailed Jagan directly.

Jagan's composure was lost. He merely said, 'Oh!' and covered his confusion with a simper.

Now the *sait* leaned forward to say with all the grimness he could muster, 'If one person does it, all the others will do it also, are you aware of that?'

Jagan's mind did not take in the implications of his statement but he felt he ought to match its sharpness and answered, 'What if they do?'

'Is that the line you wish to take?' asked the canteen man.

Jagan, wondering what there was so sinister in taking the line, mumbled some irrelevancy and suddenly shouted, 'Captain! Get four drinks for these gentlemen from the soda-shop . . .'

There were murmurs of refusal from the assembly, but they softened towards Jagan and the *sait* said, 'Oh no, don't take all the trouble, sir. We have come to talk serious business. Let us get through it first. Business first is my motto always.'

'Otherwise how can we get on? That must be the beacon-light

of conduct for all businessmen, the only philosophy,' said the canteen man, and the bearded man quoted a passage from the *Upanishads* which proved nothing.

'What are we all talking about?' asked the *sait* suddenly. Jagan and the rest said nothing. The *sait*, who was evidently the leader of the delegation, continued, 'My time is precious; at this hour I am hardly able to leave my counter, and yet I have come; does it not show the seriousness of the business that has brought us here?'

The canteen man said, 'It is nearly a year since I visited this part of the city. Where can one find the time?'

'Each man is busy in his own way,' said the bearded man.

'I am very glad to see you all here. We must all meet once in a way like this and discuss our problems,' said Jagan, feeling that he had been left out too long.

'I am very happy that you should think so,' said the *sait*, looking genuinely relieved. 'We must all learn to live together and voice our feelings nowadays; otherwise we will be left behind in the race.'

'Union is strength,' said the bearded man; he attempted to illustrate his thesis with a story from the *Panchatantra*. 'There was, once upon a time . . .' he began.

This was too much for the delegation and the *sait* cut him short with, 'Of course, Panditji, we all know the story and its moral. As I was saying,' he went on, feeling that he had the first right to speak in this assembly, 'as I was saying, we have many problems. Today we are all bewildered and we ask ourselves why we should continue in business.'

'Exactly what I have felt, but I keep it up more for the sake of my staff,' said Jagan, understanding the words in the simplest terms possible.

The *sait* felt inspired to continue, having fallen into the groove of talking shop, 'There is really no answer to our problems; people mind their own business and think that we can somehow exist and continue to exist. How they expect us to continue is more than I can understand.'

'If we close our business even for a single day, then they will know,' said the canteen man.

'It would actually be more economical to close down our business, but we cannot do it; people would suffer; innocent office-workers, labourers and students who depend upon us for their nourishment would be the real ones to suffer,' said the *sait*, feeling

as if he were a benevolent angel conferring boons on humanity.
'Our problems are numerous.'

He was excessively fond of the word 'problem'. He had
mentioned the word so often that Jagan felt constrained to ask,
'What problems?'

Both the *sait* and the canteen man turned an astonished glance
at him as if they could hardly conceive of anyone in his senses
asking such a question. Both of them started to talk at once, and the
voices clashed and became indistinguishable as they said, 'The
sales tax inspectors who will not accept the accounts we render, the
income tax people who assess arbitrarily, the health inspectors, the
food control which has practically driven everything underground—
how are we to get the provisions for our recipes? And above all, the
frying medium: we can't always use pure ghee, and the government
forces us to announce what we use; how can we do that when our
customers like to be told, whatever they may actually consume, that
they are being served pure butter-melted ghee?'

'The ideas about pure butter-melted ghee are antiquated,' said
the canteen man. 'In fact, scientists have proved that pure butter
and ghee bring on heart disease; the artificial substitutes have more
vitamins.'

'They are not much cheaper, either.'

'Their prices are going up nearly to the level of pure ghee.'

'So why not pure ghee?' asked Jagan, which really irritated his
visitors. As they were mustering their wits for a repartee, the
captain brought in four bottles of soda, opened the first one with an
enormous pop and held the bottle dripping, overflowing, whizzing
and hissing to the *sait* as the courtesy due to the leader of the
delegation.

The *sait* said with some annoyance, 'I told you, I want nothing.'

Jagan said, 'It is only soda, a lot of gas in it; take it.'

Meanwhile, like a machine, the captain was popping open the
other bottles and the bearded man was snatching each from his
hand and passing it on; the floor became wet with the effervescence.
When a bottle was offered to Jagan, he took it, but turned it
ceremoniously over to the captain.

The *sait* said, 'You wanted us to drink the soda.'

'Because I know it is good,' said Jagan.

'But why don't you drink it yourself?'

'I don't drink more than four ounces of water a day,' said Jagan, 'and that must be boiled at night and cooled in a mud jug open to the sky. I drink no other water. Even when I was in prison in those days . . .' he began, but the rest cut short his reminiscence with the question, 'Have we spent this afternoon usefully?' Jagan was not sure whose responsibility it was to find an answer, but remembering that he was the host, said, 'Of course, it has been an honour to receive you.'

'We are happy that we have understood each other now,' said the *sait*. 'I hope we can count on your cooperation.'

Without thinking what they meant Jagan said effusively, 'Certainly, surely, I believe in cooperation fully.'

The canteen man remarked, 'If it is just some temporary policy of yours, it is not for us to question you.'

'But if it's anything else,' interrupted the *sait*, 'we must all strive to maintain the tone of business; that is our common aim.'

Jagan made some indistinct sounds in his throat and they all left. He heard them drive off, and prepared to wind up for the day. The captain came in to take the iron chair back to the soda shop, and placed on Jagan's table a bill for the drinks. Jagan had emptied the cash collection into his drawer hours ago, and now proceeded to open it and was sorting out the various denominations, when the bearded man who had gone out with the *sait* came back. Jagan said, 'Forgotten anything?'

'No,' said the man, approaching and taking his seat on the stool, 'I sent them away in their car. I actually live in the next street; they gave me a lift, and I thought I might come in with them and meet you. They were so busy talking to you, I did not like to disturb your meeting.'

'I don't think I have seen you before,' said Jagan.

'I live in Kabir Street but seldom pass this way,' he said, settling down on the stool for a conversational evening.

Jagan said, 'I thought you were going with them.'

'Why should I when my house is so near?'

'I didn't know that,' said Jagan. 'I don't know your name yet.'

'People who knew me used to call me Chinna Dorai as distinct from my master, who was known as Peria Dorai. The small master and the big master—ah, in no way to be compared.'

'Who was your master?'

'How many temples have you visited in your life?' the bearded man asked.

Today everyone seemed to be firing questions at him, but Jagan answered, 'A hundred temples of all sorts, maybe more.'

'The God or gods in every one of the temples were carved by my master.'

'Oh, how wonderful to know that!' said Jagan.

'The figures of Shiva, the Destroyer, Vishnu, the Protector, Devi, who vanquished the demon Mahisha with the dreadful weapons she bore in her eighteen arms, the Dwarapalakas, gatekeepers at the shrine, and the designs on the doorways and the friezes on the walls, were alike all done by my master, all over the South.' His eyes blazed and his beard fluttered while he spoke.

Jagan was impressed by his elocution although he did not quite understand what he was driving at; it was at least a relief from the talk of butter and frying. His description of the gods made Jagan regret that he had not gone near the temple for months, being wrapped up in this monotonous job of frying and cash-counting. He declared fervently, 'Of course, I have visited every temple in this part of the universe, times out of count, and I know all the one hundred and eight gods and saints enshrined along both the banks of the Kaveri. I know the songs that Sambhandar composed in honour of those gods.' And he assumed a falsetto voice and sang a couple of pieces for sample.

The bearded man shut his eyes, listened and showered praise on Jagan's musical ability and memory; which ballast of flattery he needed today because he was beginning to have misgivings about his practical wisdom. Jagan in turn expressed approval of the other's taste in music. In all this demonstration of mutual esteem the purpose of the conversation was, as usual, lost. The bearded man sang a couple of songs himself, not in a falsetto, but a full-throated voice without inhibition, and the captain at the door peeked in to make sure that things were normal within, at this business hour, with its noise of traffic and crowds on Market Road. After the songs the bearded man returned to his main theme. 'All those gods you have seen in the temples were done by my master or his disciples.'

'What was his name, did you say?'

'Don't mind what I said. We called him "Master" and that's sufficient. There has been no other who could assume that title.'

'Was he your master?'

'Yes. In his last years he didn't like to admit anyone near him except me.'

'Where did he live?'

'Not far from here. Any day you can spare a little time, I'll take you there. It's just on the other bank of the river. You can see the trees of his garden. Do you ever go across the river?'

Jagan sighed at this reminder. For years his fixed orbit had been between the statue and the shop, his mental operations confined to Mali, the cousin and frying. He recollected with a sigh the blaze of colours at sunset, the chatter of birds in Nallappa's Grove; how he had often wandered along the river, lounged on the sands or sat on the river step with his class fellows; how Mahatma Gandhi used to address huge assemblies on the sands of the river and how he himself, a minute speck in such a crowd, had felt his whole life change when he heard that voice. Where now were those friends, whose faces and names he could not recollect—dead, flattened out by life or existing in the same place under new masks like that toothless lawyer, or that man who was so bent that he hardly looked at anyone, or a dozen other familiar faces, at one time bench companions at school and playmates around the statue every afternoon—passing each other daily but hardly uttering four syllables in twenty years? 'You have become contemplative,' said the bearded man accusingly.

'Gandhi was my master,' Jagan said. The bearded man showed no interest in the statement, perhaps because he was jealous of the term 'master' being applied to any other claimant but his own. Eager to go back to the business on hand, he asked, 'When will you find the time to go out with me?'

'Tomorrow,' said Jagan promptly, and then asked, 'Where? Come here at one o'clock in the afternoon. Are you going to show me your master's sculptures?'

'No, they are all in various temples, I told you. He was regularly besieged by temple builders. He was not the sort to keep his handiwork in his own house.'

There was such intensity in his speech that Jagan apologized. 'Oh, I didn't mean that. Where do you want to take me?'

'To show you the place where he lived and worked, that's all.'

'Do you work there now?'

'No, I told you, I live behind this road.'

'Do you make your images there?' At this, the man burst into a big laugh and said, 'Did I not tell you what I do now? I make hair-dyes. I can make the whitest hair look black. That *sait* is my best customer in the town. Once in four weeks I go and personally colour his hair, which otherwise would look milk-white. On those days he fetches me in his car; that's how I came to be with him today. A lucky day, because I have come to know your good self.'

'I'm also happy. I have never seen an image-maker before.'

'You are not seeing one now, either. I'm only a blackener of white hair. I have come, too, to ask, if you need my services. My responsibility is to make people look young. The *sait* appreciates my services. Ask him if you have doubts.'

Jagan hesitated for a moment, and said apologetically, 'I do not know if I could do it,' trying to imagine the remarks of Mali and Grace. Probably Mali would not even notice; he hardly ever looked at him. Why not try at least to amuse him? He suddenly remembered that he himself was a specialist in this and allied subjects. 'Diet has a lot to do with the colour of one's hair. My book on this subject will be out one day and then you will see for yourself; if your diet is controlled according to Nature's specifications, you will never see a grey hair anywhere.'

'That may be the reason why the bear never has a grey hair,' said the bearded man and laughed at the joke.

For Jagan, though, this was a serious line of inquiry. He said solemnly, 'I must consider that point when my book is finally prepared.'

THE POND WAS covered with blue lotus, the steps were mantled with moss and crumbling. On the bank stood a small shrine supported on stone pillars, with a low roof of granite slabs blackened by weather, time and the oven smoke of wayfarers. Over this little building loomed banyan, peepul and mango trees and beyond them stretched away a grove of casuarina, the wind blowing through their leaves creating a continuous murmur as of sea waves. The surroundings were covered with vegetation of every type: brambles, thorn-bushes, lantana and oleander intertwined and choked each other. The sun glittered on the pond's surface. The bearded man who had led Jagan to this spot remained brooding, watching some birds dive into the water.

'So quiet everywhere!' Jagan remarked, deciding to puncture the oppressive silence.

The other shook his head. 'Not as it used to be. Too many buses on the highway, ever since that project in the hills . . .' His voice trailed away. 'In those days,' he said, 'when I lived here with my master, you could not meet a soul unless you walked all the way to Nallappa's Grove and crossed into the town. In those days people did not go up the mountain as much as they do now; robbers hid themselves in the jungles, and tigers and elephants roamed the foothills.' He seemed depressed at the thought of their giving place to highway buses.

'Why did you choose to live here?' Jagan asked.

'Where else could one live? We needed all those stones.' He pointed through the thickets. 'You see the nose of Mempi? For softer panel-work that stone is excellent; for images of the inner sanctum one has to cut the stone at the belly of the hill further up, though it is difficult to hew and there are more breakages than in other portions.' His head seemed to throb with stony problems.

Jagan watched him in silent wonder and asked, 'What would one do for food, and with one's wife and children, in a place like this?'

The bearded man made a flourish as if to ward off such a petty question. 'My master never bothered about such things. He never married. I came to him when I was five years old. I don't know who my parents were. People used to say I was picked up by my master on the river step.'

Jagan wanted to ask, but suppressed the question, whether he might not have been born to a passing concubine of his so-called master who never married. While the bearded man remained thinking of his past, Jagan reflected, 'He has the whitest beard and sells the blackest hair dye. Why does he not apply it to his own beard?' He asked aloud, 'How is your business?'—a question that he must have asked every few minutes, whenever there was a pause.

The bearded man said, 'Nothing to worry about, and the sales tax people have still not come my way yet.'

'That is a real blessing,' said Jagan, remembering the visitations he had to endure, the inspectors and their minions rummaging in his desk for day books, ledgers and vouchers. In the end they accepted his accounts, unaware of the cash that grew from out-of-hour sales at the counter and filled the smaller jug, but he could no more help it than he could the weeds flourishing in his backyard. He had a habitual, instinctive and inexplicable uneasiness concerning any tax. If Gandhi had said somewhere, 'Pay your sales tax uncomplainingly,' he would have followed his advice, but Gandhi had made no reference to the sales tax anywhere to Jagan's knowledge.

The bearded man said, 'But they are bound to wake up sooner or later, when they notice fewer grey hairs around,' and chuckled.

Jagan seized this opportunity to say, 'Anyway, you are an exception to your own rule.'

'I like my white beard and so keep it. There is no compulsion for anyone to blacken his hair. I would not have dreamt of blackening people's heads if I had had a chance to work on stone. But you know how these things happen. My master supported me for years.' ('How could he not, as you were his only son by a passing concubine?' Jagan retorted inwardly.) The bearded man pointed to a corner in the pillared hall. 'He worked on those details of ornament and I had to move the block here. He lived his whole life here. All that he possessed could be contained within the palm of one's hand. I cooked a little rice for him in that corner, where you see the walls blackened. All day he sat here working on the image or we went to the quarry to hew slabs. He never saw anyone except when some temple men came to order an image. People were afraid to come here because of the snakes, but my master loved them and never approved of clearing the wild growth around. This tree was full of monkeys; you can see them now. "I'll share the fruits of those trees with them," he used to say. He enjoyed the company of snakes and monkeys and everything; once there was even a cheetah in the undergrowth. "We must not monopolize this earth. They won't harm us," he used to say, and, true to his word, nothing ever did. When he died one night I sat at vigil by a small oil lamp, and cremated his body beyond that pond, heaping on the dead wood and withered leaves. Next day I walked off to the city and lived on charity here and there, until I got the idea for my business. That is all. I have nothing in my life to complain of now, but I was well off in those days . . .' Still brooding, he walked around the small hall, peered into an alcove, 'There used to be a God in the sanctum which had been stolen years before we came here. One night my master woke me up and said, "Let me make a new God for this temple. Then it will flourish again." He had dreamt of a five-faced Gayatri, to be seen nowhere else, the deity of Radiance. He had even hewn the slab for it and knocked the first dents. It used to be in that yard somewhere. Let me look for it . . .' He became suddenly active, peeped into every corner of the hall, went round to the backyard, where oleanders and hibiscus flourished and bloomed wildly. He discovered a bamboo staff amidst a clump— 'Ah, this is still here!'—seized it and strode about, looking like a statue of many thousand years' antiquity.

Watching him in this setting, it was difficult for Jagan, as he mutely followed him, to believe that he was in the twentieth century. Sweetmeat vending, money and his son's problems seemed remote and unrelated to him. The edge of reality itself was beginning to blur; this man from the previous millennium seemed to be the only object worth notice; he looked like one possessed. He pointed to a grassy spot under a palmyra tree and said, 'This is where my master's body was burnt, that day. I can remember that terrible night.' He stood under the palmyra with his eyes shut for a moment, muttering some holy verse. 'We should not let the body deceive us as to the true nature of our being. One is not really bone and meat. My master proved it,' he declared, and as if seized with a sudden frenzy beat down every bush with his bamboo stick, startling a variety of creatures—lizards, chameleons, birds and frogs, which had lived undisturbed for years in the green shelter. He seemed to enjoy their discomfiture and inhaled noisily, with relish, the smell of crushed greenery. He said, 'I'm sure the cobras that live here must have quietly slipped away when we came; they are uncanny in their habits. Very alert, very alert and watchful . . .' Chipped-off blocks of stone and odds and ends of sculptural pieces came to view beneath the weeds. He pointed his staff at them, explaining, 'This was the pedestal of Vishnu, meant for some temple; those are the arms of Saraswathi, the goddess of learning— they could not be used because of a slight crack in the stone. My master got so upset when he noticed the defect that he flung it out through the door, and remained speechless for three days. At such moments, I used to stay away from him, shielding myself behind the trunk of that tamarind tree. When the mood passed he would call me. But where is that other block? Where is it? The two-foot-square one? It could not have grown limbs and walked off— although, let me tell you, if an image is perfect, it cannot be held down on its pedestal. I always remember the story of the dancing figure of Nataraj, which was so perfect that it began a cosmic dance and the town itself shook as if an earthquake had rocked it, until a small finger on the figure was chipped off. We always do it; no one ever notices it, but we always create a small flaw in every image; it's for safety.'

He went on talking and Jagan listened agape as if a new world had flashed into view. He suddenly realized how narrow his whole existence had been—between the Lawley Statue and the frying shop; Mali's antics seemed to matter naught. 'Am I on the verge of a new *janma*?' he wondered. Nothing seemed really to matter. 'Such things are common in ordinary existence and always passing,' he said aloud.

The bearded man, suppressing his surprise at this sudden remark, said, 'True, true, you must not lose sight of your real being, which is not mere bone or meat.' He reached up to a branch of a guava tree, plucked a fruit and bit into it with the glee of a ten-year-old urchin. 'This tree always gave the best fruit. Monkeys thrive on it, and during certain seasons the treetop would be as full of monkeys as leaves, you know.' He pulled down the branch again, plucked off another fruit and held it out to Jagan. Jagan took it out of courtesy, but did not eat it. 'I keep off sweets and salt.'

'Why?' asked the other.

'Well . . .' How to express his whole philosophy of life in a limited jargon? He concluded, 'You will find it all explained in my book.' At the mention of 'book' the other began to lose interest. He was used to inscriptions on stone and on palmyra leaf, and he was not enticed by the mention of the printed book. Jagan, unaffected by his attitude, added, 'The printer, Nataraj, do you know him at all?' The bearded man had lost interest in the subject totally by this time. Ignoring Jagan and talking on, he failed to observe that Jagan had overcome the temptation to take a bite and had let the fruit slip to the ground, unable to decide whether it would be good or bad from the point of view of dietetics. What a shame if it was good to eat and he had surrendered it, for it was attractive, with green turning yellow on top and yellow turning red in the middle, and soft to the touch. Before he had developed his theories of sane living, he used to eat a dozen of them each day and it might well be said that between seven and twelve years of age the aroma of guava had permanently clung to him! A huge tree had grown in their backyard, right over the tin shed, and one day his father took an axe and cut it down, remarking, 'These little devils will eat nothing else as long as this cursed tree stands. See how one by one they are going down with colic . . .' As he followed the other about, vaguely aware of his speech, his mind was obsessed with the fruit he had abandoned, until the bearded man asked, 'Are you listening to me?'

'Yes, yes, of course,' Jagan said.

'We have gone round and round, but not found the slab. It must be somewhere,' said the bearded man. He hugged the stick, resting his chin on it, and was lost in thought.

Jagan could not help asking, 'Why are you bothered about it?'

'Very important, very important, I tell you. When I have found it, you will know.' He unwrapped himself from the stick abruptly and said, 'Now I remember; come with me.' He moved briskly towards the pond. 'Come down with me. Mind the steps—they are slippery.' He went down the steps and up to his knees in water. Jagan lagged behind, unable to comprehend the other's action.

'Perhaps he is going to knock me into the pond and go back to the town and report, "The maker of sweets has vanished." ' The other's face was flushed with excitement as he looked up and cried, 'Won't you come down? What if your *dhoti* gets wet? You can dry it later.' His tone was peremptory.

Jagan descended the moss-covered steps, which gave him a creepy feeling underfoot. His *dhoti* did get wet and he shivered slightly as he watched with fascination bees swarming on the blue lotus. He felt a sense of elevation—it would be such a wonderful moment to die, leaving the perennial problems of life to solve themselves. While he was busy with his thoughts the other, who had stopped on all fours, looked up and said, 'Come here,' with his eyes blazing and his beard fluttering in the wind. 'There is no retreat for me,' thought Jagan. 'He is preparing to hold my head down in the water. Should I turn back and rush away? No, not a chance of retreat,' and he took a further step down. He was now wet up to his waist. 'Cold water may be good for rheumatism, but I am not a rheumatic,' he told himself. 'If I do not perish in this water, I shall perish of pneumonia. In my next life I'd like to be born . . .' His mind ran through various choices. Pet dog? Predatory cat? Street-corner donkey? Maharajah on an elephant? Anything but a money-making sweet-maker with a spoilt son.

The bearded man, still on all fours, now commanded, 'Plunge your hand in here and feel . . .'

Jagan obeyed, precariously poising himself on the slippery surface.

'What do you feel there?' the other asked imperiously.

Jagan noted that ever since they had stepped into this garden, the man had become more and more authoritarian. He was no longer the tame hair-blackener of Kabir Street, but a sort of leader of the forces, a petty chieftain used to having his orders carried out without question. Nothing like implicit obedience. Jagan plunged his arms into the water, and shuddered when something clamped its jaws on his hand. 'Oh!' he screamed. It was only the other's hand-grip. Now a smile appeared on the bearded face as he propelled Jagan's hand through the water over a stone surface. 'This is the stone I meant. Let us take it out. Hold it at your end properly. Can't you lift it? I am not surprised. If you ate normally like other human beings, or at least consumed some of the sweets that you sell, you would be in better shape. I remember my master put this stone into the water because it needed the treatment to bring out its surface grains. Do you feel the notches, the first ones he made? He had started to work on it but suddenly decided that it needed water-seasoning; he always said that the longer a stone stayed in water . . .' He looked about in despair. 'If you could only make up your mind to lift it; it is only will power you lack. This is not after all a big statue but a small one, hardly a couple of feet; when it is fully worked, it will hardly be eighteen inches. Can't you lift a stone that is going to be just eighteen inches high? I am surprised. I only want you to give me a hand, not lift it yourself. Help me.'

He was so cajoling and bullying by turns that finally Jagan began to feel that he ought to exert himself. He gritted himself for the task by tying his upper cloth around his head and tucking up his *dhoti* in a businesslike manner. He held his breath, gripped his end of the block, pausing for a moment to consider whether at his age he was well advised to carry a slab of stone up wet steps. But this was no time to consult one's own inclinations or welfare. When they reached the top of the steps, he just let go the stone, threw his entire length flat on the grass, and shut his eyes.

When Jagan revived, he found the other rolling the stone over and explaining, 'This would be the top; come closer and you will see the lines marked by my master with the bodkin, the outline of the goddess.' He scraped the moss off the stone, which was drying in patches, and stood lost in contemplation. To Jagan's eyes it was no different from any other block of stone; even the scratches originally made by the master were hardly convincing; but the bearded man seemed to feel intoxicated at the sight of it. 'This is where the goddess's hands come; she is ten-armed, and except for the one which indicates protection and the one offering a blessing, all the other arms hold a variety of divine articles.' For some time he was lost in visions of the goddess and then began to narrate a story.

'I know the story of the goddess,' said Jagan.

'Who doesn't?' replied the hair-blackener. 'But still it's always good to hear it over and over again; you will always have the protection of Devi, and everything you attempt will turn out successful.' And he broke into a loud Sanskrit song. The birds in the trees fluttered at the sudden outbreak of noise. Frogs at the edge of the pond sprang back into the water, and Jagan's gaze was held by the delicate tracks on the surface left by the newts and other aquatic creatures invisibly coursing.

'If I can devote my life to the completion of this task I will die in peace,' said the other.

'How old are you?' asked Jagan.

'Do you want to know? Then guess.'

Such speculation always embarrassed Jagan. He could never be sure whether people asking that question liked to look younger or older than their years. In either case, he felt he could not be drawn into a debate, and so said, 'I can't say . . .' observing the man's head, which was bald. ('No place for his dye there,' he thought.)

'I am sixty-nine,' said the other abruptly in a matter-of-fact manner. 'I'm prepared to die peacefully on my seventieth birthday, if I can finish that image and install it on its pedestal.'

'Will you be able to complete it in a year?' Jagan asked.

'I may or may not,' said the other. 'How can I say? It's in God's hands. With all that water-seasoning, the slab may suddenly split in the middle, and then what does one do?' Several possibilities occurred to Jagan. While he was fumbling for an answer, the other declared, 'Bury the broken image and start anew with a fresh quarrying and fresh seasoning in water, that's all.'

'If that breaks?'

'That'd be an inauspicious thought and question,' said the other grimly and added, 'The second stone does not generally crack.' They sat in silence, which the other broke, 'Ten hands! Oh, the very picture thrills me.' He burst into a song in Sanskrit, '*Mukta-vidruma-hema* . . .' When he had completed the stanza he asked, 'Do you understand the meaning of that?'

'Yes, in a way,' replied Jagan cautiously.

'It only means the goddess whose countenance has the radiance of *mukta*, that is pearl, and *hema*, that is gold, and then the blue of the sapphire or the sky, and then the redness of the coral . . .' He took a deep breath, paused and continued, 'Since she is the light that illumines the Sun himself, she combines in her all colours and every kind of radiance, symbolized by five heads of different colours. She possesses ten hands, each holding a conch, which is the origin of sound, a discus, which gives the universe its motion, a goad to suppress evil forces, a rope that causes bonds, lotus flowers for beauty and symmetry, and a *kapalam*, a begging bowl made of a bleached human skull. She combines in her divinity everything we perceive and feel from the bare, dry bone to all beauty in creation.'

Jagan was filled with awe and reverence at the picture. The bearded man sat brooding for a while, then said, 'My master always meditated on this form and wanted to create the image for others to contemplate. That was his aim, and if I can carry it out, I'll abandon all other work in life.' He came down to business. 'It's only a man like you that can help in this task.'

Jagan gave a start on hearing this. He had not thought that the task would concern him. 'How? How?' he asked anxiously, and before the other could collect his thoughts, added, 'Don't think too much of me. No, no. After all I'm a humble merchant.'

The other said, 'Why don't you buy this garden and install the Goddess?'

'I—I—do not know,' replied Jagan, thickening his armour of self-defence, and tried to laugh the question off, but the other became deadly earnest, half rose and, waving a finger close to Jagan's eyes, said, 'Very well, I understand. I only thought it would do you good to have a retreat like this.'

'Yes, yes, God knows I need a retreat. You know, my friend, at some stage in one's life one must uproot oneself from the accustomed surroundings and disappear so that others may continue in peace.'

'It would be the most accredited procedure according to our scriptures—husband and wife must vanish into the forest at some stage in their lives, leaving the affairs of the world to younger people.'

Jagan fell so heartily in agreement that he wanted to explain why he needed an escape—his wife's death, his son's growth and strange development, how his ancient home behind the Lawley statue was beginning to resemble hell on earth—but he held his tongue. He felt shy and reserved about talking of his son—like one not wishing to exhibit his sores.

CHAPTER NINE

JAGAN NOW HAD a separate key with which he let himself into his house softly, crossed the passage and shut the door between his part of the house and his son's. Then he hooked his upper cloth on a nail in the wall, stripped off his *jibba*, passed on to the backyard, poured a lot of cold water over himself and came out of the bathroom. Feeling hungry today he set a bowl of water on the kitchen oven, cut up a few vegetables, and threw them in, along with a small measure of coarsely ground wheat. The day had been hot and he preferred to remain without a vest. While his dinner was cooking, he stood before the gods for a second with eyes shut, then lit an oil wick and took out his small *charka* (wooden spinning-wheel) from behind a large bureau, inserted a hank of cotton, turned the wheel and drew a fine thread out, watching its growth with a sensuous pleasure: the slight whirring noise of the wheel and the thread growing out of it between one's thumb and forefinger was very comforting, stifling the nerves and thoughts. Gandhi had prescribed spinning not only for the economic ills of the country, but also for any deep agitation of the mind. Jagan's mind was in turmoil; at the same time he had a feeling that his identity was undergoing a change. If that was so, why should he bother or resist the idea? Committed to various things until yesterday, to the shop and the family, he was a different man at this moment. An internal transformation had taken place; although he still cared for the shop and house, this latest contact had affected him profoundly. The gods must have taken pity on his isolated, floundering condition and sent this white-bearded saviour. As he turned the spinning-wheel, sitting there in the courtyard, with the sky-reaching coconut trees of the neighbourhood waving amidst the stars, his mind analysed everything with the utmost clarity. He wondered if the

bearded man might not be a visitation from another planet—
otherwise what had brought him into his shop exactly when he
needed him? Who really needed help and from whom? The man
had said he needed help installing the image of the goddess, while
he himself thought that he was being helped. He could not solve
the puzzle easily, and so left it alone. Anyway it was a reposeful
memory: the man had really communicated a thrilling vision when
he described the goddess with five heads. Should he help him or
not to complete his task? He knew nothing about him. How could
he trust him? On what basis? After he finished the image, what
then? Live in his company in that wilderness and encourage him to
carve more images? What would happen to the hair dye? Perhaps
he'd be expected to take charge of the business and run it in
addition to his sweets. Run after white hair on a large scale, earn
more money and ruin Mali further? He suspended his reflections
and his spinning for a moment in order to attend to the vegetables
on the stove, then he came back to his wheel, thinking of the fixed
law of Nature by which wheat was cooked in exactly thirty minutes;
if it was cooked for forty minutes, it became gruel and was no good
nutritionally; in food, food-making and food-eating, what was
important was precision. It was a science—that's what he was trying
to establish in his book, which would have been in the hands of the
public but for Nataraj. Why was Nataraj so indifferent to this task,
while he had printed the prospectus for Mali with alacrity? Perhaps
he didn't like his ideas; but printers did not have to like an idea in
order to print it. He should rather be like Sivaraman, who had to fry
something even if he didn't care for it himself. The cotton got
thinner and longer as if it were the soft dough from which Sivaraman
sometimes drew fine vermicelli strands; the wheel groaned and
purred and cleared its throat. Through the open roof he could see
the crescent moon passing behind the coconut trees, a couple of
wispy white clouds racing across its face. 'Perhaps the monsoon will
be breaking earlier this year?' he reflected. 'One enters a new life
at the appointed time and it's foolish to resist.' He was no longer
the father of Mali, the maker of sweets and gatherer of money each
day; he was gradually becoming something else, perhaps a supporter
of the bearded sculptor—or was he really his ward?

There was a knock on the door, which was lost in the purring
of the spinning-wheel. The middle door opened and Mali came in,
looking like an arrival from another planet in that dim light (Jagan

had fitted ten-watt bulbs in the light sockets in order to benefit the human retina). Excited at the sight of his son, Jagan snatched a towel and hid his chest under it; if he had known that he was coming, he'd have had his *jibba* on. He left his spinning and leaped up to fetch a stool to seat Mali. Mali took it from his hand, muttering, 'What a fuss you make!', planted it in the open court and sat on it, while Jagan stood about uncertainly. 'Sit down, Father,' Mali commanded, 'but don't turn that wheel; it's noisy and I want to talk to you.'

At this Jagan felt a sinking in his stomach and smacked his drying lips. He moved away from his spinning-wheel, folded his arms across his chest, and asked, 'Now, tell me, what do you want?'

'Everyone talks about you in the town,' said Mali in a tone of accusation.

Jagan stiffened slightly but said nothing. The sinking in the pit of his stomach was gradually leaving him as he remembered that one ought not to resist when circumstances pushed one across the threshold of a new personality. 'What do they talk about?' he asked. He was beginning to shed the awe in which he had held his son. 'Who are "they"?'

'The Ananda Bhavan *sait* and a number of others were discussing you yesterday.'

Jagan did not wish to pursue the subject and so mumbled, 'Let them.' He felt unhappy having to speak in a new tone of voice to Mali, from whom he used to pine for a word; 'I am a new personality and have to speak a new tongue.' He could not judge the expression on his son's face because the crescent moon was now completely gone and his bulb enveloped everything in a pale yellow light, making all faces and all moods look alike.

Mali took a paper from his pocket, tried to read it and said petulantly, 'Why can't you have brighter light?'

Jagan replied, 'Light rays should soothe the optic nerves and not stimulate them.'

The boy smiled cynically and said, 'This cable came in the afternoon from my associates.'

When he heard the word 'associates', Jagan did not need to hear anything more. He was not scared, as he would have been forty-eight hours ago. 'In a few hours, I have undergone a lot of changes, but the boy doesn't know it,' he reflected. 'Let me be kind to him. No harm in showing him kindness. After all . . .' He felt a stab of habitual tenderness, and regret at sounding so officious to Mali. 'What does the cable say?'

Mali spread it out again to catch the light, failed and repeated from memory, 'Please cable . . . status of our project.'

Jagan looked bewildered. This was not the English he knew. Except for the word 'cable', the rest did not mean anything. He said, 'Why should they ask you to cable? An ordinary letter will do.'

The boy said, 'We have to move pretty fast in business matters. Why can't you leave that to me? I know what to do. What shall I say in reply?'

'What is "status"? Whose status are they talking about?'

Mali clenched his fists and said, 'Are we going through with our manufacturing business or are we not?'

'Do you propose to talk about it now?' asked Jagan.

'I must know about it.'

Jagan felt a sudden pity for the boy sitting there forlorn and puzzled, and he cursed the barrier which seemed to raise itself whenever they came together. He pleaded, 'Son, I'll leave you in charge of the shop, it's yours. Take it.'

The boy made a wry face at the mention of the shop; fortunately the dim light did not reveal it fully. 'I tell you once and for all, I don't want to be . . .' He merely concluded, 'I have learnt valuable things in the United States at a cost of several thousand dollars. Why can't our country make use of my knowledge? I . . . I can't . . .' Although he avoided the phrase 'vendor of sweets', his repugnance for the occupation came out unmistakably. They remained silent, and Mali added the final touch: 'In any case your business is worth nothing now.'

'Who told you that?'

'Everyone in the trade is talking about you. What are you trying to do anyway?'

Jagan remained silent. Whereupon Mali again described his fiction-writing machine in detail, and repeated the contents of his prospectus. Jagan listened while the stars ran their course. When Mali paused, having reached the end of his prospectus, Jagan just asked, 'Where is Grace?'

'Why?' asked the son.

Jagan had no answer; he was not bound to answer every question. Mali insisted, 'I have to know whether you are coming into our business or not.'

'What'll you do if I say no?'

'Grace will have to go back; we will have to buy her an air-ticket, that's all.'

'What has it to do with her?' asked Jagan; the connections were baffling, like the wiring at the back of the radio panel.

'Why would she stay here?' asked the boy plainly. 'She has nothing to do here.'

'I do not understand what you are talking about. I have never been able to understand you at all. Call her, let me talk to her.' He had got used to the presence of Grace in the house and he felt desolate at the thought of losing her.

'She has gone out,' said Mali briefly.

'Where, at this time of the night?'

'She can go where she pleases. Why should anyone question her?'

'No, it's not that,' said Jagan. Fate seemed to decree that there should be no communication between them. Some invisible force twisted their tongues when they wanted to speak and made them say the wrong things. Jagan stood up desperately, bent close to his son's face and cried, 'Where is she going? Why is she going? Is she unhappy here?'

Mali rose to his feet and said, 'Who are you to stop her from going where she pleases? She is a free person, not like the daughters-in-law in our miserable country.'

Jagan said, 'I just want to know why she is thinking of going, that's all. She is, of course, free. Who says she is not? Has anything made her unhappy?'

'What is there to keep her happy?' cried Mali. 'This is a miserable place with no life in it. She was used to a good life. She came here to work, and she is going back because she has no work to do.'

Jagan swallowed back the words he wanted to blurt out: 'But she is sweeping and cleaning the house. This is a big house and she has enough work to keep her engaged for a whole day. What more does she want?'

Mali announced, 'She came here for the project, to work with me; didn't you see her name in the notice?'

Jagan had learnt the art of ignoring questions. Mali got up, saying, 'If she has nothing to do here, she goes back, that's all. Her air-ticket must be bought immediately.'

'But a wife must be with her husband, whatever happens.'

'That was in your day,' said Mali and left.

Jagan lost his sleep that night. The obscurity of the whole business worried him. Grace was out of sight. He liked her presence in the house; it filled a serious lacuna. Where had Mali hidden her at the moment? He wouldn't even admit that he knew where she had gone. Was this how a man kept track of his wife?

CHAPTER TEN

HE HAD TO wait for his chance to meet Grace. He knew by the sound of the duster in the front part of the house that she was back, but would she come as usual to his rooms and attend to things? No. It was over ten days since she had come near him. She seemed to be avoiding him. He felt depressed at the thought. What had he done that she should avoid him? Had she shown all that consideration only in order that he might invest in their story machine? Now that he had made his position clear, the barrier between him and the other two was growing more impregnable than ever, and there was absolutely no way of his approaching her and asking for an explanation. He wondered if he could go in and talk to her, but what would be the use? With Mali there, how could he ask her for verification? It would be at best a formal greeting. Though he was ready to leave for his shop this morning, he sat on his cot vaguely hoping that either Grace would come his way or that Mali would go out on one of his errands and he could have a word with her. But there was no sign of either happening. Mali went on typing in his room; after a while the sound of sweeping ceased, and he could hear some exchange of words between the two; then even that ceased and he was left alone; a tremendous stillness reigned over the house. There seemed to be no hope. He quietly slipped out of the house and reached his shop, where life went on as usual, only the clamour at the counter destroying the peace of the afternoon. Of late, Jagan had been unable to concentrate on the *Bhagavad Gita* until the crowd had dispersed. They behaved as if they were entitled to their sweets irrespective of whether there was a stock or not, which made Jagan wonder if he had been wise in reducing the price and whether he should not go back to the original rate.

The cousin had been absent for several days. He explained, 'I had to be away in the Tirupathi Hills with the Judge's family; they had taken two of their grandchildren to the temple for their first shave. It was a grand trip; they had engaged three cottages and the whole temple was open to them—an influential man. They would not listen when I told them that I could not afford to keep away so long; they nearly abducted me.'

'You are wanted everywhere,' said Jagan. 'I have wanted you very badly since yesterday.'

'I am at your service.'

'Has the reduction in prices affected the quality of our sweets?'

'Such a thing is unthinkable, I tell you.'

'The Ananda Bhavan *sait* was here . . .'

'I know, I know,' said the cousin. 'They are talking about you all the time!'

'What do they say?' Jagan got suddenly interested in the market reactions.

'It seems you have agreed to resume your prices soon.'

'I don't know . . . I don't think I have said any such thing,' said Jagan.

The cousin said, 'At least that is what they think. It will do them good to stand in the line and see how you do things. I wouldn't be at all surprised if their men are in the crowd and buy the sweets cheap here and sell them at their own price in their shops.' It hadn't occurred to Jagan that this was a possibility. He looked desperate and the cousin had to say, 'I was only joking, don't let it worry you.'

Jagan asked, 'Have you seen Mali recently?'

'He was at the Judge's house last evening. His son is his friend. He called me aside. He is ever so fond of me as his uncle. Nothing changes him . . .'

Jagan sighed. 'Why does he not talk to me properly? He can't speak even two sentences without upsetting me.'

The cousin, pleased at the superior position he was enjoying, said rather patronizingly, 'Don't let it upset you. You are a wise man and you must not think of these things too much.'

'What did he tell you?'

'He called me into the garden while his friend had gone in to wash and told me that Grace was going back to America soon. Did you hear that?'

'Yes, yes, but I did not understand why.'

The cousin said, 'She is going on business. That's what he told me. Something to do with his machine. You see how plucky these girls are! She goes thousands of miles to settle business matters, while we do not even understand what they are doing!'

Jagan did not correct him but kept his knowledge of the facts to himself. 'Well, of course, I had heard that, but I wanted to know if there was anything more.'

'His business seems to be promising,' said the cousin. 'The Ananda Bhavan *sait* and a few others have promised to buy shares in his company.'

Jagan asked with genuine wonder, 'How does he talk to them?'

'He is all over the town and very active. I meet him here, there and everywhere.'

'I want your help,' said Jagan. 'Don't laugh at me. I have to speak to Grace and find out a few things for myself.' He explained the situation in a roundabout way without letting the cousin know too much.

The cousin knew that a lot of things were being hidden from him, but he did not mind. He said, 'I see Grace sometimes visiting Dr Kuruvilla's house. She has a friend there whom she knew in America. Shall I speak to her and say that you want to see her?'

'Won't Mali be with her?'

'Sometimes she spends her time with the girls in that house, while Mali goes out with his friends.'

Jagan had to hold his soul in peace for the next two days, while the cousin thought out ways of decoying Mali, leaving the line clear for Jagan to speak to Grace. One afternoon he arrived on his usual tasting duty. Wiping his mouth with his towel, he said, 'If you are prepared to leave the shop, you can meet Grace at home. Mali is waiting for me at the Judge's house. I have promised to go with him to look for a plot of ground on Hill Road.'

'What for?'

'For building his factory.'

'What rubbish! He is talking like a big financier! If he has the money for it, why does he ask me?'

'Everyone in the town thinks of him as a big businessman. He talks well!'

'Yes, to everyone except me,' said Jagan resentfully.

The cousin said, 'We'll talk of all that later. Will you go home? This is the right moment. Mali is going out of town and won't be back until evening. I'll stay here until you come back. There will be others to go with Mali.'

Jagan went home, washed himself, went into the *puja* room, stood before the gods and prayed, 'Please help me, enlighten me. I don't know what to do.' He stood in meditation for a second, then, reinforced in spirit, knocked on the middle door in the hall. It was unusual for him to come home at this hour; the place looked strangely different, with the afternoon sun coming in at odd corners through the open court. 'This looks like somebody else's home,' he reflected, and it confirmed his recent feeling that he was no longer his old self. He recollected the bearded man's advice during their rambles: 'At first don't hurry, but when you decide, be swift and positive.' That was more or less what he had learnt from Gandhi, but the lesson seemed to have worn out. He remembered how as a volunteer over twenty years ago he had rushed into the British Collector's bungalow and climbed the roof in order to bring down the Union Jack and plant the Indian flag in its place. Helmeted police were standing guard in the compound, but the speed of his action completely took them by surprise and they had to clamber after him to the roof, but not before he had seized the Union Jack in a crocodile grip and hugged the flagpost while attempting to plant his own flag. They had to beat him and crack open his skull in order to make him let go his hold. He opened his eyes fifteen days later in the hospital, and lay forgotten in a prison afterwards. 'There are times when a *Satyagrahi* has to act first and think afterwards,' his leaders had advised. Once a *Satyagrahi*, always a *Satyagrahi*. If one was not acting for truth against the British, one was acting for truth in some other matter, in personal affairs, in all sorts of things. His training was always there, but somehow had dimmed inexplicably. With these reflections, he reinforced his ego before venturing to knock on the door of Mali's apartment.

Grace opened the door and exclaimed, 'Father! You here at this hour! How unusual!'

Jagan went straight to the point. 'I have to talk to you. Will you come here or should I go in there?'

'Please come in. Come to the hall. The chairs there are comfortable.'

He followed her and took his seat on the sofa. She sat in her chair, one finger twirling a chain around her neck. She had a book open on a side table. She was wearing a yellow kimono and looked very much like a Japanese. 'She looks different each day!' he thought and, suppressing his impulse to ask, 'Are you sure you are not a Japanese today?' said aloud, 'What are you reading?'

'Nothing very important,' and she mentioned some title.

'Go straight to the point,' he told himself. 'You have beaten about the bush and practically lost contact with your son; don't lose your daughter-in-law too.' His first question was: 'I don't see you in my house nowadays. Why?'

She went red in the face. Her lips twitched and she remained silent.

Observing her discomfiture, he said, 'Don't bother to answer my question.' He left her a little time to recover her composure, then asked, 'Do you wish to go back to your country?'

Once again, her lips twitched, her face went red, and she cast her longish eyes down and remained silent. A crow cawed, perched on the tiles of the open courtyard. Its raucous note broke the awful silence. She muttered, 'Ah, that crow has come! Excuse me.' She bustled out, went into her kitchen, came out with a piece of bread in her hand, and tossed it onto the roof; the crow picked it up and was off. Presently more crows came and sat on the roof and cawed. 'This is the worst of it. They all clamour, but I don't really have enough for all of them,' she said.

Jagan could not help saying, 'The same thing is happening to me in my shop. The whole town clamours for my sweets, but really the sales are closed before four in the afternoon.'

She received this in silence. Jagan felt nervous. All the resolution he had made vanished without a trace. He was scared of Grace. He felt she might break down if he asked any more questions. He sensed a deep-seated disturbance in her and became anxious to leave her alone, whatever the mystery might be. When a clock struck four, he got up, saying with extraordinary clarity, 'I must be back at the shop.'

She walked to the door with him silently. When he was about to pass out, she said in a matter-of-fact way, 'Father, Mo wants me to go back.'

'Why?' Jagan asked, halting.

She hesitated. Jagan feared she might cry, but she said very calmly, 'It's all over, that's all.'

'What's over?'

She didn't answer.

He asked, 'Is it his idea or yours?'

She repeated, 'He wants me to go back. He says he can't afford to keep me here any more.' These new facets of Mali now revealed were startling and Jagan found himself tongue-tied. She went on, 'I used to work. I had two thousand dollars when I came here. All that's gone.'

'How?'

She merely said, 'Mo has no more use for me.'

'Use or no use, my wife—well, you know, I looked after her all her life.'

Grace said rather shyly, 'The only good part of it is, there is no child.'

He found some portions of her talk obscure but could not ask explicitly for explanations. He said, 'If you read our *Puranas*, you will find that the wife's place is beside her husband whatever may happen.'

'But we are not married,' Grace said simply. 'He promised he'd marry me in the Indian way, because I liked it, and brought me here.'

'And the marriage didn't take place, after coming here?'

'Wouldn't you have known it, if it had?' she said.

It was too much to swallow and digest at one sitting. Jagan wailed, 'I don't know what to make of it all.'

'Will you come back for a while and take a seat? I'll explain. I feel awkward standing here,' Grace said.

He stood looking at the girl. She looked so good and virtuous; he had relied on her so much and yet here she was living in sin and talking casually about it all. 'What breed of creatures are these?' he wondered. They had tainted his ancient home. He had borne much from them. He said coldly, 'No, I'm not coming in now. Let me go back to the shop.'

When the cousin came at 4.30 p.m. Jagan shouted, 'Come here, I am waiting for you.' The cousin held up his arm as much as to say, 'Wait till I finish my savouring duties.' While he was in the kitchen, Jagan's ardour cooled. He had mentally rehearsed a speech beginning 'Do you know . . .?' but actually, when the cousin emerged from the kitchen he asked, 'How well do you know Mali?' The cousin spent a little time gazing at the tailor across the road pedalling his sewing machine, which, as Jagan knew, was a sign that the cousin was in deep thought. He shook him out of it by saying, 'Mali is not married.'

The cousin, suppressing many questions that arose in his mind, wondered if he was expected to attempt some new matchmaking for Mali and began, 'Of course, if you give the word, people are ready to snatch his horoscope; even the Judge was mentioning that he had a brother's niece-in-law who was anxious for a match with your family . . .'

Jagan felt slightly elevated by this news, but suddenly remembered that he was not fated to live an ordinary peaceful life. 'Captain, those schoolchildren!' The captain, not knowing whether he was expected to shoo them off or give them gifts, cried back, 'What shall I do with them, sir?'

'Send them away. If you show some consideration once, they expect it for ever and ever; our people have no self-respect.'

'I know you want to reduce the price of all stuff further, but cannot,' said the cousin.

'No sense in upsetting the social balance. I don't wish to make enemies of that Ananda Bhavan *sait* or the others. There are all sorts of persons at their back.'

The cousin agreed in order to dispose of the question then and there, and let the other go on with the more interesting subject of Mali. He egged him on. 'Did you meet the girl today?'

'Why do you say "the girl" instead of "Mali's wife"?' Jagan asked with a certain amount of vicious pleasure.

The cousin, feeling trapped by this question, said generally, 'She seems to be a good girl. When I met her yesterday at . . .'

Before he could finish his sentence Jagan said, 'I am not doubting her goodness, but she is not married to Mali at all.' The cousin received the statement in silence, fearing that anything he said might smack of scandal. Jagan went on, 'She told me so herself; why should I doubt her?'

The cousin said simply, 'Then why not let her go back to her country, as Mali wants?' This sounded such a rational approach to the crisis that Jagan had nothing further to say for a long while. It was very difficult to recollect what he had meant to say or to refresh his memory with the righteous indignation he had felt. The cousin added, 'Our young men live in a different world from ours, and we must not let ourselves be upset too much by certain things they do.'

This sounded a sage-like statement, but Jagan could not accept the theory of indifference which the cousin, still not knowing the exact facts, was developing. Jagan said, 'This sort of thing is unheard-of in our family. Even my grandfather's brother, who was known to be immoral, never did this sort of thing. When he was not married he never claimed that he was married, although . . .'

'I have heard my father speak about him. He was certainly married to three wives and had numerous other women. He never shirked a responsibility.' They were deriving a vicarious pleasure from going into the details of lechery practised by their forefathers.

'I can't understand how two young persons can live together like this without being married,' said Jagan and fell silent, letting his mind revel in sensuous imaginings of what had gone on within the walls of his house. 'I feel my home is tainted now. I find it difficult to go back there.'

The cousin said, 'You have heard only one side of the story. Why not speak to Mali and find out the other?'

'He has already told me he wants her to go.'

'It is because his business is not developing,' said the cousin.

'What business?' cried Jagan so emphatically that the cook carrying a tray to the front stall stood arrested and nearly dropped it from his hand, at which Jagan glared at him and said, 'You get on with your job. I am not speaking to you.' He added in a whisper, 'These boys are not what they used to be; they are becoming awfully inquisitive. I am sure he knows all about this affair.'

The cousin now brought the matter down to a practical level, as he always did. 'Why do you let this affect you so much? It is, after all, their business.'

'But I feel it is my home that is being dirtied. Mali is my son. Grace is not my daughter-in-law.'

'Oh, that is a very wrong, selfish view to take,' said the cousin, feeling his way now and getting the measure of Jagan's mental needs. His role was to help Jagan crystallize his attitudes in a crisis. He added, 'What is all your study of the *Gita* worth if you cannot keep your mind untouched by all this? You yourself have explained to me that one should not identify oneself with objects or circumstances.'

Jagan accepted this compliment with great pleasure although, if he had questioned it, he might not have been able to find out exactly what he had said, or why or when. Obliged to admit his devotion to the *Gita* and the wisdom derived from it, he mumbled,

'We are blinded by our attachments. Every attachment creates a delusion and we are carried away by it . . .'

'Too true, too true,' said the cousin. 'Equanimity is more important than anything else in life.'

'That is what I am seeking but never attain!' Jagan wailed and quietened his thoughts for a moment. Suddenly he remembered that he had been fooled by the young people and that the house which had remained unsullied for generations had this new taint to carry. How could he live in the same house with them? He was on the point of saying, 'I have half a mind to tell them to go where they please and do what they like, but not in my house . . .' But he checked himself; it was a statement that his tongue refused to phrase. Certain things acquired an evil complexion if phrased, but remained harmless in the mind. 'How do you expect me to go on living there?'

'If you have the back door entrance, use it and don't go near their portion. Where else could they go now?'

'That is true, housing conditions being what they are. Moreover, people will talk.' He begged, 'Please don't let anyone know.'

The cousin threw up his arms in horror. 'Unthinkable. What you say to me is a sacred trust, believe me.'

Assured by this protestation, Jagan said, 'What shall I do now?'

'About what?'

'About Mali and that girl.'

The cousin gave a clearheaded statement: 'Get through their marriage very quickly in the hill temple. It can be arranged within a few hours.'

'Alas, I don't know what her caste is, so how can I?'

'Oh, she can be converted. I know some persons who will do it.'

A burden was removed from his shoulders. Jagan said, 'You are my saviour. I don't know where I should be without you.'

CHAPTER ELEVEN

JAGAN BARRICADED HIMSELF in completely. He derived a peculiar excitement in performing all the actions of a purificatory nature. He shut the communicating door between his part of the dwelling and Mali's and locked it on his side. He did everything possible to insulate himself from the evil radiations of an unmarried couple living together. There was a ventilator between the two portions of the house; he dragged up an old stool, and with the help of a long bamboo shut it tight. Now the isolation, more an insulation, was complete. He gave up the use of the front door, as it took him through a common passage trodden by the feet of the tainters. A whole morning he kept himself busy with these arrangements, dragging the stool hither and thither and shifting the ladder. After locking the back door of his house when he left for his shop, he took a side-lane which led to the main street. He noted that this path was overgrown with thorns and weeds. 'I must take out my spade and clear it,' he said to himself. Nearly fifty years had elapsed since he had traversed this lane. In those days, when his father's family had lived in a hut in the backyard and the front portion was growing up little by little, he and his brother used to hunt for grasshoppers amidst the weeds. All the blazing afternoons they would be active in this pursuit while the Malgudi summer scorched everything, and even the grasshoppers were reluctant to leave the paltry shade of the weed-plants. His elder brother carried a small tin; he cupped his palm over the grasshopper and trapped it, and, if it was a large one, transferred it to his tin as befitting an elder brother; if it was a little one, it was passed on to Jagan; but on no account would Jagan be permitted to catch one himself. He could only stand behind his brother and wait for his luck, with his own little tin in hand. This would go on all afternoon, until the grasshoppers learnt to anticipate their footfalls and to hop off to safety.

Sometimes their sister would trace them down here, and follow them doggedly, uttering sinister remarks: 'You are killing the animals here. I'll tell Father; they are found dead every day in the tins. You will both go to hell.' Jagan, afraid of this blackmailer, would plead with her to leave them alone, but his elder brother would say, 'Let her talk. No one wants her here. If she speaks to Father, I'll wring her neck,' and rear himself up menacingly, and she would run away screaming in terror. 'They never liked me,' reflected Jagan. The sister had married a wealthy village idiot, become a rustic and brought forth an ugly brood of children, and the brother had cut all contact after the division of their father's estate. Ah, how intrigued they would be if they knew the full story of Mali! Since the advent of Grace, all his relations had ostracized him. The only reminder he had had from his sister was a postcard a year ago on the back of which she had written, 'We are ashamed to refer to you as a brother. Even when you joined Gandhi and lost all sense of caste, dining and rubbing shoulders with untouchables, going to jail, and getting up to all kinds of shameful things, we didn't mind anything. But now is it a fact that you have a beef-eating Christian girl for a daughter-in-law? I can hardly call you a brother in the presence of my in-laws. No one can blame Mali, with a father like you, etc. . . .' And she had concluded with the gratifying thought that their parents were fortunately dead and spared the indignity of watching these unsavoury activities. Jagan had heard that his brother, who lived in Vinayak Street, often spoke of him in anger and shame; and he never invited him to join him in performing the anniversary ceremonies for their father. He was an orthodox man who managed the headquarters of a religious order, established ten centuries ago with a million followers, and he had begun to disapprove of Jagan's outlook long ago.

His remarks were brought to Jagan from time to time by common friends and relatives and occasionally by the cousin, whose standing was secure everywhere. The elder brother had once remarked, 'How can you expect a good type of son when you have a father like Jagan?' What would they say if they knew the latest development? They would doubtless remove themselves even further. Jagan felt grateful for being an outcast, for it absolved him from obligations as a member of the family. Otherwise they would be making constant demands on his time and energy, compelling him to spend his time in family conclaves, sitting on carpets with a lot of kinsmen exchanging banalities while awaiting the call for the feast. Thus he had escaped the marriages of his nieces, the birthdays of his brother's successive children and several funerals.

Jagan was passing the statue when the green car with Mali and Grace drove past him. Mali applied the brakes and waited for Jagan to come up. Grace opened the car door and asked, 'Want a lift anywhere?'

'No,' said Jagan and tried to pass on.

'Were you spring-cleaning your home, Father? I heard the sounds of your activity.'

'Yes, I was trying to clean my surroundings,' Jagan said, putting into the word a new meaning. Mali sat staring ahead saying nothing. Jagan noted the serious careworn look in his eyes, and felt a tug at heart. If he could have recklessly announced, 'Long live your story-writing machine! Here, take my bank book, it's yours. I have no use for it,' all problems would be at an end. No, not all problems. Marriage? These two sitting so close with their legs touching and not married! What was their relationship? Now they were saying things against each other and yet they were nestling so close!

Later Jagan confided in the cousin, 'I had half a mind to accost them then and there, but I let them go. I will find another opportunity to clear up this whole business once and for all.'

By his architectural arrangements, Jagan had isolated himself so thoroughly that he didn't notice until a fortnight later that Grace was no longer there, and that there had been hardly any movement in the front part of the house. One morning he was so intrigued by the silence that he stood beside his door and applied an eye to the keyhole, after removing a little paper ball he had plugged into it. He saw no one, but he heard some movement in another room. He put the plug back into the keyhole, straightened himself, went round by the backyard and arrived at the front window and stood peering through the half-curtain. He couldn't see anything, but Mali called from within, 'Who is it?' Jagan tried to tiptoe away. A little later, Mali opened his window, saying, 'You could have knocked.'

'No, no,' said Jagan, 'I didn't want to . . .' He tried to retrace

his steps through the side-lane. Mali watched him for a moment
then cried, 'Father!' Jagan was thrilled. After many days he was
called 'Father' again. He stopped.

The boy asked, 'Why do you prowl around like this?'

Jagan said in confusion, 'Where is Grace?'

'Why do you want her?' Mali asked gruffly.

'Because I have not seen her for a long time,' said Jagan,
feeling bold enough to make that statement.

Mali said, 'How can you hope to see anyone when you have
sealed yourself off and use the back door? It looks silly.'

Jagan pretended to attend to a jasmine bush as he noticed his
neighbour watching them with great interest. 'Ever since he bought
that house, this man has done nothing except watch our house. I
wish I had bought it when it was offered. I could have given it to
Mali. He'd have been near enough and far enough too.' Jagan was
lost in these speculations for a moment, and Mali, also noticing the
neighbour, suppressed his conversation. Jagan said, 'I want to talk
to you both; why don't you come out?'

Mali withdrew his head from the window and came out by the
front door. He wore a fancy dressing-gown, and had stuck his feet
into slippers. He seemed to cower back and recoil from the bright
Indian sunlight. It was as if he was unique and could not come out
except with a fanfare and appropriate pageantry. He approached his
father and said, 'I don't like that guy over there watching us. Don't
talk loudly.'

'All right,' Jagan whispered hoarsely. The effort to suppress his
natural tone choked him and puffed up the veins on his neck. He
was unused to secrecies.

Mali said, 'Why should we talk in the garden? Can't we go in?'

Jagan was afraid to mention the actual reason, and slurred over
it by saying, 'I thought it was pleasant here.'

'Yes,' said Mali cynically, 'with the sun scorching and all the
neighbours providing an audience.'

The sting was lost on Jagan, whose only delight was that he had
today caught his son in a talking mood. 'Let us move on to the
shade in that corner. The man won't see us there.'

'But all the passers-by will watch us,' said Mali.

Jagan asked, 'Why should not people look at us? What's wrong
with us?'

'People must respect other people's privacy, that's all. We don't do it in this country. In America no one stares at another.'

'If we avoided each other's looks, how should we understand each other? What is one ashamed of, that one's face must be hidden?' Mali could not carry on this debate. He found his father in an extraordinarily controversial mood today. He gave up his point. Jagan, triumphant, asked, 'Is Grace inside or not? I'd like to talk to you both on a matter of importance.'

'She is not here. She has gone to stay with some friends for a few days.'

'When did she go?' Jagan felt that his son was likely to resent his questioning tone, and so expanded the theme, 'I was wondering if it was not a very long time since I saw her.'

'You have sealed off the middle door and use the back door. What's your idea, Father?' While Jagan was choosing words for a plausible answer, the boy went on, 'Do you think my business is going to be dropped because you have shut the door? Our correspondence goes on and I must know where we stand. Do you imagine you have made me drop the project?'

It was a pity that they should be rushing to the edge of the precipice as usual. Jagan tried to give another turn to their talk. 'You must both be married soon.'

'What are you trying to say?' screamed Mali. Jagan explained. Mali merely said, 'You have been listening to nonsense. I never knew you could listen to such gossip.'

Jagan noted with pleasure that the boy had refrained from calling him 'silly' again. He asked, 'Does Grace gossip about herself? Anyway, I do not want to go into all that again. There is a very small temple, where you can go through a quick marriage. No one need be invited, just the three of us and a priest, and you can be done with the whole business in an hour.'

'Grace has been getting funny notions, that's why I told you to pack her off some weeks ago, but you grudged the expenditure,' said Mali. 'She is not in her right mind; she must go to a psychiatrist.'

'What's that?'

'Don't you know what a psychiatrist is? What a backwood this is, where nothing is known.' With that Mali turned and went in, leaving Jagan transfixed to the spot. He tried to recollect the words that Mali had said and to make out their meaning. There was no meaning. What was a psychiatrist? What would he do? Before he could sort it out in his mind, the neighbour edged along to the

fence, commenting, 'So rare to see you! What is your son doing?'
   'He is in business with some American businessmen.'
   'Oh, that's very good. So he will earn dollars for our country.
Very good, very good . . .' On this pleasant note Jagan tore himself
away, because he felt that the next question was going to be about
the daughter-in-law. Funny situation—not knowing whether she
was a daughter-in-law or not! He was totally at a loss to decide who
was lying.

CHAPTER TWELVE

HE WAS WORRIED. The entire day passed with his mind completely obsessed. He was functioning with only a part of himself. Sivaraman's enquiries, the coming in of cash and the arrival and departure of his cousin at the appointed hour were all mechanically gone through. His cousin ate, spoke of various things, and waited as usual to talk of Mali, but Jagan was in no mood to encourage him, and the cousin gave up with resignation. 'Sometimes he talks, sometimes he doesn't. Take him as he comes, that's all,' he thought and slipped away at the right moment.

Jagan counted the cash and made the entries, but his mind worked on one theme only: the puzzle created by Mali. At every encounter he displayed a new facet, which might or might not have relevance to the previous one. Jagan was reminded of the concept of *Viswarupa* that he had read about in the *Bhagavad Gita*. When the warrior Arjuna hesitated to perform his duty on the battlefield, God came to him in the guise of his charioteer and revealed Himself in all His immensity. On one side he was thousand-faced. 'I behold You, infinite in forms on all sides, with countless arms, stomachs, mouths and eyes; neither Your end nor middle nor beginning do I see . . .' quoted Jagan inwardly, at the same time remaining rational enough to realize the irreverence of the comparison.

That evening Jagan sat all alone on the pedestal of the statue. All the others who had congregated around it were gone. Sir Frederick thrust his top into the world of sparkling stars. The night was hot; the still air and heat were suffocating. He saw his house beyond the statue; unless he went and switched on a light, there would be no light in it. It stood up, sinister and silent. There was a time when it had seethed with life, lamps burning in every room, and during the festivals hundreds of mud lamps would be lit and arrayed all along the parapet. Theirs had been the brightest home in those days. That was long before the birth of Mali, years even before his marriage. He suddenly recollected the exact point in time when he had shed his bachelorhood, that day when he had travelled to the village of Kuppam in order to take a look at the bride proposed for him by the elders of his family. He had to go by train to Myel, a tiny red-tiled railway station set amidst emerald-green rice-fields, two stations beyond Trichy. From Myel he had to go on in a cart drawn by a pair of bullocks over a bumpy mud track, and in some places even over cultivated fields. The future bride's younger brother, who had come to meet him as a piece of courtesy, was also in the carriage. Jagan was in a happy mood and laughed uncontrollably at the way they were progressing in the cross-country run. Every time the wheels sank into a sandy patch and the cart-man got down and heaved them out with oaths, Jagan felt tickled; but the boy stuck to his seat and remained grim and silent. He had been trained to show respect to a brother-in-law by being reserved; that boy had the grimmest face in the country. Ultimately he grew a long moustache as a commissioned air-force officer, and was lost sight of in the Burma campaign of 1942.

Jagan's father had sent his elder son to accompany him and had commanded Jagan, 'Don't stare at the girl. I have seen her and I know she is good-looking. Don't imagine you are a big judge of persons.' At the end of the bumpy journey, he was received with a lot of fuss and seated on a carpet spread on the *pyol* of an ancient house. His future father-in-law and a number of his relations had assembled to have a look and measure the proposed bridegroom from different angles. They all engaged him in conversation and tried to judge his intelligence and outlook. Jagan had already been warned by his elder brother not to be too communicative, as a certain mysteriousness was invaluable in a son-in-law. Everyone kept asking as if in a chorus, 'How was your journey?' Jagan stroked his tuft with one hand, fumbled with the rim of his cap and threw furtive glances at his brother for a signal. When his brother nodded slightly, he answered, 'Oh, it was good.' 'Did you have comfortable seats in the train?' asked one examiner sitting at the farthest corner of the *pyol* and this time Jagan said on his own, 'Of course.' It was a matter of propriety to say a good word about the journey because the railway ran over their territory. 'What is your subject of study at the college?' asked another one, and Jagan answered 'History' without waiting for his brother's sanction. (Later, when they were alone his brother nudged him and said, 'You should have said "Mathematics"; I know these people would prefer a mathematical son-in-law; all the boys in this part of the country are first-class mathematicians.' To make matters worse Jagan had not only said 'History' but had also attempted some humorous explanations about his capacity in mathematics.)

While talking Jagan cast furtive glances into the hall in the hope of catching a glimpse of his future bride. He had as yet no idea what she would look like. He had been shown a rather overtouched shiny photograph of her, mounted within a floral board: a sharp-faced young person with tightly braided hair. The photographer had managed to achieve his task without revealing what the girl's eyes looked like, and Jagan when presented with the photograph had been unable to scrutinize it for long, for his father was watching him; but he was racked with a doubt whether the girl might not be squint-eyed, since it was well known that photographers tried to slur over such facts for purposes of marriage. He liked her height as she stood with her elbow resting on a corner stand with a flower vase on it; her fingers looked slender and long. She had been decorated with so many ornaments that it was impossible to guess what she really looked like, and, of course, the photographer had imparted the appropriate complexion.

Now Jagan was going to clear up his doubts; engaged in answering the questions of the assembly, he was simultaneously wondering when the call would come for him to enter the house and examine his bride. They brought a silver tray heaped with golden-hued *jilebi* and *bonda* made of raw banana, and coffee, brown and hot, in two silver tumblers, at the sight of which Jagan became hungrier than ever. Left to himself he would have gobbled up the entire lot (his food theories had not yet begun), but a glance from his brother restrained him. The protocol was inflexible: they were honoured visitors, on whose verdict would depend the future of the girl; it was a highly serious and important role, and they were expected to carry themselves with dignity and not show any emotion even at the sight of *jilebi*; even if one was maddeningly hungry one had to say, 'Oh, why all this? I cannot eat. We have just had coffee and everything in the train . . .' Jagan mumbled this sentence with the utmost reluctance, jointly with his brother, who uttered it with great clarity. All the same, the code demanded that their hosts should press the delicacies upon them. Then one would have to break off the *jilebi* minutely with the tip of one's fingers and transfer it to one's mouth, and generally display reluctance or even aversion until pressed again, and then, just to please others, eat two or three bits in succession and then take an elegant sip of coffee. The essence of behaviour in these circumstances consisted in seeming to do things for the sake of one's hosts. One left half a cup of coffee undrunk and the edibles practically untouched; one peeled a banana indifferently, broke off a couple of inches and ate it without moving a muscle, leaving the rest of the fruit to be thrown away. This was Jagan's first occasion for displaying ceremonial behaviour. At home he was well known for his gluttony, indeed his mother admired him for it. When he came home from school he always rummaged in the kitchen cupboard and stuffed his mouth with cashew nuts, coconut, jaggery, and varied fried edibles which his mother prepared for his benefit. On Saturdays and Sundays, when he stayed at home, he ate non-stop, and this always elicited the utmost appreciation from his father, who would remark, 'This son of ours must have been a rat in his last life, considering his nibbling capacity.' For one with such a reputation it was rather hard to observe the restraints of protocol; his fingers itched, his palate was agitated. However, after tasting a minute portion of the repast, Jagan resolutely pushed away the tray.

Then his future mother-in-law appeared at the doorway, unobtrusively studied the features of her son-in-law, and announced with all gentleness, 'Why not adjourn inside?' addressing no one in particular. Whereupon, the master of the house rose to his feet, saying, 'Why don't you all come in?' which was again a kind of code. Although everyone was fully aware of the purpose of the young man's visit, one had to view it casually, neither side displaying too much interest or anxiety. Everyone sitting on the *pyol* got up. Jagan's brother, a born diplomat, was the last but one to respond, and the last was Jagan, though he was burning with impatience. He was worried, too, lest he should perpetrate some silly *faux pas* and become a disgrace to his family, whose previous experience in such matters was none too happy. Jagan had become an eligible bachelor three years before and had inspected four would-be brides so far. On two occasions he had kept staring at the girls in open-mouthed wonder because they happened to be stunningly ugly; on another occasion he undisguisedly watched the legs of the girl as she walked in because she was reputed to be lame. For these lapses he had been severely reprimanded, and his action went into the repertory of family jokes. Whenever his maternal uncles or others from his mother's side arrived and gathered after dinner in the courtyard looking for scapegoats for their gossip, invariably Jagan supplied the text. This time, they had tried to prevent mistakes by sending his elder brother to chaperone him through this delicate mission. The brother was certainly not going to spare the authority vested in him; he was keeping his eye on him, commanding and manipulating him by narrowing his eyelids or opening them wide.

Next they were all led to the central hall of the village home. In honour of this visit many cluttering benches, rolls of bedding and other odds and ends had been moved to a corner and covered with a huge carpet; on the floor was spread an enormous striped carpet; incense sticks were lit so as to overwhelm the smell of the cowshed in the backyard. 'These fellows from the city are fussy and don't know how to live with domestic animals,' her father had said, or so Jagan's wife reported later in life. For Jagan the scene was heavenly; he felt a momentary satisfaction at the thought that all these preparations were for his sake (even if it was the brother who was the controller). They showed him a seat and the rest arranged themselves around. Jagan kept thinking, 'With so many around, my view is going to be obstructed and then no one should blame me if I demand a second appearance.' There could be no such thing as a second appearance, but his imagination was running wild. Some voices approached and Jagan stiffened and resolutely avoided his brother's glance. A harmonium sounded mysteriously somewhere inside, and to the accompaniment of its discordant notes a slightly masculine voice (he was to become familiar with it later in life) sang Thyagaraja's '*Telisi Rama Chintanamu . . .*' (The power of the very thought of Rama . . .). 'Ambika is singing with the harmonium; she felt too shy to sing in the presence of so many, so she is singing in the room. She can sing very well. I have got her a teacher from the town.' The father mentioned a place six miles away. Jagan was certainly not in a critical enough mood to say they should have spared themselves the trouble. The music ceased. There were stirrings inside, some arguments and protests, and then a little girl with tightly plaited hair emerged grinning with the comment, 'Ambika refuses to come out, she feels shy,' at which all the elders joked and laughed. The master of the house raised his voice and called, 'Ambika, come on, come on, there's nothing to be afraid of in these days.' And he addressed the women inside in a general way: 'Don't make fun of her, she will be all right . . .' After this preamble a tall girl emerged swishing her lace saree, facing the assembly and smiling, and Jagan's heart gave a thump. 'Not at all like the photo, so tall! I can't believe . . .' The master of the house saved further speculation by announcing, 'She is my first daughter,' and the tall girl said, 'Ambika is coming.' The rest Jagan did not hear; he lost interest in the tall girl who was only a sort of advance guard for her younger sister, who came with downcast eyes and bowed head and moved across the arena so fast that Jagan could not take in any detail. 'Not short nor tall, not fat nor puny . . .' Jagan could not arrange her in any clear outline. The details overlapped, but producing only impressions of an agreeable nature, and not provoking aversion as on the previous occasions.

'How is she to know what I look like if she flits by so fast?' Jagan speculated. 'I don't care what my brother is going to say later; for the present I am going to stare, gaze and study. I don't care what anybody thinks.' He stared unwinkingly at the girl. She had a thick wad of wavy hair, plaited and decorated with flowers, and many pieces of jewellery sparkled on her person. She wore a light green saree which suited her complexion. Was she fair or dusky? Who could say? His vision was clouded with a happy haze and he might keep peering at her a whole day with none to disturb his study, yet he could never clear his doubts about her personality. During these muddled moments, she shot one lightning glance at him, which somehow, through the fates, coincided with a look he was himself shooting at her; their eyes met, and Jagan's heart palpitated and raced, and before he could do anything about it, it was all over. The assembly was on its feet, people were leaving and the vision was gone.

All through their journey back, Jagan remained pensive. His brother did not try to disturb his mood. Their train was due to arrive two hours later, but the double bullock cart had put them down at the little railway station before sunset and had returned to the village. Jagan sat on a weighing platform, looking away at a range of mountains beyond the green fields. His brother, who was pacing up and down impatiently, stopped by for a minute to say, 'Why should they have dumped us down here so early?'

Jagan merely said, 'They have their own reasons, I suppose. I heard the young fellow say that the bullocks had some difficulty at night . . .'

'Ah, you are already assuming the role of their spokesman? Does that mean . . .?'

Jagan nodded an assent somewhat shyly and stood up and asked eagerly, 'How will they know? Should we not tell them?'

His brother stood stiff and said, 'I hope you have not been a fool, telling anyone that you like the girl. One doesn't cheapen oneself.'

'No, no,' protested Jagan. 'I was with you all the time and never spoke to anyone except to say goodbye . . .' When he had had to leave at last his feet had tarried and moved at a snail's pace in the hope that the girl would peep out of the doorway, at least to prove that she loved him as conveyed by her lightning look; he wanted somehow to assure her that he would marry her and that he was not in the least prejudiced by her harmonium music; in his excited state of mind it seemed to him a matter of the utmost urgency to convey to her his message, and if she really cared for him she would show some slight sign at parting. He had never expected that such factors as train-times and the poor sight of bullocks would tear him away from his beloved's aura so unceremoniously.

On the train journey, he remained brooding. He was troubled by the feeling that he had missed the chance, somehow, to say farewell to his beloved; the thought of her was extremely comforting, soothing and also in a quiet way thrilling. His brother, now having no policing to do, was asleep in his seat, leaving Jagan free to go back to the village in his thoughts and roam unfettered. Thinking it over, Jagan felt charmed by every bit of the expedition: their house was nice and cosy, their hall smelt beautifully of incense which somehow blended successfully with the cowdung smell from their cattle shed; the harmonium was out of tune, but it would not be proper to judge her music from it. Her voice was gruff because she had had to adjust it to that horrid instrument; he was sure that she really had a sweet voice to suit her face . . . Then he too fell asleep during the rest of the journey. They had to get off and change into another train at some junction and they arrived at Malgudi station early in the morning. His brother hailed a *jutka*, haggled with the man, and they started out for their ancient home at Lawley Extension. Milkmen were out with their cows, a few cyclists were on the move to reach the single textile mill of the town by the time its doors should open. Except for these the city was still asleep.

When the brothers arrived home, their mother was sprinkling water on the front doorstep and decorating it with flour. While his brother was still arguing with the *jutka* man who was demanding two annas more than the agreed fare, Jagan picked up his little bag and passed into the house. His mother just smiled at him but asked no questions. His father was drawing water from the well in the backyard; he glanced at Jagan and went on with his work. His sister was circumambulating the sacred *tulsi* plant in the central yard and grinned at him mischievously, while her lips were muttering prayers. Jagan retired to his room, asking himself, 'Is no one interested in my opinion of the girl? No one is prepared to inquire whether I like her or not. Does it mean that they are all opposed to the idea?' Nor did his brother pause to enlighten anyone, but proceeded to the backyard in order to help his father at the well.

But somehow the information leaked out and his sister was the first to come to his room when he was about to leave for the college, her eyes glittering with mischief. 'Aye! Hai . . .' she cried and clicked her tongue provocatively. 'Someone is getting married soon . . .' The house was in great excitement. His brother's wife had been summoned from her parents' house in order to help with the arrangements for the wedding. Stage by stage the tempo increased. His father wrote numerous postcards every day between noon and three and carried them to the railway station in order to make sure that they went by the mail train. He had many relatives whom he highly respected, elders without whose sanction he never proceeded in any matter. Every day the postman's arrival was awaited by him at ten o'clock. In those days a postcard cost only three paise, but one could cram on its face and back as many hundred words as one pleased. After receiving the approvals from his elders, Jagan's father carried on several consultations with his wife in whispers in a far-off corner of the second courtyard. Jagan, as became a junior, was careful not to show too much personal interest in his marriage, but he was anxious to know what was going on. He would have been snubbed if he had inquired. He had to depend upon his younger sister, who stood about casually while the elders talked, eavesdropped, and brought him news. She would seek him out as he sat at his desk apparently studying, and then whisper to him,

'Grand-uncle has approved.' 'Father is writing to the bride's people tomorrow; they are waiting for an auspicious time.' 'Father wants a dowry of five thousand rupees,' which really worried Jagan. Suppose the other refused? Then what? 'They want to have the marriage celebrated in September.' Only three months! Jagan felt scared at the thought of becoming a married man in three months. It was all right as long as one dreamed of a girl and theoretically speculated about marriage, but to become a positive and concrete husband, it was a terrifying reality. 'Why do they want to have the marriage so soon?' he asked.

Father's letter of approval went to Kuppam village. Many, many letters passed between the parties. A voluminous correspondence grew which Jagan's father harpooned methodically on to a long iron spike with a circular wooden stop at one end, by which system they had preserved their family correspondence from time immemorial. One evening the bride's party arrived with huge brass trays covered with betel leaves, fruits, saffron, new clothes, a silver bowl of fragrant sandal paste, a huge heap of sugar crystals on a silver plate and a pair of silver lamps. A dozen priests were assembled in the hall. A few neighbours and relatives had been invited and Jagan was given a new *dhoti* and made to sit in the centre of the assembly. They then unfolded a sheet of paper, on which they had previously spent a considerable time drafting the exact wedding notice, getting the names down correctly. The senior priest of the house, a gaunt old man, stood up and read the notice aloud, his voice quivering with nervousness. It announced that Jagannath, son of so-and-so, was to marry Ambika, daughter of so-and-so, on the tenth of September, etc. etc. The father of the bride handed this important document ceremoniously to Jagan's father, together with an envelope in which he had put currency notes, half the dowry in advance, and gently suggested, 'Please ask your elder son to count the cash.' Jagan's father made some deprecating sounds, but passed the envelope on to his elder son for counting, who lost no time in performing the task and confirming, 'Two thousand five hundred.' 'It was not necessary to count,' said Jagan's father gracefully, 'but since you insisted on it . . .' 'In money matters it is best to be assured. How could I be sure that my counting was perfect? I always like to get cash counted again and again,' said Jagan's father-in-law, at which everyone laughed as if it were a brilliant piece of humour. Then they all adjourned for a grand feast prepared by a company of expert cooks. Huge plantain leaves were spread out in the second court, with silver tumblers and bowls for each guest and a dozen delicacies and side dishes in addition to heaps of softly-cooked ivory-like rice. A pipe-and-drum party seated in the front part of the house created enough din to make it known to the whole town that a marriage was being settled. The house had been brilliantly lit with numerous brass lamps as well as gas lamps, which shed an enormous amount of greenish illumination everywhere. Jagan felt overwhelmed by the celebrations. He kept thinking, 'All this for my marriage! How seriously they have taken it; no backing out now.' By the midnight train the bride's party were seen off. When they were gone, Jagan's mother and her relations went in and lost no time in assessing the value of the clothes and silver left by them as presents. They were satisfied with the weight and design of the silverware. Mother expressed her utmost approval by telling Jagan, 'Your father-in-law is not a mean sort; see how solid all the presents are!' Jagan, identifying himself with them, felt personally complimented.

The house wore an appearance of extraordinary activity as September approached. Jagan lost count of time. His end-of-term examinations were over and his father had permitted him to take time off from college and assist the people at home. Mother went about saying, 'Although we are the bridegroom's party, we cannot spare ourselves; there are things to do.' Clothes had to be chosen for the bride and others, for which purpose Mother and her relations went to the Universal Saree Emporium and spent eight hours at a stretch examining gold borders, fabrics and hundreds of sarees. Jagan spent much time at his tailor's shop measuring himself for silk shirts and a dark suit; his mother and the others seemed keen that the bridegroom should appear in a suit during the wedding procession. Jagan would have preferred to be clad in his *dhoti* and *jibba*, but he was forced by everyone to accept a tweed suit. His elder brother was very vehement on the subject, having himself gone through it all some years ago. He also took charge of the printing of invitation cards and ran between Truth Printing and their home and prepared an elaborate list of addresses. Father harassed everyone about the list, asking if so-and-so had been included, and, if not, to do it at once. He woke them up at midnight to suggest a name just occurring to him. He did not want any friend or relation remotely connected with Jagan to be overlooked. No one had ever suspected that Father would be such a keen sender-out of invitations or could collect or recollect so many names, although he was never sure whether the name or initials were correct (sometimes he knew a person only by a pet name), whether so-and-so was living at that address or even whether he was alive at all.

They sent out three thousand invitations. The result was that an enormous crowd turned up by every bus, train and vehicle, at the wedding in Kuppam village. Jagan's whole time was spent in greeting the guests or prostrating himself at their feet if they were older relatives. The priests compelled him to sit before the holy fire performing complicated rites and reciting sacred *mantras*; his consolation was that during most of these he had to be clasping his wife's hand; he felt enormously responsible as he glanced at the sacred *thali* he had knotted around her neck at the most auspicious moment of the ceremonies. He was overwhelmed by the scent of flowers and jasmine garlands and holy smoke, the feel of expensive silks and lace on his person and the crackling new sarees in which his wife appeared from time to time draped as in a vision. Her voice was not so gruff as it had sounded in the company of the harmonium; she had an enchanting smile, voice and laugh and she spoke to him with shy reserve whenever he was able to corner her and snatch a little privacy in the house which was crowded every inch with guests and visitors. He found the company of so many a bother and distraction. Whenever he found a moment to talk to his wife someone or other would butt in with the remark, 'Come on, come on, enough; don't get attached to the apron strings yet; you have a whole life to sit and admire your wife, whereas you will lose sight of us after the marriage.' These were routine jokes and interruptions in any marriage party, but Jagan felt particularly martyred, and felt he would have been happier with fewer relatives and friends around. The noise, the music of drums and pipes, the jokes and feasting went on for three days and ended with a photographer organizing a huge group with the bride and the bridegroom seated in the centre. The celebrations, on the whole, concluded peacefully, although at one stage a certain bitterness arose over the quality of the coffee supplied to the bridegroom's house by their hosts, and one of Jagan's uncles, a very elderly man, threatened to leave the marriage party.

There was one other embarrassment on the night of the wedding feast. Someone who held the highest precedence in the family hierarchy (Jagan's father's cousin, a seventy-five-year-old man who had come all the way from Berhampore for the marriage) was given a half-torn banana leaf to dine on and was seated in the company of children instead of in the top row. This threatened to develop into a first-class crisis, but the girl's father openly apologized for the slip and all was forgotten. Something that upset all the womenfolk of the bridegroom's party was that the bride was not provided with the gold waist-belt that had been promised when the original list of jewellery was drawn up, the goldsmith in the town had delayed and finally, when the piece was delivered, it was found to be made not of one gold-sheet, but a number of little gold bars intertwined with silk cords. The women felt that this was downright cheating. 'They are saving the gold!' they commented angrily. They would have even gone to the extent of stopping the marriage, but for the fact that Jagan did not approve of all this hullabaloo over a gold belt, explaining to his mother, 'This is the latest fashion; nowadays the girls do not want to be weighed down with all that massive gold.' At which they became very critical of him, saying that he had already become henpecked, and was already an unpaid advocate for his wife's family. Even his brother managed to take him aside during this crisis and say, 'Don't make a fool of yourself so soon. Why don't you leave these problems for womenfolk to discuss in the way they want?' Jagan had the temerity to reply, 'It is because they are criticizing my wife, poor girl!' At this demonstration of loyalty his brother left him with a wry smile, saying, 'You are obsessed, it is no use talking to you.'

Jagan was given a room in the middle block. When he and his wife shut the door, they were in a world of their own within the confines of the heavy four-poster. At the performance of the consummation ceremony, Jagan's father had insisted on the nuptial suite being furnished properly at the expense of the bride's party. In one corner of the room Jagan was supposed to have his study (he still had his examinations to face). When they were alone, Jagan spent all his time in love-making. He lost count of time. He found his education a big nuisance, cut his classes, and came back home and sneaked into his room and failed in every examination, forcing his father to comment that Ambika should be sent back to her parents' house at least for six months if Jagan was ever to take his degree. At home Jagan spent very little time with his sister, mother or brother, as he used to, but shut himself in and awaited his wife's arrival. But she had her own duties in a large joint household; she had to do her share of work in the kitchen, helping her mother-in law in cooking, serving, scrubbing and sweeping the house, washing vessels and finally awaiting her mother-in-law's company for every meal. It would be unseemly for a daughter-in-law to seek her husband's company when the others were busy in the house in various ways; the elder daughter-in-law set the model for these codes of conduct, modelling herself on Jagan's mother, who had had her training early in life when she entered the family as a daughter-in-law. Ambika often enough reminded Jagan of her obligations as a daughter-in-law, but he was blind to everything except his own inclinations. When he came home and waited in his room for his wife's company and she was busy elsewhere, he sulked and quarrelled with her or pretended to be absorbed in his studies when she came. His wife always liked to have him in a pleasant mood and sooner or later would yield to his inordinate demands. His father severely reprimanded him when he found him indifferent to his studies. His mother often commented, 'A son is a son until the wife comes,' feeling sore that he could spare so little time for the others at home. His younger sister said, 'Who may you be, stranger? We have forgotten your face.' And his wife herself often said, 'Please don't create all this embarrassment for me. At least pretend that you are interested in the others.' His elder brother took him into the garden and advised, 'I know how you feel about things. I have passed through it all myself. If you spend four hours in your bedroom, at least give the others an hour now and then; otherwise you make yourself unpopular at home.' With one thing and another Jagan's stock was pretty low at home, but he did not care, as he lived in a perfect intoxication of husbandhood. Later, when his wife failed to have a baby and there were whispers and rumours, Jagan told his wife, 'I wish people could see us now on this side of the door, and then they would stop talking.'

Despite all his bragging there was no outside proof of his manhood. They had been married for almost ten years now; he had failed repeatedly in the Intermediate and was now failing in the BA class and still there was no sign of a child in the house. His brother had moved off to Vinayak Street with his entire family, which had become quite a crowd now. His sister was married and had gone to her husband's house. The big house had become silent and people began to notice how empty it was. Jagan's mother began to grumble that there were no children at home; it was one more stick to beat the daughter-in-law with. When she was tired with housework, such as washing and scrubbing the floor of the entire house, she went about muttering, 'All one asks of a girl is that she at least bring some children into a house as a normal person should; no one is asking for gold and silver; one may get cheated with regard to a gold belt even. Why can't a girl bear children as a million others in the world do?' All this was heard by the daughter-in-law scrubbing another part of the floor; she went on with her work without replying and took it out on Jagan when the door shut on them for the night. Sometimes she treated it as a joke as they sat, he with his BA text before him and she on the edge of the table with her legs swinging: 'I dread the monthly periods nowadays. They will start commenting . . .'

'Why don't you pretend, as some modern girls do, that you are not in the month?' But that was a frivolous suggestion. In an orthodox household with all the *puja*s and the gods, a menstruating woman had to isolate herself, as the emanations from her person were supposed to create a sort of magnetic defilement, and for three days she was fed in a far-off corner of the house, and was unable to move about freely. Jagan was very irritated and cried, 'Are they not satiated with children? My brother has provided enough children for several houses and my sister has begun in the true tradition with three children in four years. Why can't they be satisfied with affairs as they are now?'

'Because your mother would have nothing to comment on if we had a child,' Ambika suggested, then mumbled, 'As far as our family is concerned, all my sisters have many children, and your mother's insinuation that I am infertile . . .'

Jagan at once rushed to the defence of his own family. 'On our side too there can be no misgiving. Do you know there is a group photo of my grandmother at the centre of all her children and grandchildren, and do you know how many heads you can count?'

'Forty? Fifty?' asked Ambika. 'We also have a group photo in our house with our grandmother; do you know how many children and grandchildren and great-grandchildren there are?'

'One hundred and twenty?' asked Jagan mischievously.

His wife replied, 'No, don't try to joke about it; one hundred and three; and the photographer, it seems, charged four times his usual price.' She was reddening under her skin, her temper was slightly rising as she said, 'We are not an impotent family.'

Jagan was irked by her suggestion and looked up from his book with consternation. He had no answer to give. His devotion to bed had unconsciously diminished lately. Thinking it over, he recollected how often he rolled up a carpet, took a pillow and went out to sleep on the veranda, grumbling about the heat. 'It is getting to be very hot here; shall I sleep on the veranda? Would you be afraid?' 'Afraid of what?' Ambika would ask jokingly at first, but gradually, as time went by, with irritation. He hardly noticed her mood and went out and slept. This had become a more or less permanent arrangement except for when she returned, after a long absence, from her father's house, when he would give her passionate attention for a week running, hardly worrying about whether he was adequate; it was a question that he never at any time asked himself or his wife. He felt fatigued by all the apparatus of sex, its promises and its futility, the sadness and the sweat at the end of it all, and he assumed that his wife shared his outlook. Moreover, he had read in a book that Nature had never meant sex to be anything more than a means of propagation of the species, that one drop of white blood was equal to forty drops of red blood, and that seminal waste and nervous exhaustion reduced one's longevity, the essence of all achievement being celibacy and conservation.

It had become imperative for him to produce a child, and he didn't know what more he could do about it. Ambika herself was beginning to crave one. He had to do something about it. She sulked and blamed him with her looks. When she saw him rolling up his carpet, she said rather bitterly, 'Why don't you go and sleep at the foot of Lawley statue? It must be much cooler there.' When she taunted him thus, he felt extremely confused and attempted to joke it off with, 'That statue was not built for us to sleep on,' which even as he was uttering it sounded extremely silly in his own ears. When she taunted him further, he would put out the light, and pull her to the bed, and roll about, imagining himself to be the 'Sheik' in the Hollywood film in which Rudolph Valentino demonstrated the art of ravishing women.

His father suddenly said one morning, 'Next Tuesday we are going to the temple on Badri Hill. You had better apply for two days' leave from your college. Your wife will also come.' When Father said anything so specific there could be no discussion of the subject. Jagan was about to leave for his college. His father, who generally spent his time in the back garden, had come up to the middle part of the house to tell him this, which itself indicated the seriousness of the situation. Still, Jagan had the hardihood to ask, 'Why are we going to that temple?'

His father said, 'The temple is known as Santana Krishna; a visit to it is the only known remedy for barrenness in women.'

Jagan blushed. He wanted to assure his father of his wife's fecundity and describe to him the group photo in their house with her grandmother and the one hundred and three others, but he felt tongue-tied; one didn't discuss these things with one's father—nor with one's mother. He was a determined student this year, having made up his mind to pass his BA in order to prove that husbandhood was quite compatible with scholarship; that would at least prevent people from blaming his wife for his failure. Whenever the results came out and he had failed, there were pointed references within Ambika's hearing, so that the moment the bedroom door was shut she would say, 'Why don't you pick up your books and go away to a hostel? Your mother seems to think I am always lying on your lap, preventing you from touching your books.'

She looked so outraged that he felt like mitigating the seriousness with a joke of his own brand: 'If I have been failing it is because I don't believe education is important, that is all.'

'Your mother remarked that, being uneducated myself, I want to drag you down to my own level.'

'Why don't you put your fingers into your ears whenever Mother talks in that strain?'

'Why don't you use your intelligence and pass your examination?'

He said, 'Yes, that is also a good idea,' and applied himself to the task with all his might. He never arrived late for his class, never missed a lesson, and drew up a general chart of subjects and a working timetable. He sat at his desk and studied far into the night. Into this nicely readjusted life his father came crashing with his plan for visiting the temple.

Jagan pleaded, 'Can't we go after the examinations?'

His father glared at him and said, 'We have waited long enough,' and then, feeling that he sounded too commanding, added, 'This is the only month when we can go up the hill; if the rains start we shan't be able to get there. Full of leeches and such things. Ten months in the year it is raining up there.'

The base of the hill had to be reached by bus. The party consisted of Jagan and his wife, his father and mother. He felt touched by his father's solicitude in offering to climb the hill at his age. His mother looked extraordinarily pleased at reaching a solution at last for the barrenness of her daughter-in-law. She kept on saying, 'Good things only come with time. Otherwise, why would I not have thought of all this earlier, last year for instance?' She was bawling over the noise of the bus as they occupied a long seat, clutching their little bundles. Ambika felt a little shy. Some other woman in the bus asked across the aisle, 'Where are you going?'

'To the temple on Badri Hill . . .'

'Ah, the right time to go, and you will be blessed with children.'

'Not me,' said Jagan's mother, 'I have enough.' And they all laughed.

A man sitting beside the woman leaned forward to say, 'If the god blesses you, you may have twins. I know from experience!' And they all laughed again.

'One does not ask for twins; they are difficult to tend. We once had twins in the house of a distant relative, and the parents just went mad, both the babies demanding feed at the same moment or rejecting it at the same moment. I shall be happy if my daughter-in-law has a child, the next following in the normal way,' said Jagan's mother.

'How many sons have you?' asked the woman and they went into details of their family arrangements. Someone on the back seat was sick and the bus had to be stopped every now and then for him to lean out and relieve himself. Ambika, as became the daughter-in-law of the house, sat beside Jagan's mother, and Jagan sat beside his father, who had the businesslike aspect of someone going out to negotiate a contract.

Jagan would have enjoyed his wife's company rather than his father's, but it would be unthinkable for women to sit with men, and Ambika had to keep her mother-in-law company out of courtesy, so that Jagan was forced to sit by his father. It was a long seat running end to end below the windows. On Jagan's other side, there was a man from the forest with a string of beads around his neck, holding on his lap a small wooden cage containing a mottled bird, which occasionally let out a cry, sounding like doors moving on ancient, unoiled hinges. When it made this noise, it drowned the conversation of the passengers (quite fifty of them in a vehicle expected to accommodate half that number legally, some with tickets, some without, for the conductor pocketed the cash and adjusted the records accordingly, for which purpose he was constantly pulling out a pad and making entries). Remarks, inquiries, advice, announcements, the babble of men's talk, women's shrill voices and children crying or laughing, formed a perfect jumble and medley of sounds constantly overwhelmed by the shriek let out by the mottled bird. Jagan's father was engaged in a prolonged conversation with a peasant on his right, who was cracking groundnuts and littering the floor with shells, on the subject of manures and the technique of well-digging. Jagan glanced up at his wife and noticed that she was tired, the noise and the rattle were wearing her out. He wished he had her at his side. He would have pointed out and said, 'See those trees, and those hills? Aren't they beautiful? Are you aware that this trip is for your benefit?' And she would probably have retorted, 'For yours, let us say. I don't need a miracle to conceive. Remember the group photo in our house.' And then he would have teased her, pinched her back and so forth, which would have ended in a quarrel or in her laughing over it all. One couldn't say definitely. After all these years of married life, he could not really anticipate her reactions. Sometimes she took things easily, with the greatest cheer, sometimes she stung him and glared at him for the same remark. She was a model of goodness and courtesy and cheerfulness generally, but she could lash with her tongue when her temper was roused.

A few weeks before, Father had complained that something was wrong with the sauce; it turned out that it was over-salted. An on-the-spot inquiry was held. The mother-in-law demanded, 'Ambika, did you add salt to the sauce?' Ambika said, 'Yes, of course, Mother,' in a polite tone from inside the kitchen. Mother was serving the men in the dining hall. At her daughter-in-law's admission, she dropped the plate in her hand and went in, demanding an explanation. 'Who asked you to put salt into it?' The girl replied haughtily, 'I don't know,' at which they heard the elder lady saying, 'Should not anyone have the sense to ask whether a thing is already salted or not? What's to happen when several hands add salt? The stuff is fit only for the street gutter, not for eating; this is how everything gets wasted and ruined in this house, I know. I know how it all happens . . .' 'Bring some more rice,' said Jagan's father from the dining hall. Ambika took the rice and served, leaving her mother-in-law to continue: 'One doesn't ask for extraordinary things;

they are not for us, we are not destined to enjoy the spectacle of a gold waistband, like hundreds of others, but one wants at least a sensible . . .' She did not finish her sentence. Ambika was heard to cry, 'I don't care,' and dropping the dish, retired from the scene. She shut herself in her room and refused all food, throwing the whole house into a turmoil. She complained that she was not feeling like eating, that was all. Later in the week, when the situation had calmed down, she explained to Jagan, 'Do you know what I said to your mother? "Why are you so obsessed with the gold belt? What has it to do with salt or sugar? Have you never seen a gold belt in all your life?" ' Since that day, his mother had been very sparing in her remarks, particularly with reference to the gold belt. They had all along underestimated Ambika's temper.

The bus deposited them in a village at the foot of the hill. It was probably the smallest village on any map, consisting of two rows of huts and a couple of wooden stands made of packing cases on which a little merchandise was displayed, mainly for the convenience of pilgrims going uphill—coconuts, bananas, betel leaves and flowers.

Mother was evidently tired after the journey and sat on a boulder to rest herself, while Father carried on interminable negotiations with the coconut-sellers over the price, trying to beat them down. Finally he yielded, grumbling that these villagers were spoilt nowadays and had become exploiters of the worst kind, and flourished his fists in anger. 'We have come from twenty miles away. Should we not expect some consideration for our trouble? If I had known the price of things here, I'd have brought all the stuff from home,' he cried irascibly.

Mother interposed from where she sat, 'That is not permitted. Custom requires . . .'

'Yes, yes, it was written in the *Vedas* ten thousand years ago that you must be exploited on this spot of earth by this particular coconut-woman. True, true,' he said cynically, glaring at his son and daughter-in-law sitting on another boulder, hinting that if only people displayed normal fecundity, one would not have to buy coconuts at an exorbitant price. Jagan squirmed at the look his father gave him and felt more impotent than ever, but Ambika, at whom he glanced, looked defiant, as if ready to bring out the group photo of a hundred and three.

But for the fact that he was a coward, Jagan would have asked his parents, 'Haven't you enough grandchildren? Why do you want more? Why don't you leave me alone?' Meanwhile the coconut-woman was saying, 'Don't grudge a little extra expense; the grandson will bring you a lot of good fortune when he arrives.' At which the old gentleman softened and asked, 'How are you sure it'll be a son, not a daughter?' 'No one who prays at that temple is ever disappointed with a daughter,' she replied.

As if in fulfilment of the coconut-seller's prophecy, Mali was born. The very minute he was delivered (in the village home of his mother) he was weighed on a scale-pan, even before the midwife could clean him up properly, and an equivalent weight in gold, silver and corn was made up to be delivered to the god on Badri Hill, according to the solemn vow made during their visit.

When she came home, bringing the three-months-old baby, Ambika's parents had sent with her an enormous load of gifts, as prescribed in the social code for the first-born.

A huge feast was held to which a hundred guests were invited; they had to cover the floor of all three segments of the house with dining leaves. Mali still looked puny and hardly able to bear all the gold and jewellery the fond grandparents had heaped on him. After dinner, chewing betel leaves with great contentment, Jagan's father looked very happy. The house was filled with the babble of guests and laughter. Women in groups simultaneously carried on conversations at several pitches. The baby, passed from hand to hand, cried, unable to bear the disturbance around him. A smell of incense, flowers and sandalwood filled the air, as on any auspicious occasion. The two grandfathers retired to a corner for a moment, leaving the other guests. 'Mali,' said one, 'will have a deposit of a thousand rupees, earmarked, to which we will add a hundred on each birthday. This has been the practice in our family for generations whenever a child is born.'

'So is it with us,' said the other. 'After all, we must provide for the new one and give him a good start in life.'

'A new son in the house is a true treasure in this life and beyond life.'

'I was dreading Jagan would be without issue,' said Jagan's father.

'I was in no doubt at any time. Barrenness is unknown in our house.'

A look of triumph glowed on Jagan's face as he went from guest to guest, prostrated at their feet, and received blessings. Ambika followed him, prostrated, and was also blessed by everyone. She held herself up proudly, having now attained the proper status in the family. She looked especially gratified that she had enabled them to add, if it could somehow be done, one more figure to the group photographs on the walls of both the houses.

CHAPTER THIRTEEN

BROODING ON THE past, Jagan must have dozed off at the foot of the statue. He was awakened by the clamour of birds alighting on the head of Sir Frederick Lawley. Jagan bestirred himself and looked at his house, now touched by the morning light, its heavy cornices emerging into view. 'A little brighter now than at night,' he said to himself, 'but it has an unhappy look; it will never get back the light and laughter of other days. Who's there to brighten it? Not my son, nor his so-called—what do we call her, really? What name shall I give her? Anyway, where are they? Lost sight of. They don't come home. Where do they go? Never tell me. They are both alike. They are not the sort to make a home bright, unlike my mother or even Ambika when she was well. On the contrary, they blacken their surroundings. Probably they will be happier without me there.'

Jagan felt it would be impossible for him to get back to that house. 'It's tainted, but it is not my house that's tainted. It is his. Who am I to grumble and fret? I am sixty, and I may live for only ten or fifteen years more, whereas Mali, with or without his story-machine, will have to go on for sixty or more years in that house. May he be blessed with longevity!' Jagan revelled for a moment in visions of Mali at eighty, and that profoundly moved his heart. But the immediate thought was: 'Where will Grace be when Mali is eighty? Still in the same situation?' Perhaps Mali would succeed in sending her back. It was the best possible solution—if they still spurned his suggestion for a quick solemnization in the hills.

He felt hurt at the recollection as if a needle had probed a wound. 'I have probably outlived my purpose in this house. If I live for ten or fifteen years more, it will have to be on a different plane. At sixty, one is reborn and enters a new *janma*.' That was the reason why people celebrated their sixtieth birthdays. He remembered his father and mother, his uncle and aunt and a score of other couples celebrated a man's sixtieth year like a wedding, with pipes, drums and feasting. People loved to celebrate one thing or another all the time. He had had his fill of them, and had nothing to complain of. Mali had proved that there was no need for ceremonials, not even the business of knotting the *thali* around the bride's neck. Nothing, no bonds or links or responsibility. Come together, live together, and kick away each other when it suited them. Whoever kicked harder got away first. Kick? Where was the kick? They sat in the green car with their legs intertwined in spite of what they had said of each other. Puzzling over things was enervating. Reading a sense into Mali's actions was fatiguing like the attempt to spell out a message in a half-familiar script. He had no need to learn anything more. No more unravelling of conundrums just as there was not going to be any more feast or music in that shuttered house before him. When his sixtieth birthday came, it would pass unnoticed. A widower had no right to celebrate anything. He was fit only for retirement. What a magic word! If one had to shake off things, one did it unmistakably, completely, without leaving any loophole or a path back.

He still had to pay his visit to his house, to collect a few things he needed, though he would prefer to walk off, just walk, as the Buddha did when he got enlightenment. It was five o'clock, his usual hour for the bath for half a century.

An hour later, after his morning ablutions and nourishment, he came out of his house, carrying a little bundle, in which among other things was included his *charka*. 'It's a duty I owe Mahatma Gandhi. I made a vow before him that I would spin every day of my life. I have to do it, whether I'm at home or in a forest.'

The sunlight, the cold bath and the gruel he had had, mitigated somewhat the ardour of his renunciation. He still had the key in his hand. 'Must leave it somewhere,' he thought, 'with someone. I can't take it with me . . . But why not, after all, it is the backdoor key. The main key must be with Mali. If he never opens the door again, well, it's his business: it's his house that is going to become haunted with evil spirits, which might throw things about with a clatter.' Jagan did not fully believe in it, but he knew instances of deserted houses where such things happened. After all, evil spirits too needed accommodation somewhere. He chuckled at the thought

of his inquiring, inquisitive neighbour. 'Let him ask all the questions
he likes of the ghost storming my house.'

He still felt bothered about the key. 'Why can't I leave it with
my brother? It will be a good excuse to visit him.' He toyed with
the idea. Engage Gaffur's taxi, run to Vinayak Street and leave the
house key with his brother. Years ago, when he was chosen to take
part in the National Struggle, he took elaborate leave of everyone
before volunteering for arrest. How his brother had tears in his eyes.
The entire family were moved by his self-abnegation, accompanied
him in a body halfway down the street, although they disapproved
generally of his patriotic acts. He sighed for those warm and
crowded days, and longed for a similar send-off now. When they
could show such intense feelings for a jail-going man, they could as
well display a little of it to one retreating from life—even more so
since this was going to be a kind of death actually, although he'd
breathe, watch, and occasionally keep in touch, but the withdrawal
would not be different from death. He longed for a nice, crowded
send-off now. But only his brother was left of an entire generation.
He felt a longing for a glimpse of him. He had lost all his teeth
according to the cousin and Jagan felt curious to know what he
looked like now. He felt nostalgic for his brother's gruff voice
uttering clipped sentences; ever a positive man and a born leader
of younger brothers. The whole street was likely to crowd around
Gaffur's taxi to look at one who was reputed to have become the
father-in-law of a girl of outlandish origin. His brother would
probably keep him standing in the street and tell him to throw him
the key from a distance since Jagan's shadow was likely to taint the
threshold. He might have to shout his explanation across, 'I am off
to a retreat. I'm sixty and in a new *janma*.' He might have to speak
about Mali too. 'It's not only his marriage, but you must know the
latest truth that they are not married at all, but carry tales against
each other, although they sit close in a motor car.' And his brother
might shout back, 'Get away, you polluter of family reputations.'
And that crowd surrounding his taxi might jeer and laugh, obstruct
his taxi, and force him to miss his bus at the Market Gate. Thus he
would get caught again in the day's routine, and another day's and
another day's. Impossible thought. 'Better carry away the key. After
all, it's the back door.'

When passing Sir Frederick Lawley, he saw his cousin riding
down clumsily on a bicycle, his tuft flying in the wind, his wheels

zig-zagging perilously on to the edge of the storm drain and
retracting miraculously to the centre of the road. Jagan stood
arrested by the spectacle as he had never seen the cousin on a
bicycle before. The wheels seemed to come straight for him.
Shouting incoherent inquiries, Jagan stepped aside. The cousin
helplessly dashed past him a dozen yards, and fell off the saddle,
leaving the bicycle to bolt away by itself to a ditch. He picked
himself up as Jagan got over his wonderment and demanded, 'What
is this circus-feat so early in the day? At your age! You may kill
yourself.'

'Don't I know?' panted the cousin, dusting off the mud on the
scratches at his elbow. 'I was in a hurry to meet you and so
borrowed the bicycle from my neighbour. If you don't mind, I'll
leave it in your house. I dare not ride it back.'

Jagan said, 'I have locked my house and am not going back.'
The unmistakable firmness of his tone made the cousin proceed
straight to business. 'Come with me. Our lawyer is waiting. Mali
needs immediate help.'

'Ah! What has happened?'

'Mali is in prison since last evening . . .'

Jagan came to a dead stop on the road and screamed, 'Oh God!
Why?'

'He was found with half a bottle of alcohol in his car.'

'Siva!' cried Jagan. 'That's why I discouraged his idea of buying
that horrible car!' He vented his rage against the green automobile
until the cousin interrupted, 'A bottle could be sneaked in
anywhere . . .'

'You don't understand. It's the motor car that creates all sorts
of notions in a young fellow,' said Jagan and found an agreeable
escape into this theme. 'Everything would have been well if he
hadn't bought that car.'

'Don't interrupt me, listen,' said the cousin. 'You must get him
out of the police lock-up at once. It's not a good place to be in. We
could have got him out last night, if you had not disappeared.
Where were you?'

'I was only sleeping on the statue,' Jagan said and remembered
his wife's taunts whenever he proposed to sleep out.

'Fine time you chose to give the statue company while I was
searching for you everywhere!' exclaimed the cousin. 'We could
have got Mali out last night.'

'Oh, what can we do now? Poor boy! In the lock-up! He won't feel comfortable: he has always slept on a spring mattress, since he was seven. How can I get him out?' Tears blurred his sight, until the cousin looked distorted, corrugated and dwarfish. The cousin watched him calmly and said, 'Come, come. Don't let that vagrant see the tears in your eyes.' The cousin was extremely practical and knew exactly what should be done. No wonder he was in such demand, thought Jagan, all over the town. Any crisis in any house, a funeral, marriage, accident or a litigation, brought to the surface the best in the cousin. Jagan asked, 'Which lock-up?'

'In the sub-jail, until the trial begins. Get up, get up. Let us go and see if . . .'

Jagan felt giddy. He pressed his temples with his palms: 'Don't pile on so much. I can't stand it.' He felt faint and stretched himself flat at the foot of the statue.

The cousin said, 'Let us go back to your house.'

'No,' said Jagan resolutely.

'You need rest. Don't worry. I will manage everything for you . . .' The cousin patted his shoulder tenderly and said, 'Don't lose your nerve; what is all your philosophy worth if you cannot bear this little trial?'

'In the sub-jail . . .' Jagan wailed. 'I know the place; it is very dirty, prisoners urinate in a corner of the lock-up, or have they improved the conditions since my days?' he asked, blowing his nose.

'Naturally, it is all different now.'

'Oh, yes, it must be different, I know, though it was so awful in those British days.'

The cousin went on, 'The first thing I did was to go out to the sub-jail and plead with the warders there. I saw the boy and spoke to him. I managed to get him a cup of coffee also.'

'Did you give him anything to eat? He must have been hungry.'

'They'll treat him specially. I know the District Collector, and so we can get things done. I got the news at six o'clock. I was returning from the house of the Superintending Engineer where I had gone to fix up a home-tutor for their son. At the turning near the General Post Office an orderly from the Superintendent's house gave me the news. The green car was halted at the Mempi outpost where they generally check for prohibition offences, as they find a lot of illicit distilling and traffic in the jungles high up. A policeman seems to have stopped Mali's car and found hidden in it half a bottle of some alcoholic drink, and you know how it is . . . The police immediately seized the car, sealed the bottle before witnesses, and have charged the inmates of the car under the Prohibition Act.'

'Who else was there?'

'Two of his friends.'

'Oh, his friends have been his ruin. Where is the car now?'

'They drove it down. It will be kept at the police station till the case is finished.'

Jagan sat up, shut his eyes and remained silent, his lips moving in a prayer. 'I . . . I didn't know the boy drank,' he said, coming on a fresh discovery about his son.

'One doesn't have to drink to be caught by the Prohibition. It is enough if one's breath smells of alcohol. There are some fever mixtures which have an alcoholic flavour. A doctor has to certify that he had administered two doses of a fever mixture earlier in the day, that is all.'

'Who would be that doctor?'

'Oh, you are wasting time. Come on, let us go,' the cousin cried impatiently. 'The lawyer will manage all that. Trust him and leave it in his hands . . .'

'What was the green car's business in the hills?'

'That's beside the point . . . Anyway, Mali had gone up to confer with some parties on his business, undisturbed at the Peak House. He was expecting someone representing his foreign collaborators.'

Jagan recovered his composure. 'Ah, foreign collaborators! Impressive words. No one in India knows about business. Always foreign! Well, accepted, sir. But the bottle? How did it get in?'

'Someone left it there. A stranger stopped the car on the mountain road, asked for a lift, got off on the way, and perhaps left the bottle behind.' Jagan felt partly relieved at such possibilities. He studied his cousin's face to judge the quantum of truth in his explanations, but that man avoided his eyes, and said generally, 'Anything is possible these days. You can't trust people, especially strangers. When I didn't find you in, I went in search of Ganesh Rau, our lawyer, the best in our district. Though he is up to his neck in work, he has accepted our case; he knows Mali and admires his plans. He seems to have promised to buy shares in Mali's company when the time comes.'

'Does he believe Mali's machine can write stories?'

'I'd no time to discuss all that, but he said, "Why not?" when I mentioned it.'

Jagan became reflective. The cousin said, 'All that apart, the case is very strongly in our favour. We sat discussing all the possibilities until two o'clock in the morning. I could find no time for sleep at all. At five o'clock I borrowed the bicycle and fell off it four times before reaching you.'

'Don't go on a bicycle again. You may kill yourself,' said Jagan pontifically.

The cousin said, 'He is also looking into the antecedents of the policeman who checked Mali's car at the outpost. That stranger who accosted them could have been the policeman's accomplice. They must have had a grudge against you.'

'Why?' asked Jagan. 'Why should any policeman bear a grudge against me?'

'For a hundred reasons,' said the cousin. 'People are generally bad. He might have been demanding free packets of sweets from your shop; after all, poor fellows, they are so ill-paid that they do seek favours from shop-men. You might not remember it now; but you will have to try and recollect how you threatened to report him to his officers.'

'I have never seen a policeman in my shop . . .'

'Or he might have marked you in those days when you violated the laws . . .' Jagan laughed at this idea.

'If a grudge was to be borne, we had greater cause than the police.'

'Very well, it could be so . . .'

'But Mahatma Gandhi trained us not to nurse any resentment. . . Anyway, the policeman of our days must all be senile or dead now.'

'Or he might have had a brush with Mali some time. Policemen are generally prejudiced against young people driving scooters or cars, you know. This is all just casual talk, that's all; the lawyer will instruct you on what to say. We should depend upon his guidance. One thing is certain. Just answer his cross-examination as he directs you. The whole issue will turn on your evidence.'

Jagan said briefly, 'If what you say is true, well, truth will win. If it is not true, there is nothing I can do.'

'No, no, don't say so. We must do our best to get Mali out.

They could sentence him up to two years under this Act.'

'Who are we to get him out or to put him in?' asked Jagan philosophically. He had recovered from the first shock totally, and spoke even impishly now, although his voice was still a little thick with grief. 'Truth ought to get him out, if what you say is true,' he repeated.

'But the lawyer will have to build it up and establish it,' said the cousin, 'with proper evidence. He is thinking of ways and means. If he is able to establish the malafides of the policeman, we may even file a counter-case in order to strengthen ours.'

Jagan's mind had attained extraordinary clarity now. He threw a look at his bag, lifted it lightly and said, 'I wish you all luck; you and your lawyer and his distinguished client and also that poor soul—the policeman who had the misfortune to stop the green car; but don't expect me to take any part in it. Leave me out of it completely; forget me and I'll go away without asking too many questions.'

'Where, where are you going?' asked the cousin anxiously.

'I will seek a new interest—different from the set of repetitions performed for sixty years. I am going somewhere, not carrying more than what my shoulder can bear. All that I need is in that bag . . .'

'Including the bank book, I suppose,' asked the cousin, 'which is a compact way of carrying things. How far are you going?'

Jagan described the retreat across the river. The cousin was aghast: 'I know that place near the cremation ground. Has that hair-dyer been trying to sell it to you? Forgive me if I say, "Keep away from him." He is a sorcerer: knows black magic and offers to transmute base metals into gold . . .'

'I don't care what he does. I am going to watch a goddess come out of a stone. If I don't like the place, I will go away somewhere else. I am a free man. I've never felt more determined in my life. I'm happy to have met you now, but I'd have gone away in any case. Everything can go on with or without me. The world doesn't collapse even when a great figure is assassinated or dies of heart failure. Think that my heart has failed, that's all.'

He gave the cousin a bunch of keys and said, 'Open the shop at the usual hour and run it. Mali will take charge of it eventually. Keep Sivaraman and the rest happy; don't throw them out. You can always come over to the retreat if there is anything urgent, or to render an account. I'll tell you what to do. At the Market Gate buses leave for Mempi every four hours starting from eight-thirty in the morning. You are a busy man, but please help me now.'

'Yes, I'll do anything you say,' said the cousin, rather intimidated by Jagan's tone. 'The lawyer wanted two thousand rupees for preliminary expenses. He will arrange the bail. Mali should be out before this evening.'

'A dose of prison life is not a bad thing. It may be just what he needs now,' said Jagan, opening his bag and taking out his cheque-book. Resting it on his knee, he wrote out a cheque and handed it to the cousin.

'If there are further charges?' asked the cousin.

'We'll pay them, that is all. You can ask me whenever you like. I am not flying away to another planet.' The cousin was amazed at the transformation in Jagan, who kept repeating, his eyes still wet, 'A little prison life won't harm anyone. I must not miss the bus at Market Gate at eight-thirty. I don't want to ask questions, but tell me, where is she?' he asked, rising and shouldering his bag.

'She has friends who have found a job for her in a women's hostel,' began the cousin, but Jagan dismissed the subject halfway through the other's explanation and said, 'If you meet her, tell her that if she ever wants to go back to her country, I will buy her a ticket. It's a duty we owe her. She was a good girl.'